ROYAL

By Danielle Steel

Royal • Daddy's Girls • The Wedding Dress • The Numbers Game
Moral Compass • Spy • Child's Play • The Dark Side • Lost And Found
Blessing In Disguise • Silent Night • Turning Point • Beauchamp Hall
In His Father's Footsteps • The Good Fight • The Cast • Accidental Heroes
Fall From Grace • Past Perfect • Fairytale • The Right Time • The Duchess
Against All Odds • Dangerous Games • The Mistress • The Award
Rushing Waters • Magic • The Apartment • Property Of A Noblewoman
Blue • Precious Gifts • Undercover • Country • Prodigal Son • Pegasus
A Perfect Life • Power Play • Winners • First Sight • Until The End Of Time
The Sins Of The Mother • Friends Forever • Betrayal • Hotel Vendôme
Happy Birthday • 44 Charles Street • Legacy • Family Ties • Big Girl
Southern Lights • Matters Of The Heart • One Day At A Time
A Good Woman • Rogue • Honor Thyself • Amazing Grace • Bungalow 2
Sisters • H.R.H. • Coming Out • The House • Toxic Bachelors • Miracle
Impossible • Echoes • Second Chance • Ransom • Safe Harbour
Johnny Angel • Dating Game • Answered Prayers • Sunset In St. Tropez
The Cottage • The Kiss • Leap Of Faith • Lone Eagle • Journey
The House On Hope Street • The Wedding • Irresistible Forces
Granny Dan • Bittersweet • Mirror Image • The Klone And I
The Long Road Home • The Ghost • Special Delivery • The Ranch
Silent Honor • Malice • Five Days In Paris • Lightning • Wings • The Gift
Accident • Vanished • Mixed Blessings • Jewels • No Greater Love
Heartbeat • Message From Nam • Daddy • Star • Zoya • Kaleidoscope
Fine Things • Wanderlust • Secrets • Family Album • Full Circle • Changes
Thurston House • Crossings • Once In A Lifetime • A Perfect Stranger
Remembrance • Palomino • Love: *Poems* • The Ring • Loving
To Love Again • Summer's End • Season Of Passion • The Promise
Now And Forever • Passion's Promise • Going Home

Nonfiction
Pure Joy: *The Dogs We Love*
A Gift Of Hope: *Helping the Homeless*
His Bright Light: *The Story of Nick Traina*

For Children
Pretty Minnie In Paris
Pretty Minnie In Hollywood

Danielle Steel

ROYAL

MACMILLAN

First published 2020 by Delacorte Press
an imprint of Random House
a division of Penguin Random House LLC, New York

First published in the UK 2020 by Macmillan
an imprint of Pan Macmillan
The Smithson, 6 Briset Street, London EC1M 5NR
Associated companies throughout the world
www.panmacmillan.com

ISBN 978-1-5098-7817-8

1 3 5 7 9 8 6 4 2

A CIP catalogue record for this book is available from the British Library.

Typeset in Charter BT
Printed and bound by CPI Group (UK) Ltd, Croydon, CR0 4YY

MIX
Paper from
responsible sources
FSC® C116313
FSC
www.fsc.org

Visit **www.panmacmillan.com** to read more about all our books
and to buy them. You will also find features, author interviews and
news of any author events, and you can sign up for e-newsletters
so that you're always first to hear about our new releases.

To my beloved children,
Beatie, Trevor, Todd, Nick,
Samantha, Victoria, Vanessa,
Maxx, Zara,

Never give up your dreams,
Be grateful for who you are,
And what you can be,
Don't settle for less than you deserve,

Don't give up!! Dare to be!!
Be True to Yourself!
And always know how very much
I love you!
Bigger than the sky!

All my love,
Mom/d.s.

ROYAL

Chapter 1

In June of 1943, the systematic bombing of England by the German Luftwaffe, targeting Britain's cities and countryside, had been going on for three years. It had begun on September 7, 1940, with heavy bombing of London, causing massive destruction in the city, at first in the East End, then the West End, Soho, Piccadilly, and eventually every area of London. The suburbs had also been severely damaged. Buckingham Palace was bombed on September 13, six days after the daily raids began. The first bomb landed in the quadrangle, a second crashed through a glass roof, and another demolished the palace chapel. The king and queen were in residence at the time.

Other historic places were rapidly added to the flight path of the German bombers. The Houses of Parliament, Whitehall, the National Gallery, Marble Arch, various parks, shopping streets, department stores, Leicester, Sloane, and Trafalgar Squares were bombed too. By December of 1940, almost every major monument had been injured in some way, buildings had collapsed, and countless citizens had been injured, rendered homeless, or killed.

The intense bombing raids had continued for eight months, until May of 1941. Then a period called "the lull" set in with daily attacks, but with less intensity than in the earlier months. The damage and deaths had continued. For the past two years, Londoners had done their best to get used to it, spending nights in air raid shelters, helping to dig out their neighbors, volunteering as air raid wardens, and assisting with the removal of millions of tons of debris to make streets passable. Limbs and dead bodies were frequently found in the rubble.

During the first year of the bombing, eighteen other cities were bombed as well, several suburbs, and in the countryside Kent, Sussex, and Essex had suffered grievously. As the years went on, the coastlines had been heavily bombed too. Nowhere appeared to be truly safe. Prime Minister Winston Churchill and King Frederick and Queen Anne did their best to keep up morale and encourage their countrymen to stay strong. England had been brought to its knees, but had not been defeated, and refused to be. It was Hitler's plan to invade the country once it had been severely damaged by the constant bombing raids, but the British government would not allow that to happen. By the summer of 1943, nerves were stretched, and the damage was considerable, but the English people refused to give up.

The Germans were fighting hard on the Russian front as well, which gave the English respite.

The ear-shattering sirens had sounded again that night, as they did almost every night, and the king and queen and their three daughters had taken refuge in the private air raid shelter that had been set up for them in Buckingham Palace, in what had previously been the housekeepers' rooms, reinforced by steel girders, with steel shutters on the high windows. Gilt chairs, a Regency settee, a large mahogany table gave them a place to sit, with axes on the wall, oil lamps, electric torches, and some minor medical supplies. Next door there was a shelter for members of the royal household and staff, which even included a piano. With over a thousand staff members in the palace, they had to use other shelters as well. They waited for the all clear and had been in the shelter close to a thousand times by then. The two elder royal princesses had been sixteen and seventeen when the first air raids had started.

Families had been urged to send their children to the country for safety, but the royal princesses had stayed in London to continue their studies and do war work as soon as they turned eighteen. And when the bombing was too severe, their parents sent the royal princesses to Windsor Castle, for a break. Princess Alexandra drove a lorry now, at twenty, and was a surprisingly competent mechanic, and at nineteen, Princess Victoria was working at a hospital doing minor tasks, which freed up the nurses to tend to the severely injured. Their younger sister, Charlotte, was fourteen when the bombing began, and the king and queen had considered sending her to Windsor, or Balmoral, their castle in Scotland, but their youngest child was small, and had delicate health, and the queen had preferred to keep her at home with them. The princess had suffered from asthma since she was very young, and the queen did not wish to part with her, and preferred to keep her close. Even now, at seventeen, she wasn't allowed to do the war work her sisters were engaged in, or even the things they had done at her age. The constant dust from fallen buildings and the rubble in the streets were hard on her lungs. Her asthma seemed to be growing steadily worse.

The day after the most recent bombing, the king and queen discussed Charlotte's situation again. Although she was Queen Victoria's great-great-granddaughter, a fairly distant connection, Charlotte had inherited her diminutive size from her illustrious ancestor. It was unlikely that Charlotte would ever be on the throne, since she was third in line after her two older sisters. She chafed at the restrictions her family and the royal physician put on her. She was a lively, spirited girl, and a brilliant rider, and wanted to make herself useful in the war effort, despite her size and her asthma, but her parents had continued to refuse.

The dust in the air was particularly thick the next day. The queen gave Charlotte her medicine herself, and that night, she and the king spoke yet again about what to do with their youngest daughter.

"Sending her to the countryside would encourage others to do the same," her father said with a pained voice while the queen shook her head. Many families had sent their children away in the last four years, since war was declared, at the government's insistence. A shocking number of children had been killed in the bombing raids, and parents had been urged to send their children to safer areas. Some concurred, other parents were afraid to let their children go, or couldn't bear the thought of being parted from them. Travel was difficult and frowned on, with heavy gas rationing, and some parents who had sent their children away hadn't seen them for several years since they'd left. Bringing their children home for holidays was strongly discouraged, for fear that the parents wouldn't send them away again. But unquestionably London and the other cities were more dangerous than the rural areas where they were being housed by kind people who had opened their homes to them. Some hosts took in a number of children.

"I don't trust Charlotte to take her medicine if we send her away.

You know how she hates it, and she wants to do the same work as her sisters," her mother said sympathetically. Charlotte's oldest sister, Alexandra, who would inherit the throne one day, understood their mother's concerns perfectly, and insisted to Charlotte that she respect the limitations of her health. Her sister Victoria was less compassionate. She had always felt a rivalry with her younger sister, and occasionally accused her of faking the asthma attacks in order to shirk the war work that Charlotte wanted to do desperately, and had been forbidden from doing so far. There were frequent verbal battles between the two girls. Victoria had resented Charlotte since the day she was born, and treated her like an intruder, much to her parents' dismay.

"I don't think she's any better off here. Even *with* her medicine, she still has frequent attacks," her father insisted, and his wife knew there was truth to it.

"I don't know who we'd send her to anyway. I don't want her at Balmoral alone, even with a governess. It's too lonely there. And I can't think of anyone of our acquaintance who is taking more children in, although I'm sure there are some we're not aware of. We could let it be known that we have sent our youngest child away, to set the example, but it would be dangerous for her, if people knew precisely where she was," Queen Anne said sensibly.

"That can be handled," the king said quietly, and mentioned it to Charles Williams, his private secretary, the next morning. Charles promised to make discreet inquiries, in case the queen changed her mind, and decided to let the princess go away. He understood the problem completely. She would have to stay with a trusted family that would not reveal her true identity, in some part of England that hadn't been as heavily bombed as the towns close to London.

It was two weeks later when Charles came to the king with the name of a family that had a large manor house in Yorkshire. The couple were older, titled aristocrats, beyond reproach, and the private secretary's own family had recommended them, although he hadn't told his family any details about the situation or who might be sent away, only that the hosts had to be unfailingly trustworthy and discreet.

"It's in a quiet part of Yorkshire, Your Majesty," he said respectfully when they were alone, "and so far, as you know, there are fewer air raids in the rural areas, although there have been some in Yorkshire as well. The couple in question have a very large estate, which the family has owned since the Norman Conquest, and there are several large tenant farms on the estate." He hesitated for a moment, and told a familiar tale. "In all honesty, they have been somewhat in difficulty since the end of the Great War. They're land rich and cash poor, and have struggled to keep the estate intact, without selling off any part of it. I've been told that the house is in poor repair, and even more so since all the young men left for war four years ago. They're running the place with very little help. They're older parents, she's in her sixties, the earl's in his seventies, and their only son is Princess Charlotte's age. He's due to go into the army in the next few months, when he turns eighteen. They took in a young girl from a modest home in London at the beginning of the war, to do their patriotic duty. I believe they would be willing to offer Princess Charlotte safe haven, and perhaps . . ." He hesitated, and the king understood. "Perhaps a gift of a practical nature would help them with the running of the estate."

"Of course," the king said.

"I think she would be safer there," Charles added, "and with papers in another name from the Home Office, absolutely no one except the earl and countess hosting her needs to know her true identity. Would you like me to contact them, sir?"

"I must speak to my wife first," the king said quietly, and his secretary nodded. He knew the queen was loath to send her away, and Princess Charlotte herself would object strenuously. She wanted to remain at Buckingham Palace with her family, and hoped to convince her parents to allow her to do war work the moment she turned eighteen, in a year.

"Perhaps if you let her take one of her horses to Yorkshire with her, it would soften the blow a bit." Princess Charlotte was horse mad and an excellent rider, despite her asthma and her diminutive size. Nothing kept her away from the stables, and she could ride any horse, no matter how spirited.

"It might help," the king said, but he also knew that Charlotte would present every possible argument not to go. She wanted to stay in London, and hoped to do whatever she could as soon as she was allowed, like her sisters. But even sending her away until she turned eighteen in almost a year would relieve her father's mind. Between the constant bombings and his daughter's health, London was just too dangerous for her, or anyone these days. His two older daughters were doing useful work, which justified their being there, but they were not as delicate as Charlotte by any means.

He suggested the plan to the queen that night. She presented almost as many arguments against it as he expected from Charlotte herself. Queen Anne really didn't want to send her daughter away, and perhaps not even be able to see her for the next year, which they both knew was more than likely. They couldn't single her out for special treatment, or people around her might suspect her true identity, which would make the location dangerous for her. She had to be treated like everyone else, and just like the young commoner from London who was already staying there. Also the queen didn't like the fact that her would-be hosts had a son nearly the same age as Charlotte, almost a year older. She thought it inappropriate, and used that as an argument too.

"Don't be silly, my dear." Her husband smiled at her. "I'm sure all he can think of is joining the army in a few months. Boys his age are begging to go to war, not interested in pursuing young girls at the moment. You won't need to worry about that until after the war. Charles Williams says it's an excellent, entirely respectable family, and he's a very nice boy." They also both knew that their daughter was far more interested in her horses than she was in men. It was her next oldest sister, Princess Victoria, who was an accomplished flirt, and her father was eager to get her married as soon as the war was over and the boys came home. She needed a husband to manage her, and children to keep her busy. Victoria had had an eye for men since she'd turned sixteen, and he worried about the men she met now doing war work, but he knew it couldn't be helped. They all had jobs to do, and the queen kept a close eye on her. Princess Alexandra, on the other hand, had never given her parents a moment of concern. She was serious and responsible, and never lost sight of the duties she would inherit one day as monarch. She was a solemn young woman much like her father. It always intrigued him how different his three daughters were.

The following day, after taking a walk beyond the palace gates with her governess, Charlotte had an asthma attack as soon as she came home. She took her medicine without complaint, as it was a fairly severe attack. That night her parents spoke to her of their intention to send her to stay with the Earl and Countess of Ainsleigh in Yorkshire. Their family name was Hemmings. Charlotte looked horrified at the thought. She had pale blond hair, porcelain white skin, and enormous blue eyes which opened wide when she heard her parents' plan for her.

"But why, Papa? Why must I be punished? In a few months, I can do the same work as my sisters. Why must I be banished until then?"

"You're not being 'banished,' Charlotte, and it's more than a few months before you turn eighteen. It's nearly a year. I suggest that you stay in Yorkshire peacefully until your birthday, getting strong, and if your asthma improves in the country, we can talk after your birthday about your coming home to volunteer for the war effort, like your sisters. Your mother, your doctor, and I all agree that the air in London is not good for you, with all these buildings coming down, and heavy dust in the air. You're still young, Charlotte. If there wasn't a war on, you wouldn't be out of the schoolroom yet, not until you turn eighteen. You still have studying to do."

Charlotte set her chin stubbornly, prepared to do battle with them. "Queen Victoria was eighteen when she took the throne and became queen," she used as an argument her father didn't accept.

"True, but she wasn't seventeen, there wasn't a war on, and the Luftwaffe wasn't bombing England. This is a much more complicated situation, and a dangerous one for everyone, particularly for you." Her father knew that she had been fascinated all her life by her great-great-grandmother Queen Victoria, perhaps because people compared Charlotte to her because of her size, and because she had a plucky spirit, and was a brave girl like Queen Victoria, who had been Queen of England a century before. Charlotte knew that as third in line to the throne, she was unlikely to ever become queen, but she greatly admired her illustrious ancestor, and thought of her as a role model in life.

By the end of the week, the king and queen had made the decision, despite Charlotte's strenuous objections. She was only slightly mollified when they told her she could take her favorite horse with her. And to emphasize the validity of their plans for her, a larger scale attack occurred again, targeting the center of the city, which strengthened the king's resolve to send Charlotte away.

The king asked the Home Office to provide the papers they needed to protect Charlotte's identity. The earl and countess knew who she was, and had promised to tell no one, and with new identity papers she would be using the name Charlotte White, not Windsor, which would give her anonymity.

The plan was explained to both of Charlotte's sisters the night before she left, and Charlotte sat with them and their parents silently, with tears in her eyes, trying to be brave. Princess Alexandra put her arms around her, to comfort her, and Princess Victoria smiled wickedly, delighted to be rid of her younger sister for a year.

"I hope they don't treat you like Cinderella, and have you sweeping out the hearths. They've probably lost their help like everyone else. Will you really be able to keep the secret of who you are?" Victoria said meanly, obviously in doubt.

"She'll have to," her father answered for her. "It wouldn't be safe for her there if everyone knew who she was. We intend to say that she is being sent away to the country, like many children, but we will not reveal where she is. No one will discover her identity, and only the earl and countess and Charlotte will know."

"You'll be back before you know it," her older sister reassured her kindly, and came to her bedroom later that night to bring Charlotte some of her own favorite sweaters to take with her, and several books. She took a little gold bracelet with a gold heart on it off her own arm and put it on her sister's wrist. "I'll miss you terribly," Alexandra said and meant it. She had been protective of her since the day Charlotte was born. Victoria had often been a thorn in their sides, but Charlotte had a happy disposition, and Alexandra was a gentle soul, and stronger than she appeared. She would have to be one day when she was the sovereign, after their father was no longer king. Victoria had a jealous nature, and had often been envious of both her older and younger sister. She resented the easy bond they shared.

Alexandra was as dark as Charlotte was fair. Victoria had red hair, and all three of them had delicate aristocratic features, typical of their bloodline. Both of Charlotte's sisters, and her parents, were considerably taller than she. Like her great-great-grandmother Queen Victoria, Charlotte was barely five feet tall, but perfectly proportioned. She was just very small, and very graceful.

The family gathered the next morning in the queen's private sitting room to say goodbye to Charlotte. Charles Williams, the king's secretary, and her elderly governess Felicity had been assigned to make the trip with her. Both were trustworthy with the secret of the princess's whereabouts for the next ten or eleven months. The earl and countess were expecting them after the four- or five-hour drive from the city. They drove in Charles Williams's personal car so as not to attract attention. He had a simple Austin, and there were tears on Charlotte's cheeks when she got into the backseat. A moment later, they drove away, and rolled circumspectly through the gates of the palace, as Charlotte wondered when she would see her home again.

She had a terrible sense of foreboding that she would never be back. But everyone in London felt that way now, living from day to day, with bombs falling all night long and their homes and loved ones disappearing and dying.

"It's just for a year," she whispered to herself, to stay calm, as they drove past newly ruined buildings on their way out of the city. She had her medicine with her, but they kept the windows rolled up so she wouldn't need it, but either from the emotion of leaving her family or the dust outside, her chest felt so tight she could hardly breathe. She closed her eyes as she thought of her parents and sisters, fighting valiantly to make herself stop crying.

Charlotte dozed on and off during the long drive from London to Yorkshire. Felicity, her old governess, had brought a picnic basket with things for them to eat. Military Intelligence had advised Charles Williams that it would be best not to stop at pubs or restaurants along the way in case Her Royal Highness might be recognized, and give people a hint as to where she was going. An announcement was going to be made in a day or two that she had been sent to the country for an extended time, to avoid the London bombings, until her next birthday. Both the Home Office and MI5 were anxious not to give any clues to her whereabouts in Yorkshire. They didn't want that information falling into German hands either, which was another factor they had to consider. The Germans capturing the princess or worse, killing her, would have decimated British morale, and the royal family.

Charlotte ate the watercress and cucumber sandwiches the cook had prepared for her, along with some sliced sausage, which was a rare delicacy now, even on the queen's table. She fell asleep several times, bored with watching the countryside slide by.

Eventually, they reached the rolling hills of Yorkshire. It was a warm sunny day. She looked at the cows and horses and sheep in their pastures, and tried to imagine what her life in Yorkshire would be like. Her horse, Pharaoh, had been sent down with the assistant stable master and one of the stable boys three days before, and when they returned, they reported that the spirited Thoroughbred Charlotte liked to ride had settled well into his new home. He seemed to like the grazing land available to him. There was only one very old man, previously retired, and a fourteen-year-old boy managing the stables at Ainsleigh Hall, the Hemmingses' estate, and the Earl of Ainsleigh's seat. They had reported that there were few horses left in the stables. There was one hunter for the Hemmings boy to ride, and a few older horses. Neither the earl nor the countess rode anymore. The earl had been master of the hunt, but all of that ended with the onset of the war, and the countess had had a bad fall ten years before, the ancient stable master told them, broken her leg badly and hadn't ridden since. It reminded Charlotte of what Charles had told them, that the Hemmingses were not young. Their son, Henry, had come to them as a surprise late in life, when the countess was forty-nine. She was sixty-seven now, and the earl in his early seventies.

Charles had mentioned that the boy was the love of their life, and they were dreading when he would leave and go to war in a few months. He had joined an infantry regiment, and was waiting to be called up right after his eighteenth birthday, which wouldn't be long now. By Christmas, he'd be gone, and the Hemmingses would be left with their two young female guests for company.

Charlotte knew almost nothing about the girl who'd been staying there for two years, only that she came from the East End of London, and both her parents had been killed in the bombings right after she left. She was an orphan now, like so many other British children. She was the same age as Charlotte, which would be pleasant for her, if they got along, and Charlotte couldn't imagine why they wouldn't.

Charlotte had never gone to a proper school herself, and had been tutored at home. It was tedious at times, particularly once her sisters left the schoolroom, and she had to do her lessons alone, with a French governess who tutored her in French, drawing, and dance. A professor from Eton College taught her history and the basics of mathematics, and another from Cambridge taught her literature, all by British writers and poets. She hoped that she wouldn't have to continue her studies in Yorkshire, although she had promised her father she would read all the books available to her, and a few he had given her about the history of Parliament, to take with her. He wanted all his daughters to be well versed in the process of British government. He said it was their duty as daughters of the king.

Charlotte much preferred riding her horses, and needed no lessons there. She was a bold, skillful rider, and had joined her father numerous times at the royal hunts he'd attended before the war. Her sisters were far less adventuresome. She intended to ride astride in a normal saddle now, like the men, instead of sidesaddle, with no one to stop her or complain about the impropriety of it. She'd been reprimanded every time she'd tried it at Windsor, with her own and her father's horses. She couldn't do it at the royal training centers, but she could occasionally at their country retreat, but whenever her parents found out she was scolded and told to ride sidesaddle like her mother and sisters.

Queen Anne was an avid rider too, but not as much so as her youngest daughter, and the queen was content to ride sedately in their park. The king and queen frequently rode together, while Charlotte rode early in the morning with one of the grooms, so no one could observe her pushing her stallion to his limits and riding like the wind. She planned to do some riding in Yorkshire, and hoped that the earl and countess wouldn't organize schoolroom lessons for her, if they didn't have a teacher for her, which she fervently wished would be the case. She wondered if her young female contemporary liked to ride as much as she did, or even knew how. If not, perhaps she could teach her.

They arrived at Ainsleigh Hall as the Hemmingses were finishing lunch, and the earl and countess and their son, Henry, came out to greet her and introduce themselves. They introduced Charlotte as "Charlotte White." Lucy Walsh, the girl from London, brought up the rear and hung back, too shy to speak to Charlotte at first, when the Hemmingses introduced her. She was content to watch her from a distance. She noticed Charlotte's simple dark blue dress, and the well-cut coat she wore over it. Charlotte was wearing high heels and a small elegant dark blue velvet hat, gloves, and her hair was combed in a loose knot at the nape of her neck. She looked well dressed and very fashionable, as she greeted the Hemmingses and Lucy politely, and she thanked them for letting her stay with them. Their son, Henry, stared at her in fascination, without saying anything. He had never seen a girl quite like her, and hadn't been to London since he was a little boy. His parents preferred their country life, and he wasn't old enough to go into society yet, and would miss his chance now by going into the army. All that went with his rank and title would have to wait until after the war. It was the same for all of his friends. He was struck by how small Charlotte was, which surprised him, having seen her horse in the stables. He was intrigued to think she could ride such a large, lively horse. She looked so dainty and demure, and somewhat shy as they walked into the house. She glanced at Lucy with a smile, and never spoke directly to Henry. Charlotte wasn't accustomed to speaking to boys. The earl appeared to be very jovial, and welcomed her warmly. He looked older than he was, and the countess walked with a slight limp after her riding accident. She had a kind face and snow white hair, and seemed old to Charlotte, compared to her own mother, who was considerably younger. She thought the Hemmingses seemed more like Henry's grandparents than his parents.

"We're delighted to have you with us, Your Royal Highness," the countess whispered to her out of everyone's hearing, as Charles Williams took charge of Charlotte's bags, and a young hall boy from one of the farms carried them upstairs. A meal had been set out in the kitchen for Felicity and Charles to eat before they left. Charlotte said she had eaten on the way, and was hoping for a ride on Pharaoh in the warm weather. Once they settled her into her room, her governess and father's secretary would have nothing left to do there.

"You have a very fine mount," Henry finally said, as he walked into the house beside her, and she thanked him, with her eyes cast down. His parents could see immediately how impeccable her manners were. She was every inch a princess, although they would not be using her title from now on, so as not to alert anyone to who she was. Their son had no idea who she was either, and merely thought her the daughter of some aristocrats his parents knew in London, who wanted their daughter out of harm's way in Yorkshire.

Lucy didn't speak to her at all, as she followed the Hemmingses and Charlotte into the house. Then she disappeared into the kitchen, where she was more comfortable. Henry paid no attention to her, and seemed riveted by the new arrival. She seemed very grown up to

him, and he joined her and his parents for tea in the library, and then left to ride over to one of the farms, where he said he was helping repair a fence since there was no one else to do it. He said he worked on the farms a lot now, and enjoyed it, to keep busy.

"We're a bit shorthanded, I'm afraid, in the house as well," the countess said apologetically. "It's never been quite the same since the last war, and I fear that this one will finish off estates like ours. Many of the young people never came back and stayed in the cities last time when the war was over. I fear it will be the same, or worse, when it ends this time. With women needed in the factories, even the young girls have deserted the farms and gone to the cities. Lucy has been a great help to us. We'd be lost without her. We're hoping she'll stay, since she has no one left in London now. Very sad all that. She lost both her parents in the bombing when their apartment building collapsed. It's fortunate that she was here." Charlotte nodded and felt sorry for her without even knowing her. She seemed like a very plain, shy girl. Charlotte hoped they could be friends, since they were the same age.

After they finished tea, the countess took Charlotte up to her bedroom, and for an instant she was shocked.

"I wanted to give you one of our guest rooms, Your Royal Highness," she said in a soft voice, "but we don't want to make anyone aware of your position. Your mother particularly asked me not to, in the letter she sent me, so we gave you the room next to Lucy." It was one of the old servants' rooms on the top floor, with a view of the hills, the forests, and the lake on their estate. The room was just big enough for the bed, a chest, a small desk and a chair, and had been used for one of their maids before the war. There were only two of the women left now. Their rooms were down the hall, and no better

than Charlotte's. Since she had never visited any of the maids' rooms in any of her parents' palaces, she had no idea how it compared to theirs. But this was a small, dark, cheerless room with nothing to distinguish it, and nothing on the walls. On the way upstairs she had noticed that the manor was in need of paint, many of the curtains were shredded by the sunlight, and some of the rugs were threadbare in several places. The furniture was handsome, but the house itself was dark and drafty, cool in the summer months, but undoubtedly freezing cold in winter, heated only by the fireplaces in the rooms downstairs. It was not at all the kind of room that Charlotte was used to, and she still looked startled when she came downstairs to say goodbye to Felicity and Charles. They left as soon as they had eaten, to get back to London by that night, before the blackout. They were in a hurry to leave. Charlotte shook hands with both of them, and thanked them for accompanying her. Charles had to stop himself from bowing, and Felicity forgot herself and curtsied to her, but only the countess saw it. No one else was with them.

Charlotte went back upstairs then to unpack her bags. She had to leave some of her clothes in her suitcase, for lack of closet and cupboard space, but she didn't mind. She changed into her riding clothes, and was putting on her hat when Lucy walked into the room, and studied her keenly. Her riding habit was simple, but it was obvious that everything she owned was of the highest quality, perfectly cut, in fine fabrics, and fit Charlotte's tiny form impeccably.

"Are they your parents?" Lucy asked, referring to Felicity and Charles, and Charlotte shook her head, not sure what to say, and how to explain them. She noticed Lucy's East End accent immediately.

"They're friends who offered to drive me here, since they have a car, and my parents don't, and they couldn't leave London." It was all

she could think of to say, to explain them, but a closer look would have identified them as employees, which Lucy hadn't noticed. The thought never occurred to her, although she could see that Charlotte must be wellborn, from her manners, her accent, and her clothes. She was very pleasant to Lucy. "Do you ride?" Lucy responded by shaking her head with a look of panic.

"I'm afraid of horses. They look like big frightening beasts to me. What do your parents do?" She wanted to know more about the intriguing newcomer. They spoke with very different accents. Charlotte with the distinct diction of the upper classes, and Lucy's was pure London commoner. They came from two very different worlds.

There was a pause as Charlotte sought rapidly for an answer to Lucy's question about her parents. She hadn't thought of what to say if anyone asked her. "My father works for the government as a civil servant, and my mother is a secretary." It was a long way from the truth, but the best she could come up with. Lucy was a tall dark-haired girl with a plain pale face, and she seemed fascinated by Charlotte, though not particularly warm, and somewhat awkward. Charlotte felt like an intruder on the young woman's turf, which was how Lucy viewed her. Everything had been perfect there till then, and she had Henry's attention for herself, although he didn't speak to her often or at great length. At dinner, he spoke mostly to his parents about the farms, and ignored her.

"That sounds fancy," Lucy commented. "Where do you live?"

"In Putney," Charlotte answered quickly, and Lucy nodded, satisfied with her response. It was a pleasant middle-class neighborhood, and she believed her.

"My father was a cobbler and my mother was a seamstress. She used to help him at the shop sometimes." Lucy's eyes filled with tears as she said it, and Charlotte wanted to reach out to her but didn't dare. "Do you have brothers and sisters? I don't have none. I'm alone now, and I will be when I go back to London after the war."

"I'm so sorry," Charlotte said as Lucy nodded and turned away, as she wiped the tears from her cheeks, and Charlotte adjusted her riding hat, and said she had two sisters, and then picked up her crop and gloves, to go out to the stables. She could hardly wait to see Pharaoh, bringing him here was almost like having a friend from home with her. Charles had told her that her father was paying for his upkeep, so as not to be a burden on the Hemmingses. Her mother had told her that they were paying for her to stay there too. The Hemmingses were grateful to have the assistance, although slightly embarrassed to take it. They had no income from the farms at the moment, since all of what they grew was controlled by the government's Ministry of Food, and they ate whatever was left. Several of the wives on the farms had planted home gardens, and kept chickens and rabbits to eat. And their daughters had joined the Women's Land Army and become Land Girls.

Lucy watched her go as Charlotte ran lightly down the stairs in her impeccable, perfectly shined riding boots. She saw the earl dozing in the small drawing room as she left. The countess had gone upstairs for a nap, and there was no one around, as she left the house and walked the short distance to the stables, circled by beautiful old trees. The gardens along the way were in need of attention and were sadly overgrown. The gardeners had been among the first to leave. One of the grooms was walking what appeared to be a very old horse, which Charlotte assumed was the Thoroughbred that the earl rode, when he still did. The countess had mentioned that he suffered from arthritis and seldom rode anymore.

She strode into the stables, and heard Pharaoh whinny the moment she walked in. He recognized her step and sensed her, and she found his stall easily. He nuzzled up next to her, and she saddled him with the saddle and tack the palace grooms had brought to Yorkshire for her, and then changed her mind. She removed the sidesaddle, and took one of the ordinary men's saddles she found in the tack room, so she could ride astride. She shortened the stirrups to the right height for her. She found a groom to give her a leg up, and a moment later, she was heading down a path toward the lake, passing under splendid tall trees which provided shade along the path. She was warm in her jacket but didn't care, as she reached a field and gave Pharaoh his head. He was as happy as his mistress as they took off at full speed. They galloped for half an hour, rode past the lake, and then doubled back at a slow canter, as she smiled at the scenery around her. It was a beautiful place, and she didn't feel quite so far from home with Pharaoh to ride. As she slowed to a trot on the way back, Henry Hemmings approached on his horse and caught up with her. He looked at her admiringly.

"You're a bruising rider. I saw you galloping in the fields before. He's a splendid animal, fit for a queen," he said smiling at her, and for an instant, she wondered if he knew who she was, but she was sure he didn't.

"He's a good boy. He was a gift from my father," she said.

"I'll race you when you get used to the terrain around here," he offered and she nodded, looking pleased. "Although Winston is no match for him, but we'll try." She laughed and smiled as she looked at him, feeling more comfortable than when she arrived.

"It's lovely here," she complimented him, as he rode the big gray horse, who was a fine specimen, but didn't have the bloodline Pharaoh did, and would have a hard time beating him. She noticed that Henry had warm brown eyes, and a shock of dark hair. His riding clothes were old and worn, and she suspected had been his father's from long ago, since they were of another era. There was nothing fashionable about Henry, but he was open and friendly, and happy to have another young person there, and he couldn't ignore the fact that she was a beautiful girl. He knew that Lucy had a crush on him, but it wasn't reciprocal, so he ignored it and pretended not to know. She was a big, awkward, plain girl, and not very interesting to talk to. Her education in a London school had been brief, and her interests were limited. She had helped out in her father's shop every day and sometimes with her mother's sewing, she had told them, which didn't interest Henry. She hated horses, which were his passion, as they were Charlotte's. He liked Lucy. She was a decent girl, and he could sense that she was lonely and wanted to talk at times, but they had nothing in common. And in contrast, he was dazzled by Charlotte, who seemed like a bright shining star to him. She had a much bigger presence than he had expected judging from her size. And she was a remarkable horsewoman.

They picked up the pace, and cantered the rest of the way back to the stables, jumping over several brooks and some logs along the way. They were evenly matched as riders, and it was fun riding with him. They unsaddled their horses after they dismounted, and Charlotte brushed Pharaoh, and fed him some oats and hay, and then she and Henry walked back to the house together. It was almost time for tea, which was their evening meal. She had stayed out for a long time, and went to change. She met Lucy on the stairs, in a plain blue cotton dress, on her way to the kitchen, to help get tea ready for the family. She didn't mind serving them and thought Charlotte would too.

"You can come to the kitchen to help as soon as you change," Lucy said in a curt voice. She had seen Charlotte and Henry from her window as they rode home, and she worried when she saw them. She still hoped that one day, with time, Henry might reciprocate her feelings for him. In light of that, Charlotte's arrival wasn't a happy development for her. Lucy had spent two years hoping that Henry would become enamored with her, and she could make this her home forever, and she didn't have much longer to woo him, before he went to war. Henry would be leaving in a few months, and now this pretty elfin girl from London had shown up. Charlotte hadn't tried to charm him, but she didn't have to. Everything about her was so enchanting that Lucy was sure Henry would fall in love with her, and Lucy's chances would be dashed forever.

She looked glum as she set the table, and banged a few dishes down on it, angry about something Charlotte couldn't guess at. Charlotte arrived a few minutes later in a navy pleated linen skirt, a white cotton blouse, and flat shoes. There was nothing of the seductress about her. She was all innocence, but she was a very beautiful young girl, which the two ancient kitchen maids had noticed too. One of them did the cooking, which was a challenge because they were so limited by rationing. The full brunt of that hadn't hit Charlotte until now, but it did here. At the palace, their chefs were artful about making up for what they lacked for the queen's table, but here in Yorkshire, it was going to be a slim meal. She wasn't a hearty eater so she didn't mind.

The earl and countess came downstairs to the dining room on

time, and the girls sat down with them. They were generous about having Lucy eat with them, and had been since she arrived. It had improved her manners considerably, and she also helped in the kitchen, and served most of the meal. Charlotte tried to help but was embarrassed to realize she had no idea what to do, how to carry the platters in properly, how to set the table, or serve. She was used to everything appearing, with no thought given to how the servants did it, and she knew that here she'd have to learn in order to make herself useful. The countess looked embarrassed when she saw Charlotte carrying in a bowl of thin stew made with pork from the pigs on their farms. She started to tell Charlotte that she didn't need to serve, and the earl gave her a cautioning look. Her Royal Highness would have to be one of the normal people here, pitching in as everyone else did, so no one would suspect her true identity. She was Charlotte White, a commoner now, but nothing about her demeanor made that convincing. She was a princess to the core, and looked it, even in simple clothes. After the meal, she and Lucy carried the plates back to the kitchen. Charlotte looked as though she might drop them but she didn't, much to everyone's relief.

They all retired early and kept country hours, since they woke at dawn. Henry often left to help on the farms before sunrise. He walked Charlotte back to her room that night, and offered to lend her a book about Arabian horses that he had just read, and she thanked him. After he left, she sat down at the small desk in her room to write to her mother. The countess was going to mail her letters for her so no one would see who they were addressed to. With a sigh, Charlotte picked up her pen, wondering what to say to them. She didn't want to shock them by telling them about serving dinner, or worry them, nor tell them about the tiny room that would be hers in the drafty dark manor for the next year. She was anxious to hear from them soon, Alexandra had promised to write too.

"Dear Mama and Papa," she wrote in her elegant penmanship, and began telling them about riding Pharaoh in the beautiful Yorkshire hills. That was something they would understand at least, and she could tell them honestly that she hadn't been troubled by her asthma on the first day there, and didn't need her medicine. She told them about Lucy and said she was very nice. She didn't mention Henry, who had been pleasant to her too, but it didn't seem proper to write about him. She talked about the earl and countess, and their hospitality. It took her an hour to finish the letter, and there were tears in her eyes when she sealed it. Her family, and the palace, and all the problems in London seemed so far away. It was going to be a very long ten or eleven months until she could return. For now, Pharaoh was her only reminder of home in this unfamiliar world. Lucy seemed almost too withdrawn to become a friend, and Henry was a boy, so they wouldn't be close. The earl and countess were kind but seemed so old. She missed her parents and sisters fiercely as she left the letter on her desk and undressed for bed in the tiny room. She had never felt so alone in her life, and the year ahead seemed like an eternity, as she cried herself to sleep that night.

Chapter 2

Charlotte rapidly fell into a routine of leaving the house at dawn every day, and riding Pharaoh through the fields and along paths in the forests for several hours before coming back to the house. There were no morning chores she had to do, and no one objected to her going out riding. Henry saw her leaving the stables one morning, when he was late going to a nearby farm, and asked if he could ride with her. Neither of them could resist the temptation to race each other, and Charlotte always won, because of Pharaoh's extraordinary speed, and her ability to urge him on.

"You shouldn't ride out alone," he chided her gently. "I know you're a very fine rider, and Pharaoh is sure-footed, but if anything ever happens, there would be no one to help you." In part because of her size and the fact that she was a girl, he felt protective of her.

"I don't want to be slowed down by a groom on an old horse," she said, and he laughed.

"Maybe I should ride with you every day." She blushed when he offered, and didn't answer. She could tell that he liked her, but more than anything they liked riding together. Charlotte never flirted with him. She told him about her sisters sometimes, without saying who they were, and he never suspected anything. Charlotte was the companion he would have liked to have had for the last two years, not Lucy. He and Charlotte always found something to talk about, unlike Lucy, with whom he never knew what to say. She was so obviously besotted with him, it embarrassed him, and he felt awkward trying to respond. She was becoming increasingly dour as the friendship between Henry and Charlotte grew. She knew there was no way she could compete with Charlotte's beauty and innocent charm, and within weeks, it was equally obvious to the countess that her son was falling in love with their royal guest. They were becoming inseparable. He now left for the farms later, and came home earlier, changed for dinner, and was always on hand to help Charlotte, even with carrying in the heavy platters for their meals. He had never offered to help Lucy with the same tasks. Charlotte was learning how to make herself useful in the kitchen. She never tried to shirk from the menial tasks, or even the disagreeable ones, like scrubbing the pots, or washing the kitchen floor, which Henry insisted on doing for her. It caused a deep resentment between the two girls, not on Charlotte's part, but Lucy could see easily what was happening. The only one who seemed unaware of the meaning of his intentions was Charlotte. She seemed oblivious and entirely innocent. He was her riding partner, and her friend, as far as she was concerned, and nothing more.

The countess mentioned it to her husband one night in their room, with a look of concern. "Have you noticed how attentive Henry is to our royal guest?" Their bedroom was the only place she could allude to who Charlotte really was.

"What do you mean?" The earl was surprised.

"He's besotted with her, George. Surely you're aware of it?"

"They're just like pups playing together. It doesn't mean anything," he said blandly.

"Don't be so sure. He's not a child anymore, and she's a very appealing young girl. I think she's as oblivious as you are, but I don't want anything to happen between them. I owe it to her parents to keep her safe, not just from enemy bombs, but from my son as well." She looked genuinely worried and her husband laughed.

"You make Henry sound dangerous," he chided her. "They're just having fun. All he thinks about is joining the army. He's not serious about any girl."

"He could be very dangerous for her, if things get out of hand. We have a responsibility to the king and queen. Don't forget that. She's not just any girl."

"It's impossible to forget, my dear. Everything about her is regal. From the way she walks and the way she holds her head, to the way she speaks, and even her kindness to Lucy. There is an innate modesty and grace to the child. She's a lovely girl, and if something did happen between them one day, I certainly wouldn't object and you'd be foolish if you did. Wouldn't you like to have a daughter-in-law like her?"

"Of course. I'd like nothing better. But if that's ever to be, it has to happen in the right way, after the war. They're both much too young, and I doubt very seriously that Their Majesties would be pleased with a surprise betrothal at this point, based on proximity and nothing more sensible. I think they'd be furious with us if something were to come of this now."

"Wars make people grow up very quickly, and inspire deep feelings. Perhaps this is the right match for both of them," he said, and the countess sighed again.

"It is not the right time, or the right circumstances," she said emphatically. "I've tried warning Henry about that, but he has no wish to hear it, and it would be indelicate and presumptuous of me to talk to Charlotte about it. But her mother isn't here to warn her. I think they're both completely innocent, and falling in love. That could be dangerous for them, and for us, if Their Majesties get upset about it."

"This isn't the dark ages. They're not going to lock us in the Tower, Glorianna. I think you're unnecessarily concerned. They're both innocents, children really, and he won't be here for much longer. He'll be eighteen soon enough and in the army."

"They'll be here long enough for them to get themselves in deep water," she reminded her husband. The earl shook his head, got into bed, and a moment later, he was asleep. The countess lay awake, worrying about Henry and Charlotte for several hours.

She tried to speak of it discreetly to her son a few days later, and he looked shocked. "Mama, do you think I would try to seduce her? I would do no such thing." He was deeply offended by her implication. He was a gentleman, but also a healthy young man.

"I wasn't suggesting that you would. But you're both very young, and love is a powerful force at your age. It could lead you into situations neither of you are prepared for, and must avoid at all costs."

"You do Charlotte a disservice, ma'am," he said haughtily. "She would never do something inappropriate, nor would I." Henry was chilly with his mother for the next few days, and he never mentioned her comments to Charlotte. They were just having fun, and enjoyed riding together. All of his local friends were in the army now, and he was anxious to go too. His plans to go to university had been canceled, and would have to wait until after the war. His only friend whom he considered his equal was Charlotte. He could talk to her about almost anything, which was a first for him with a girl. She was his only close female friend or even friend of any kind now, with the war. She let him ride Pharaoh once, to see what a smooth ride he was, and he was stunned by the power of her horse, and her ability to control him with ease. She made it look effortless. She was an extraordinary horsewoman, which was only one of the many things he liked about her.

Henry's mother continued to keep an eye on them, but there was nothing she could really complain about. She was just uneasy about how close they had become. Charlotte only mentioned him in passing in her letters to her parents, with no particular details. She didn't think it was important, and he was leaving soon. She felt sorry for the Hemmingses about how sad she knew they would be once he was gone. He was their only child, and the light of their lives, just as Charles had said. Her mother and oldest sister had already written to her and given her the latest news from the palace and London. Charlotte pounced on the letter with glee the moment the countess handed it to her. She was starving for news of them. And they said how much they missed her too. When she finished reading her mother's letter, she placed it in a leather box her mother had given her for papers and letters, before she left. The box was her mother's, made of fine brown leather, with the crown embossed on it in gold and her mother's initials in small gold letters inside. It was a reminder of home just seeing it on her desk, and warmed her heart and made her homesick at the same time. To anyone not knowing who had given it to her, the gold crown just looked like a handsome decoration. The queen's own father had given it to her on her eighteenth birthday and it was a smaller version of the daily boxes of official documents Alexandra would receive one day as queen. And now Charlotte could keep her correspondence in it, the letters from her mother and sister. Victoria hadn't written to her yet.

There was a heat wave at the beginning of August, six weeks after Charlotte arrived. She felt at ease on the Hemmingses' estate by then, and in their home. Henry took Charlotte swimming in a stream at the back of the property, near one of the farms, and they cavorted like children, splashing each other, and laughing as they doused each other. Charlotte had thought about inviting Lucy, but she had promised to stay with the countess, to clean up some of the gardens with one of the farm boys. The countess had decided to try and do what she could, and Lucy was willing to help, so Henry and Charlotte went swimming without her, and didn't tell her where they were going so she didn't try to join them. They felt guilty saying it, but agreed that Lucy was dreary company, although she was helpful to Henry's mother, but no fun for them. And she couldn't swim.

They were sitting on the bank of the stream, their horses tied to a tree, and Henry lay back in the grass, admiring her in her bathing costume.

"You're so beautiful, Charlotte. I think you're the prettiest girl I've ever seen." She blushed and looked away, not sure how to respond. She didn't think of him in that way, just as a boy, and a friend.

"Don't be silly," she brushed off the compliment. "My sisters are much prettier than I am, especially Victoria. She's a real beauty." Something occurred to him then, an odd coincidence.

"Did your parents name the three of you after the royal princesses?" He had never thought of it before, and the question startled her. She was silent for a moment and then shrugged.

"I imagine they did. I never gave it any thought."

"It can't be an easy life, being royal," he mused. "I would hate it. All those official events they must have to attend. And you have to behave all the time."

"I suppose so," she said vaguely, and then threw a handful of water at him to distract him, which proved to be effective. They got back in the stream again and swam some more. They were both smiling when they got out, and dried off in their bathing suits, and Charlotte noticed him looking down at her. He was very tall, which made her feel even more diminutive next to him, and before she could say anything, he slipped his arms around her, pulled her close to him, and kissed her. He hadn't meant to do it, but couldn't stop himself. A wave of passion for her had just washed over him. At first she was too shocked to react. Then she melted into his arms and kissed him back. When they stopped, she stood staring at him with a serious look in her eyes. She seemed even more beautiful to him.

"Why did you do that?" she asked in barely more than a whisper, and she was stunned at herself for responding so readily. She had never been kissed by a boy before.

"Because I'm in love with you, Charlotte, and I wanted you to know it. I'm going away soon, in a couple of months. I didn't want to leave without your knowing how I feel about you. Maybe we could get engaged before I go," he said hopefully, sounding innocent and childlike, and a ripple of fear and reality ran down her spine.

"I can't do that. My parents have never met you."

"Could we go to London to see them?" he suggested naïvely.

"You know we're not supposed to travel. We can't just go running down to London to see them, and they can't come here. They're too busy. If we ever get engaged, it would have to be after the war." He looked disappointed, but willing to accept it. People were not moving around the country with ease, so she made sense. "Besides, we're too young. We're both just seventeen," she reminded him.

"I'll be eighteen soon, and you'll be eighteen next year."

"That's too young to get engaged. My parents would be upset," she said sensibly. She hesitated for a moment then, and looked at him. He could see that she wanted to say something more, but he had no idea what it was. "Besides, there are things you don't know about me, about my parents, and my family. Maybe things you wouldn't like." He was surprised by that and tried to guess.

"Has your father ever been to prison? Has he murdered someone?" he teased her and she shook her head. "Is he a spy? Or a German?" She hesitated then and nodded.

"Not a spy, but we have German ancestors, quite a lot of them in fact." The British royal house and her family tree had been heavily intertwined with Germans for centuries. Most of the Windsors, including Queen Victoria, were originally Saxe-Coburg-Gothas. There were German Coburgs on every throne and in nearly every royal house in Europe.

"My parents wouldn't like that, about your having German relatives," he admitted. And then he looked at her. "I don't care what skeletons you have in your closet, and I don't care that your father doesn't have a title, if you're worried about that. My parents would prefer it if he did, but they're falling in love with you too. And if we marry, you'll have my title one day." She smiled. It never dawned on him for an instant that she might have a title herself, far more important than his. "None of that makes any difference to me, and it shouldn't to you." He kissed her again then, and in spite of her concerns, she kissed him with abandon, and they were both breathless when they stopped.

"We should get back," Charlotte said modestly. "I promised to help Lucy set the table when she finishes with your mother in the garden." She put her riding clothes over her wet bathing suit and he did the same, and he gave her a leg up onto her powerful stallion. The horses had stood peacefully by, tied to the tree, grazing on the grass. His mare and her stallion were fast friends by now, and always pleased to see each other on their morning rides.

On the way back, Henry looked at her curiously. "Were there other things you wanted to tell me?" he asked her cautiously. He had a feeling that there were, and there were things she wasn't saying that were weighing on her. She shook her head. She didn't feel ready to tell him who her parents were. It was too big a secret to share so soon. He knew her only as Charlotte White, the daughter of a civil servant and a secretary in London. She knew he would be profoundly shocked by the truth. She would have to tell him eventually, but not yet. And his parents knew, even if he didn't.

They left their horses in the stable, and hurried into the house. It was later than they'd thought, and there was suddenly an unspoken intimacy between them that one could sense, now that he had kissed her. Lucy was aware of it when they walked into the kitchen, and Henry's mother when she saw them that night. As time went on, she worried more and more. They were so close and so comfortable with each other. Too much so, in her opinion. And Lucy was mournful and silent all evening. She felt left out by the two of them, as though they had a secret from her.

That night, Charlotte sat at her desk in front of a blank page for a long time, wanting to tell her mother about him, but she hated to do it in a letter, and wasn't sure what to say. That she loved him? That he loved her? That he wanted to ask for her hand one day? Perhaps they could make a pact just between the two of them before he left, and then get engaged after the war. But he had to meet her parents first. She was thinking about it, and still hadn't started the letter to her mother when she heard a soft knock on her door. She tiptoed to it, and opened it a crack, and Henry was standing on the other side, in the moonlight, and smiled at her.

"I wanted to kiss you good night," he whispered. "Can I come in?"

"You shouldn't," she said, her heart pounding with excitement, but opened the door anyway. He walked in quickly on silent feet, and closed it behind him, and an instant later she was in his arms, and they were kissing again. His kissing her that afternoon by the stream had changed everything between them, and his admissions about his hopes for them had opened the floodgates that had been closed until then.

"I love you, Charlotte," he whispered in the dark. Her whole body was shaking when she answered him. She didn't want Lucy to hear him in her room.

"I love you too," she whispered back. "Now you have to go." No matter how much she loved him, she didn't want to do anything foolish, and after several more kisses, reluctantly, he left. She didn't write to her mother that night, but lay down on her bed, thinking about him. She closed her eyes for a minute, her heart full of him, and it was morning when she woke up.

They all went to church in the village that day, and Charlotte earnestly prayed not to do anything with him that she'd regret, and even more earnestly that he'd survive the war, and nothing bad would happen to him. Lucy had gone to church with them, and they all had lunch in the garden afterward, in the part that Lucy and the countess had worked hard to clear the day before, and the countess praised how hard she had worked, which cheered her up a bit. Afterward, Henry and Charlotte took a long, slow walk down to the small lake near the house. There was a larger one they often rode to. They didn't invite Lucy to come and she looked hurt.

"I meant what I said yesterday, you know," he said seriously to Charlotte once they were alone. "I'd like to get engaged before I leave, and I want to marry you one day, after the war. I don't want to get off on the wrong foot with your parents, if you think they'd be angry at your getting engaged to someone they don't know." He had thought about it all night, and in church, and so had she. "Do you think I should write to them, to ask their permission?"

She almost shuddered at the thought. "They'd be *very* angry if we got engaged without their meeting you. And I don't think you should write to them. I know they would say we're too young." It was true. "I want you to meet them. But there won't be any opportunity before you go. We talked about why. They can't come here, and we can't go to London, so we have to wait." She was very firm about it. There was no way they could get engaged now. "They're much too busy at their jobs."

Henry narrowed his eyes then, and smiled at her, as they sat down on the grass. "I think your father must be a spy of some kind. You're very mysterious about him. Does he work for MI5 or MI6?" He was fascinated by military intelligence himself and she laughed and shook her head.

"No," she said simply, "and he's not a spy. I told you he works for the government." But she knew Henry would have keeled over if she said he was the king, and probably not believe her.

"That doesn't explain anything. He could be a mailman for all I know." She laughed.

"He's *not* a mailman. I can promise you that. He serves his country and the people of Great Britain, and he's very dedicated to his job."

"He sounds like a good person."

"He is," she said solemnly, "and I think he will like you very much. And so will my mama. And Alexandra, my older sister. I can't tell about Victoria. She'll probably hate you because you're my friend. Victoria never approves of anything I do, just to be difficult."

"I want to be more than your friend," he said and kissed her and they lay side by side in the grass and he pressed his body against her, and despite all her resolve, she didn't resist or stop him, as his hand slipped under her dress. No one could see them in the tall grass, but she was afraid that what she was doing was wrong, and knew it was, but it was impossible to resist him. Suddenly, all she wanted was to be with him, and lie in his arms.

They walked back to the house with his arm around her shoulders, and they looked as though they were lost in another world. Fortunately, no one was around when they returned. His parents were taking a nap, and Lucy was in the kitchen, helping to prepare dinner. They had both regained their composure when they sat down for their evening meal with the others.

He knocked on her door again that night, and she let him in, and they lay on her bed and kissed and fondled each other for a long time, and she finally forced herself to stop and whispered to him that he had to leave and was sorry when he did.

His late visits to her room became a nightly occurrence, and they inched closer and closer to the edge of reason day by day. She couldn't stop him anymore and didn't want to, and the inevitable finally happened. The heat wave had persisted, and it was steaming hot in her room, right under the roof. He slowly peeled away the thin cotton dress she was wearing one night and she took off his shirt. The feel of their skin touching ignited like dynamite, and suddenly their clothes were on the floor and they were naked in each other's arms and couldn't stop this time. All they wanted was each other. They did everything they could not to make any noise and their lovemaking was exquisite agony as their bodies joined with all the passion and tenderness they felt for each other. There was no lock on her door, and Charlotte was terrified someone would come in and discover them, but no one did. No one ever came to her room at night except Henry. Lucy was a heavy sleeper and heard nothing from next door.

Henry finally tore himself away from her, and left her just before the sun came up. Before that, they lay in bed awake, after they made love, talking about the future they would share, and all the things they would do together after the war, once they were married. He wanted to take her to Paris for their honeymoon. The birds were already singing, as though celebrating their union. Charlotte knew she was his now forevermore, and whatever would come, she was ready to face it at his side. She could survive anything now, with the added strength of his love. Their youthful passion and desire had overtaken them and they became adults in a single night.

She sat quietly at breakfast the next day, with a dazed look on her face. Henry had already left for the farms, and his mother thought that Charlotte looked strange.

"Are you all right? Are you ill?" Charlotte shook her head, and didn't say a word. All she could think of was what had happened the night before. She had no regrets and only wanted more. The countess was alarmed at how remote she seemed and disconnected from everyone around her. She tried speaking to her husband, who once again laughed at her concerns.

"Even if they fancy themselves in love," he reassured her, "it doesn't mean anything at their age."

"It's different in wartime, George. There's a kind of desperation that sets in when people are no longer sure how long they'll live."

"They'll both live a long time, and fall in love many times after this. This is child's play, my dear. You have no cause for concern." He didn't see the looks in their eyes when they gazed at each other, but his wife did. Charlotte went to bed early that night, and they made love again as soon as they thought everyone was asleep. They were noisier this time than they meant to be. Lucy woke up with a start when she thought she heard a muffled scream. She heard the floorboards creak an hour or so later, opened her door a crack and peered out. She saw Henry tiptoeing to the stairs, with his shirt off, wearing only his pajama bottoms, and guessed instantly what it meant. She closed her door just as softly, with a deep anger burning inside her, and raw hatred for both of them. She felt cheated of all her dreams. Charlotte had stolen them from her. Lucy didn't know what she would do about it, but she knew her time would come one day to get even with them.

As it turned out, retribution came in another form, within weeks. A month later, Charlotte appeared at breakfast looking green. She rushed away from the table within minutes and was violently ill. When the countess came to her bedroom afterward, Charlotte told her that she felt sure she had eaten something spoiled the night before. The countess was worried and sympathetic, and offered to call the doctor, but Charlotte insisted she was fine and it wasn't serious.

Two weeks later, in mid-September, she was just as ill, even more violently than she had been at first. She hadn't been out on Pharaoh in weeks, and despite their innocence, both Charlotte and Henry could guess what had happened. The waistband of her skirt was already tight, and she was so nauseous, she could barely eat. The only time she felt better was in Henry's arms. He spent every night with her now, and didn't want to leave her feeling so ill.

"What are we going to do?" she asked him one night, as tears slid down her cheeks. There was no doubt in their minds. She was six weeks pregnant by their calculations. She must have gotten pregnant immediately. They were both young and healthy, and nature had taken the upper hand once they lost control. Now they would have to ride the wave until the end. Or she would. He was leaving soon. His birthday was only weeks away, in October, and the army would take him soon after.

"We have to tell my mother," he said, sounding determined. "She'll know what to do. Do you think something is wrong that you're so sick?"

"I don't know. I've never known anyone who had a baby, and my mother never talks about things like that. We should really tell her too. But I don't want to tell her in a letter, and we can't just show up in London and give her this news. It would kill her, and my father too." And they had told her not to call them, the lines weren't secure, and there were always many people listening on the lines at the palace. Everyone would know instantly, and she would be disgraced.

"And they'd hate me forever," he said, worried.

They told his mother the next day. Like two children who had committed an unpardonable crime, they went to her study together after breakfast and told her the truth. She closed her eyes for a minute, trying to stay calm, and gather her wits about her. How was she going to face Queen Anne, or worse the king, with this piece of news? They had entrusted her with their daughter, and her son had gotten her pregnant, at seventeen. There had been no sign of her asthma since she'd arrived, but what she had now was much worse. The countess was desperately trying to think about what was the best thing to do in the circumstances, and how to handle it. They were innocent children in a dangerously adult situation, which could easily become the scandal of the century. And Charlotte couldn't sit down with her parents and discuss it face-to-face. This was wartime, and nothing was simple, let alone for a pregnant seventeen-year-old princess. The countess could guess that her parents would be devastated.

"Do you want to go home?" she asked Charlotte quietly. It would create a scandal ultimately, but she might prefer to deal with this at home, with her own parents, instead of his.

"No, I don't," she said firmly. "They want me to be here. I know they'll be furious at first, but maybe the best thing is to tell them afterward. There is nothing they can do about it then."

"I'm not sure that's fair to them," the countess said sternly, "to confront them with a fait accompli, a love child after the war." The thought of it made her cringe. She wanted to do the right thing, and so did Henry. He was an honorable young man and deeply in love with Charlotte. They were babies having a baby.

"I can't just write to my mother and tell her this, and they don't want me in London, they want me here. There's nothing they can do

to stop it now." There were indeed several options, but in her innocence Charlotte was aware of none of them, and an abortion was far
too dangerous for a royal princess entrusted to their care, so the
countess didn't suggest it. The countess thought of something else
then, which might mitigate the circumstances somewhat when they
would finally have to face the king and queen.

"Do you want to get married, or do you plan to have the child out
of wedlock?" she asked them, shaking at the thought. "A legitimate
baby fathered by the son of an earl might be considerably more pal-
atable to your parents than an illegitimate child after the war."

"Can we get married, Mama?" Henry looked shocked. It hadn't
occurred to him since they were both underage. "Do we have to go
to Scotland?" It was still where most people went to elope.

"You can get married here, with your father's permission. You're
almost eighteen. And we have a document giving us the right to
make decisions for Charlotte in the event of an emergency, and I'd
say this is. We can give her our consent to marry. I think we should
do it quickly. You may have to report for duty very soon after your
birthday," which was only weeks away, and then he would be gone,
and it would be too late to legitimize the child.

"Will you marry me?" Henry asked her, looking straight at Charlotte, and she nodded, looking stunned. It hadn't occurred to her either, without her parents' knowledge or consent, but at least the
child would be legitimate when she told them what had happened.
They wouldn't be pleased, but they would be even less so if faced
with what they would consider a bastard child. She knew her mother
would be hurt that Charlotte hadn't told her, but she would forgive
them if they had done the right thing, and Henry was respectable.

They would all avoid disgrace if they married immediately, and it was Henry and Charlotte's fondest wish anyway for the future. The future had just speeded up at a rapid rate in the form of a baby.

"Yes, I will marry you," Charlotte said clearly, suddenly sounding very grown up, even though she looked like a child.

"I'll speak to your father," Glorianna Hemmings said to her son. "I imagine there will be hell to pay with your parents eventually because I let this happen," she said to Charlotte, "but I pray they will forgive me. I agree with Charlotte," she said to her son, "we can't write them about this kind of thing in a letter. It's too complicated to call her parents, and they asked us not to. And if you marry, you'll have done the right thing. It's the best we can do in this situation, since you've both been so foolish. I was afraid of something like this happening. Your father didn't believe me," she said to Henry, and he nodded, embarrassed at the mess they had made. Neither of them had expected this to happen, nor knew how to avoid it. They had thrown caution to the winds, and somehow thought they'd get away with it. They realized now that Charlotte must have gotten pregnant immediately, possibly the first time they made love. His mother wasn't pleased but she felt sorry for them both.

George Hemmings agreed to give his permission for both of them to marry by special license, but he insisted that the marriage be kept secret. If it somehow got out that Princess Charlotte Windsor had gotten married in haste, it would expose the reason for it, and the scandal for sure. And he didn't want the king and queen hearing it as a rumor or idle gossip that would spread like wildfire, and even wind up in the press. He was adamant that their marriage, and eventually the baby, must be kept secret until after they met with the king and queen, which wasn't possible now and wouldn't be for some time. He was calm and sensible about it. And he wasn't entirely sorry, as he told his wife. Charlotte was an excellent match for his son, to say the least. His wife scolded him for it. They all agreed that both the marriage and the pregnancy had to remain a secret between the four of them. Under no circumstances did they want Charlotte's parents to find out about it before they had a face-to-face meeting with the Hemmingses, who intended to beg their forgiveness for the foolishness of their son. And until then, no one was to know that anything was afoot. Henry's father impressed that on both of them, and both young people agreed, with deep remorse for the situation they had created and gratitude for his parents' help.

They met with the vicar the following afternoon, and he agreed to marry them by special license since Henry would be leaving so soon to join the army. He thought it very touching and romantic. The Hemmingses did not tell him about the pregnancy, or who Charlotte really was. Their special license said only that her name was Charlotte Elizabeth White, which was on her identity papers provided by the Home Office.

The ceremony was conducted in secrecy and privacy at the church, with Henry's parents standing beside them. Charlotte wore a simple white wool dress that she had brought with her, and carried a bouquet of white flowers from the countess's garden. Henry looked tall and handsome and suddenly more mature in the role of groom. Then they all went home and had dinner together. Nothing more was said about the marriage. And Lucy knew nothing about their secret wedding, although she knew that Henry spent his nights with Charlotte, but she said nothing to either of them and kept the information to herself for future use.

Lucy had started eating dinner in the kitchen with the two elderly servants a while back, and barely spoke to Charlotte anymore. Her eyes burned with the fury of a scorned woman anytime she saw Henry, and he paid no attention to her. He had bigger things on his mind. And he had no patience with Lucy's fantasies about him, and her petty jealousies of Charlotte. Charlotte was his wife now. It changed everything in his eyes. He was her protector, and had vowed to be forever. His parents were relieved that they had done the right thing for the child Charlotte was carrying, even if it meant facing the ire of Their Majesties at some point once they knew. Hopefully they would forgive them, although it seemed inevitable that they would be angry at first, with their daughter getting pregnant at seventeen and rushing into a hasty marriage, no matter how respectable the Hemmingses were.

The one thing Henry didn't understand was why it was impossible to call them.

"You don't tell people something like this on the phone," his father said and refused to explain it further, much to Charlotte's relief. Henry still had no idea who she was.

Henry and Charlotte retired early on their wedding day, and she slept in his room discreetly that night with his parents' permission. They had to do something to acknowledge their wedding night. Charlotte was still feeling ill, but she looked happy as she sat next to him on the bed, and he smiled at her. She had tiptoed down the stairs after Lucy went to bed and she felt sure she was asleep.

"So, my darling, we are now secretly married, and are having a secret baby. Do you think your parents will forgive us?"

"Eventually, though it won't be easy at first." She knew her father's temper but also his spirit of forgiveness. And they loved her, and would ultimately accept him and the baby. They had no other choice.

"I don't know why it has to remain such a dark secret. We're married now, our child will be respectable," Henry said, looking pleased.

"It has to remain secret because my parents don't know about it yet." His parents understood it better than he did. "It's a matter of being respectful of them, we don't want a rumor to get back to them before we can see them in person and can tell them ourselves, about the baby and our marriage."

"Why would it become a rumor? It's not so remarkable really. Charlotte White married Henry Hemmings, son of the Earl of Ainsleigh. I should think they'd be pleased. The daughter of a civil servant will be a countess one day." He acted as though it was a gift he had given her. But she had a far more important title of her own.

"Not exactly. It's not quite as simple as that," Charlotte said quietly, looking at her husband, who was half man and half boy. She felt like a woman now. She had grown up overnight, faced with the surprise pregnancy, and it meant a great deal to her that she was now his wife. She took their marriage very seriously, no matter how it had started.

"Why isn't it that simple? Are they anti-monarchists?" Henry was surprised, thinking about his father's title.

"On the contrary." She smiled at him. "It's about who my parents are."

"A civil servant and a secretary. You still haven't told me what branch of the government your father works for," he said casually, as he leaned over and kissed her.

"Your mother and father know who my parents are," Charlotte said mysteriously.

"Then why can't I know too?" He looked petulant. He hated secrets that didn't include him. And she could think of no way to break it to him other than just tell him. It was time that he knew who they were, and who she was, even if they didn't know about him.

She took a breath and said it simply and directly. "My father is the King of England, King Frederick, my mother is the queen consort, Queen Anne." There was dead silence in Henry's bedroom after she said it and he stared at her, and then started to laugh.

"Very funny. All right. Now tell me the truth. Are they communists or spies?" He couldn't stop laughing at the joke she was playing on him, but she looked oddly serious.

"That is the truth," she said in a quiet voice.

"And that means you are Her Royal Highness Princess Charlotte Windsor." As he said it, he stopped and stared at her again. "Oh my God, you're not . . . are you?" She nodded. "Charlotte, why didn't you tell me? Your sisters, Alexandra, Victoria, and you. I should have known. Oh my God. How could you not say anything before this? Your father will have me hanged for getting you pregnant." He looked genuinely terrified at the thought.

"No, he won't. He's a very kind man. They'll be upset at first because of how it happened, and that I didn't tell them. But we're married now, and the baby will be legitimate. That will be very important to them," and it was to her too, and to Henry and his parents.

"Charlotte! You're a royal princess? I never even guessed. I thought your father was a spy or something. Does anyone else know here?" He looked bowled over by her news. He had thought her sisters' names were a coincidence. The truth seemed enormous to him now.

"Only your parents know, and now you," Charlotte said. "It doesn't change anything, but it complicates things a bit. No one is supposed to know I'm here, which is why I'm using a different name, at the request of the cabinet and the prime minister, to ensure my safety."

"And you live in Buckingham Palace?" Henry was still staring at her in disbelief, as it all came clear to him.

"Yes, until I came here," Charlotte said quietly.

"Am I supposed to call you 'Your Royal Highness' now?" He looked nervous and she laughed.

"Hopefully not." She smiled at him. He sat looking into the distance for a moment, trying to absorb what she had just told him. It all felt so unreal, especially when he fell asleep that night with his arms around her, and realized again that his new parents-in-law, whom he'd never met, and knew nothing of his existence, were the King and Queen of England, and his wife was their daughter.

"Good night, Your Royal Highness," he whispered to her as they fell asleep. She laughed and cuddled closer to him. It was even more shocking to realize that the baby they would have would be fourth in line to the throne. In his wildest dreams, Henry had never imagined anything like this happening to him. He was married to a royal princess, and he was only seventeen. It sounded like a fairytale to him. But all that mattered to both of them was how much they loved each other, for better or worse, and Charlotte was now his wife.

Chapter 3

Two weeks after Charlotte and Henry's clandestine wedding in the little village church, they celebrated Henry's eighteenth birthday at dinner. Lucy sat at dinner with them that night, and drank a little too much of the wine the earl had opened for the occasion. Because of the war, it was a bittersweet event.

Charlotte was sleeping in her own room again, after their wedding night in Henry's room. Henry was spending every night upstairs with her. They tried to be as quiet as possible, so Lucy didn't hear them, but she was well aware that Henry was in the room next door with Charlotte, and more than once she peeked into the hall in time to see Henry head down the stairs before everyone else got up. Lucy fully understood what was going on, or thought she did. She was sure that Henry and Charlotte were having an affair, and she had guessed that Charlotte was pregnant because she threw up consistently. They had admitted nothing to anyone, and Lucy was biding her time to see what they would do. She had no idea that Henry's parents were aware of it, or that the two young people had gotten married. And she had no suspicions at all about Charlotte's royal birth. She thought she was just a fancy London girl, possibly with rich parents, judging by her accent and clothes. It had occurred to her immediately that the information about their affair, and possibly an illegitimate baby, might prove useful to her one day. She had to think of her future and what she would do when the war was over. She had nowhere to go. Maybe they would pay her to keep quiet. And she wondered if Charlotte would give the baby away and have it adopted in secret when it was time for her to go home. Lucy thought she wasn't likely to keep it at seventeen. Lucy wasn't normally a conniving girl, but alone in the world now, she had to think of herself. And Henry's loving Charlotte instead of her still stung. She would have liked to be the one in his arms every night. And she thought she might have been if Charlotte had never come.

Charlotte had given up her morning rides on Pharaoh ever since she realized she was pregnant. She missed riding him, and meeting Henry along the way.

A week after his birthday, Henry received the notice he'd been expecting for months. He had to report for training in five days, at Catterick Camp in North Yorkshire, the largest training camp of the British Army. He'd already had a physical exam in Leeds, with an A1 designation. His training would last six weeks, and at the beginning of December, he would ship out, and he had no idea where. It was suddenly very real, and Henry and Charlotte spent every night wide awake, making love and talking until nearly dawn. His going to war terrified them both, especially now that they were married and had a baby on the way. The whole house was subdued, with the prospect of Henry leaving for the army. His mother looked panicked, and his father seemed to have aged overnight.

Charlotte's letters to her parents and sisters were brief during Henry's last days at home. She explained that the Hemmingses' son was reporting for duty, as had been expected, and that they were all upset to see him go. Her mother wrote back sympathetically and wished him well. It was the first time Charlotte had mentioned him in any detail and Alexandra commented to their mother that Charlotte sounded sad about his leaving too.

"You don't suppose Charlotte is in love with him, do you?" Victoria commented to them when they got her most recent letter, which sounded extremely serious. The queen brushed it off as an absurd idea.

"Of course not. He's just a child, and so is your sister. If she was in love with him, she'd have mentioned it before. She's barely said two words about him until now. I do feel sorry for his mother, though. It must be very hard to see your only child go to war. They sound like lovely people from the correspondence I've had from his mother. Charles said they're older, and the countess has suggested her husband is in poor health. I do hope Charlotte isn't a burden to them. Maybe she'll cheer them up once their boy is away."

"He may be barely more than a boy, but that's who's fighting this war, Mother," Victoria said tartly, but she decided that her mother was right. Charlotte had hardly ever mentioned him, and she certainly would have if he mattered to her, which made a romance seem unlikely, and Victoria always thought her younger sister childish and overprotected by their mother because of her asthma, which had apparently improved in Yorkshire, or so she said in her letters. Victoria had enjoyed the last four months without her younger sister afoot, although she was starting to miss her, not acutely, but she admitted to Alexandra that she missed arguing with her, which seemed perverse.

The Hemmingses took Henry to the station on the appointed day with the train warrant the army had sent him. Charlotte and Lucy came too, to see him off. Lucy looked longingly at him, and dared to kiss his cheek when she said goodbye to him, and then Henry took Charlotte in his arms and kissed her in front of everyone, as though they had nothing to hide, which made Lucy furious, although she didn't show it. She would have liked him to kiss her that way, but he never had. She silently blamed Charlotte for stealing her rightful place in his affections. She had caught him by sleeping with him and being a whore.

"Take care of yourself," he whispered to Charlotte. He was hoping to come home on a brief leave before he shipped out, but he had no idea if they'd allow him to or if there would be time. This might be the last he saw of them for a very long while. He kissed his mother's cheek, shook hands with his father, wished Lucy well and kissed Charlotte again, and then boarded the train, and stood waving from the compartment. He opened the window so he could lean out and see them until they disappeared from sight.

They were a somber, silent group when they went back to the house, each of them lost in their own thoughts about him. Lucy went into the kitchen as she did every night, with tears in her eyes now, thinking of Henry, and Charlotte went to lie down. All she wanted to do was think about him and keep the image of him in her mind.

His parents retired to their room, and the countess looked red-

eyed when they came down to dinner a few minutes late. The earl
was subdued and barely talked. Life at Ainsleigh Hall was going to
be very different without Henry. The vitality seemed to have slipped
out of the place. Everyone went to bed right after dinner that night.

For Lucy, it was a relief not to see Henry hovering over Charlotte,
or know that he was next door in her arms at night. She could cher-
ish her fantasies again, now that he was gone, and hoped he missed
her. She and Charlotte hardly spoke to each other anymore, just to
chat. The rivalry between them, for Henry's affections, had been too
strong. Lucy had never been in that race, no matter how hard she
tried, but she chose not to see it that way. She still believed that
Henry would have fallen in love with her eventually if Charlotte
hadn't come along. As she saw it, Charlotte had stolen her dreams
from her.

For the next six weeks, their days were spent waiting for letters
from him, which were brief and to the point. He said the training
was arduous and he was exhausted every night, but he was well and
hoped they were too. He wrote to Charlotte separately and told her
how much he loved her, and how happy he was to be her husband.
She put his letters in a drawer tied with a ribbon, and his parents
shared the letters they'd had from him. They were proud to have a
son serving the country. At the end of his training, he was allowed to
come home for two days, before he shipped out. He still had no idea
where he was going, and couldn't have told them anyway.

Henry looked tall and handsome in his uniform when he came
home on leave. His hair was short, and had been shaved at the beginning of his training, he had trimmed down, his shoulders looked
broader, and every moment he spent with them was precious. He
managed to share himself equally with his parents and his wife, and

even spent a few minutes chatting with Lucy, and asked her to take care of Charlotte, which stung. Henry had no idea that Lucy still cherished romantic fantasies about him. She hid them well.

They shared an early Christmas with him, and his mother gave him a few things he could take with him. Then forty hours after he'd arrived, he was gone. Charlotte stood freezing on the platform in frigid weather, watching him go. His eyes never left hers as the train pulled out, and she watched him until he was only a tiny speck in uniform, and then she got in the car and went home with his parents. Charlotte was four months pregnant by then, and it was starting to show, but it didn't really matter since no one knew who she was, and she hardly ever left Ainsleigh Hall. All they could do now was wait for his letters and pray that he was alive and well. Charlotte never mentioned the pregnancy to Lucy and the others, but they could see it now.

Christmas was quiet and dismal without him a few weeks after he left. Charlotte had three letters from him in January, and she guessed that he was somewhere in Italy or North Africa, but he couldn't say, and there were several lines blacked out by the censors when he said too much. The days seemed interminable without him, and Charlotte was homesick for her family now too. Yorkshire suddenly seemed a long way from home. And as her pregnancy became more pronounced, she missed her mother and sisters, although they knew nothing of what was happening to her. Only Henry spoke of their baby in his letters, and then in the beginning of February, his letters stopped. His father suggested that his division was probably on the move from one location to another and reassured his wife and Charlotte that the letters would start again soon. They believed him for several weeks, and then the dreaded telegram came, informing them that Henry had died a hero's death, in battle with the enemy. They regretted that it was impossible to bring his body home. He had died and his body had been lost at Peter Beach in the Battle of Anzio. The War Office extended their sincere sympathy to his parents. His father was inconsolable, and took to his bed immediately. Charlotte felt sick when she read the telegram again and again, and it sank in that her baby would have no father. She was bereft. She reported his death to her parents, and they wrote a personal letter of condolence to the earl and countess.

The earl's health deteriorated from the moment Henry died. He'd had a bad cough for weeks, which rapidly turned into pneumonia, and three weeks after they learned of his son's death, George Hemmings died too. They were all in shock, with one death on the heels of the other. It left the earl's widow and Henry's to console each other. Glorianna Hemmings had lost a husband and a son, and Charlotte her husband and the father of her unborn child. She was less than two months from her due date when her father-in-law died at the end of March, and a widow at seventeen when Henry died in February. Lucy heard her sobbing in her bed at night, and Charlotte looked ravaged. She wrote to her parents of the countess's grief and how sad they all were, but it never occurred to them and she never said that she was grieving for Henry too, and that he had been her husband and the father of her unborn baby. It infuriated Lucy that the countess was aware of the baby and didn't seem to mind. She was even pleased about it.

"You'll be going home in a few months, after you have the baby, when you turn eighteen," her mother-in-law said sadly one night.

She couldn't imagine life without Charlotte now. They sat together by the fire every evening, while she told her stories of Henry's childhood. Glorianna had a distant look in her eye most of the time now, remembering the two men she had lost. Waiting for Henry's child to be born was the only ray of sunshine in their lives. And alone in her room, Lucy cried for Henry too. It was a time of loss and sorrow for them all. The countess moved Charlotte to a bedroom close to her own as the due date approached.

The weather warmed slightly in late April, just before Charlotte's due date in May. Buds began to appear in the countess's garden. She and Lucy had worked hard to clear away the weeds, and plant some flowers, which were the first sign of spring. Charlotte put them in vases on the table when they had dinner, trying to cheer them all up. All she could think about now was Henry and their fatherless child. He had been much too young to die. It seemed so pointless. She read his letters to her every night.

The Germans had increased their air raids since January, and the bombing of London was severe again. Charlotte wondered if her parents would still let her come home even after her eighteenth birthday, since the bombing was worse again. For once, although she missed her parents, she was glad not to be in London, so her baby could be born in the peaceful Yorkshire countryside, without bombs falling every night among air raid sirens. And in their letters, her parents and sisters sounded busy and anxious about the war. They were relieved that she was safe. But at her end, Charlotte was sad not to be able to share the progress of her pregnancy with her mother and sisters, although her mother-in-law was very kind. She missed her own mother terribly and clung to Henry's as the only mother at hand.

It was the second week of May when the pains finally began. She had written to her mother the night before, and wished she could tell her about the baby, but knew she couldn't until she saw her, hopefully sometime in the next few months, and then she would tell her everything that had happened, about marrying Henry and how much she loved him. She was a widow now, and all she wanted was to see their baby and for it to arrive safely.

The countess sent for the doctor as soon as Charlotte told her that the contractions had started. He arrived quickly, and had been concerned for the past several weeks that the baby had grown too large for her tiny body. There was a hospital nearby, and he hoped she wouldn't need a cesarean section, which was a complicated operation for both mother and child, and one or both frequently didn't survive it. He had shared his fears with the countess, but said nothing to Charlotte, not wanting to frighten her. Her belly was huge in the final weeks of her confinement. She looked so uncomfortable that at the last Lucy wasn't even jealous of her, to be having Henry's child. Until then, it had irked her constantly.

The pains were already powerful when the doctor got there after labor began. Glorianna was sure she'd come through it. She was healthy and young. The doctor sat by Charlotte's bedside from morning to nightfall, and her mother-in-law stayed with her. It was an arduous birth, and after sixteen hours of hard labor, there had been no progress. The baby appeared to be too large to come down the birth canal, and the countess and the doctor exchanged a worried look. It was midnight by then, and Charlotte was too far gone to move her to the hospital, even by ambulance. Glorianna applied damp cloths to her brow, while the doctor tried to maneuver the baby down. The maids and Lucy could hear Charlotte's screams throughout the house, and the doctor looked at the countess in dismay twenty-four hours after labor began.

"Charlotte, you have to try harder," her mother-in-law told her with a sense of urgency now. Charlotte was getting weaker and she couldn't push anymore. "The baby is big, and you have to push it out. Think of Henry, and how much he loved you. You have to do this for Henry. You have to push the baby out." Charlotte renewed her efforts, and the physician attempted to turn the baby to ease its passage, which only made Charlotte scream louder. She was doing the best she could, but getting nowhere. Lucy had peered several times into the bedroom where Charlotte was laboring and disappeared just as quickly at the sounds of her agony. It seemed so much worse than she'd expected and it frightened her.

Charlotte renewed her efforts then, and used every ounce of her remaining strength to move the baby down, and slowly, it began to emerge, and the doctor gave a shout of victory when he saw the baby's head, which made Charlotte try that much harder as she clenched her mother-in-law's hand and they cheered her on. It took another two hours of agonizing pushing, while Charlotte hung between consciousness and oblivion and felt as though she was drowning, as her baby finally came into the world with the cord tangled tightly around her, which was what had been holding her back. The doctor cut the cord and freed her, and he held her up, cleared her airway with a suction bulb, and the baby gave a hearty cry. Charlotte smiled weakly when she saw her. It was a girl, a very big baby. It was difficult to imagine that a child that size had emerged from such a tiny person, and when they weighed her, she weighed just over nine pounds. Charlotte had slipped into merciful unconsciousness by then, just after the baby was born, and he had given her drops for the pain which allowed him to repair the tears the baby had caused before Charlotte woke up again. She was bleeding heavily, which he assured the countess was to be expected after such a difficult birth, with a baby that large, and he said the bleeding would soon stop.

"What are you going to call her?" her mother-in-law asked her with a gentle smile as she kissed Charlotte's cheek when she awoke. She had been so brave. A nurse the doctor had brought with him was holding the baby, who had been cleaned and swaddled by then, and was staring at them with wide-open blue eyes, while Charlotte gazed at her with unbridled love, wishing Henry could see her. Seeing her baby now made all the agony worthwhile.

"Anne Louise, after my mother, and one of my great-great-aunts. One of my German relatives," Charlotte said, in barely more than a whisper. The doctor was observing her closely, relieved that both mother and child had survived, which he had begun to doubt in the last few hours of the delivery. Charlotte was very weak now, and spoke in a whisper as she glanced at her daughter. "She's so beautiful, isn't she?" She drifted off to sleep again then from the drops the doctor had given her. He left an hour later, after checking her pulse several times. It was thready and weak, but it didn't surprise him after all she'd been through. He told the countess to let her sleep, and said he would be back to check on her in a few hours, and the nurse would check on her from time to time. She took the baby to the room they had set up as a nursery, next to the bedroom Charlotte was occupying, down the hall from her mother-in-law. The countess went to her room to rest too. It had been a frightening night, and like the doctor, the countess had feared that neither Charlotte nor the baby would survive, but was grateful that they had.

The countess lay down on her bed without getting undressed, and fell asleep instantly. She woke up two hours later, and decided to check on Charlotte, to make sure that she was doing well, and not in pain. She opened the door to her room, careful not to waken her, wishing that Henry were alive to see his daughter, and as soon as she entered the room, she saw that Charlotte was ghostly pale, even more than she had been during the birth. Her lips were blue, she was peacefully asleep, but ghostly white, and as Glorianna approached her bed, she could see no sign of Charlotte's breathing. She reached for her wrist to find a pulse and could find none and saw no sign of movement at all. She pulled back the bed covers instinctively, and saw that Charlotte was lying in a pool of blood. She had bled to death after the delivery, while the nurse was with the baby. Her skin was already cold to the touch. She was dead at seventeen, from a childbirth that her parents knew nothing about. Her mother-in-law's heart was pounding as she looked at her. What was she going to tell them? Their precious child was dead. She had died giving birth to a baby they didn't know existed. She called the doctor with trembling hands, and he returned immediately. She had told no one what had happened, and couldn't believe it herself. First Henry, then her husband, and now this, poor Charlotte, and the poor little girl with no mother now, orphaned at birth.

The doctor confirmed that Charlotte had died of a severe hemorrhage from trauma during the delivery. It couldn't have been predicted, although she'd still been bleeding when he left, which he said was to be expected. And he said hemorrhages like that happened very quickly. It had struck Charlotte even before the nurse could return to the room to check her again. All Glorianna could think of now was how to protect Charlotte's memory, and Henry's, and to spare her parents further grief, until they knew about the baby later.

She looked pointedly at the doctor with an idea. "Would it be possible to list the cause of death on the certificate as pneumonia or in-
fluenza, perhaps with the complication of asthma, which she suffered
from before? Her parents don't know about the baby," she said in a
whisper. "I will tell them about her later of course. But for now, this
seems like the least painful course for them, without adding the
shock of a child to the death of their daughter." The doctor hesitated
only for a moment and then nodded. What difference did it make
now? The poor girl was dead, and he assumed the baby had been
illegitimate if her own parents didn't know about it. Perhaps it was
why she had come to Yorkshire, to conceal an illegitimate birth. The
countess wanted to protect them from the truth, and the girl's reputation. And why cause her parents further grief to have lost their
daughter to a child born out of wedlock? It never dawned on him
that Charlotte might have been married, and the countess didn't say
it, since the marriage was a secret too because of who Charlotte was.
And despite being a princess, she was just a child herself and now
she was dead. Yet another tragedy after too many recently.

"Of course, your ladyship, whatever I can do to help in the circumstances. This is most unfortunate." He looked deeply troubled about
it too, and wished he hadn't left, but she'd appeared to be doing well
enough when he did. And she might have died even with a cesarean
with such a large baby.

"Her parents will be heartbroken." Glorianna knew only too well
how they would feel, having lost her son too.

"At least they'll have the infant to console them, once you tell
them—if they're willing to accept her," the doctor said kindly. It was
clear to him now that the baby was illegitimate, and the countess
said nothing to correct him. It didn't matter what he thought, only

that the press didn't get hold of the story before she could tell the king and queen face-to-face about the baby, and that Charlotte and Henry had been married. Other than the vicar, she was the only one who knew now. And the vicar knew nothing of Charlotte's true identity. Only Glorianna did. To everyone else, she was Charlotte White. The doctor had guessed that the baby's father was the countess's son, and now the baby was an orphan, with both its parents dead.

"I want to wait until I see Charlotte's parents, to explain the entire matter to them. For now, all they need to know is that they've lost their daughter. They don't need to know the true reason why immediately. It won't change anything." She spoke with the authority of her rank, trying to make the best of a terrible situation.

"Of course, your ladyship, whatever you think best." He had a death certificate in his medical bag, and filled it out listing pneumonia with complications from asthma as the cause of death, as she had suggested. He promised to register it at the county record office, and called the funeral home for her. He wanted to do all he could to help.

Looking dignified and grief-stricken, the countess told Lucy, the housekeeper, and the maids of Charlotte's death. Lucy looked shocked as tears filled her eyes, and the maids burst into tears and went back to the kitchen, and Lucy joined them. None of them had expected Charlotte to die. She was so young and healthy, despite her size.

The funeral parlor came to get Charlotte an hour later, and Glorianna kissed Charlotte before they took her away. Lucy stood in the hall crying with the maids, as they carried Charlotte out on a stretcher, covered with a black cloth. The countess stood in the library alone afterward and poured herself a glass of brandy with shaking hands, before she dialed the number she had for emergencies at Buckingham Palace, and asked for the queen's secretary. A man came on the line after she said her name. She hadn't thought to call Charles Williams, whom she had met when he'd brought Charlotte to them. It seemed more appropriate to call the queen's secretary in this instance, than the king's. She had corresponded with Charlotte's mother but never her father. She explained that it had all happened very quickly. Charlotte had caught a bad cold, which set off her asthma. It had turned to pneumonia within a day, she had been seen by the doctor, and before they had a chance to call the palace, she had a massive asthma attack and succumbed. The countess sounded distraught herself, and offered her deep condolences to the king and queen, and Charlotte's sisters. She offered to bury her in their small cemetery on the estate for the time being, until the royal family had a chance to bring her home for burial, most likely after the war.

The secretary thanked her, and promised to call her after he discussed it with the family, and would inform her of their wishes. Charlotte had died just weeks before her eighteenth birthday. No one had expected this. Other than her asthma, she was a vital, healthy young woman. And Glorianna had fully expected her to withstand the rigors of childbirth, not bleed to death.

She mentioned to the queen's secretary as a detail at the end of the conversation that they would pack all her belongings to return to the palace, and were willing to stable her horse until they came for him with everything else. The secretary thanked her and they hung up. He had a grim task to face, breaking the news to the royal family that Princess Charlotte was dead.

The only consolation for Glorianna was that she knew that Charlotte's reputation, and Henry's, were safe. There would be no scandal about the baby, a rushed marriage, two young people who had been in love and foolish. She would tell Charlotte's parents the whole story when she saw them, but it wasn't a story she wished to tell them in a letter or on the phone. Once they knew it all, she would show them the baby, and respect whatever they wished to do about her, let them take her or care for her herself. But for now, the baby was safe in Yorkshire, with her, until the royal family was ready to acknowledge her existence and welcome her.

The countess went to see her a few minutes later in the makeshift nursery. She sat holding her as she slept peacefully. A wet nurse had already been arranged from one of the farms. The housekeeper had taken care of it. As she held her, the countess mourned the infant's mother, who had brought sunshine to their lives for a year, and had loved her son. And thanks to Charlotte, part of Henry would remain. She was grateful for that. She couldn't believe that Charlotte was gone now too, and she knew that, like Henry, Her Royal Highness Princess Charlotte would live on forever in this child, who was her flesh and blood too. The countess felt a powerful bond with the helpless infant, Princess Anne Louise, named by her mother before she died. Glorianna hoped that fate would be kinder to her in the future than it had been so far, with no parents now to love her. She had come into the world in sorrow, not in joy.

Chapter 4

For weeks after her birth, they all hovered around the nursery, to make sure that the infant Anne Louise would survive the rigors of her birth, and her mother's death. The doctor came to see her every day. He found a nurse for them who would stay, and despite the loss of her mother, she was a thriving, healthy, normal baby, with a hearty appetite and a lusty cry. She was the only ray of sunshine in the somber house.

The royal family had been grief-stricken by the news of Charlotte's death. And the doctor had obligingly done as the countess had suggested in listing the cause of death as pneumonia and asthma. They knew nothing about a clandestine marriage, death following childbirth, nor about the surviving child.

The royal family had gratefully accepted temporary burial on the Ainsleigh estate, with the intention of moving Charlotte's remains immediately after the war, rather than bringing her back for burial now, while London continued to be bombed. They preferred to leave her belongings and horse in Yorkshire too, until they came for her, which the countess said was fine. The secretary said that the thought of burying her in the midst of the ongoing air attacks was more than they could bear.

Both of Charlotte's sisters were as heartbroken as their parents. Princess Victoria suffered even more than her older sister, remembering all the times that she had tormented her, belittled her, and argued with her.

A formal announcement by the palace was made on the radio and in the press that the king and queen's youngest child, Her Royal Highness Princess Charlotte, while staying in the country to avoid the bombing, had succumbed to pneumonia and died shortly before her eighteenth birthday. It said that the royal family was in deep mourning. Everyone at Ainsleigh Hall heard the broadcast, and none of them made the connection with Charlotte White, who had died shortly after childbirth at Ainsleigh on the same day.

"Strange, isn't it?" Lucy had commented to the housekeeper after the broadcast, as they all sat in the kitchen. "She died the same day our Charlotte did, though from a different cause." Everything seemed to be about death these days, in the war, in the cities, and at Ainsleigh. Lucy was spending all her time in the nursery, and loved holding the baby. She was a last link to Henry. She would sit and hold her for hours. She was there when little Anne gave her first smile, and was more adept at calming her than anyone in the house, when she cried for hours sometimes. The nurse said it was wind, but the countess always wondered if she was keening for her mother. Lucy was sorry that Charlotte had died, but she loved the baby.

The funeral for Charlotte in their cemetery had been simple and brief. The countess, Lucy, the housekeeper, and the maids attended.

The vicar who had married her and Henry said the funeral service and was genuinely sad over the death of someone so young, and such a lovely person who had brought happiness to all. No one knew exactly what had happened or why, but they knew that there were mysterious circumstances surrounding the baby's birth. No one except the countess and the vicar knew that Henry and Charlotte had gotten married, although they had all guessed easily who the baby's father was. And now the poor child had only her grandmother, since both her parents were dead. The countess shared the baby's history and royal lineage with no one. Charlotte's parents deserved to hear it first, and what they chose to tell after that was up to them. Her birth was respectable, but her conception had been less so, with parents who were so young and unmarried at first.

The countess was particularly glad now that she had encouraged them to get married. There would have been no chance of the royal family ever accepting or acknowledging the child if she had been illegitimate. For now, she was the countess's secret, but at least she was legitimate.

The countess was anxious for the bombing in London to end, so she could go to London with Anne Louise, show her to the queen, and tell her the whole story. It was hard to imagine that she would reject an innocent infant, who was the last link she had to her youngest child, who had died at such an early age. She had sent them a copy of the death certificate, and had received a handwritten letter from the queen, saying how heartbroken they all were, and thanking the countess for her kindness to Charlotte, despite her own grief for her husband and son. They had all suffered too many losses. But it cheered Glorianna a little knowing that the baby would console them all in the end, if the Windsors were willing to accept her, and she felt sure they would. She wasn't the first Windsor, or royal, to be born with unusual circumstances surrounding her birth.

The mood of the public was bleak again. The bombs dropping all over England were distracting and depressing them all with constant deaths and ravaged cities. It was as bad now, or worse, than at the beginning of the war. The Luftwaffe's attacks were relentless, as Hitler continued to hammer Britain with all the force he had.

Yorkshire was still one of the safer spots in England, although that could change at any time. And they had had their share of bombings too, though less severe ones than London.

The nurse had to leave them in September, when her mother got sick in Manchester, after their home was bombed and she had a stroke. Anne Louise was four months old, and Lucy was quick to volunteer to take care of her. The countess was impressed by how loving and efficient she was for one so young. Lucy adored the baby, and every time she held her, she thought of Henry, her one true love. He had been indifferent to her in his lifetime, but now she could lavish all her love for him on his child. She was tireless in what she did for the baby, and never let her out of her sight. Wherever Lucy went, the baby went too, and the countess was grateful to her. Lucy slept in the nursery with her at night.

The countess hadn't been well since Charlotte died. She had had too many shocks in a short time. Three deaths in the space of four months. Everyone she loved had died, except for her granddaughter, who was the only bright spot in her life.

The countess had been melancholy for months, and when winter set in, despite her injured leg from her previous accident, she began riding again for the first time in years. She said it gave her time to

think, and in truth, she no longer cared about the dangers. Sometimes she went for long walks on the grounds, and stopped in the
cemetery on the way back, to tend to her husband's grave or Charlotte's. They had put up a marker for Henry, although his remains
weren't there and had never been sent home. George's parents were
there as well, and ancestors for several generations. It brought her
comfort to visit them. She seemed particularly pensive one afternoon
when she came home, stopped in at the nursery, and saw the baby
fast asleep in Lucy's arms. Both Lucy and the baby looked entirely at
ease with each other. She left the nursery without disturbing them,
and was grateful again that Lucy had made herself so useful. There
was a reason now to let her stay after the war, which was a relief for
Lucy and the countess. She could be Anne Louise's nurse, unless the
queen wanted other arrangements, and decided to bring her home to
the palace, once she knew about her. The countess was anxious for
that time. The fate of the child was a heavy burden for her alone, and
was meant to be shared. She was eager to do so with them, if they
were willing and welcomed the baby.

A few days before Christmas, one of the maids went to wake her
ladyship, as she always did, and bring her her breakfast. She threw
back the curtains on a bleak December day. There was snow on the
ground, and most of the house was bitter cold. The maid made a
comment about it, as she turned to smile at her employer, and saw
her lying peaceful and gray in her bed. She had died during the night
of a heart attack that killed her in her sleep. The past year had been
too much for her. The vicar and funeral home were called, and after
some consternation, the housekeeper called Peter Babcock, the Hemmingses' attorney in York. She remembered his name from when the
earl was alive. It was a dilemma knowing what to do next, since no

one knew of any living relatives, but they assumed that the attorney would know who was the heir to the Ainsleigh estate. Henry had been when he was alive, but he was their only child. Neither the earl nor the countess had siblings, so presumably it would fall into the hands of distant cousins now, as often happened with old estates. They often passed on to relatives they'd never even met.

The attorney came to see who was staying at the house, and found two maids and a housekeeper, and a young girl from London living there, and an infant he assumed was her child. No one had told him otherwise. They weren't sure what to say, since Charlotte was dead, and no one had ever confirmed to them for certain who the father was, although they could guess, but they weren't sure and it had never been openly said.

So the attorney attributed the infant to Lucy. No one told him that the baby was the countess's grandchild, since she had taken none of them into her confidence. They had no idea who would take responsibility for the child now. It appeared no one would. The whispers were that Charlotte's family knew nothing about the baby, or didn't approve, since none of them showed up when the baby was born, or even when she died.

There were two men in the stables, one old, and one barely more than a boy. The tenant farms were well occupied. The countess had enough money left to pay their wages for quite some time. She'd been running the estate on a pittance, without extravagance. Once the lawyer knew that all was in good order, he agreed to pay the wages from the estate account, until the lawful heir could be found, which could take time.

It took the attorney two months to locate a distant cousin, by running ads in the York and London papers. He finally received a letter responding to one of his ads. It was from a third cousin of the earl, who had moved to Ireland during the war, since it was neutral. He seemed most surprised to learn that he had inherited the estate. He hadn't seen the earl since he was a boy, and the heir was even older, had never married, and had no children. He wrote that he wasn't eager to return to England while the war was on, but said that he would come to inspect the property as soon as the war ended, or earlier if possible. In the meantime, he authorized the Hemmingses' attorney to continue paying the meager wages to the staff who remained. He said he was sorry to hear that the entire family had died. He seemed unsure about keeping the estate, and said he might put it up for sale, once he'd seen it. He had purchased a large estate in Ireland, a castle, and intended to stay there after the war. He had no real use for Ainsleigh, particularly once he was told it was in need of repairs and required a larger staff to maintain it properly.

It was another three months before the war in Europe ended in May, much to everyone's relief. It had been an agonizing five years and eight months, with such crushing loss of life in England and all over Europe, as well as in the Pacific. Europe in particular was battle-scarred after the bombings on both sides. Anne Louise turned a year old a week after Germany surrendered.

It was June, a month after the surrender, when Lord Alfred Ainsleigh arrived from Ireland to meet with the lawyer from York and inspect the estate. The heir was quite elderly, and was discouraged to see the condition of disrepair of the manor house itself, and to note how much work and expense it would take to modernize it, add central heating, redo the plumbing and electricity, which were old and rudimentary at best. The park was sadly run-down, the gardens in need of replanting, although the grounds were beautiful, and the tenant farms would spring back to life quickly when the men re-turned from the war. But he said he had neither the energy, nor the youth required to bring the Ainsleigh estate back to what it had been before the Great War. There were thirty years of deferred mainte-nance repairs to do, due to lack of funds, and he thought the most sensible solution was to sell the property, at the best price he could get. He had no desire to live in England, he and the attorney dis-cussed it at length, settled on a price that seemed reasonable to them, and put it on the market, with realtors in London and York. It was Lord Ainsleigh's hope that an American would buy it, or some-one with enough money to restore it to what it had once been. It was a long way from that now. He went back to Ireland after that, and Peter Babcock, the attorney, promised to keep him informed.

Lord Ainsleigh's visit and decision to sell had caused a stir among the remaining staff at Ainsleigh Hall. All of them were worried about what a new owner would mean for them.

"I guess that's it for us," one of the two maids said in her heavy Yorkshire accent, looking glum. She had worked there all her life, and been faithful to the earl and countess for the forty years of their marriage, and all of their son's life. "The new owner will probably sack us all," she said grimly, "and put young ones in our jobs," she predicted. "They'll be lucky if they can still find anyone willing to be in service. I don't think any of the girls are going to be in a rush to give up their factory jobs with better conditions and better pay than we have here. They'd rather live in the cities now than in the coun-try."

Her colleague responded hopefully. "They're going to need some-one to clean the place. We might as well stay, and see who buys this place." The housekeeper agreed and said she was staying until they fired her. She loved the house, and had grown up on one of the farms. "What about you?" she asked, turning to Lucy. She wasn't an employee, but she wasn't family either, and she would need a place to go too, now that the earl and countess were dead and the place was being sold. She had no living relatives anywhere now, with her parents dead. She had a small amount that had come to her when her parents died, after her parents' apartment building was bombed, and their insurance paid her something. She couldn't live on the money forever, but it would last her for a while. Her dream was to return to London and find her way. She liked the idea of working on an estate like this one, maybe in Sussex or Kent. Yorkshire was a little too remote for her. She had just turned nineteen, and had been there for four years. It was the only home she had now. The big question for her was about Anne Louise. They were both orphans now. Annie, as Lucy called her, was thirteen months old. Lucy loved her like her own, and had cared for her entirely ever since the nurse left when Anne Louise was four months old.

"I want to go back to London," she said quietly, and they nodded. It made sense to them. It was where she was from, even if she had no family left there now. There would be better jobs there, and the surrounding countryside, than in Yorkshire. Others would be going back to their original cities once they got out of the army, or returned from the places where they had taken refuge from the bombs being showered on the cities for the past five years. A new era of renewal and reconstruction was about to dawn, and Lucy was energetic and young. "I thought I'd take Annie with me," she said, to see what they'd say, if they'd object or be shocked, or say she needed someone's permission. But the countess was gone, and an elderly distant cousin was the heir. He didn't want the place, and none of them could imagine him accepting a baby, whose parents and grandparents were dead, and whose parents hadn't even been married, as far as they knew. She was an orphan, and presumably a love child, or a bastard, even if the countess had protected her. And illegitimate, she couldn't inherit the estate one day. There was no member of the family to take her now, and if they spoke up to the new Lord Ainsleigh, they were all sure the baby would wind up in an orphanage. They all agreed that she was better off with Lucy, who loved her and took such good care of her, than among the thousands of orphans all over England, who would be struggling for a place to live and on public benefits. Whatever happened, Lucy would take care of her, and it was obvious how much she loved her. She didn't care that she was illegitimate.

"That sounds like a good idea to me," the housekeeper said to Lucy in a matter-of-fact tone. "She'll be safe and loved with you. She has no one else, and you're the best mother she'll ever have." Lucy smiled at her praise, and the other two women agreed. Lucy was the obvious choice to take the child. She had cared for her almost since her birth, and was the only mother the child had ever known. Putting her in a public orphanage, or giving her to an old man in Ireland who didn't want her, seemed wrong to all of them. And even if they had all guessed that Henry was her father, he wasn't there to take responsibility for her. And she had no claim on the estate as heir, so Lucy acting as her mother seemed like the answer to a prayer for both of them. Lucy needed a family and Annie a mother.

"When are you thinking of leaving?" one of the two maids asked her.

"Soon," Lucy said. She had her savings to tide her over, and she was going to look for a job where they would allow her to bring a child, perhaps as a nanny, or a nursery maid, or a housemaid on a large estate. She knew the kind of work that would be required of her, and she planned to say she was a war widow with a child when she applied for jobs. There would be plenty of them on the market now, widowed women with children, and no one was going to ask her for a marriage certificate or Anne Louise's birth certificate. She could always say her papers had been lost in the bombing.

"I'll give you a character if you like," the housekeeper offered, and Lucy was delighted. It was all she needed to get a good job. With that in hand, she could take her pick of whatever was available. She had read in *The Lady* magazine about an agency in London that helped men and women find domestic jobs, and planned to go there.

That night, after everyone went to bed, Lucy went upstairs to the large guest room Charlotte had occupied in the last weeks of her life, before Anne Louise was born. Her things had been moved down from the attic room next to Lucy's to the large guest bedroom, and Lucy knew that all her papers would be there. She wanted to take them with her, not to show to anyone, but in case she ever needed them. She had never known much about Charlotte's history. She had always been vague about it whenever Lucy asked her, and Lucy had always sensed that there was a secret there somewhere, just as there was surrounding Anne Louise's birth. A mystery of some kind.

When she got to the room, she had an eerie feeling, knowing that it was where Charlotte had died over a year before, the night of Annie's birth. The room hadn't been used since. The shades and curtains were drawn. She sat down at the desk, opened the drawers, and was relieved to find they weren't locked. This was easier than she had thought it would be. The drawers were all full, and there was a large brown leather box on her desk. It had a crown embossed on it in gold. Before she examined its contents, Lucy went through each of the desk drawers. Two of them were filled with stacks of letters tied with thin blue ribbons. She removed the ribbons, and opened the letters, and saw the crown on the stationery. They were all signed "Mama," the initials engraved at the top of the page were "AR," and handwritten in the upper right-hand corner, under the date, in a neat elegant hand were the words "Buckingham Palace." A few said "Sandringham," some "Windsor," and several others said "Balmoral." Lucy frowned as she read the locations and wondered if it was a code of some kind. And then she read several of the letters, and suddenly her heart gave a jolt. "AR" could mean Anne Regina, Queen Anne, the crown was the crown of the Royal House of Windsor, and they had been written from all of the palaces that the current royal family used most often. But that wasn't possible. How could it be? Charlotte had said that her father was a civil servant, and her mother was a secretary. Had she been lying? Or was her mother a secretary to the queen? It seemed unlikely she'd use so much of the queen's stationery for letters to her daughter, unless she was the queen.

She began to read the letters more carefully and nowhere did Charlotte's mother, the woman who had signed herself "Mama" in the letters to Charlotte, nowhere did she mention Henry, or the fact that Charlotte was expecting a baby. She obviously didn't know. Charlotte had clearly kept the baby a secret from her mother, presumably because Anne Louise was illegitimate and she didn't want to tell her mother of her disgrace. But the countess knew about the baby and had kept the secret for her.

Lucy vaguely remembered then hearing that the youngest royal princess had been sent to the country to escape the bombing in London. Maybe she had come here. But Charlotte's last name was "White," not "Windsor." There was no doubt in Lucy's mind that the letters signed "Mama" were from the queen, written from Buckingham Palace, and all the palaces where they lived. The envelopes showed that they were addressed to the countess, but the letters were to Charlotte.

She read the letters right to the last ones, and several from her sisters. She looked for mentions of a baby coming, and there were none. Lucy tied the letters up again, then found the packet of letters that Henry had written her shortly before he died, telling her how much he loved her, and mentioning the baby that was about to be born and how pleased he was. It made Lucy's heart ache to read them, remembering how she had hoped that one day he would love her. But now she had Annie, and he was gone. There were several photographs of him in the desk, and one of him with Charlotte that his mother must have taken, in a small heart-shaped silver frame.

After Lucy finished reading the letters, she carefully opened the leather box with the crown embossed in gold on it. There was a key in the lock, but the box was open, and Lucy was astounded by what she found. Their marriage certificate, for the marriage by special license that they had kept secret as well. So Anne Louise wasn't illegitimate after all, which came as a shock to Lucy. Everyone assumed she was. The queen apparently didn't know about her, but Henry and Charlotte had gotten married before he left, not long before. Glorianna Hemmings had signed it as a witness, so she knew, and so had the earl, but they had waited to tell the queen, and must not have gotten around to it by the time Charlotte died, hours after the baby's birth, because the queen's letters never mentioned the marriage or the child. Perhaps they'd been waiting until Henry returned from the war to face the royal family with the news of a marriage and a baby conceived out of wedlock at seventeen. For whatever reason, the queen appeared to be entirely unaware of Anne Louise's existence, or Charlotte's hasty marriage, after she was pregnant, and before he left. So they had legitimized the child, but kept her a secret. And most shocking of all, Charlotte had been a royal princess. The king and queen's youngest child. Lucy was sure of it now. Things had obviously taken an unexpected turn when she came to Yorkshire and she and Henry fell in love. She had kept that a secret from her family as well. He was never mentioned in a single one of the queen's letters, until after his death when she said how sorry she felt for his mother, but she appeared to have no idea that Charlotte was mourning him as well.

Her travel papers were in the leather box, in the name of "Charlotte White." There was nothing in the box to identify her as "Charlotte Windsor," or as a royal princess, except the letters from the queen signed "Mama," sent from Buckingham Palace and their other homes. There were letters in the letter box too, from Charlotte's mother and both her sisters and a few signed "Papa." The box was too full to contain all the letters. The rest were in the desk drawers. And when she took all the papers out to read them, she saw that there were initials inside the box at the bottom. They weren't Charlotte's initials, they began with "A," presumably the queen's. Charlotte had kept a multitude of secrets until her sudden death, and in the end, had taken them to her grave. The countess had known the whole story, but hadn't told the queen either, since she didn't seem to know. Perhaps she was afraid of the king's and queen's reactions to their seventeen-year-old daughter getting pregnant by the Hemmingses' son, and married in secret without her parents' permission, to prevent her child from being born illegitimate. Some of the mysteries remained unsolved and would be forever, but Lucy could guess. Charlotte was almost surely the youngest princess who had been sent away from London to escape the bombs, and the same one who had died, supposedly of "pneumonia," on the same day that Charlotte White had died in Yorkshire, shortly after childbirth at seventeen. It wasn't a coincidence. Lucy was certain now that she was the same girl.

There was also a copy of Anne Louise's birth certificate, with her father's last name, and the death certificate of Charlotte White, apparently put there by the countess, with "pneumonia" listed as the cause of death, not hemorrhaging after childbirth. It was all there. And when she peered into the box for a last look, she saw a narrow gold chain bracelet with a heart dangling from it and put it on her wrist. She felt like a thief taking it, but she'd never had anything as pretty and couldn't resist. She would give it to Annie one day. She remembered Charlotte wearing it and had noticed it when she arrived.

As Lucy sat back in the chair at Charlotte's desk, contemplating the piles of papers in front of her, she realized that she had everything she needed to blackmail the Royal House of Windsor, if she wished to do so. It was a powerful feeling that she knew about a secret marriage, a baby conceived out of wedlock by their seventeen-year-old daughter, and the child that had resulted from it, and she knew the real cause of Charlotte's death, and she was sure that the royal family were aware of none of those things. Lucy knew everything they didn't. How much would they pay for the information, and to keep her quiet, and not create a scandal involving their dead daughter? But she had gotten married, and the baby had been born legitimate.

But she didn't want money, she wanted Annie, the baby that she loved, and they didn't know existed. They would never miss her, and if Lucy gave her up now, she knew it would break her heart. Remaining silent now would mean depriving Annie of life as a royal princess, but whatever she did now, Annie's mother was still dead. She could give her up to a life of palaces and royal blood, but Lucy firmly believed she could give her a mother's love as none of the royals would. And if things had been different and Henry had loved her, Annie would have been their child, not Charlotte's. This was a way of keeping Henry close to her forever, but more important, she could lavish love on his child. Annie would never know that she was the granddaughter of a king and queen, and if she took Annie's birth certificate with her, no one would ever know. They would never know that there was a child, when they came to get Charlotte's belongings and remains, and Annie would never know of the life she had missed. Only the earl and countess and Henry and Charlotte had known the truth of who Annie was, by birth, and now Lucy had discovered the secret. She stared at the birth certificate long and hard, and her hands shook as she decided what to do. She knew she had no choice. All she wanted in the world was within her reach. She could let the servants at Ainsleigh continue to believe that Annie was an orphaned love child with no relatives except the very remote cousin who had inherited the estate and wouldn't want her either.

The royal family knew nothing about Annie's existence, and never would. There was no one left alive to tell them, and no one in the world knew that the baby's mother had been a royal princess, third in line for the throne. If Lucy took Annie with her, no one would ever suspect that she wasn't Lucy's child. The king and queen would never come looking for a baby they didn't know anything about, the servants at Ainsleigh didn't know of her royal connections or who her mother really was, and there was no one to stop Lucy now. Whatever she could have gotten for selling Charlotte's secrets to them, the baby she loved as her own was worth far more to her.

With sudden determination, she decided to keep the letters and documents, the marriage certificate and Annie's birth certificate, and carefully put them all in the royal leather box. She took one of the blue ribbons off the letters from the queen to her daughter, locked the box with the key, slipped the key on the ribbon, and put it around her neck, where no one would take it from her.

In the box, she had everything she needed to guarantee that Annie would be hers forever. All trace of her bloodline had been removed, thanks to Charlotte keeping all her secrets to herself. Everyone who had known the whole story was now dead. The only remaining evidence was the infant herself, and Lucy intended to bring her up as her own, her very own royal princess. Her Royal Highness Anne Louise Windsor. Lucy would always know that the little girl she loved was royal. Her very own princess, whom even the king and queen knew nothing about. Their youngest child was dead, but her baby daughter was Lucy's now, to love forever, and no one would ever take her away. Lucy couldn't bear the idea of another loss if she gave the baby up. For her sake, and Annie's, Lucy was certain she was doing the right thing, and told herself she was. A mother's love was more important than riches and royal lineage. She would love Annie to her dying day as they never could. To Lucy, it justified everything. She realized that she could have destroyed the contents of the box, but the papers seemed too important to do that. She wanted to keep them in the box.

With an iron will, and no hesitation, she picked up the locked leather box, containing all the letters and papers. The desk was empty. Lucy carefully turned off the lights in what had been Charlotte's final bedroom, and all her secrets belonged to Lucy now, along with her child. There was an element of revenge, since Charlotte had stolen Henry from her. But she forgave her for that now. She had Henry's daughter, which meant more to her than Annie being a princess. Annie was Henry's final legacy to her. The child that should have been theirs. Annie was her baby now, and always would be. No one could take Annie from her. Once back in her room, she put the locked leather box in her suitcase, and touched the key around her neck. She had Charlotte's gold bracelet with the heart on her wrist. Annie was asleep in the crib in Lucy's room, where she had slept for months now, and from that moment on, Annie, the little princess no one knew about and never would, was hers.

Chapter 5

Two days after Lucy had packed all of Charlotte's papers into the leather box and slid it into her suitcase, she announced that she was leaving. She said she was ready to go back to London. She bought a gold-plated wedding band in a jewelry store in York, slipped it on her finger in her new role as war widow, and the next day, she packed up Annie's things, said goodbye to the staff at Ainsleigh Hall, with a character from the housekeeper, and took Annie with her on the train to London. Her heart was pounding when she left, afraid someone would try to stop her. But no one did. The remaining maids, housekeeper, and hall boys all thought it was a good thing that Lucy was taking Charlotte's baby with her. Without Lucy, where else would she go? Most likely to an orphanage. They hugged Lucy and Annie, and wished her luck. She promised to let the housekeeper know when she found a job. But no one would be writing to her in the meantime. The only people she knew were the staff at Ainsleigh Hall. All of her school friends had died in the bombing of London, and she'd had few friends anyway, working at her father's cobbler shop every day.

The toddler was fascinated by the people on the train, and Lucy sat watching the countryside slide by, remembering when she had come to Yorkshire four years before, at fifteen, and now she was returning to London to make her way and find a job, with a baby of her own. The war had been good to her, after four years at Ainsleigh Hall, and the kindness of the Hemmingses. She had all of Charlotte's papers in her suitcase, and life as a war widow would open new doors for her. There were plenty of girls pretending to be war widows, who had never married, and had babies by the men they met during the war. But none, she was sure, were absconding with a royal princess, pretending it was their own. She had won the prize with little Annie, and no one would ever know that she hadn't given birth to Annie herself. She had everything she'd ever dreamed of. Now all she needed was a job, and a home.

She checked in to a small hotel in the ravaged East End. The streets were still littered with rubble and debris, and everything was dusty as she walked around holding Annie. She went back to see the building where she had lived with her parents, and there was no sign that anything had ever been there. It was a sad, empty feeling, as though further proof that they were gone. The apartment building had vanished the night it had been bombed and the explosion had killed her parents. She clung to Annie for comfort as she walked around the neighborhood for a while, and then went back to her hotel. The memories were too powerful and the sense of loss in their wake. It made her even more grateful that she had Annie now. None of the neighbors had survived the bombing and her father's shop was gone.

The next day she went to the agency she'd read about in *The Lady,* to look for a job. She explained that she would have to take her daughter with her. Before the war, no one would have hired her with a child, now there were many girls like her who had no other choice, and employers would have to make allowances for it. The widows with children had no one to leave them with, and had to bring them along. Employers desperate for help in their city and country homes had to find a way to accommodate them, and many were willing to be creative and give it a try. The woman who ran the agency suggested three jobs to her. One employer wasn't willing to hire anyone with a child, the other two expected her to find someone to care for her baby by day, but were willing to let the child sleep at their home at night. One was in the city, in Kensington, and the other was at a country estate in Kent, which sounded more similar to the life she had led at Ainsleigh Hall, on a grander scale, and seemed more interesting to her.

The woman at the agency called the potential employer, and arranged for an interview for Lucy the next day. The position was as a housemaid, at what the agency claimed was a magnificent estate. Ainsleigh had been more of a manor house, and nothing had been formal there with so little help during the war. The estate in Kent was much more elaborate, with a separate house for the servants, and cottages for the married ones, if both spouses worked for them. The woman at the agency said that they'd been hiring people in droves for the past month, to re-staff their home after the war. They wanted footmen, both a senior and under butler, a fleet of maids. They had excellent stables with experienced grooms and a stable master, and had just hired three chauffeurs and a chef.

Lucy was excited when she took the train to Kent from Victoria Station for the interview the next day. She had paid a maid at her hotel to babysit for Annie, but had made it clear to the agency and employer that she had a little girl. She had mentioned that her husband had been killed at the Battle of Anzio, and she had lost her own family in the London bombings as well. The war had taken a heavy toll on many young women like her, and her story was entirely believable, although much of it wasn't accurate. She hadn't been married, she wasn't a widow, and Annie wasn't her child. She almost believed her own story now, and it had the ring of truth.

One of the chauffeurs picked her up at the train station in a Bentley, and they drove through the imposing gates of the estate twenty minutes later.

The interview was conducted by the head housekeeper, a daunting looking woman with a thin, sharp face, wearing a severe black dress, with a heavy ring of keys on her belt. The head housemaid appeared at the end of the interview to walk Lucy through the house, which was as elegant and grand as the agency had said. The owner of the estate was the proprietor of one of the largest and finest department stores in England. They were commoners and extremely wealthy.

Some experienced servants who had been in service before the war preferred working for titled families, but Lucy didn't care. Her potential employers had four young children, two nannies, and a nursery maid, but Lucy had applied for a job as a housemaid, which she knew she could do well. She wasn't afraid of hard work.

She was told that the wife of one of the tenant farmers was willing to babysit for the housemaids' children for a small fee during the day. It sounded like a perfect arrangement to Lucy. She would get one day off a week from morning, after her employers' breakfast, until just before dinnertime, and she would be handsomely paid. It was exactly what she needed, and when they offered her the job before she left, she accepted immediately. She didn't want to lose the opportunity, and it seemed like the ideal household for her to bring up her child. The chauffeur told her how much he liked working there on their way back to the train station. They had asked her to start the next day and she'd agreed.

She packed when she got back to the hotel, checked that the leather box with Charlotte's papers was still in her suitcase, and felt for the key around her neck. The box of Princess Charlotte's papers was Lucy's insurance for the future, if it ever became advantageous to her to share the information in it with the queen. But for now, it was safe, and she was only going to use it if she had to. All she wanted now was to start a good job, and lead a good life.

They had told her that Annie could sleep in a crib in her room, or on a cot later when she outgrew it. Two of the housemaids had young children there as well. Their employers were supposedly modern and very flexible, but expected them all to work diligently and for long hours. They gave house parties nearly every weekend, dinner parties frequently, and balls in their grand ballroom several times a year. Unlike the more distinguished, aristocratic Hemmingses, with diminished funds, they seemed to have unlimited money to spend. It sounded like a very pleasant life and work experience to Lucy, and she could hardly wait to start the next day. She would be given her uniforms when she arrived, and a seamstress would fit them to her.

She took the train to Kent the next morning, and was picked up again, this time by a different chauffeur, who was even more pleasant than the first one. They stopped at one of the farms so she could drop Annie off for childcare, and once at the main house, he took her to see her room, on the top floor of the house. The chauffeurs and stablemen had already filled the rooms in the staff building, and the cottages were only available to couples, of which there were several on staff.

"What about you?" the young chauffeur asked her. "A husband or boyfriend?" He had looked her over thoroughly before he asked. She had an ordinary face, but a voluptuous figure, which would definitely appeal to some. She was a buxom girl and looked well in the black uniform and lace apron their employer expected them to wear. It made her look older than her nineteen years, very serious and professional, with a little white lace cap.

"All I have is my little girl." Lucy answered the chauffeur's question in a neutral tone. "My husband died in the war."

"Oh, I'm sorry to hear that," the chauffeur said kindly. "Maybe you'll meet a new man here," he commented, and she smiled.

"That's not what I'm here for. I'm here to work." And she meant it. By nightfall, after working all day, every inch of her hurt and felt strained, as it never had before, but she knew she had done a good job, cleaning, scrubbing, waxing, and polishing all day. She had helped two footmen carry tables, had vacuumed several large reception rooms, and set the table impeccably for an informal dinner for twelve. She learned quickly from her coworkers, and liked their employers' style. She hadn't met them yet, although she had been told that the lady of the house was very fashionable. "Informal" to them meant the silver service, not the gold one they used for formal events.

The housekeeper had checked on Lucy several times throughout the day, and corrected her whenever she thought it necessary. She didn't like the way Lucy fluffed up the cushions on the small drawing room couch, or the way she arranged the curtains after she opened them, and she reminded Lucy to wear a fresh uniform and apron every day, and if she got one dirty, she was to go to her room and change. Lucy was startled at the end of the day when she went outside for some air and bumped into one of the stable boys walking a horse back to the barn. He smiled as soon as he saw her.

"When did you arrive?" the stable boy asked, clearly admiring her. He was taller and broader than she was. He had piercing blue eyes, brown hair, a strong face, and a warm smile.

"About six hours ago," she answered him, slightly out of breath. "I haven't sat down all day since I arrived."

"They'll work you hard, but they're fair employers," he informed her. "She can be difficult, but he's a great guy. He made a fortune and she spends it lavishly. He doesn't seem to mind. He's a generous man. He's got a few dollies on the side, but you never see them unless she's away with the children."

"That must get interesting," she said, enjoying the gossip with the stable boy. He was a nice-looking man with a warm, outgoing personality that made him even more attractive.

"I'm Jonathan Baker, by the way, and I'm going to run these stables one day. My boss is twenty years older than I am, and he's going to retire before long. I want to be there to pick up the pieces." She could easily believe he would. He seemed like an enterprising guy, and had a bold upbeat way about him, without being offensive. Just the way he looked at her and smiled made her like him. He looked to be a few years older than she was, he wasn't handsome in a classic sense, but he had a kind face, and she liked his powerful broad shoulders. She introduced herself, since he had, and they went on chatting for a few minutes. It was easy to feel comfortable with him.

"Do you like horses, Lucy?" he asked her.

"Not really," she said. She had wanted to learn to ride while she

was at Ainsleigh in order to get closer to Henry, but he had never offered to teach her, and she felt foolish asking him. And then Charlotte had arrived, with her remarkable skill as a horsewoman, which
had impressed him, and Lucy had retreated to the kitchen. "They
look like big, dangerous beasts to me. I never learned to ride when I
was younger. The cobbler's daughter doesn't get riding lessons." She
smiled at him.

"Neither does the blacksmith's son usually. I fell in love with them
as a boy. They're not frightening once you get to know them, the
good ones. I can teach you about them."

"I doubt that I'll have time for riding lessons. It looks pretty busy
to me around here. And I have a daughter. I'll need to spend my time
off with her. She's thirteen months old. I'll be leaving her at Whis-
tlers' farm while I work."

"War widow?" he asked her, "or do you have a husband tucked
away somewhere?"

"He died right before she was born, three months after he joined
the army."

"There are too many stories like that one. I was in France myself
on D-Day. They died like flies all around me, the poor devils. I got
lucky, I guess. I just got back a month ago. I grew up here. My grand-
father was a tenant farmer to the previous owner, and my father was
the blacksmith. We've been here longer than the current owners.
They bought the place seven years ago, right before the war. The
previous ones went broke, after the last war. They hung on as long as
they could, and finally sold. All three of their sons were killed in the
Great War. I like working in the stables. I want to run them one day."
The horse he'd been leading started to get restless then, and they
both had other things to do. "It's been nice talking to you. I'll keep a

lookout for you. The stable hands don't eat in the servants' hall. We have our own kitchen here, and cook our own food."

"See you again sometime." She smiled at him again. He led the horse back to the barn, and she went to pick up Annie after work. She was crying and fussy when Lucy got there in her uniform, and she walked all the way back, holding her, thinking about what a good place this was going to be for Annie when she got a little older. The Markhams' estate in Kent was a perfect place for a child and anyone who didn't mind being in service, which didn't bother Lucy. She had a roof over her head, plentiful meals three times a day. The Markhams treated their servants well, and everyone said that the wages were better than they had been before the war. There were forty or fifty employees in various positions around the estate, gardeners, chauffeurs, stable hands, as well as those who worked in the house. The newcomers had more staff than most of the original owners, except in the days before the Great War. It had changed everything on the big estates, as money began to run out and the order of things changed.

The new owners could afford to maintain the properties the way the old owners no longer could. It was new money, which the aristocrats looked down on. They had no titles unless they bought them, which some did. Some of the more desperate landowners sold their titles along with their estates, but the Markhams were commoners and didn't mind it. They made up in wealth what they lacked in blood and ancestry. But Lucy knew she trumped them all. She had a royal princess as a daughter, and her grandparents were the King and Queen of England. It didn't get better than that, even if no one knew it. Lucy did, which was all that mattered to her. It always thrilled her when she thought about it. It was so surreal, and an enormous secret. Her baby was a Royal Highness, and Lucy was going to give her the best life she could, worthy of any princess, to the best of her ability. Working for the Markhams was the first step. Maybe she'd rise to housekeeper one day, with a ring of keys on her belt like Mrs. Finch, who ran the Markhams' home with an iron hand, but despite her odd, stiff ways and stern face, Lucy liked her. She was from the northern border of Yorkshire, and had the accent that had become familiar to Lucy while she stayed with the Hemmingses at Ainsleigh.

She settled into her job, determined to work hard, and had a letter from the housekeeper at Ainsleigh a few months later. She had let her know where she was, and told her she'd found a good job. The housekeeper from Ainsleigh reported that the estate had been sold to an American. The old servants had all been let go. The new owner was going to spend a year or two remodeling everything and modernizing the place, and would hire a new staff after they did, probably some of them American. They had bought the place for very little.

Her big news was that two palace secretaries and the queen's equerry had come from London shortly after Lucy left. They had exhumed Charlotte's casket and taken her remains back to London for a service there, and it turned out that Charlotte had been a royal princess. It had all been arranged very quietly, and the palace emissaries hadn't said much about it. No one at Ainsleigh had suspected that Charlotte had apparently been a member of the royal family. It made what they thought was her illegitimate love child even more shocking. And out of respect for the Hemmingses, sympathy for Charlotte, and loyalty to Lucy, no one had breathed a word about Annie. The housekeeper wrote that they hadn't asked about the baby, and she had the strong feeling they didn't know about her, which was probably just as well. Henry and Charlotte were both dead. Annie was illegitimate and she was in good hands. The whole matter was better left buried and forgotten. There was no point maligning the dead and causing a scandal. She also mentioned that they had taken her big horse back to London with them.

Lucy still believed she had done the right thing, taking her because she loved her, particularly since they didn't know about Charlotte's clandestine marriage to Henry Hemmings. It would all be forgotten now, and she and Annie could go on with their lives. She had left just in time, which was providential. She didn't write back to the housekeeper, and didn't want to pursue a friendship with them and maintain a connection. She wanted to put Ainsleigh behind her. It was history now. And they could have exposed her. Fortunately they didn't know about the marriage, which would have changed things if they did, Lucy had turned the page and started a new life where no one knew her. At the Markhams', she was just another war widow with a child. There were thousands of them all over England, some of whom had truly been married, and some not and only claimed to be. There were too many of them to ask questions or garner much interest. The Ainsleigh servants were happy for Lucy and Annie.

And no one at the Markham estate had questioned Lucy about Annie. They just thought she was a pretty little thing, and they never commented that she looked nothing like her mother. Lucy was a tall girl with a big frame, and despite her size at birth, Annie already had the delicate frame and features of her natural mother. Lucy could already see how much she looked like Charlotte. She had the face of an angel and white blond hair, with sky blue eyes. She was going to be a beauty one day, and she was already small for her age, which

Lucy blamed on rationing and how little food they'd had in Yorkshire at the end of the war. The restrictions of rationing hadn't been lifted yet, but they ate well at the Markhams', who managed to feed their employees plentifully. And Lucy gave whatever treats she had to Annie. She never minded depriving herself for her baby. Lucy had convinced herself by then that Charlotte's family would have rejected her because of how her birth came about, and everyone at Ainsleigh believed it too. Annie would have been the child of a regrettable mistake, a disgrace they would have buried and probably put her somewhere with people who didn't love her as Lucy did. Lucy had no trouble justifying what she'd done by taking her. Her love for the child made it seem right to her. In her mind, love was stronger than blood or ancestry. She might not have a royal life, or live in a palace, but little Annie had a mother who loved her deeply. What more could she want or need? Lucy had no regrets. She never let herself think about it now. Annie was her baby. And anything she'd had to do to become her mother seemed right to her. And like Charlotte, she would go to her grave with her secrets.

The service for Princess Charlotte was a private one with only her sisters and parents present. They buried her at Sandringham because she had loved it. The queen was devastated when they brought her home, and Victoria mourned her even more deeply than the others, remembering every unkind word and criticism she had ever uttered, which cut through her now like knives, each time she remembered one of them. She had even accused her of fakery with her asthma, and in the end it had killed her. It was a sad day for all of them when Charlotte came home at last. The king felt it acutely. She had been his most favored child because she was the youngest and had such a light spirit and gentle manner. It was hard to imagine that she would never dance through their palaces again, and her delicate little face wouldn't make them smile.

It was more than a year after her death when they buried her at Sandringham, and seeing her casket lowered into the ground tore at their hearts. She would be forever mourned by the family that loved her. The queen blamed herself for sending her to the country, but how could they have known what terrible fate would befall her there? It still shocked them that the earl and countess had died as well, and their son. It was a tragic story, and a loss none of the Windsors would forget. Her mother visited her grave every day, until they went back to London. Then life went on, with their duties to their war-torn country, but Princess Charlotte would live in their hearts forever. And the joy she spread around her in her short life would burn brightly. And none of them imagined even for an instant that she had a child who was the image of her, living as the daughter of a housemaid in Kent. The child was unknown to them, and lost forever.

Chapter 6

B y Annie's second birthday, Lucy felt as though they had lived on the Markham estate forever. They were exemplary employers, and Lucy had worked for them for a year by then. She was diligent in her duties, and Mrs. Finch, the housekeeper, had increased them. Lucy was twenty, and was mature beyond her years, with the added responsibility of being a mother so young, and having no family of her own. Annie was the darling of the other servants, who loved to play with her and spoil her. She had a sunny, loving personality, and they frequently said she looked like a little fairy, dancing around her mother with her big blue eyes and light blond hair. Lucy always said she looked just like her father, to explain why she looked nothing like her. She looked remarkably like Charlotte, and it appeared that she had inherited her diminutive size as well. Lucy was big-boned and solid.

The rest of the house staff was always knitting something for her, or making a bonnet, or carving little pull toys she could drag along behind her. She would clap her hands and chortle with delight whenever they gave her something or hugged her. They loved seeing her when Lucy brought her back from the farm at night after dinner. She let her play in the servants' hall for a few minutes and then took her upstairs, bathed her, and put her to bed. Lucy sang to her as she fell asleep, and would look at her adoringly in her crib during the night. She still seemed like an angel who had dropped from the sky to Lucy, and she thanked heaven every day for the gift of this child. Annie was her passion and the love of her life. She loved her as she would have Henry, if he'd let her. But now, that no longer mattered. He was gone, and she had Annie, for the rest of her life. What she felt for her was better than the love of any man.

She ran into Jonathan Baker from the stables from time to time, when she had reason to leave the house on an errand for Mrs. Finch, or for their employers. Annabelle Markham was spoiled and expected a great deal from her employees, but she was also a fair and generous woman and rewarded them when appropriate. They gave all of their employees handsome gifts at Christmas from the store they owned. She loved her home, her husband, and her children, took no interest in the business, which her husband ran so efficiently, and was so lucrative. It was the most successful store in London. She had a fifth child a year after Lucy had come to work for them, and Lucy saw the baby nurse walking in the gardens with the fancy pram. She let Lucy bring Annie to see the new baby, and commented on how prettily Annie was dressed. Lucy had made the dress herself, copied from children's clothes she saw in magazines.

"She looks like a little princess," Annabelle Markham remarked one day, as Lucy smiled proudly.

"She *is* a princess," Lucy always said firmly, as though she believed it. And Jonathan gave Annie rides on the pony the Markhams had bought for their children. She always squealed with delight when Jonathan set her on a horse of any size and held her. She had no fear of horses or anything else, and she would cry when he took her off. Lucy worried that she'd be horse mad like her mother, which was a luxury she couldn't indulge in and didn't want to. She still thought them dangerous beasts.

Jonathan took them to a nearby lake to go swimming that summer when he had a day off, and taught Annie to swim like a little fish. She had no fear of water either, and it touched Lucy to see such a big man so gentle with a child as young as Annie. He loved the time he spent with her, and with Lucy, and he said it made him dream of having children of his own.

"Do you ever think of marrying again and having more?" he asked her shyly when they were at the lake.

"No, I never think about it," she said, not wanting to talk about it with him. "Annie keeps me busy, and I've had to bring her up alone."

"You wouldn't have to if you married again." She had just turned twenty-one, and marriage was the farthest thing from her mind, or so she claimed. He was twenty-six, and had just gotten another promotion. It was clear now that when the stable master retired, Jonathan would take over for him. It was no longer just a wish, it was a sure thing. He was the most responsible man Lucy had ever known, and in many ways he reminded her of her father, who had been a good husband and father and a good man. But she didn't want any man interfering with her relationship with Annie. She had assiduously avoided any involvements or entanglements with men. She had years ahead of her to bring up Annie, and Jonathan said he didn't want to think of settling down until he was the stable master, and then he would have a cottage with his job. There would be plenty of time to think about marriage then, but not before that.

In spite of their determination not to marry, and caution about getting too involved in a romance, Lucy and Jonathan's attraction to each other evolved slowly into a deep mutual respect, and a long, slow romance that became harder and harder to deny. When Annie was four and he had at long last become the stable master and earned one of the better cottages, he proposed. Lucy was twenty-two and he was twenty-seven, and he told her it was time. He wanted to marry and have children with her, which worried Lucy more than she wanted to admit.

"I'm not sure I could ever love another child as much as I do Annie," she said when he mentioned children to her. "Everything about her is perfect, and I love her with my whole heart."

"I think all parents feel that way, until they have the second child in their arms, and realize that they can love another baby as much," he said sensibly.

"I'm not sure I could," she said thoughtfully. To make up for the royal life Annie would never have, Lucy had devoted her whole life to her, heart and soul.

"It would be good for Annie to have a brother or sister. It will be lonely for her growing up as an only child," he said, trying to convince her, but Lucy wasn't sure. He kissed her to seal the deal then, and Lucy felt stirrings she had never felt before, which frightened her too. She wasn't going to let passion run away with her as Charlotte had, and end up with an unwanted pregnancy. And what if she died in childbirth? Who would take care of Annie then?

"I would," he said without hesitating when she shared her fears with him. He was surprised by how frightened she was of going through childbirth again. "You're not going to die," he said gently. "You're a strong girl, Lucy. You've been through it before and survived. Women have babies every day and come through it. I'm sure it's not easy, but it can't be that bad or no one would ever have a second child. Was it very bad when you had Annie?" he asked, and she was touched by the compassion in his eyes. She couldn't tell him that Annie's mother had bled to death, but Charlotte was a tiny woman, and Annie had been a big baby. And the medical care was excellent in Kent. There were several very good midwives in the area, a number of fine doctors, and a hospital, they were close to London, and to reassure her, Jonathan said she could see a specialist there. "And I'd be with you." He knew that her husband had already been dead before Annie's birth, which must have made it hard for her too. She was young. Now he felt she could endure it, with good medical care and his help. He wanted desperately to marry her and have children of his own, although he loved Annie as though she were.

"How would you feel about her if we had other children? Would you love her as much?" Lucy questioned him, and he didn't hesitate.

"Of course I would. I wouldn't stop loving her, or love her less because we had another child. Will you think about it? We don't have to have a baby right away. But I want to be married to you." He had an excellent job as stable master, and their employers were pleased with them. "It would be wonderful to live together in our cottage. My mother could take care of Annie when you're at work. And any other children we have." His mother still had a cottage on their old farm on the estate. He made it sound very appealing, but Lucy wasn't sure. She had her life in perfect balance and control. She made a good salary and could provide for Annie. Adding a man to it, and possibly other children, sounded complicated to her. But Jonathan was so gentle and convincing, so loving, calm, and reliable that he eventually wore her down, and won her heart.

They were married at the local church just after Annie turned five, and Lucy twenty-three. She felt ready to take on a husband and all that it entailed. They fixed up his cottage together, and he painted a bedroom pink for Annie, who said it was her favorite color. They were married in the presence of their coworkers and employers, and everyone was happy for them. He was such a lovable man, and Lucy was a good woman, even though she was quiet and not as gregarious as he was. The wedding breakfast afterward in the church hall was a lively occasion. They left Annie with his mother, and went to Brighton for the weekend for their honeymoon. Rationing had finally eased up, and life had almost returned to normal, so traveling was possible. Lucy was nervous about their wedding night, because she didn't want Jonathan to realize she was a virgin. She told him it was her time of the month when they got to the room, and he said he didn't mind, and hoped she didn't either. She gritted her teeth and didn't let herself make a sound. The pain was sharp and brief, Jonathan was unaware that she'd lost her virginity to him, and when they made love again in the morning it was easier.

The war had ended four years before. The memories of tragedy had dimmed, and the scars had begun to heal. She no longer had nightmares about her parents dying in the bombing, which she never spoke of but were very real. She'd had them all during the war. She still dreamt of Charlotte sometimes too. Lucy's worst fear was that Charlotte's family would find out what had happened, learn of Annie's existence, find them, and take her away. She couldn't have survived losing Annie. They had lived with the story Lucy told for four years now, and Lucy had almost come to believe it herself. She knew she could never say anything to Jonathan about it. He would never understand, and he would be shocked. He still knew nothing of the real circumstances of Annie's birth, and Lucy had no intention of telling him. It would be too difficult to explain, and he didn't need to know. He still believed the fantasy of her being married to a man named Henry, and Annie being their child. He could never have imagined that Annie was a royal princess and another woman's child. It was a secret Lucy intended to take to her grave. As Lucy planned it, no one would ever know, not even Annie when she grew up. Lucy was afraid that one day, if Annie found out, she might feel that Lucy had cheated her of a better life. She had done it purely out of love for her, and to some degree out of love for Annie's father, but Annie might not understand it and long for everything she'd missed, grandparents, aunts, cousins, a family, and a royal life.

After their honeymoon, they settled into real life, as a working couple. His mother came to take care of Annie every day, or they dropped her off at her cottage. Jonathan's mother loved having a grandchild.

Lucy had spoken to a local doctor about how to avoid getting pregnant at first. He had recommended condoms or a diaphragm. Jonathan agreed to use condoms for a while, and she tried to avoid conception with the rhythm method, avoiding sex at times. But six months after they married, fate intervened. They enjoyed a particularly energetic night of lovemaking, when Annie stayed with her adopted grandmother, and Lucy discovered afterward that the condom had broken. Her greatest fear was realized a month later when she missed her period and realized she was pregnant. It seemed so unfair to her that with only one slip she had conceived, and she cried when she told him. Jonathan could see how frightened she was, which made no sense to him since she'd been through it before. And all Lucy could think of was Charlotte bleeding to death hours after the birth, and she was terrified it would happen to her, perhaps as retribution for taking a child that wasn't her own. But she had given her a good life, and a wonderful father in Jonathan, which she told herself compensated for what she'd done.

Jonathan had found her locked leather box when she moved into his cottage, and he asked her what it was. He wasn't a nosy person, but it was an imposing looking box and beautifully made. She responded brusquely that it was some old letters, and mementos of her parents, and she put it on a high shelf at the back of a closet and left it there. He forgot about it. She kept the key hidden and no longer wore it around her neck. She thought of destroying the papers and letters in it at times so no one would ever see them, but for some reason never did, and gave no further thought to the contents of the box. There was no question in her mind now, no matter who had given birth to her, Annie was hers. And her other family ties were irrelevant, since Lucy had chosen to keep her away from them, for life. And she had convinced herself that Annie's life was happier the way it was now, with Jonathan and her, and a brother or sister on the way.

Lucy's fears about the pregnancy abated slowly over time, with Jonathan's loving reassurance. He was excited about the new baby, and both of them were surprised by how fast it grew. By the time Lucy was three months pregnant, the baby looked huge. She wondered if something was wrong and compared it to Charlotte's pregnancy with Annie, where nothing had showed for several months.

But Charlotte was so tiny, she had concealed it easily. By the time Lucy was five months pregnant, she looked as though she was about to give birth. She was a big woman, and the baby was too. Annie was excited at the prospect of having a brother or sister. It was due at the end of the summer, which seemed a lifetime away to Lucy, carrying a heavy load. A month later, when she saw her doctor for her six-month checkup, he looked concerned and sent her for an X-ray, which explained the way she looked. She was having twins. Jonathan was beside himself with joy at the prospect of having two babies, and Lucy had nightmares about it, and was even more terrified of the birth. She couldn't imagine surviving it, in spite of all her husband's reassurance, and his mother was going to help take care of them. Mrs. Markham was understanding about it, and they gave them double supplies for a layette, and she told her to take as much maternity leave as she needed. Lucy was a valued employee, and head housemaid by then.

Annie was even more excited about twins, and wanted to help name them and take care of them. She was hoping for twin girls, while her parents liked the idea of one of each. Jonathan told her that it was fine with him if it was boys since they already had the best little girl in the world. He let her help him get the nursery ready, and paint the crib a friend had given them.

Lucy continued to work but was miserable all through the summer. They had a series of heat waves that made it even worse, and she lay in their cottage at night, feeling like a beached whale, but she wanted to work for as long as she could. She tried to do things with Annie too, but she was exhausted all the time, so Jonathan took Annie out on special outings. When Lucy wasn't working, the three of them went to the movies. Annie loved being with them. And Jonathan took her to the stables with him whenever he could, which was always a thrill for Annie, and what she loved best, even more than movies.

Jonathan had a busy summer at the stables. John Markham had bought six new Arabians that Jonathan was training for him. Annie would sit and watch him for hours. Annie was six, and said she wanted to train horses like him one day. He had been giving her riding lessons for the past year, and he told her mother she had a gift. She had a remarkable way with horses, and was utterly fearless. Lucy knew where it came from, both her parents, and made no comment. But she went out to the ring one day in the barn, and was struck by how graceful and elegant Annie looked on horseback. She was a natural like her mother. Jonathan had her jumping obstacles by the end of the summer, and with Lucy's permission, put her in a local horse show, where she won a blue ribbon. He went riding with her whenever he had the chance. She was an extraordinary rider, even at the age of six. She always said she wanted to be a horse trainer like him when she grew up.

"That's not a job for a girl," he said gently. "You should be a mother and a wife, or a teacher or a nurse." She made a face when he said it and he laughed.

"Nurses hurt people and give them shots. And I don't want to be a teacher. I hate school," she said staunchly. Nothing ever swayed her from wanting to work with horses when she grew up.

"I hope you don't hate school. It's very important," he said as he put her through her paces, which she accomplished with ease. She had real skill going over the jumps he set for her. Nothing frightened her as long as she was on horseback, and she wanted to ride the bigger horses, which he said she wasn't ready for yet, and she was so small. She looked like a four-year-old in the saddle, which made her ability even more startling. She had the hands of an adult while handling the reins, and an unfailing eye for the jumps. She never missed one, and rarely knocked one down.

"Someone in your family must have been an expert rider," he said to Lucy one day after Annie's lesson. "It's not possible to ride the way she does at her age. She has an uncanny knack for anything to do with horses. Are you sure no one in your family rode? A grandparent maybe?"

"Positive," she said and changed the subject, but it struck her too that Annie looked more like Charlotte every day. The Windsor genes were strong. If possible, she was even smaller and more ethereal looking than her mother. People always guessed she was younger than she was, until they spoke to her. She was very bright, and Jonathan gave up trying to keep her out of the stables.

Annie headed for the barn like a homing pigeon, and was never happier than when she was on a horse. Riding with her, when he had time, was a pleasure. She kept up with him, galloping across the fields and jumping streams. Her horse was smaller than his, but she had no trouble matching his speed, and got the best out of every horse she rode. She had an uncanny communication with them, and seemed to sense their every thought and anticipate every move. He loved riding with her, and her lessons were a pleasure for him. He was very proud of her, as though she was his own.

It was a long hot summer for Lucy, the babies were due in September, and in the last week of August, she could hardly move anymore, and their employer sent her home to rest. She would have continued to the end, but even the doctor had told her to slow down. There was a chance the twins would come early. She'd had no problem with the pregnancy so far, but the delivery was likely to be more difficult with twins. Once she stopped work, she hardly got out of bed, and Jonathan was cooking their meals at night, with Annie's help. He made bangers and mash, and shepherd's pie, stew, and all the things he liked to eat and his mother had taught him to cook. Annie loved assisting him in the kitchen, and everywhere else. She was his shadow in the barn, and he would turn around and find her beside him as he checked on the horses, or called the vet for a horse that had been injured or seemed sick, and when he couldn't find her, she was either currying a horse, taking one a treat, or in their stall.

The nursery was ready. They had a tiny third bedroom in their cottage that was barely bigger than a closet. It was going to be the twins' room. Jonathan didn't want to take away Annie's bedroom that she had had since they moved in, and he had painted pink for her. He treated her as their firstborn, with all the honor and respect that went with it.

Lucy was at his mother's cottage the night she went into labor. It started off with a bang when her water broke, and by the time they got to the hospital, she was unable to speak through the pains. The doctor examined her when they arrived, and spoke to them as Lucy clutched her husband's hand and tried not to scream.

"If this was a single baby, I'd have said it was going to be very fast. But it never is with twins. We can give you something for the pain, Lucy, but we need your help. I can't give you much. We can put you out when it's over, but we're going to need your cooperation, so you'll need to be awake and alert, especially for the second twin. We don't want too much time between the two deliveries. How long did your last labor take?" he asked, and Lucy looked stunned for a minute and didn't know what to say.

"I can't remember," she said vaguely, and the doctor looked surprised.

"It can't have been too bad then." He smiled at her. "Most women remember every minute of it. It won't be long now for the first one. I can feel the baby's head." He examined her again, and that time she screamed, and the doctor asked Jonathan if he wanted to leave the room and he shook his head and didn't move.

"I've helped a lot of mares give birth," he said calmly, and although he said it was unusual, the doctor let him stay. He was worried at how severely Lucy was reacting, and thought she'd need all the support she could get. Jonathan was quiet and calm, and didn't seem inclined to panic. He sat next to Lucy, while she cried, until they took her to the delivery room, and Jonathan stayed near her head. The doctor was right. Lucy sounded like she was dying, but the doctor had the first twin in her arms after half an hour of strenuous pushing. It was a boy. Then the contractions stopped for a few minutes, before they started again with a vengeance, and Lucy begged them both to do something to stop it. They put an oxygen mask on her while she pushed. The second twin took an hour and was much more difficult. He was bigger and gave a powerful cry when he was born. Jonathan held him for a few minutes, while the doctor tended to Lucy, and then he cut the cord. They gave her a shot for the pain the moment both babies were out, and she was groggy as she looked at Jonathan and seemed dazed. But everything had gone well. The first twin had weighed nine pounds, and the second twin weighed just over ten. She had been carrying nineteen pounds of baby, and felt as though she had given birth to twin elephants. They were strapping, healthy baby boys, no matter what they had cost their mother.

"I'm not going to die like Charlotte, am I?" she asked Jonathan with glazed eyes.

"You're not going to die, my love. I'm so proud of you. We have two big beautiful boys. Who's Charlotte?" he asked her then, and she shook her head and cried, as the doctor put another mask over her face and gave her a whiff of chloroform to put her out.

"She'll sleep for a while now," he said softly to Jonathan. "She did very well. Twins aren't easy. And you have two great big boys there. I'm surprised she went full term." They were fraternal twins, not identical, but they looked very similar to their father. "You can go to the nursery now if you like. We're going to clean her up, and take her to a room. The nurse will call you when she's awake." Jonathan thanked him, and followed his sons to the nursery. It was the happiest day of his life, and he couldn't wait to show the twins to their big sister.

He took turns holding them in the nursery, and he was sitting at Lucy's bedside when she woke up. She looked as though she had been through an ordeal, and she had. He kissed her as soon as she was awake.

"I thought I was going to die," she said in a hoarse voice.

"I wouldn't have let you. We all need you too much." He had never thought there was a risk of that, and the doctor seemed calm throughout. "Who's Charlotte?" he asked her again, now that she was awake.

"Why?" She looked panicked at the mention of her name.

"You asked if you were going to die like her."

"She's a woman I used to know, who died a few hours after she gave birth."

"That's not going to happen to you," he said firmly, as a nurse came in and asked her if she was going to nurse her babies. Lucy said she was, although it seemed daunting with twins, but she wanted to try. Now that she had survived it, she wanted to enjoy her baby boys to the fullest. She had been terrified for nine months.

"Did you nurse last time?" the nurse asked her, since she was listed as a second-time mother on her chart.

"No, I didn't," Lucy said, and seemed awkward about it. "But I want to this time." The nurse told her how to do it with twins. It sounded complicated and she was going to need all the help she could get when she went home. But her mother-in-law had promised to be there, and Jonathan would help her at night.

She spent five days in the hospital, and the babies were nursing well by the time she went home. Annie couldn't wait to meet them. They let her hold them, sitting down, one at a time. Jonathan was a natural father, and managed to make Annie still feel special too. He even cooked her favorite dinner of shepherd's pie, and ice cream. Overnight they had become a family, with a mother, father, and three children. Their cottage felt as though it was bursting at the seams, and Jonathan enjoyed it thoroughly. Lucy was overwhelmed, but Annie did little chores for her, and her mother-in-law was a huge help. Three children were a lot for Lucy to cope with, and it was even harder than she expected. In comparison, Annie had been so easy. Twins were a lot to deal with. One was always hungry and crying, and sometimes both of them.

A month after their birth, Lucy was relieved to go back to work. All of her colleagues had come to see the twins while she was at home, and Mrs. Markham had sent them lovely gifts, in duplicate, with little matching outfits. But it was nice getting out of the house and going back to her job. She stopped nursing when she did, and she went home at lunchtime to help her mother-in-law give the twins their bottles. After the terror of the last nine months, thinking she would die like Charlotte, she hadn't, and Lucy felt complete with the family she and Jonathan had. She was emphatic about not wanting more children. Annie remained special to both of them, and the twins were like whirling dervishes going in opposite directions as soon as they could walk, which one of them did at nine months, the other at ten. Annie was the perfect big sister, patient, loving, responsible. She told her parents she would teach her brothers to ride one day, and she admitted to her grandmother that as much as she loved her baby brothers, she still liked horses better.

"She certainly doesn't take after you," Jonathan's mother commented to her daughter-in-law, laughing. Blake, one of the twins, was the image of Lucy and looked just like her, and Rupert was identical to his father. And Annie looked nothing like any of them. She was fine-featured, tiny, and seemed to float when she walked. She had a regal air and grace even at six. And looking at Lucy's large frame, and plain facial features, at times it was hard to imagine she was Annie's mother. They looked and acted nothing alike.

"The fairies must have left you on your mom's doorstep," her grandmother teased her. Annie loved that idea, and Lucy didn't comment when she heard her say it.

Chapter 7

When Blake and Rupert were eighteen months old, they were running everywhere, and it took Lucy, Jonathan, Annie, and their grandmother to control them. They knocked things down, pushed over lamps, climbed up on tables. They got into mischief everywhere, and the only time Lucy and Jonathan had peace was when the boys were asleep at night in the crib they shared. They slept in one crib, and cried when they didn't, so whichever of them woke first invariably woke the other, and then the fun began.

Jonathan and Lucy had no time for long, lazy mornings, or romantic nights. The twins were like a tornado that hit the cottage every day, as soon as they got up. Jonathan thoroughly enjoyed them, and Lucy loved them too, although Jonathan had more patience with them. They wore Lucy out and she told Jonathan that the twins and Annie were enough for her. He would have liked one more, but she said he'd need another wife to pursue that plan, and he graciously conceded, and settled for three children. In his opinion, Annie and the twins were the best things that had ever happened to him. He was a happy man. He loved his wife, his family, and his job. He loved working on the estate where he'd grown up, even with new owners. He had never hungered for distant shores or great adventures. He had exactly the life he wanted and was content.

Three months after the twins turned two, he gave Lucy a Christmas present that she said was the best one she'd ever had. He bought her a television, one of the big fancy floor models with the widest screen they made. It came in a piece of furniture, and was the pride of their living room, even though the images were black and white. They hadn't invented color TV yet, but he promised to get Lucy one whenever they came out with it.

Lucy had favorite programs she turned on every night when she came home from work. Jonathan watched sports matches on the weekends, and there were even suitable shows for Annie early in the evening. She was eight years old. Whenever there was a horse show on TV, she ran to see it. It really was the best gift he'd given the entire family. The boys were still too young for it, but soon they'd be able to watch it too. The gift was particularly meaningful that year because King Frederick had died in February, and his oldest daughter, Alexandra, had become queen. Her coronation had been postponed for sixteen months, for assorted political reasons the public wasn't privy to, and her coronation had been set for June of the coming year. For the first time in history, it was going to be televised, so millions of people could watch it in their homes around the world. Lucy was going to be one of them. She had been saying for months that she was going to take the day off from work to watch it, wherever she had to go to find a television, and now, thanks to her generous husband, she had her own.

It had always amused Jonathan that Lucy was obsessed with royalty, and in particular the British monarchy. She subscribed to *The Queen* magazine, and any publication that wrote about the royals. She read every news report about them. The coronation of Queen Alexandra was going to be the high point of her obsession with the monarchy. Jonathan's well-timed Christmas gift would allow Lucy to watch Queen Alexandra's coronation at home in June.

The new queen was a young woman, the youngest to ascend the throne since Queen Victoria had become queen at eighteen in the nineteenth century. Queen Alexandra was twenty-nine years old when she became queen, had been married for five years, and was expecting her third child when her father died. She gave birth to her third son the week after her father's funeral. So the succession was now assured with an "heir and two spares" as the British liked to say. Queen Alexandra's three sons were in line for the throne after her, with her oldest son first in line. Fourth in line to the throne was Queen Alexandra's younger sister Victoria, a year younger than the new monarch, and unmarried. She had always been somewhat wild in her romantic choices, and had the personality to go with her flaming red hair. Alexandra and Victoria had had a younger sister who had died tragically at seventeen during the war, in 1944. She'd died of complications from pneumonia. Queen Alexandra's mother, Anne, was now the Queen Mother since the death of her husband, King Frederick.

Jonathan had always been ignorant about the royals, and somewhat indifferent to them, until Lucy filled him in on all the details. She seemed to know everything about them and read up on them constantly. Queen Alexandra had a German husband who was prince consort, His Royal Highness Prince Edward, just as her great-great-grandmother Queen Victoria had had in her husband, Prince Albert.

Although allegedly very much in love with their husbands, neither queen had ever requested the government to make her husband king, and both men had remained with the more limited status of prince consort. But as both were German-born, it was unlikely that the cabinet would have approved of their being made king. So both queens reigned alone. Queen Alexandra's coronation in June promised to be a dazzling affair, complete with the legendary historic golden coach in which she would travel to the ceremony, while wearing an ermine robe over her coronation gown, and her heavily jeweled crown was said to weigh forty pounds.

Monarchs from all over Europe and dignitaries from every country would be in Westminster Abbey, by highly coveted invitation, to see her crowned. And now Lucy could see every last detail of the ceremony too, sitting on her couch in her own home.

Jonathan had often teased her about her fascination with the monarchy, and now he had made her dreams come true. Her new television was her proudest possession.

Annie didn't share her mother's obsession with the royals, and at eight years of age, she was still much more interested in horses than Royal Highnesses. She would turn nine in a few weeks before the coronation and Lucy correctly suspected that her daughter wouldn't bother watching it, although she was slightly intrigued by the horses that would be part of the ceremony, and those that would be drawing the golden coach. Other than the horses, Annie had no interest in it.

In June, the coronation, which Lucy watched on TV for several hours, from beginning to end, lived up to all her expectations. It was the high point of her passion for all things royal.

It was not lost on Lucy, although no one else in the world knew it, that Annie was now fifth in line to the throne, though it was unlikely the succession would ever get that far down the list. The young woman who had just been crowned Queen of England was Annie's aunt, and the late Charlotte's oldest sister. The young queen's three sons were Annie's cousins, and the Queen Mother, Anne, was her grandmother. They were Annie's family by blood and birth, although she didn't know it, and they had no knowledge of her existence. But it was a thrill for Lucy to know it, as she watched them on her television screen. The child she considered her daughter, and always would, was part of the royal family because of her mother, the late Royal Highness Princess Charlotte, who had died hours after giving birth to Annie. And the only person who knew was Lucy herself. The proof of it was still locked in the leather box that had belonged to Charlotte, and Lucy had taken from her room before she left Yorkshire with Annie when she was a year old. All the pomp and ceremony in Westminster Abbey, the golden coach, the fabulous horses and gowns and glittering crowns were all part of Annie's heritage. She was a Royal Highness too, just as her mother had been. Lucy never allowed herself to think that she had deprived her of it. She had given her love instead. The thought that the royal family might have loved her too, although they knew nothing of her existence, never occurred to her. She had never regretted her decision, or doubted her judgment, even once.

Annie headed for the stables to find her father while her mother was still watching the coronation on television.

"What's your mom up to?" he asked Annie when she climbed under the fence. She was still noticeably small for her age, having just turned nine, and looked more like a six-year-old, but she rode like a man, her father liked to say. Her riding skill was as much part of her birthright as the ceremony in Westminster Abbey, but no one except Lucy knew that either. Lucy had kept her dark secrets for nine years now, ever since she had left Yorkshire and Ainsleigh Hall with Annie as a baby, and had pretended that she was her own, and had erased all trace of Annie's existence so the royal family would never find her.

"She's watching that thing on TV," Annie said with a roll of the eyes. "The coach was pretty cool though. And the horses are gorgeous."

"I think your mom is more interested in the crowns and gowns." They both laughed, but Jonathan was happy for Lucy that she was enjoying it, and was sure she would talk about it for days. Televising the coronation had been a stroke of brilliance and had brought it into the common man's living room. Women like Lucy could have a front row seat, on the couch, with a cup of tea.

By the time Annie was twelve, she had won ribbons at every horse show Jonathan entered her in. She was much more interested in speed than in the precise maneuvers of dressage or jumping competitions.

And at thirteen, she and her father had several serious arguments, and he had banned her from the stables for a week, after she snuck out with John Markham's wildest new stallion, not even fully broken yet, and rode him hell for leather across the fields. Her father noticed the horse was missing a short time after she'd taken him, and he'd gone looking for her. What he'd seen was heart-stopping. He was sure she'd broken some kind of speed record, but she could easily have broken her neck or lamed a horse who over his lifetime might prove to be worth millions. He had brought her back looking chastened and mollified. She begged every day to be allowed to come back to the stables, and he had stuck to the week restriction to teach her a lesson. To his knowledge, she never did it again, but he wasn't entirely sure. Annie was smart as a whip, and in love with horses, the faster the better.

At fifteen, to complicate matters further, she saw a horse race on television. Instead of aspiring to be a horse trainer or a stable hand, she announced that she wanted to be a jockey when she grew up. The televised horse race had convinced her. She was the right size, but the wrong gender, her stepfather informed her. Women were not allowed to be jockeys. Horseracing was a man's sport, and he told her it was much too dangerous. It was 1959, and the idea of women jockeys was unheard of. Jonathan told her that females were allowed to compete in some amateur events, but in his opinion they would never be allowed to race in professional ones.

"I want you to grow up to be a lady," her father told her, "not an amateur jockey at sleazy, second-rate events. I love what I do, but you have to aspire to more than just being master of the stables, a job no one is ever going to give a woman anyway. Your mother wants more for you too." Lucy had been a housemaid, and more recently housekeeper for the Markhams, but she had greater ambitions for the daughter she always referred to as her "princess." Oddly enough, Annie looked like one when she wasn't riding at full speed. She had a natural grace and elegance and a strangely aristocratic look to her in spite of her small size.

"All I want to do is what you do, Papa. Train horses and work with you, unless I can be a jockey one day."

"You can't," he repeated. And Lucy wanted her to be more than a mere housekeeper. A teacher, a nurse, any respectable profession for a woman, and eventually a wife and mother. Annie told her that her aspirations were pathetic. And the only thing that interested her was anything involving horses. Nothing had changed.

At eighteen the battle raged on, when Jonathan insisted she go away to school and further her education. She'd attended the village school. She'd never been interested in her studies, only in horses. But she lost the battle and went away to university to please him and her mother. Her grades were less than stellar and Jonathan eventually discovered that she had lied about her age and ridden in several minor amateur horse races as a jockey. He went to visit her at school to discuss it with her, and all she wanted was to drop out and come home to work with him in the Markhams' stables. She'd been hanging around the local stables and the only friends she'd made were there, which her parents considered unsuitable. She had no interest in pursuing school.

Despite mediocre grades, she managed to graduate in three years under duress, and in the end, came home to work as an apprentice stable master and trainer. John Markham commented frequently to Jonathan about how talented she was.

"It doesn't matter what we do, I can't keep her away from horses," Jonathan told his boss, sounding discouraged. Markham laughed at him. He had his own problems with six spoiled wild children by then, and an expensive wife.

"Maybe you should stop trying to keep her away from horses," John Markham said with a wry smile. "Give her her head and see what she does with it."

"She wants to be a female jockey, which isn't even legal. She'll break her neck and my heart one of these days." He worried about her. In contrast, the twins, who were fifteen by then, had showed very little interest in horses. They took after their mother. Blake wanted to be a banker and Rupert wanted to go to vet school, which was at least closer to his father's interests. Jonathan hadn't been able to get Annie interested in veterinary school either. All she wanted was speed, although she admitted that one day she might be interested in horse breeding, though not yet. She followed the bloodlines of several stables, including the queen's, which was her only interest in the royal family, unlike her mother, who was obsessed with everything about them, from what they wore to the kind of tea they drank.

"Kids do what they want to in the end. So do wives," John Markham said before he drove off to London in his new Ferrari. He was as obsessed with speed as Annie, but it was more appropriate for him than for a twenty-one-year-old girl.

But a month later, they had other things on their minds. Lucy suddenly fell ill with severe stomach problems, and lost a shocking amount of weight. She lost fifteen pounds in a month, and Jonathan took her for tests at the local hospital, and then to see a specialist in London, at the Markhams' suggestion. They were worried about her too.

The tests were inconclusive at first, and the diagnosis vague. She lost another ten pounds, and looked like a shadow of her former self when the doctors finally told them she had stomach cancer. It had metastasized to her liver and her lymph system, and the prognosis was not good. Jonathan was in shock when they told them. They suggested exploratory surgery, but as soon as they opened her up, they closed her up again. The cancer had spread too far and too quickly. There was nothing they could do. It didn't seem possible.

She was thirty-nine years old, and the twins were only fifteen. What would they do without their mother, and Jonathan without his wife?

They administered a round of chemotherapy followed by radiation to slow things down. And after the treatment, she seemed better for a while, and they gave her morphine for the pain. Jonathan wanted to cling to her to keep her with him. He had loved her for twenty years and couldn't imagine his life without her. He was desperately in love with her. She was such a good person, and a decent woman, and her illness and suffering were so unfair. She still went to work, directed the Markhams' housecleaning staff, and supervised household repairs. She could only manage a half-day now, and some days she couldn't go to work at all. They had nurses come to the house when she needed them, and the nights were hard when she was in a lot of pain. Jonathan gave Annie more responsibility in the stables so he could spend more time at home with his wife, and nurse her himself. At other times, Annie stayed home with her so Jonathan could work. She sat with her mother for hours, watching TV with her, and prepared meals she thought she'd like. She didn't want to lose her mother either and was afraid she would. She took care of her brothers, did the family laundry, and tried to do as much as she could. To thank her, Lucy took a small box out of a drawer one afternoon and put a gold bracelet on her wrist, with a gold heart dangling from it. Annie remembered her mother wearing it many years ago.

"I want you to have it," Lucy said in a tired voice, and Annie smiled.

"I love it." She kissed her mother and went to check on her brothers.

The Markhams were very understanding, and heartbroken for

them. Everyone on the estate was aware of how sick she was. Whenever Lucy was at home, she sat staring at the TV. She had her favorite
shows, and particularly one about the royals. She watched it one
night and Jonathan could see that she was in pain. He was tempted
to have a drink himself to calm his nerves, but he wanted to be alert
for her, in case she needed him in the night. She had trouble sleeping, and he often stayed awake all night to keep a watchful eye on
her, and give her morphine when she needed it.

She seemed agitated when he put her to bed. She was having
trouble breathing, and he was terrified that the cancer was spread-
ing, and he could see that she had lost more weight.

"I have to talk to you," she said in a whisper, as she looked intently
at him. She seemed worked up about something, and he was afraid
that she wouldn't sleep. She was often anxious now, as the illness
progressed at a rapid rate.

"We'll talk tomorrow. You need to rest," he said gently.

"No, I don't. It's important. We need to talk." He could see that
arguing with her would only make things worse. He couldn't imagine what was so important that it couldn't wait till morning, and he
wanted to give her a morphine pill for the pain. "Listen to me," she
said sharply and then closed her eyes for an instant.

"I'm listening to you." He didn't want her to get upset, but he
could sense that she already was. There was an urgency to everything now, as though she were fighting for more time. But he was
afraid it was a fight she couldn't win. "What is it, love?" he said
gently, fighting back tears. She looked so ill.

"It's about Annie. I've never told anyone, but now I think maybe I
should have." He suspected that she was about to tell him that she
had never been married to Annie's father during the war, and wasn't

a proper war widow, which was something he had wondered about anyway. So many women who had had babies during the war had never been married to their children's fathers. And afterward, they just claimed to be widows. There were so many that no one ever questioned it. It didn't matter now, and never had to him. He loved her whether she'd been married to Annie's father or not.

"It's not important," he said kindly.

"Yes, it is." She stopped talking for a long time, a full five minutes, and then whispered to him. "She's not mine." He hadn't been prepared for that, and suspected that she was confused. The doctors had warned them the cancer might spread to her brain. He wondered now if it had.

"Of course she is," he said gently.

"No, she isn't. I didn't give birth to her. Her mother died a few hours after she had her." He wondered if it was true or some kind of delusion she was having. "Her name was Charlotte. She was staying at Ainsleigh Hall at the same time I was. I didn't find out who she was until after she died," she said, and he recognized the name from what she'd said the night the twins were born, and for an instant he wondered if it was true. "She was royal," Lucy said with eyes like daggers staring into his. She seemed very intense and anxious to tell him. "Annie is royal too. Charlotte was the youngest sister of the new queen." He vaguely remembered that one of the young princesses had died during the war, but he was convinced now that Lucy was hallucinating and confusing it with one of her TV shows. "Charlotte's parents sent her to the Hemmingses, to get away from the air raids, the way mine did, and she fell in love with their son. She got pregnant, and they never told the king and queen. I read the queen's letters to her after she died. The queen didn't know about the baby, she never mentioned her existence. I think the countess was probably going to tell them later face-to-face, but with the war still on, she never got to it. I think they didn't want to tell the queen in a letter. The Hemmings boy was Annie's father, they were both seventeen. He turned eighteen and left for the army, and was killed before Annie was born. I thought they'd never married and she was illegitimate, so they hid the whole story. But after Charlotte and the countess died, I read all the letters from her mother and from Henry. I found their marriage certificate. So they were married in secret. But by then, everyone had died, Annie's parents and the earl and countess, an old cousin had inherited the estate and was selling it. And the Windsors, Charlotte's family, didn't know about her, I thought they wouldn't have wanted her, because she was born of a disgrace. And I loved her. I thought the Windsors would have sent her away. I was nineteen, and I took all the letters and documents, so they wouldn't find out about her when they came for Charlotte's things. I said the baby was mine and I was a war widow. She was only a year old when we left Yorkshire, and I came here. She's mine now, Jon, as if I gave birth to her. But sometimes I wonder if I should have told her. She's a Royal Highness, a princess, the queen's niece. I'm not sorry I took her. She's had a good life with us, and you're a wonderful father. But she's not really ours, she never was. Her mother was as horse mad as she is." Lucy smiled and closed her eyes to catch her breath. "The Windsors never knew that she existed, that Charlotte had a baby, or that she married the Hemmings boy in secret once she was pregnant. So I took Annie and raised her as my own. They still don't know that she exists. The Queen Mother is her grandmother, and was Charlotte's mother. The death certificate says she died of complications from pneumonia, but she didn't. She died after childbirth. Jonathan,

Annie is a royal princess, and they know nothing about her. I think now that maybe what I did was wrong. I loved her, and I didn't want to lose her. When they all died, I just took her. I talked to the housekeeper and the maids about it. They didn't know she was royal or legitimate, but I did when I left. It's all in the leather box with the crown on it. I want you to read it, and tell me what I should do. You have a right to know too. I don't want to lose her, but she has the right to a life we can never give her. Read it. Read it all. The key to the box is in an envelope in my underwear drawer." She was clearly out of her mind, and Jonathan spoke to her firmly, as he would have to a child.

"You need to rest. I want you to take a pill."

"The leather box," she said again, her voice fading. "You have to read the letters. I should have told you years ago. The box is in my closet, on the shelf."

"It doesn't matter now," he insisted. "Annie is your daughter. Our daughter. I love her too."

"They must have been heartbroken when they lost Charlotte. I read all the letters from her mother to her for the entire year. The queen loved her, and they don't know she had a daughter. Maybe they deserve to know and so does Annie." She was getting increasingly wound up, and Jonathan couldn't distract her. "Promise me you'll read what's in the box." She fixed her eyes on him almost fiercely and he nodded. Her eyes were sunken deep in their sockets with dark circles under them.

"I promise." It killed him to see his wife in this condition, and now she was losing her mind either from the pain or from her illness. She suddenly looked like an old woman, and nothing she had told him made sense. He loved Annie too, and she was a wonderful girl, but she wasn't royal. If she was, they would have known about her. Their daughter would have told them about her, or the countess would have. He was sure that she couldn't have gotten married and had a child without her family knowing, particularly the royals. It just wasn't possible. The royal family didn't go around losing princesses. He knew his wife. Lucy would never have stolen someone else's child, even at nineteen. She was the best mother he'd ever seen to Annie, whoever her father had been, and to their sons, who were devastated over their mother's illness too.

He gave Lucy some of the drops for pain then, since she refused to take the morphine, and a few minutes later, her eyes closed and she drifted off to sleep.

He went to sit in the living room for a while to gather his thoughts. It broke his heart to see how mentally disordered she had become. She had never been irrational before, and now suddenly she was caught up in some kind of obsessive fantasy about Annie being royal, and the circumstances of an allegedly royal princess's death, who probably wasn't a princess at all, and just some young girl from London staying in the country to avoid the air raids, as Lucy had done. Nothing she had shared with him made any sense. He wondered if the box she was talking about was empty. He had seen it once, years before, when Lucy first moved in, and never since. To put his mind at ease, he went to look for the box, and found it where Lucy had said it would be. Then he looked for the key in the envelope in her underwear drawer, and found that too. He brought it back to the living room, took the key out of the envelope, and fitted it into the lock. He noticed the gold crown on the leather, as the key turned easily, and he lifted the lid and glanced inside. The box was crammed full of packets of letters tied with ribbon, and there was a sheaf of documents. He saw a birth certificate, a marriage certificate, a death certificate, and some photographs. For an instant, he stared at it, not wanting to read through the letters, but at least this much was true.

He picked up one packet of letters and untied the ribbon to get a sense of what they were, and immediately saw the Windsor crown, the queen's initials, and her elegant hand, dating the letter, with the words "Buckingham Palace" under it, and he frowned. Maybe there was a kernel of truth to something Lucy had said, and the rest was hallucination from her illness. He wondered again if the cancer had gone to her brain. He read the first letter, saw that it was to someone named Charlotte, obviously her daughter, and the letter was signed "Mama." And as he set it down in the box again, his heart was beating faster. Without meaning to, or wanting to, he had opened Pandora's box, and he was afraid of what he would discover next.

Chapter 8

Jonathan went in to check on Lucy several times while he read through the contents of the box. It was late and everyone in the house was asleep. It was a quiet time for him. Lucy was sleeping soundly from the drops, and made an occasional noise. He would watch her for a minute, gently touch her or stroke her hair, and then he went back to the living room to continue reading.

He had read all of the queen's letters to her daughter, and, like Lucy, he had no doubt that they'd been written by the queen.

He remembered now the royal family sending their youngest daughter to the country during the war, to set an example to others and get her away from the air raids in London. And her tragic death at seventeen a year later, of an illness, he thought. It was also remarkable that the princess and Lucy had ended up in the same place. War was the great equalizer. There was also no mention of a baby, a pregnancy, a marriage, or even a romance, so whatever had gone on in Yorkshire, Charlotte's parents had apparently been unaware of it. Perhaps, as Lucy said, they were going to tell her all of it when they saw each other again, when Charlotte returned to London. But she seemed not to have shared any major news in the meantime. She also couldn't tell her mother anything shocking on the phone, since phone lines were not secure during the war, and the palace switchboard would have been equally unreliable, with others listening in on conversations and talking about it afterward. For government business and military intelligence, they had used scramblers and codes, but Charlotte wouldn't have had any of that available to her. Her news would have been that of a seventeen-year-old girl. In this case, one who had gotten pregnant, and then secretly married. News that would not have been easy to share with her parents at a distance, particularly as a royal princess.

Jonathan read Henry's letters to Charlotte after that, which referred to both the baby before it was born, and their marriage in haste and secrecy before he left. They were obviously deeply in love with each other, and had gotten themselves into a very awkward spot.

The official documents in the box told their own tale. Their marriage certificate by special license, signed by the countess and earl, which Charlotte's parents knew nothing about, under the name she must have been using to guard the secret of her identity for a variety of reasons. But it seemed reasonable to believe that Charlotte Elizabeth White was in fact Charlotte Elizabeth Windsor. It was also reasonable to believe that they might not have been too upset about the Hemmings boy in other circumstances, but a marriage at seventeen due to an unwanted pregnancy was enough to upset any parent, royal or not. They sent her away for a year, for her safety, to respectable people, and she got both pregnant and married in that order. It would have been a lot for them to swallow.

He could see why neither Charlotte nor the countess had told them, and were probably waiting for the right time to do so, but that time had come and gone, with the death of the baby's father in war-time, the deaths of both the earl and later the countess, and Charlotte's own death after the baby was born. The entire situation had gotten out of hand, which left an infant whom they knew nothing about an orphan of the royal family. The circumstances had been perfect for Lucy to simply sweep the baby up, tuck her under her wing, and take off with her, with no one more mature to reason with her and stop her. Her ill-judged though well-meant action at the time had resulted in a royal princess who had been deprived of her family and her birthright, and a royal family who had been deprived of their late daughter's child. Knowing that Princess Charlotte had left a daughter behind when she died might have offered them some comfort in their grief at the time. It wasn't too late to set things right, but it was going to be awkward now. Their suddenly coming forward with a lost princess was going to be highly suspect and not easy to pull off without causing a major uproar, or Lucy even being accused of a crime, child theft or something worse, on her deathbed. And there was no one left to corroborate the story.

Jonathan suspected that Lucy no longer knew where the Hemmingses' servants were, since the property had been sold, or even if they were still alive since more than twenty years had passed. Also, who knew if the doctor who had delivered Annie was still alive, or the vicar who had married them? Twenty-one years was a long time, and Henry Hemmings and his family were all dead. The entire mess was not going to be easy to unravel, but Jonathan was convinced it had to be, for the Windsors' sake, and also for Annie's. She had a right to know who she was, and what had happened, and that Lucy loved her, but was in fact not her mother. Jonathan had no idea how Annie would react to the news, not to mention the Windsors' reaction. And he wanted to clear Lucy's name and protect her. What she had done was very wrong, but also naïve, and she had been suffering from the loss of her own family, and clinging to the infant for love and comfort, however misguided.

It was a most unusual story. Lucy was not delusional, she was trying to repair the mistakes of the past at the eleventh hour. They were not small mistakes. Whether she meant to or not, Lucy had stolen Annie from the Windsors for more than two decades, her entire life so far, and had deprived Annie of the life she had been born to and had a right to, with her royal family, in a palace, not the life of the child of a housemaid and a stable master in Kent. The biggest question of all was how to get the information to the queen now, without causing a scandal, and catching the attention of the press, and then leaving the royal family to handle it as they wished. Jonathan didn't want Lucy to be punished for an enormous error of judgment she had committed at nineteen. And what would Annie think of Lucy once she knew, and found out that the mother she loved in fact wasn't? She had lived with a lie all her life, and was someone else entirely than she thought she was.

One thing was certain in Jonathan's mind. The Windsors would want to see Annie. And the other thing he felt sure of was that Lucy had made a terrible mistake, and taken it too far. He was grateful she had told him, and he lay awake thinking about it all night. He was sitting next to her on their bed, when she woke up the next morning. In spite of the drops that had made her sleep, she remembered immediately what she had asked him to do, and she searched his eyes as soon as she woke up.

"Did you read it all?"

He nodded, with a serious look. "I did. That's quite a story. You got in over your head through a series of unusual circumstances, and some bad decisions on your part, made from the heart."

"I don't regret it, I love her. But now I wonder if she'll hate me for keeping her from the life she was born to. We should tell her, but I don't want to just yet."

"We both love her, and she won't hate you," he said quietly. "But she has a right to know where she comes from." He was the only father she had ever known, and Lucy the only mother, but in fact she had an entire family of aunts and uncles and cousins, a grandmother who had loved Annie's rightful mother. She was a royal princess, and no matter where she had grown up, that could not be denied. He wasn't sure how Annie would feel about it. She was hard to predict at times, and could be stubborn too. He didn't know if she'd be angry or only shocked, and it was shocking, even to him. It was hard to believe that his wife could do such a thing, and had gotten away with it, but she had. For almost twenty-one years.

They were still talking about it when Annie came in with a breakfast tray for both of them, and her stepfather stared at her as though seeing her for the first time. Suddenly her natural grace and elegance made sense, as did her skill as a rider, even her passion for horses, which the royal family was famous for. She was heavily influenced by her bloodline. He was looking at her intently, thinking of what they would all have to face when the truth surfaced, and Annie stared back at him, confused.

"What? Do I seem weird or something? You're looking at me as if I have two heads."

"Not that I'm aware of." He smiled. She left the room then and he glanced at his wife. "Do you want to tell her?" But Lucy shook her head. She knew she had to, or thought she should, but she was exhausted and didn't feel up to it. Jonathan didn't want to press her, but he didn't know how much time they had, and he thought Annie should hear it from Lucy first, so she could understand why she had done it. Only Lucy could truly explain what had motivated her to do such a thing.

"Don't tell her now. I will," she said weakly, and he nodded and went to take a shower and dress for work. When he came back, she was asleep. He told Annie he was leaving, so she could check on her mother. And when he returned to see her at noon, she was weaker, and that night she felt too ill and was in too much pain to think or speak. The next morning she was worse. Annie came and sat beside her, while her mother slept. Lucy seemed to be sliding downhill quickly. Jonathan sat with her all the next day and didn't go to work, and by that afternoon, Lucy was in a coma. The doctor had come several times and left a nurse. And Annie was in her room crying all afternoon. There was nothing she could do and the boys were at their grandmother's. Jonathan had sent them there.

He lay next to her holding her hand, as the nurse checked her and Annie came and went. That night, the boys came home, and Annie sat with them, and as Jonathan lay beside his wife, she silently slipped away without ever regaining consciousness. They never got to say goodbye. And she never got to tell Annie the story that was essential now.

The pain of the loss was shocking, and more brutal than he could have imagined. He went through the motions of making the arrangements while trying to console his children, who had lost their mother. Annie was devastated, and the boys couldn't stop crying. Jonathan held himself together for their sakes, and two days later, as they left for the funeral in the church where he and Lucy had been married, he thought about the contents of the box Lucy had revealed to him before she died. He was grateful she had told him about it, but now it was up to him to try to reach out to the Queen Mother, and tell her what had happened to her daughter and granddaughter. And after that, he would have to tell Annie. But he wanted to know the royal family's reaction first. And this was not the right time to tell Annie. She was shattered by her mother's death. She needed time to catch her breath, before another shock. He had loved Lucy unconditionally, but she had left him the hardest job of all at the end. How was he going to explain it to Annie, and the Windsors? He had no idea where to start.

He thought about it all through the funeral, and for days afterward. He missed Lucy like the air he breathed. She was his lover, wife, best friend, and companion of twenty years. Now he had to find a way to return a lost princess to the Windsors, without breaking Annie's heart or dishonoring Lucy's memory. It was the hardest task he'd ever faced. Without Lucy now, he had to keep his family together, while tearing them apart.

Chapter 9

The weeks after Lucy's funeral were like a fog which enveloped Jonathan and the children. He felt as though he was swimming underwater and everything around him felt surreal. He kept telling himself he had to put one foot after the other, go through the motions of his daily life, and be there for his children. But nothing made sense without Lucy. He felt now as though he was in a free fall through the sky with nothing to stop him, no parachute.

Annie was no better. She barely spoke, except to talk to her twin brothers. They argued with each other constantly, which was their fifteen-year-old way of coping with the loss of their mother. They took it out on each other. Annie took care of them as best she could. Jonathan's mother came to cook for all of them. Their nightly meals were deadly silent. No one talked and they hardly ate. Jonathan was inconsolable and Annie looked shattered, although she pulled herself together for the twins.

All Annie felt able to do was exercise the horses. It was usually the stable hands' job, but she was grateful to have something to do that she could cope with. Sometimes she walked them slowly through the fields and let them graze when they wanted, and sometimes she rode them at full speed. Jonathan saw her do it, but for once he didn't say anything about it to her. He knew she needed the release.

It was weeks before he was able to focus again on what he had read in the leather box two days before Lucy died. He knew he had to do something about it. If he didn't, Lucy's secret, and the secret of Annie's very existence, would die one day with him. He couldn't let that happen, for Annie's sake, and the Windsors'. Not knowing what else to do, he tried the simplest way first. He got the number from information for Buckingham Palace, which was ridiculously easy, like calling the White House in Washington. Getting the number wasn't difficult. It was what happened after that that mattered.

He asked for the queen's private secretary, and got the runaround from start to finish. The names they gave him were for inconsequential underlings who put a smokescreen around the queen's secretary. His attempt to get through to the Queen Mother was equally fruitless. And after nearly an hour of waiting for half a dozen people, he got nowhere, and finally hung up. He should have known better, but it was worth a try. He realized now that he had to be more ingenious and find another way to gain access to the queen, or her personal secretary. He needed to be put in touch with her, on a deeply personal matter, like the fate of the sister she had lost more than twenty years before, and the niece she was entirely unaware of.

After thinking about it for several days, he decided to try channels he was more familiar with. He couldn't just march up to the gates of Buckingham Palace and demand to see the queen, or even send her a letter which might never reach her, and end up in a file of crackpot mail she'd never see. Instead, he asked John Markham if he was acquainted with the queen's horse trainer, and his employer looked instantly worried.

"Are you looking for a job?" He was seriously concerned. Jonathan was the one employee he didn't want to lose. Jonathan shook his head.

"No, not at all. It sounds crazy, but I'm trying to get access to either the queen or the Queen Mother, about a matter that happened twenty years ago. I spent an hour on the phone yesterday, trying to get through to her secretary. I thought I might have better luck through her horse trainer. At least it's a world I understand. Do you know him personally?" Jonathan asked, and Markham seemed relieved.

"I've met her royal racing manager a few times. He's an important man. He's responsible for all her racehorses. He's a little grand and my name probably won't get you far, but you can give it a try."

"I thought I'd tell him we're interested in their stud services, to get my foot in the door. I don't really want to talk to him, I need the name of the queen's private secretary. It's a personal matter." John Markham gave Jonathan the number, and later that afternoon, Jonathan called, and reached a secretary who wanted to know what it was about. "I run John Markham's stables. We're interested in stud services for several of our mares, and John asked me to discuss some possibilities with him." The secretary sounded more interested, and a moment later, he put him through to Lord Hatton directly. It went a lot more smoothly than his futile call to the palace previously.

He spent a few minutes mentioning the mares they allegedly wanted services for, and the stallions that might be available. Lord Hatton was interested, and talked for some time about the virtues of the various stallions they were using for stud at the moment. At the end of the conversation, Jonathan casually mentioned that John Markham had asked him to get the name and direct line of the queen's private secretary, about an event he wanted to invite her to on his yacht. Hatton took the bait and gave Jonathan the name and number he had been unable to discover before when he called the palace. It had all been so simple in the world he was accustomed to, in the language he spoke well. Jonathan was respected in horse circles, and his employer was well liked. He thanked Lord Hatton for the information, and said he would get back to him about the studs they preferred, after he discussed it with John Markham.

He took a deep breath when he hung up, and dialed the palace after that. He got straight through to the queen's personal secretary this time, Sir Malcolm Harding, who answered the phone himself on his direct line. Lord Hatton had given him the secretary's private line, and for an instant Jonathan was a little shocked. He tried to stay calm, and not get flustered or he'd sound like a freak.

"I'd like to request a private audience with the queen, at her convenience. My wife died recently, and entrusted me with some documents which I believe belong to Her Majesty, or the Queen Mother, and date back to the war. They're of a personal nature, and I would like to return them personally. They relate to the queen's late sister, Charlotte. She and my wife were personal friends, and my wife held on to the documents out of sentiment for a very long time." There was a pause at the other end of the line, while the queen's secretary digested what Jonathan had said to him. He didn't want to turn him away, nor did he want to give him instant access to the queen.

"Would it be possible to entrust the documents to me and allow me to have a look at them? If the queen feels an audience is warranted, I'll be happy to arrange it. We don't want to waste your time."

More to the point, they didn't want him to waste theirs. "You could send them to me by post if you like."

"I'd rather not. I'd rather put them in your hands. Lord Hatton gave me your name and number, and I'd be happy to give them to you to have a look at. There's a personal side of the story as well, I'm afraid. I won't take up much of her time, but I believe it's a matter that would be of great interest to Her Majesty." Jonathan wondered how many people said that to him every day. Dozens probably, but in this case it involved a long lost relative who had been stolen from them. He couldn't say that to him, but he intended to write up a brief summary of what had happened, what had remained hidden for such a long time and what remained. He had no idea what their reaction would be after so long, or if they would suspect him of trying to blackmail or extort the royal family. They might refuse any further contact with him entirely, but at least he had to try, for Annie's sake and theirs.

"Could you bring the documents to me tomorrow, sir? Say at two o'clock? I promise to put them in the right hands." The mention of the queen's horse trainer's name had greased things along, as Jonathan hoped it would.

"I'd be delighted to." The secretary told him which entrance to come to, who to ask for, and the inside line for his office, and they agreed to meet at two the next day. As soon as Jonathan hung up, he sat down to write a brief summary of the facts, to simplify things. It was almost painful to write the details.

He mentioned the romance between Princess Charlotte and Henry Hemmings, before he left for the army, and the unexpected result that the princess had gotten pregnant, but didn't have the opportunity from Yorkshire to share the information with her mother. He then gave the date of their marriage by special license, and the subsequent date of the young man's death. He said that she had given birth to a baby girl, and had died three hours after delivering her. He listed the dates of both the earl's and the countess's death, which left no one to care for the infant, once orphaned, and no one knowing what to do with a child who was in fact legitimate but whose existence was entirely unknown to Their Majesties, Charlotte's parents. And for better or worse, a young girl who had been staying with the Hemmingses to escape the bombing raids in London had cared for the child herself, and had then taken the infant to live with her as her own. Jonathan did not deny that poor decisions had been made by the young person involved, whom he had subsequently married. He had said that the information had only fallen into his hands two days before his wife's death, several weeks before. And the most important piece of information of all of it was that Princess Charlotte's child was alive and well, living with his family in Kent. She currently had no knowledge of the circumstances of her birth, or her connection to the royal family, of which she was in fact a member, as the niece of the current queen, and the granddaughter of the Queen Mother.

Jonathan said his only interest was to reunite Anne Louise with her family. He would be happy to bring her to meet them, if they were so inclined. It was confusing at best, but the story was familiar to him now, and he tried to make it as simple as he could. He made copies of everything that was in the box, made a package of all of it, put it in a large envelope, and sealed it, with the information on how to reach him, should they wish to. He respectfully thanked Their Majesties for reading the material he sent, hoping that they would. It occurred to him that he could get arrested for interference or blackmail, or if they thought he was trying to extort money from them, or had sequestered the girl against her will for over twenty years, or worse, was trying to pawn off an imposter on them. There was risk involved in trying to be the go-between, and set things right, after Lucy had let it lie in the shadows for so long. He made no attempt to excuse his wife's behavior, and said she had died with deep remorse for keeping Her Highness Princess Anne Louise away from them for so long.

He took the train to London the next day and asked Annie to cover for him. He said he'd be back that night.

"Where are you going?" she asked, curious.

"To London, to see the queen," he said, sounding as though he was teasing her, but he wasn't. "Just like the nursery rhyme says."

"Very funny," she said.

He caught the train on time, and arrived promptly for the appointment with Sir Malcolm Harding, shook hands with him, and handed him the package.

"These are all copies. I have the originals, but I don't want them to get lost. I'll be happy to turn them over to you, if it's of interest to the queen, or the Queen Mother." The secretary thanked him politely and set the bundle on his desk, and a moment later, Jonathan was back on the street, looking up at the palace where Annie's mother had grown up.

He took the train back to Kent and arrived in time for dinner. He was very quiet, and Annie noticed that he had worn a suit to go to town, and he seemed very formally dressed for a simple errand, but Jonathan volunteered nothing about how he had spent the afternoon. He wasn't ready to tell her yet.

The phone rang in his office in the stables, at nine o'clock the next morning. Jonathan was startled to hear from Sir Malcolm so soon. He went straight to the point.

"The queen would like to meet with you tomorrow, at eleven in the morning, and she would like you to bring the girl." They weren't dignifying her with her title yet, and weren't sure if she was for real. Jonathan hesitated for only a fraction of an instant, thinking that he would have to tell Annie the whole story sooner than he was ready to, but now there was no choice. He had until eleven A.M. the next day to do it.

"Of course," Jonathan responded about bringing Annie with him. He wondered if he was going to be arrested when he got there, and wind up in jail. Anything was possible, but he was too far down the road to back out now, and he didn't want to. He had a bumpy stretch of road ahead of him, when he told Annie about her history, and tried to explain why Lucy had taken her in the first place, and never contacted the Windsors until now.

He waited until he saw Annie return from exercising one of the horses, and then asked her to have lunch with him as she walked the horse back to his stall.

"Something wrong?"

"Not at all. I just have something I want to discuss with you," like the fact that you're a royal princess and part of the royal family, just a little thing like that.

He made two sandwiches, put them on plates, and set them down on a picnic table near the barn, where they could talk.

"Something's up," she said, looking suspicious after they had both sat down. "Is it something to do with Mom?" she asked.

"Yes, and no. It's actually old news, but your mom only told me about it two days before she died. I think you should know about it too."

"She left each of us a million pounds," she teased him, and he laughed.

"That would have been nice. Actually, it's more complicated than that." He wasn't sure how to broach the subject with her, so he just plunged in and told her the story and the circumstances surrounding her birth. It got complicated here and there, but Annie followed, and at the end of his recital, she sat and stared at him, as though she'd seen a snake.

"Stop. Let me see if I got this right. Mom was not my real mother, she didn't give birth to me, and the woman who did died a few hours after I was born. She was a royal princess, and her mother was the queen when I was born. And the woman who is the queen now is my mother's sister, and my grandmother is now the Queen Mother. If any of that is true, it sounds totally crazy to me. And what does that make me, if it is true?" she asked, visibly confused and more than a little overwhelmed.

"It makes you a Royal Highness," he said quietly. And it made Lucy, the woman Annie knew as her mother, an infant thief, a young girl who had stolen a baby and kept it a secret for more than twenty years. But Annie hadn't absorbed that part of the story yet, and she loved the woman she knew as her mother, and the memory of her, no matter what. And Jonathan hoped she always would. Annie had been suffering terribly from her mother's death.

"Wait a minute," Annie said holding a hand up, as though to stop traffic. It was all coming at her too fast. "You're telling me that I'm a princess, that I'm royal, and related to the queen and the royal family." He nodded and then she stared at him in disbelief. "And how did Mom get away with that for so long?"

"Because no one knew that you existed. Tragically, everyone died, your mother, your father in the war, and both his parents. The only other family you have are the royals. And me, of course." He smiled at her. "And I want you to know that I think what your mother did was wrong. She did it because she loved you, but just taking a child is not the way things should be done. She told me about it two days before she died. I think she would have told you herself if she hadn't been so ill. I'm not judging your mother, but what came clear to me is that you have a right to meet your relatives, and at least know who they are. And your mother felt that way too at the end, which was why she told me the whole story. What you do after that is up to you."

"What if I don't want to be a princess, Papa. I don't think I'd like it. And what if they hate me on sight? Or don't believe you?"

"They might not. But why would they hate you? You're the daughter of their beloved sister and daughter. They owe it to her to be civil to her child, and welcome you after you've been lost to them for so long. They never knew that you were born."

"I wasn't lost. I was with you and Mama, where I belong. I don't want to be a princess, Papa," she said, sounding like a little girl.

"You don't have that choice. That's who you are, and who you were born. We don't get to pick and choose our families, although being related to the Royal House of Windsor is a pretty cool thing to be."

"When am I going to meet them?" She looked afraid.

"Tomorrow at eleven A.M., at Buckingham Palace."

"Oh my God," she said and immediately looked panicked. "I don't

think I want to be a princess, Papa. It sounds hard. I think I'll re-
nounce my title. Can I do that?"

"Technically, yes. In real life, I wouldn't. Why not enjoy it and try
it out for a while? And get to know your Windsor relatives first. You
might all love each other, and somehow I think it would make Lucy
happy."

They threw away their paper plates from lunch then, and Annie
left him to walk slowly back to the house. She needed time to think
about everything her father had said. She was a royal princess, and
had been stolen at birth by the woman she knew and loved as her
mother. It sounded like a fairytale, and Annie didn't know what to
believe.

Jonathan saw her walk into the barn later that afternoon and saddle up one of the horses. She took a horse he had discouraged her
from riding before. He was a stallion who was barely broken, skittish
and hard to manage, although she had never had any trouble with
him. He saw her leave, heading toward one of the trails at a slow
trot, and then he saw her take off across the hills at a blistering gallop, riding as hard as she could. He stood watching her for a minute,
hoping no harm would come to her, as she flew across the meadow
at breakneck speed, and for once, knowing what she was wrestling
with and had to face the next day, he didn't blame her a bit, or try to
stop her. She was riding like the wind.

Chapter 10

Annie was almost silent on the brief hour's train ride from Kent to London. She sat staring out the window, thinking of the only mother she had ever known, trying to understand who she had been at nineteen, to take a baby she believed no one wanted, and claim it as her own for twenty years. Annie couldn't fathom why Lucy had never told her the truth. She had done it out of love for Annie, and in time, the lie had become too big to admit. She had in fact been a wonderful mother, and perhaps she had been right and saved her from an orphanage, if the royal family had rejected her as an infant. She would never know now what they would have done.

Annie could even less understand her place in the family she had inherited overnight. She was suddenly a royal princess with all the burdens, responsibilities, expectations, and confusion that entailed. She had no idea what was expected of her, if they would accept her, or accuse Jonathan of having concocted a lie, and Annie of being an imposter. What if the royal family didn't believe them? Annie still couldn't believe it herself.

And what had her "real" mother been like? Princess Charlotte, who died at seventeen, hours after Annie was born. She didn't know what to think, or believe, or who she was now. It was all so confusing, and she wondered if they would treat her like a fraud at the palace. Why would they believe a history as complicated as hers? She was twenty-one years old, and it was a lot to absorb. Whatever would happen at Buckingham Palace, both of her mothers were dead now. She felt like the motherless orphan she was as she stared out the window, and then turned to Jonathan with an unhappy expression.

"I want to go to Australia," she said in a dead voice.

"Now? Why? What brought that on?" It was an odd idea to him.

"Female jockeys can ride in amateur races there. I want to see what it's like and sign up."

"How about an apprenticeship at the queen's stables here instead? She has some fabulous racehorses and the best stables in the country. You could do worse." They might be open to that idea, if they believed her story at all.

"I'd rather go to Australia," she said, trying not to think of the meeting they were going to. She had worn her only appropriate dress to meet the queen, who was supposedly her aunt. It was the black dress she had worn to her mother's funeral, and Jonathan recognized it immediately. It suited Annie's somber mood, as they headed for their fateful appointment in London. He was nervous too, but tried not to show it. He wanted to give Annie the courage to face whatever came next. His worst fear was that they would be blamed for Lucy's youthful but very grave mistake. However innocent her intentions, she had robbed them of a child. It explained to him some of Lucy's obsession with the royals.

"I can't afford to send you there," Jonathan said apologetically about Australia. "I think you should stick around here for now, until you get things settled."

"What if they think I'm a fraud?"

"They might. But then you'll be no worse off than you were before." He had brought the original documents with him, at their request, and all the letters, and kept handwritten copies and photographs of the documents and letters for himself, and a set made for Annie too. He had brought the leather box with him in a bag too, in case it added to their credibility.

"Do they pay you to be a royal princess?" she asked with a mischievous look and he laughed.

"They give you an allowance. The entire royal family gets an allowance. It would be nice for you." There was an upside to this for her, if Lucy's story was true and they believed her.

"Is that why you did this?" She was worried when she said it.

"No, I did it because they're your family, and you deserve to know them, and they have a right to know about you." It had crossed his mind that if they accepted her, she might not want to live with him anymore. He wasn't her father and he had never adopted her officially. It hadn't seemed necessary, but he might lose her in the process. Even if he did, he knew that what he was doing was correct, for her. She had a right to a life he couldn't give her, and they could. He wanted the best for her. And in her own naïve way, Lucy had too. Jonathan was just grateful that Lucy had told him the truth before she died. Otherwise, they would never have known.

They were both quiet as they got off the train, and he could see that Annie was anxious, and so was he. People probably tried to claim that they were part of the royal family every day. He wasn't sure who would be there, the queen or the Queen Mother, or only the queen's secretary.

They took a cab from the station to Buckingham Palace, to the same entrance he had used two days before, when he had dropped off the copies of the letters and documents.

A security guard checked their ID papers at the desk and called Sir Malcolm and told him they were there. "Miss Walsh and Mr. Baker." She hadn't been accepted as royal yet, and a moment later Sir Malcolm hurried down a hall, and they followed him into an elevator after Jonathan introduced Annie. He saw the secretary staring at her, as Annie gazed at the floor, and then they walked down a long carpeted hallway with portraits of members of the royal family all the way back through several centuries. They stopped at a tall door, where two uniformed palace guards opened the door and announced them, and Jonathan could feel his heart catch as he realized that at the end of the room Queen Alexandra was sitting at her desk. She stood to greet them as Jonathan bowed and Annie curtsied, and she invited them to sit down. An older woman walked into the room, and they both recognized Queen Anne the Queen Mother, for whom Annie realized now she had been named, since she was her grandmother. She was wearing a simple black suit. Jonathan and Annie stood and bowed and curtsied again. The Queen Mother had a photo album with her, and after a few moments of polite superficial conversation, she handed it to Annie.

"Would you like to take a look?" she asked, and Annie nodded, almost too intimidated to speak. "They're photographs of your mother as a little girl and before she went to Yorkshire. You're only a few years older than she was then." Annie's eyes grew wide as she carefully turned the pages. The photographs were old, but it was easy to see that Annie was the image of her. They looked like twins. The Queen Mother had seen it too when she walked into the room, and Queen Alexandra spoke to Jonathan and Annie then. She noticed the leather box that Jonathan was still holding, and she asked to see it. He handed it to her, and she opened it carefully, moved some of the contents aside to look for the initials, and stared at Jonathan with amazement when she found them.

"My father gave me this box on my eighteenth birthday. I gave it to Charlotte for her correspondence when she left for Yorkshire," the Queen Mother said quietly. She looked deeply moved when she said it. "It's a very unusual story," the queen admitted. "But wartime can create some very odd situations. Our phone lines weren't secure then, and Charlotte and our mother communicated entirely by letter during the time she was away. The news of her early marriage, and your impending arrival," she smiled at Annie as she said it, "is not the sort of thing you want to write about to your mother at seventeen. She was meant to stay in Yorkshire for a year, to get away from the air raids in London, and she suffered from severe asthma. But things apparently got out of hand while she was away. It must have been an awkward situation for the countess too. It was a heavy responsibility shepherding young people that age. I don't envy her." She smiled at both of them again. "The tragedy for us was when she died, whatever the cause, whether from pneumonia, or . . . other causes in the circumstances. We knew nothing about you, Anne, until two days ago," she said solemnly, and Annie nodded. "It's been a shock for my mother." The Queen Mother appeared to be fighting back tears when Annie handed the album back to her. "And for my sister, and for me as well. Charlotte died twenty-one years ago, but it seems like yesterday to us. We're going to authenticate the documents your stepfather brought to us. Her Majesty, my mother, recognized the letters, and the leather box with the crown. They're genuine. And once we verify the documents, so there can be no doubt about who you are, and if indeed you are my niece, and Her Majesty's granddaughter, we'd like to introduce you to the rest of the family. But we need to be sure first. I trust that's agreeable to you," she asked, looking at Jonathan, and he immediately agreed.

"I'd like to make one thing clear, Your Majesty," he said to the young queen. "There is nothing I want from this for myself. If in fact everything checks out, your niece should be restored to you. You all lost a great deal and it was a tragedy when Her Highness Princess Charlotte died, and Anne should know who she is and who her relatives are. There is nothing more we want from any of it."

"Is that true for you as well?" she asked Annie directly, and she nodded, in awe of the woman who was allegedly her aunt. She looked every inch a queen in a navy velvet suit with a string of pearls around her neck.

"Yes," Annie confirmed in barely more than a whisper, and then, "My father says you have wonderful horses. I would like to see them one day."

"That can be arranged." The monarch smiled at her. "Do you like horses?" Annie beamed and her father laughed and relaxed a little. The meeting had been very formal so far.

"It's the *only* thing she cares about," he answered for her. "She's been horse mad ever since she could walk. She's a bruising rider, and extraordinarily skilled."

"I want to be a jockey," Annie added bravely, "but women are not allowed."

"Maybe you will be one day. And I'd be happy to arrange a tour of our stables in Newmarket with Lord Hatton, the royal racing manager." She smiled at them both. "We have some rather famous horses there. I'm horse mad myself. And your mother was too. She was just about your size. If the papers are genuine, you both take after my great-great-grandmother Queen Victoria, who was no taller than you are. You're the perfect size for a jockey if they ever change the rules."

"I hope they do," Annie whispered and the queen smiled and stood up, and then something caught her eye.

"You'll be hearing from us as things proceed," the queen said formally, but she was staring at Annie's arm. She was wearing the gold bracelet with the heart that Lucy had given her. "May I look at your bracelet?" she said in a voice softened by emotion as Annie extended her wrist. Queen Alexandra recognized the bracelet immediately as the one she had taken from her own wrist and given Charlotte when she left for Yorkshire. "May I ask where you got that?"

"My mother gave it to me. My mother Lucy," she explained. There were tears in the queen's eyes when she nodded. "I gave it to your mother, my sister Charlotte. It was mine." There was silence for a moment, as the Queen Mother cried silently and Jonathan spoke up.

"Thank you for seeing us, Your Majesty. I know it's a visit we'll never forget," he said with a bow, and Annie curtsied deeply to both Majesties, her grandmother and her aunt.

"If things go well, the first of many visits, I hope," the queen said generously, and her secretary appeared from nowhere, and all three of them backed out of the room, and the two palace guards in livery closed the door, as the queen turned to her mother with a sigh. They had left the leather box, and its contents, with them to authenticate.

"She looks just like Charlotte, doesn't she?" The Queen Mother nodded and wiped the tears from her cheeks. "Don't get too excited, it could all be a trick. People are too clever sometimes. They may have noticed the resemblance and decided to take advantage of it. It could be purely coincidental. I hope that's not the case, but it's possible. It would be lovely to have Charlotte's daughter in our midst. She seems like a very sweet girl." Seeing the bracelet had shaken the queen and gave her hope that Annie and the strange story were real.

"Her stepfather is a simple man, but polite and without pretension. He seems to care about her a great deal. I thought he was sincere," the Queen Mother commented in a serious voice. The meeting had been deeply emotional for her.

"Let's hope they're honest people and it all turns out well."

They had spent half an hour with her, which was longer than the queen normally spent with non-cabinet visitors, but she and her mother had been anxious to see the girl. Princess Victoria was in Paris, so hadn't come, but had wanted to meet her too when the queen told her sister about her. Nothing like this had ever happened to them. Long lost relatives didn't just turn up, or never had before. She was hopeful that they were telling the truth. It was like having a piece of Charlotte back after so many years.

Annie was smiling broadly when they got into a cab and headed for the station, after thanking the queen's secretary for his help. He had been charmed by Annie, who looked more like an elf or a fairy than a girl her age. She was so small and delicate, and looked like the photographs he had seen of Princess Charlotte in the Queen Mother's rooms. He had worked for her before when she was queen.

"They were so nice," Annie said, looking awestruck, and Jonathan was impressed too. It was the high point of his life so far. They had been to Buckingham Palace to meet the queen.

"Maybe if she's really my aunt, she'd let me ride one of her horses one day," she said with dreams in her eyes.

"Oh Lord," Jonathan said. "She has racehorses worth millions. You'd be a lucky girl if that ever happened. Just seeing them at close range would be a gift."

She smiled at him then. "I'm lucky anyway. I love you, Papa. Thank you for bringing me here." All he could think of as they rode toward the station was again how grateful he was that Lucy had told him about the leather box, and let him see its contents, before she died. Whatever she had done, for whatever reason, and no matter how wrong it was, she had redeemed herself. With luck, Annie would be restored to the family where she belonged. Even if he lost her as a result, it was his fondest hope for her. To atone for his wife's sins, out of love for his stepdaughter, was a sacrifice he was willing to make.

Chapter 11

Their visit to the queen and Queen Mother at Buckingham Palace had a fairytale quality to it. Even if nothing came of the authentication of their documents, and whatever investigation they were sure to conduct, it was exciting to have been to see the queen. No one knew that they had been there. Their life in Kent on the Markham estate seemed like drudgery after that. Annie exercised the horses as she always had, and Jonathan was working with the new horses to break. Their life was hard without Lucy, and their evenings sad. Annie missed Lucy terribly, her warm contact and their brief conversations when they saw each other at the end of the day. Annie took over from her grandmother and cooked dinner for her father and the twins every night, and the boys complained about her cooking. But Jonathan and Annie agreed that family meals were important.

The house seemed so dreary without her mother. And it was a rainy spring, which made it worse. They felt as though they hadn't seen the sun in months.

There was no word from Sir Malcolm Harding, the queen's secretary, for nearly two months. Jonathan wondered if that meant the documents had been discredited or rejected, but they heard nothing either way. It was almost as though nothing had happened, and they'd never been to see the queen. Annie began to suspect she wasn't royal after all. It didn't really matter. She was happy as she was, living with her father and brothers. She had more work to do than before, trying to step into her mother's shoes, doing the laundry and the cooking, picking up after them. They tracked mud into the house, grumbled about doing homework. She felt like the mother of two teenage boys since her mother's death. There were days when it all seemed like too much. Too much energy, too much work, too much complaining, too many men in the house who messed everything up as soon as she cleaned it. There was no woman she was close to. She saw only the grooms in the stables, who were her age, and her father and brothers at night.

They went to dinner at a local restaurant in Kent on her birthday, and the day after, Sir Malcolm called to tell them that all of the papers appeared to be authentic.

The handwriting on the Queen Mother's letters had been verified. The letters from Henry Hemmings appeared to be all right. The town hall county record office near Ainsleigh had registered all the documents. Charlotte's cause of death on her death certificate had been a discrepancy, and the doctor who had attended the birth was long dead, but a nurse who had worked for him remembered how distressed he'd been when Charlotte had hemorrhaged shortly after the delivery. She had died after childbirth, but the nurse recalled that the countess had asked the doctor to list the cause of death as pneumonia to spare her parents embarrassment, since neither the pregnancy

nor her marriage were known to her parents at the time, so the doctor had agreed. The marriage certificate was genuine. The vicar was
still alive and had verified it, and said they were lovely young people
and very much in love on the eve of his going to war, and Henry died
shortly after, so the vicar was glad that he had married them, and
had therefore legitimized Annie's birth. And Her Majesty the queen
had instantly recognized the little gold bracelet Annie was wearing,
that the queen had given to her sister Charlotte. Annie could have
gotten it from someone else, which all of them thought unlikely. It
was credible that she got it from Lucy, who probably found it among
Charlotte's things after she died, along with the papers and letters.
And the Queen Mother had acknowledged the brown leather box as
hers as well.

Everything was in order, so far, and MI5 was doing some further
investigation, but Sir Malcolm did not explain it. He promised to stay
in touch and call when the investigation was concluded.

Annie wondered after she hung up if Lucy would have felt betrayed by their trying to have Annie recognized as a member of the
royal family, or if she would have been pleased. She had gone to such
lengths to make Annie her own, that Annie felt guilty about it at
times, but Jonathan kept telling her that it was her birthright, and
encouraged her to see it through to the end. And Lucy had told him
the story herself and wanted to right the wrong she'd done. Nothing
had been leaked to the press about it. The royal family was keeping
it quiet in case she turned out not to be related to them after all.
None of them wanted the embarrassment of discovering that Princess Charlotte wasn't her mother, in which case Annie didn't know
who was, maybe Lucy after all. It was hard to guess the truth after

silence for so long. And if Annie wasn't Charlotte's daughter, what had happened to the infant born to Charlotte at Ainsleigh Hall, now that they knew the rest?

It was another two months before Sir Malcolm called again. None of the Ainsleigh Hall servants were still alive, but they had spoken to the daughter of one of the maids, a hall boy, and the doctor's nurse again. Blake and Rupert were screaming over a soccer match on TV when Sir Malcolm called. Annie could hardly hear him, and shouted at the boys to turn it down, and stop screaming. They were rooting for opposing teams and driving her insane. They had just turned sixteen, and the cottage seemed too small now for four of them. They were turning into big, brawny men, and they left a mess in their wake everywhere, which Annie constantly cleaned up for them.

"I'm sorry," she apologized, "I couldn't hear you. My brothers were behaving like savages." She glared at them as she said it, and turned off the television. "Could you repeat that?" she said to Sir Malcolm, as her brothers left the room, grumbling.

"Your Royal Highness." It struck her as odd when he said it. "The investigation has been concluded to everyone's satisfaction. Her Royal Highness Princess Charlotte was your mother, and you bear a remarkable resemblance to her." He was smiling as he said it, and much to her own surprise, Annie had tears in her eyes, and sat down suddenly, feeling dizzy. She had wanted this result and didn't even know it. It was now confirmed that she was Her Majesty's niece and the Queen Mother's granddaughter. "Her Majesty is very pleased. We will be releasing a statement in the next few days. You might want to prepare for some media attention. They can be quite intrusive, no matter how discreetly we frame the news. It's liable to cause consid-erable excitement." Her heart was pounding as he said it. She was a member of the royal family after all. And she had no idea what would come next.

"What are you going to say in the announcement?" She was curious about it.

"Her Majesty's press secretary is handling it. We want to keep it as discreet as possible, so it doesn't raise too many questions of a delicate nature. It will say that you've been living abroad with distant relatives who brought you up, since your parents' tragic deaths during the war, you've completed your education, and you have now returned to England to take your rightful place with the royal family. Her Majesty is immensely pleased at the return of her youngest sister's daughter. It's hard to make much of that, but the press will always try.

"Her Majesty also wanted me to let you know that the cabinet will be deciding on your allowance next month, and she'd like you to come to Balmoral for a few days this summer, to meet the rest of the family. Her boys are close to your age, and they'll be home from school then. And Her Royal Highness Princess Victoria always spends a week or two there on her way to the South of France, where she spends the month of August. It's a bit chilly in Scotland, but I'm sure you'll enjoy the palace. The Queen Mother and Her Majesty have always loved it. The Queen Mother would like to have you to tea in the coming days. And Her Royal Highness Princess Victoria would like to meet you when she returns from the trip to India she's on now." Annie felt dizzy when she hung up, her head was spinning, and she sat staring into space for a minute. Her father came in from the stables in time for dinner, and saw the look on her face, as though she'd seen a ghost.

"Did something happen? Did the boys break something?" Jonathan asked, looking worried. They'd come back into the room and were screaming at the soccer match and threatening to kill each other again, as she shook her head and stared at her father.

"I've been authenticated," she whispered. "It's all true, Charlotte is my mother. The cabinet is voting on my allowance next month, and the queen wants me to come to Balmoral this summer to meet the others. Oh my God, Papa, I'm for real!" He put his arms around her and hugged her with tears in his eyes.

"You've always been real to me," he said gruffly.

Then her face clouded for a minute. "Do you think Mama would be upset about it? Or pleased? It seems so disloyal after everything she did for me." Suddenly Annie had two mothers, but both were dead.

"She must have wanted this to happen or she wouldn't have told me," he reassured her. "This was meant to be. She had you to herself for twenty years. They're your family. I think she thought it was time to make a clean breast of it, before she left us. I think she would be happy for you. I suppose this means that you don't have to play Cinderella for me and your brothers anymore." He smiled at her. "Will you be moving to one of the palaces?" he asked her innocently. But Sir Malcolm hadn't said anything about it. Only about tea with her grandmother and aunt.

"Of course not. I'm staying here with you. But it would be nice if those two Neanderthals could pick up after themselves occasionally, and stop screaming when they watch a match on TV," Annie said, exasperated.

"Good luck with that, and you don't have to stay here, Annie, if you don't want to."

"Where else would I go? You're my papa, and I want to live with you." He looked pleased. He hadn't lost her after all. He had been afraid he might, but it hadn't stopped him from pursuing the truth for her. He had done what was right.

She put dinner on the table a few minutes later. The hamburgers were overcooked and she had burned the potatoes, but her hungry brothers ate it all anyway. She sent them upstairs after that, so she and her father could enjoy a peaceful end to the meal. "I'm so happy for you, Annie. And I really think Mama would be too."

"I hope so. I'm not sure I'm ready to be a princess yet. They're going to make an announcement to the press in the next few days."

Neither of them was ready for the onslaught of photographers and TV cameras that assaulted them, invaded the stables, and generally drove everyone nuts for a week following the announcement. They tried to get pictures of Annie doing her chores, with her father and brothers, on horseback. The announcement was as discreet as Sir Malcolm had said it would be, but the press was wildly excited. A lost princess was big news.

It said simply that Her Royal Highness Princess Anne Louise, daughter of Her Royal Highness Princess Charlotte and the son of the late Earl and Countess of Ainsleigh, the late Lord Henry Hemmings, had returned to England after living abroad since her parents' tragic deaths during the war. It referred to the fact that Princess Charlotte had died in Yorkshire at seventeen, that she had married and had a daughter during the year she spent in Yorkshire, and that due to the war and constant bombings, the family had waited to announce it after the war and by then, the young couple were both dead, and their daughter grew up in seclusion, under the supervision of the royal family, until she came of age. And she was now brought home to her aunts, uncle, grandmother, and cousins, and she would be publicly presented soon. In the meantime it said that the queen was extremely pleased to have her niece home in England again. And she was residing at an estate in Kent, which was how the press found her. They checked every large estate until they did. They reported that before that, she had been living with distant relatives on the Continent, and having completed her studies and reached her majority, she had returned to take her place with the royal family, as Her Majesty's niece, as well as the niece of Her Royal Highness Princess Victoria, and the granddaughter of Queen Anne the Queen Mother. It said everything pertinent about who she was related to, and where she'd been for the last twenty-two years without bringing up anything that might prove to be controversial or embarrassing. It was all very clean and direct and established her as a Royal Highness. And it acknowledged her father as having died a hero's death at Anzio at eighteen.

The Markhams saw it in *The Times* the next morning at breakfast and were stunned and recognized who it was instantly. Annabelle Markham dropped by to congratulate Annie on her newly elevated rank, and recognition as a royal princess. It was an extraordinary story that had taken them by surprise.

"Will you be moving to London now?" she asked her. At twenty-two, as the newly recognized niece of the queen, she couldn't imagine Annie wanting to hang around in Kent in their cottage for much longer. She had the world at her feet now, or would soon.

"I'm staying here, as an apprentice to Papa in the stables," Annie said firmly. "Where else would I want to be?"

"Silly girl, dancing your feet off at a disco in Knightsbridge, if you had any sense," Annabelle teased her.

"My father and the boys need me here, or the house will look like the stables." But two days later, she got a call from Lord Hatton at the queen's stables, with an offer that was seriously tempting. He was inviting her to tour the stables and view Her Majesty's racehorses, and he offered her a summer internship if she was interested. It was an offer that was nearly impossible to resist, and her stepfather insisted she had to take it. He said she'd never get another offer like it, and she was inclined to agree. So she called Lord Hatton back and said she would be delighted to work for him for August and September if he wanted her. July was already almost half over. He said he could use the help, and was sure that she'd enjoy it. Who wouldn't? With the queen's racehorses all around her. She hoped he would let her exercise them.

Her recognition by the royal family had brought nothing but happy changes to her life, in spite of the brief furor in the media, which calmed down within a week after the paparazzi got enough pictures, which Annie hated. She didn't like being a media star. She wrote the queen a note to thank her for the internship at her stables. She was sure that Her Majesty had put in a word for her with Lord Hatton. Lord Hatton reported that the queen was very pleased with Annie's dignified handling of the press.

"This is going to be a seriously fun summer," Annie said, beaming at her stepfather, as she walked into the stables. Balmoral to meet her family, and an internship at the royal stables. The queen wanted to give her time to adjust to the changes in her life, which suited Annie too. She wasn't ready to leave home yet, except to work at the queen's stables instead of the Markhams'. And all the current excitement balanced some of the sadness of Lucy's death.

She took one of their stallions out to exercise him that morning and rode like the wind across the meadows. She was inheriting the life she had been born to. It was almost too wonderful to be true.

Jonathan delivered Annie to the queen's stables in Newmarket himself. It had taken just under two hours from Kent, and they chatted on the way. She was excited by the internship Lord Hatton had offered her. She didn't care if she had to muck out stalls, or curry horses, or simply sponge them down after a run. Just being there was an honor, surrounded by the kind of horses the queen owned.

Newmarket was the center of Thoroughbred horseracing, and the largest racehorse training center in Britain. Five major races took place there every year. Tattersalls racehorse auctions were held frequently, and there were excellent equine hospitals. The queen had five main horse trainers to train her horses in different locations. The famous trainer Boyd-Rochfort was one of them. She kept horses at the Sandringham Estate too, and in Hampshire before they were sent to Newmarket to train. There were more than fifty horse-training stables and two racetracks in Newmarket. A third of the town's jobs involved horseracing. Most of the stables were in the center of the town. The top trainers in England were there.

Lord Hatton was very gracious to Annie and her father when they arrived, and he already knew that Annie was the queen's long lost niece who had recently turned up. Jonathan was the stepfather who had brought her to them, the only father she'd ever known, and was the stable master for the Markhams, who had impressive stables too. Though the queen's horses surpassed them all. While Lord Hatton and her father talked about the stud services for the Markhams' mares again, Annie walked around, and stopped to admire each of the queen's racehorses. She had some of the finest horses in England.

She was halfway through her quiet private tour going from stall to stall, when she noticed a striking-looking young man leaning against a wall and staring at her. He was wearing white jodhpurs, a crisp white shirt, and tall black riding boots. He had jet-black hair, and a surly expression as he watched her. He didn't greet her or approach, and then finally when she reached the last stall, he ambled over. He seemed very pleased with himself.

"How old are you?" he asked when he got to her, without introducing himself or asking her name.

"Why?" she asked him, annoyed by his bad manners, supercilious style, and arrogant attitude.

"Because you don't look tall enough to ride a decent-sized horse. Do you ride ponies?" He was almost laughing at her, and she was furious but didn't show it.

"I'm twenty-two, and I can ride anything you can. I'm going to be a jockey one day," she said, sticking out her chin.

"Oh please, not another feminist. It's my personal belief that women aren't made to be jockeys. They don't have the nerves for it."

"Really? When was the last time you saw a successful male jockey taller than I am by the way? At least we know you'll never be one." He was six feet three or four, and irritatingly good-looking, in a kind of studied way. He looked as though he considered himself God's gift to women, an opinion Annie didn't share.

"I have no desire to be a jockey, and spend my life with a mouth full of mud, my face covered in dirt as I cross the finish line." He looked immaculate in his white jodhpurs, and Annie had taken an instant dislike to him.

"I suppose the white pants work well for you. Do you play polo?" He looked the type, a spoiled rich boy whose main interest was showing off to women. He looked vaguely familiar but she didn't recognize him, and she didn't think they'd ever met before.

"Yes, I do play polo. I take it you don't?"

"It's not my sport. It's too tame."

"Don't be so sure. Polo can get rough too."

"Mostly at cocktail hour when you talk about it."

"Are you visiting?" he asked her.

"I'm going to be working here for the next two months," she said proudly.

"That should be interesting. I'll be working here too. Maybe we can have some fun, and exercise the horses together, if you think you can handle them."

"What makes you think I'm such a sissy?"

"You're such a little girl. I'd be afraid you'd get hurt."

"Let's have a race sometime. It would be fun to see if I can beat you," she said, smiling at him.

"Trust me, you can't. I've got the biggest horse in this stable. He's the only thing here that has longer legs than I do." She wanted to slap him just listening to him.

"I accept the challenge. Little People against Big People. The difference is I'm not afraid to get mud in my hair or my teeth, as you pointed out earlier."

"You must look charming when you race."

"I'm not interested in how charming I look. All I care about is winning."

"At least you're honest about it. Most women like to pretend they don't want to compete with men." She looked too small to him to be a man-eater, but she sounded like one. Normally she wasn't, but she hated men like him. They put women down constantly, and thought themselves superior. "What's your name by the way?"

"Anne Louise," she said simply, and it didn't ring any bells for him.

"No last name?" he asked, supercilious again, and this time she let him have it.

"Windsor. Your Royal Highness to you." She laughed at him then and walked away, as he blushed purple. Lord Hatton and her father found her then, and the queen's stable master glanced at the tall young man in the white jodhpurs.

"I see you've met my son, Anthony Hatton. I saw you talking to each other. No mischief together please. Tony likes to ride the fastest horses we have here, and your father tells me you're a demon when it comes to speed too. I expect you both to behave and not egg each other on, if you exercise the horses together. This is not a racetrack." He was serious and Annie promised to act responsibly, while his son rolled his eyes and looked amused.

"The horses need real exercise, Father, you can't just trot them around a ring when they're used to racing."

"Let's just be clear about it. If you lame one of our horses, I'll shoot you, and have you hanged for treason." He looked at Annie then, appearing demure as she admired the horses. "I'm shorthanded this month, and Anthony offered to help me out. That usually means he does exactly what he pleases and rides anything he wants. Your father tells me you're a hard worker and I can count on you, Your Royal Highness. I need someone like you around here."

"You can call me Annie while I'm here." She was still getting used to being a Royal Highness, and she didn't think it necessary while she was working for him, although it was her title now, and people were obliged to use it.

"I'm not uncomfortable using your title, ma'am. Her Majesty and I are old friends, since her childhood. My younger brother went to school with her. I knew your mother too," he said gently, and Annie smiled at him. She liked him a great deal better than his son, who had sauntered off without saying goodbye and disappeared.

She had been assigned a room in the luxurious guest quarters behind the stables, and they'd given her one of the best rooms. Her father carried her bags upstairs for her, and she had a large comfortable room, with antique furniture and a desk. But she was dismayed to see from his open door that Anthony Hatton was two doors down from her. He was standing in the middle of the room, and had just added a well-cut blazer to his outfit with the white jodhpurs and still had his boots on for a sporty look. He was obviously going somewhere. He hurried down the stairs and a few minutes later, she saw him drive off in a red Ferrari.

"Handsome guy," her father whispered and winked at her.

"He's a jerk. He acts like he owns the place."

"Actually, his father does." Her father laughed at her. "He's partners with the queen on these stables, and they buy most of the racehorses jointly. He and the queen are close friends. There have been a few rumors about them."

"How would you know that?" She looked amused. Her father almost never repeated gossip.

"Your mother kept me well-informed about the royals. She read everything about them." He missed her now more than ever. She had made a colossal mistake in her youth, absconding with Annie, but other than that, she had been a wonderful wife to him, and a devoted mother to their children, including Annie. "Well, don't get into any mischief," he warned her as he hugged her and kissed her goodbye. Her dinner was going to be brought to her on a tray. They had a chef especially for royal guests and VIPs, and she was both now, and she'd been told the food was delicious. The chef was French, and she was looking forward to it.

"I love you, Papa," she whispered when she kissed him goodbye. He waved and headed down the stairs, and five minutes after he left, her dinner arrived. The first course was caviar and blinis, followed by lobster salad, with profiteroles for dessert. She felt like she was at a dinner party all by herself as she sat in the handsome room, enjoying the meal. She was excited about spending the next two months here. The only fly in the ointment so far was Anthony Hatton, but she was sure that she could beat him any day, no matter what he rode. She was determined to prove it at the earliest opportunity. There was a man who needed to be put in his place, and she would have given her right arm to do it, or whatever it took.

Chapter 12

Annie was up and dressed and in the stable at six the morning after she got there. She wanted some quiet time to familiarize herself with the horses. There were three large horse barns, with state-of-the-art facilities and equipment. One was for breeding, another was for their most illustrious racehorses, and the third was a mixture of the very fine horses they owned, some that had already won several races, others that were ridden but had never raced, and perhaps never would, or might someday but weren't ready yet. Some horses the queen kept there because she enjoyed riding them. She was an avid and talented rider and had been all her life, as was her mother before her, and most of her relatives for generations, even centuries. It was in their blood, both on the German and British sides. The queen knew as much about breeding horses as her business partner Lord Hatton did, and sometimes she knew more, as he readily admitted. He was one of her greatest admirers and closest friends, and valued the companionship they shared.

Annie made her way quietly through the three horse barns, patting a neck or a muzzle here and there when the horses in their stalls stuck their heads out to see her. Sometimes she just stood and admired them. They were each the finest of their breed. In the racing barn, she was in awe, reading the names on each stall. Some of the greatest racehorses in history were in that barn. Just being near them felt like having an electric current race through her. They were not only incredibly valuable, they were horses with spirit and history and the best possible bloodlines, and also heart to win the races they had. It made her eyes water thinking of some of their victories. She was admiring one of them, when she heard a step behind her and turned. It was Lord Hatton, enjoying his universe before the day began. He was impressed to find her there. He could see in her eyes what it meant to her to be there, and was moved by it.

"They're so beautiful," she said, awestruck.

"Indeed. There is some extraordinary horseflesh in these barns. I'm fortunate to have the partner I do." Annie knew he meant the queen. "Her father was one of the finest riders I've ever known. He picked some of the greatest racehorses we've had. You can't learn that kind of judgment. It's a gift. She and I have spent years trying to figure out some of his decisions. I've never known him to make a mistake. I can't say the same for myself." He smiled at her. "It's not just about speed, it's about heart and courage and endurance. You have to believe in them. They know it when you do and they rarely let you down." He pointed to some of the horses she'd been looking at, as examples of what he meant. She felt grateful to be there, and wanted to learn all she could. Most of her feelings about horses were based on pure instinct, not always on what you could see. Jonathan had taught her that too.

"You have to love them. People are like that too," he said wisely, as they walked out of the last barn. "Is there any horse you'd particularly like to ride today?" he asked generously, "except for the queen's. She's particular about that." He smiled tenderly, and Annie could see both respect and affection in his eyes. "She has a keen eye for horseflesh. We've made some interesting choices together. We balance each other. Horses can teach you a great deal about life. Your stepfather tells me you want to be a jockey. Why is that? It's a tough business. Most men think women aren't suited to it. I disagree. I think women will be better at it, once they're allowed to ride professionally. That day will come. It's not far off, if you're serious about it."

"I am," she said, as they stopped at a coffee machine and he filled a mug and handed it to her. "I like the excitement and the speed," she said, taking a sip of the strong brew. "But I like the calculation and the theory along with what you have to know about the horse you're riding. There's so much soul to great racehorses, maybe that's what I love about it. They try so hard and they're so brave. It's not just about winning, it's about how you get there. Everything about it appeals to me. And the combination of rider and horse is so important. I think jockeys lose races, not horses." It was a fine point, something he always said himself. You could put some jockeys on a mule and they'd win a race, and give others the finest racehorses in the world and they'd lose every time.

"You'll be a fine jockey one day if you think that way," he said, getting to know her better. "Horses are a lot less complicated than people," he commented, and she remembered that he had been married three times. "We have a new horse you might like to try. I'd be interested to hear what you think of him." In theory, he was much too big for her, but instinct told him that she could manage almost any mount, her stepfather had said the same, and she liked a challenge. She was an amazing girl, and with her history, something of a dark horse herself. She had come from nowhere, and was suddenly the surprise of the hour. It was all about breeding and courage and bloodlines, and perseverance, and she had them all. The queen had said as much when she recommended her to him, and he trusted her judgment implicitly. And she had turned out to be a fine monarch.

He led Annie to the stall of the horse he was thinking of for her. He was a magnificent stallion, and her eyes lit up as soon as she saw him.

"I'm not sure he'll ever win a race for us, but he's an interesting ride. We've had him for about a month. I don't know him well enough to tell. He doesn't trust us yet. He has a slightly dodgy history, but fabulous bloodlines." She could see it in the way he stood and moved, even in his stall. "You can take him out now if you like." She finished her coffee, put the mug in a sink, and went to get a saddle. She walked into his stall with confidence, and led him out. His name was Flash, and she looked ridiculously small beside him, which didn't occur to her at all. She had him saddled in a few minutes, led him to a mounting block, swung up easily, and let herself into one of the rings, as Lord Hatton watched. She had a light hand on the reins, and her legs were short but powerful. She was guiding him with her knees as much as her hands, and had a fluid grace that blended with the horse. She rode him around the ring to get a sense of him, changed directions several times, and then eased him into a gallop. The horse seemed to be enjoying it as much as she was. He balked at a sound nearby which didn't faze her, and her confidence and poise calmed him, as Lord Hatton watched her, fascinated. She had all the instincts he looked for in a rider, and was unaware of them herself. She had the powerful horse in her full command, and he could tell that the stallion trusted her, which was half the battle.

"He's a beautiful ride," she said admiringly.

"Yes, he is. Inconsistent, though. He's a moody guy. Everything has to line up just right for him. He threw one of our best riders the other day, and we couldn't figure out why." But he was as docile as a lamb with Annie astride him. She took him through his paces again and Lord Hatton left them and went to his office. He liked getting an early start, when everything was calm. Once he left, Annie rode Flash for an hour, and then dismounted and took him back to the barn. Both rider and mount were pleased with the time they'd spent together. After she'd removed his saddle, she put him back in his stall, and went to join the trainers she saw gathering outside the racing barn. They were handing out assignments for the week, and she was assigned to shadow one of the head trainers.

They were busy after that until lunchtime. There were a dozen assistant trainers, each with special skills that were suited to the functions they performed.

She didn't see Anthony again until after lunch. He looked as though he had just gotten up, and had had a rough night. He'd been assigned to exercise one of the horses who had had a pulled tendon for several weeks, and was told to go easy on him. As soon as she saw him riding the horse around a ring, she saw that he had heavy hands. He had no instinct for the horse he was riding, just impeccable training, and an elegant style, but he wasn't at one with the horse. She didn't comment. She walked over to the rail, and he stopped to chat with her for a minute.

"I hear my father let you ride Flash this morning. Scary devil, isn't he?"

"He was a gentleman with me," she said noncommittally.

"Don't count on his being like that again. He tried to kick me when I walked into his stall the other day, and bucked when I rode him."

"A personality clash perhaps," she suggested, smiling at him.

"Would you like to have dinner with me tonight? There's an amusing pub nearby. It's pretty quiet here at night." She didn't mind that, but she could sense easily that he did. She didn't want to be rude, but she would have preferred having dinner in her room.

"That would be nice," she said politely, and she had the feeling that he was as insensitive with women as he was with horses. It was all about getting them to do what he wanted, not figuring out who they were and what they needed.

She went back to the trainer she'd been assigned to then, and he had her exercise two of the horses. Flash was the high point of her day, and Anthony stopped by and told her he'd pick her up at seven.

She changed into slacks and a sweater before they left for dinner, and was surprised when he turned up still in his riding clothes with a rakish look. "You don't mind, do you?" he asked as they got into the Ferrari she'd seen the night before. She had no experience with men like him, and far more with horses. Her romantic life had been nonexistent so far. She'd spent all of her time around stables and with her father, except for the boys she'd gone out with at university, but had never fallen in love with any of them. They just seemed young and foolish to her, and she didn't flirt the way the other girls did, nor did she play games with them. She was simple and direct, and without artifice. She spoke to Anthony like one of the guys at the stables when they got to the pub, and he laughed after she talked about the racehorses she'd seen in the barn.

"Do you ever think of anything except horses?" he asked her after they ordered dinner and a bottle of wine.

"Not often," she admitted with a smile. "I was a disaster in school. I rarely went to class at university. I begged to come home the entire time. All I ever wanted to do was train horses and work with my father. You don't need a degree for that. I thought about vet school for a while, but it takes too many years. I'm basically lazy," she said modestly, and he laughed.

"I doubt that. You're just not an academic. Neither am I. My father studied physics and psychology at Oxford. I don't know how he wound up in a horse barn. He can quote Shakespeare for hours. He says he wanted to be an actor. He's a Renaissance man."

"And what about you? What are you passionate about?" she asked. She had a feeling it wasn't horses, although he had been around them all his life because of his father. But it wasn't a love affair for him. It seemed more like something to do between parties.

"I just invested in a nightclub with a group of friends. It's a lot of fun. I like people more than horses, and women in particular." He gave her a look that was meant to melt her heart, or her knickers, but it didn't. "I'd like to own a restaurant one day. Or a small hotel, maybe in the South of France. I lived in Paris for a year. It was a fantastic experience. I'd like to live there again one day."

"I've never been," she said innocently. She hadn't been anywhere, although that was about to change in her new life. Until then, she had spent most of her life in Kent on the Markham estate, and Liverpool where she went to college. "I'd like to go to the States one day.

It seems so exciting." There was something about her openness to new experiences which touched even him. She was very young, and seemed even younger than her years. There was an Alice in Wonderland quality to her, which was accentuated by her girlish looks and tiny size, and at the same time there was something very old and wise in her eyes.

She was an odd mix of naïveté and experience. She was different from the women he knew. They all seemed so jaded and sophisticated compared to her. He liked the childlike quality about her, much to his own surprise. She had a lot of growing up to do, and a lot of the world to see. "I've been thinking about going to Australia to race there. And I'd like to see the Kentucky Derby one day."

"I went with my father once. We had a horse in the race. He didn't win though. Kentucky is an odd place. We bought a horse there. I like New York better." America was a mystery to her, as was his way of life. He had mentioned that he was thirty years old, and the difference in their ages and life experience was enormous. He had gone to Eton and Cambridge, had traveled extensively, and moved in a fast crowd. They had nothing in common. "So when are we going to race?" he asked her halfway through dinner. "It should probably be sometime when my father's not around. There will be hell to pay if he catches us. He's going to an auction in Scotland next week. Maybe then, if I'm not in London. I'm going to Saint Tropez for a weekend. I have a friend who has a yacht there." He would have asked her to come, she was pretty enough, but it would be like taking his little sister. There was nothing racy about her, and he could sense that she had no interest in the fast life of fashionable beach towns and yachts. All she cared about was horses, and her dream of being a jockey. "And after horses, what?" he asked her. "Marriage and babies?" She seemed like that kind of girl. He had no interest in either one for now.

She looked blank when he asked her. "I never think about it. I just think in terms of horses right now."

"I have a half-sister like you, from my father's second marriage. She breeds horses in Ireland. She and her husband have a big operation there. My father helped them set it up. They have seven kids. Scary thought," he said and she laughed.

"I have twin brothers. They're sixteen, and they drive me crazy. I've been helping my dad with them since my mother died . . . my stepmother," she corrected, in her new life. "Actually, my world is a little confusing right now. I thought she was my mother all my life, and I loved her that way, and now it turns out she wasn't. My real mother died when I was born, but I never knew about her until after this mother died, and it all came out. Now suddenly I'm a Royal Highness, and the queen is my aunt. I haven't sorted it all out yet. I'm going to Balmoral to meet the rest of the family for a weekend at the end of August. I suddenly feel like two people, or one person in two worlds, my old life and my new one. The only constants in my life at the moment are horses and my stepfather. He runs the stables for John Markham. Most people in horse circles know John." She was so honest and open about everything that he didn't know what to say. There was no artifice about her. She was a straightforward person who had been cast into a new life that would have daunted most people. It forced him to be real with her too, which was new to him and unfamiliar. He was used to much more complicated girls who always wanted something from him. She didn't, which was refreshing.

"It must be a little strange to suddenly be a Royal Princess."

"The queen and her mother were very nice to me when I saw them. I haven't met Princess Victoria yet." And the queen had gotten her the highly coveted internship.

"She's more exciting than her sister. She's never married or had children, but she's had some exotic romances, with the Aga Khan, an American senator, a few married men no one talks about, except the tabloids. She was in love with someone who died when she was young. I think she decided to pursue a different life after that. She's very amusing," Anthony volunteered. "I see her in nightclubs a lot. She actually went out with one of my friends a year or two ago. She and her sister are chalk and cheese. She's the racy one. The queen is all about duty and the job. I think the crown is heavier to wear than one thinks. It can't be a lot of fun."

"I wonder what my mother was like in the midst of all that. She died when she was so young."

"So did mine," Anthony said quietly. It was the first serious side of him she'd seen.

"I'm sorry, I didn't know."

"You wouldn't," he said with a forgiving look. "You haven't been around for all the scandals. She left my father for another man when I was eight. They were killed in a car accident in the South of France shortly after. I went off to boarding school a few months later, and that was the end of family life as I knew it. She was my father's third wife, and he never married again. He's always had women in his life, but no one he's serious about. He's probably closer to the queen than anyone else. She's his best friend. I'm not sure he ever got over my mother. He doesn't talk about it. He's a decent father, though he probably likes his horses better than his children. Very British, you know." It made her realize how lucky she was to have Jonathan in her life. He was warm and loving, and the only father she had ever known, and she would always think of him as her father, even though they weren't related by blood. "I can't really see myself settling down, not for a long time anyway. I have no role model for it. I hardly remember my parents together before she left. They were always out somewhere. He didn't start his horse operation until after she was gone, and that's really his first love now. I don't think he'll ever marry again."

"I'm not sure I will either," Annie said, looking pensive. "My parents had a good marriage and they loved each other, but it seems complicated. I grew up in a tiny cottage with them and my brothers. My mother was the housekeeper on the estate where my father works. Marriage doesn't seem to work out for most people. I'm not sure it's for me. Horses are a lot easier," she said, smiling at him.

"Or wine, women, and song. That works for me," he teased. But underneath the glib exterior, the good looks, and the charm, she had the feeling that he was afraid of getting close to anyone, maybe because his mother left when he was so young, or he was having too much fun now. The kind of life he led was a mystery to her and didn't seem very appealing. But he wasn't as arrogant as she had thought when she met him. There was a soft side to him. Outwardly, he was just the stereotype of the handsome playboy. She couldn't imagine going out with someone like him, or with anyone for now. The hub of her life and her only interest were the stables.

He drove her back to the horse farm after dinner, and they walked into the guesthouse together. He invited her to his room for an after-dinner drink, and she didn't think it was a good idea. She was worldly enough to be cautious about going to men's rooms with a bottle of scotch for easy sex. She was still a virgin, and had no intention of changing that for him.

"I have to be up at five-thirty," she used as her excuse. "I promised to exercise Flash again at six."

"You're the only girl I know who'd rather be with a horse than with me," he said, laughing, and she thanked him for dinner, and went to her room. It had been a nice evening, and for some reason, even with all the trappings, the fancy car, his good looks, and the racy life he seemed to lead, she felt sorry for him. He'd had a lonely childhood and no mother to love him. She'd been better off growing up as the daughter of a housemaid and a stable hand who both adored her. It had been a simple life, but they were real, and she knew how much they loved her. She never doubted it. The life he led seemed empty to her. He was a lost boy in a glittering world that had no appeal at all to her.

In his room, Anthony poured himself a glass of scotch and wondered what would become of her. She was like a child, and a breath of air. A little too much so for him. The women in his world were more exciting, and what they wanted from him was easy to give. What you'd have to give a girl like her was beyond him, and would have terrified him.

Annie was back in the stables at six o'clock the next morning, and had Flash in the main ring ten minutes later. He was more skittish than he had been the day before, but her steady routine and soothing voice calmed him, and by the time she brought him back to his stall at seven, he was peaceful and easy to manage again. She saw Lord Hatton go to his office as she walked Flash back to the barn. She was at the trainers' meeting on time, and got her assignment for the day. She heard a rumor from the other trainers that there were photographers lying in wait for her, and then was told later that Lord Hatton had chased them away. He didn't want Annie harassed by anyone, nor their collective privacy invaded. It was a great relief to Annie.

She'd exercised five of the horses by the end of the afternoon, and passed Anthony in the hall of the guesthouse. He was on his way out, looking very dashing. He obviously had a date or was going to a party.

"My father's going to London tomorrow. Shall we race?" he said enticingly, and she hesitated.

"Will we get in trouble?" she asked him with wide eyes.

"We might," he admitted, "but not if you don't tell him." The challenge was too great for either of them to resist, and they agreed to meet at seven the next morning. She was tempted to ride Flash, but knew he wasn't stable, although she could have run any race with him. She didn't want to win badly enough to damage a horse that wasn't settled yet, and decided to ride a horse she'd exercised that afternoon, that was tried and true and easier to predict.

They settled on the meeting place, and she hoped no one would see them and tell Lord Hatton. It was a risk that seemed worth taking and she was looking forward to it.

She exercised Flash the next morning, and switched horses in time to meet Anthony. The idea of racing him was exhilarating. He was a good rider, but his skill was more mechanical, without passion. He had learned about horses and had been taught well, but didn't "feel" them in his gut the way she did, or love them. She was smiling when she met up with him, in anticipation of what was to come. They left the more populated area sedately, and didn't start the race until they were well out of sight. She gave her horse its head, and coaxed everything out of him he had to give. She wasn't going to let Anthony

beat her, and she calculated her horse's strengths well, and won easily. Anthony looked angry when they finished, but got control of himself quickly.

"You're a hell of a rider, Your Royal Highness," he said grudgingly.
"Rematch tomorrow?" he pressed her and she laughed. It had been
an easy victory for her.

"Where will your father be?" They were like two naughty children, but she was pleased with beating him, and wanted to do it
again. She'd outsmarted him as much as outrun him.

"He won't be back till tomorrow night," Anthony said.

"Then you have a deal. Same time, same place," she said, and they
headed back to the barns, with no one any the wiser for what they'd
done.

She met him again the next day. She had chosen a different horse
this time, one that was faster and more spirited. He danced around
a bit on their way to where they had raced the day before. They were
both wearing helmets, which would have been a tip-off to anyone
who knew either of them that they were up to mischief, but no one
had seen them leave the barn and ride off.

She got a good start on him as she had the day before, and they
pounded across the meadow, and raced toward the cluster of trees
that had been their finish line the day before. They were almost there
when her horse shied from something he'd seen. She kept control of
him, but he almost stumbled, and with no warning, she came off and
flew through the air like a doll and landed hard, as Anthony reined
his horse in, and raced to where she lay, suddenly realizing how foolish they had been. She lay lifeless on her back when he got there,
and he grabbed her horse's reins on the way, and tethered the two
horses to each other as he jumped down and knelt next to her. She

was breathing, but looked deathly pale. He took her helmet off and tried to decide what to do, and as he started to panic, she opened her eyes and couldn't speak for a minute. She was badly winded, and when she tried to sit up, he stopped her.

"Stay still for a minute. I was an idiot to suggest this. Can you move?" he asked her. She gently moved her arms and legs and smiled up at him as she caught her breath enough to speak to him.

"It was fun, until I fell. I haven't come off in years."

"I should have known better. I'm older than you are." He took off his jacket and folded it under her head, looking deeply concerned. "Do you think you can sit up?" He could tell that she wasn't paralyzed but had difficulty moving. She'd had a hard fall.

"Should we finish the race?" she asked as she sat up and saw stars for a minute, and then her head cleared. She had a slight headache, but nothing serious, and nothing was broken. She had been lucky. She'd been going at breakneck speed, but the ground had been soft enough to cushion her fall.

"You're insane. Do you think you can ride back, or do you want to ride with me?" he asked as he helped her to her feet. She was as light as a feather.

"I'm fine," she said gamely, but she looked unsteady to him. He held her arm until she seemed solid on her feet, and he gave her a leg up back into the saddle, and he watched her closely to make sure she wasn't dizzy, and stayed close to her. He knew she had to be feeling badly bruised from the fall, but she was steady in the saddle, and never complained. She was much tougher than she looked.

"You are one hell of a rider, and damn brave. I thought you were dead for a minute," he admitted, still shaken by the sight of her flying through the air like a leaf on the wind.

"So did I," she said and grinned at him.

"You could have broken your neck. I'm not racing you again." She was too daring to be safe.

"You're just afraid I'll beat you. I probably would have if the damn horse hadn't tripped."

"You were not going to beat me this time. I was two lengths ahead of you."

"One, and I was catching up. I hadn't gotten Mercury up to full speed yet."

"Don't be a sore loser," he teased her with a broad grin, grateful that she hadn't been injured. It seemed like a miracle that she wasn't. "You probably came off just to get sympathy. That's women riders for you. And you want to be a jockey? In what, the powder puff races?" He teased her all the way back, but he had unlimited respect for her now. She was the ballsiest girl he'd ever met. "You're a hell of a lot stronger than you look," he complimented her, and even he could recognize that she was a better rider than he was. She was at one with the horse at all times, even if she'd flown off. If the horse hadn't stumbled, she would have won in the end, and he knew it. "Let's ride again sometime," he suggested, "but no racing."

"That's no fun." She looked disappointed and he laughed at her.

"I happen to like you, Your Royal Highness. I don't want to kill you. I think you're the craziest damn rider I've ever seen, and the bravest girl I've ever met. I'd rather not see you dead if you come off again."

"Thank you," she said for the compliments and smiled at him. She'd had a hell of a fall, and knew she'd be hurting by the end of the day. She already was but wouldn't admit it. But she'd won something better than she had the day before when she'd beaten him. They were friends now. And she needed one in her new world. He was different from the men she had known in her previous life. More complicated, more spoiled, and surprisingly more interesting. She liked him better now than she had when they met.

They smiled at each other and walked the horses the rest of the way home, and he saw her wince when he helped her dismount, but she didn't say a word and marched into the barn and unsaddled the horse herself.

"Good exercise session?" one of the trainers asked them as they put the saddles away.

"Not bad," Annie answered and smiled at him, and Anthony watched her as she walked out of the barn. She was a devil on horseback, but he liked that about her. He liked her better than any girl he'd met in years. Maybe she would be a jockey one day. She had the guts for it, and the heart. And she was the best damn rider he'd ever seen. His father had thought so too. He had plans for her, but hadn't told her yet. He wanted to speak to Her Majesty first. And then they would see.

Chapter 13

August flew by as Annie settled into her duties at the queen's stables. She wasn't aware of it, but Lord Hatton observed her whenever possible, and frequently asked for reports from his other trainers. All reports confirmed what he'd glimpsed from the first. She had a rare talent and a gift, a passion for horses, and a sixth sense of them that even her ancestors and new relatives didn't have. And the queen was pleased with what she was told. The new addition, and previously undiscovered princess, was conscientious, hardworking, modest, and well liked by all. She expected no special favors because of who she was, and was tireless in accomplishing the tasks she was assigned.

She seemed to have no special friends among the people she worked with, but was polite and respectful to all, which was how she had been at the Markhams' too. She kept her distance and was un- failingly dignified and discreet, even more so now. As a royal prin- cess, she felt an even greater obligation to be responsible and private at all times. She felt she owed the queen her good behavior. Her only friend at the queen's stables was Anthony, and she called Jonathan to say hello several times a week. And from what Lord Hatton had heard, she never went out at night, except once or twice with his son. She appeared not to have a wild side, unlike some of her new relatives, and Lord Hatton knew it wouldn't go far with Anthony, who was a rake of the first order, occasionally to his father's chagrin. At thirty he had already been involved in several scandals, and had a penchant for married women who were as outrageous as he was when it suited them. He liked showy women and had little respect for the rules governing polite society, whereas in contrast Princess Anne Louise was fearless with horses, but demure and somewhat shy in the world. She proceeded with caution and a careful step, and was respectful of her new role, however unfamiliar to her.

Annie took criticism well, which no one would have said of Anthony Hatton. If nothing else, his father thought Annie would be good for him, even as a friend, just as his own friendship with the dignified Queen Alexandra had tempered him. They were good contrasts and counterpoints to each other.

The queen was pleased with everything she'd heard, both from her old friend, and others who encountered the princess. It was difficult to believe that she'd grown up as simply as she had, brought up by people who were essentially servants, but her stepfather was known to be of high moral character. The royal family thought less of his late wife after what she'd done. And it amazed everyone in the family that Princess Anne Louise had gone undiscovered for so long.

She was excited and nervous about her upcoming weekend at Balmoral Castle in Scotland, to meet the rest of the family. The queen had purposely moved slowly to include her to give Annie time to adjust to her new life, and not overwhelm her, and she had convinced the Queen Mother to be patient too. And it made sense to her as well. This wasn't Charlotte returning from the dead. To Annie, everything and everyone around her was brand new.

Balmoral was said to be the most relaxed of the queen's homes, where she enjoyed a proper vacation every summer, with family picnics and barbecues, and fishing for all, which was why she had chosen it for Annie's family debut. Annie spoke to Jonathan about it, and was anxious about what it would be like, and how she should behave. It was all new to her, and no matter what her lineage, she was the stranger in their midst. Everyone had been gracious to her so far, particularly the Queen Mother, her grandmother, and the monarch herself, who treated her like any other young girl, with ease, and chatted with her when they met at the stables.

The queen was a frequent visitor at the stables when she had time, in order to discuss recent and future purchases, which of the stallions they were using for stud services, which was a lucrative business for them, and upcoming races. It was a going concern and did well, and a serious business interest of the queen's, although the rumor was that the prince consort didn't share her passion, and only came to major races under duress. He was never seen at the stables with her, but he would be at Balmoral when Annie was there. She hadn't met him yet, or her aunt Victoria, who would be staying there on her way to or from the South of France for more hedonistic pursuits.

Annie gleaned whatever information she could from Anthony about Balmoral, since he and his father were frequent visitors there, but he was much more excited about his own trip to Saint Tropez. He wished Annie luck when she left for Scotland by train. Jonathan's best advice had been to just be herself, which didn't give her much help. She wasn't even sure what kind of clothes to bring, and had no woman to ask. All Anthony said was to bring some nice dresses and you'll be fine.

"What kind of 'nice'?" she pressed him over dinner at the local pub a few days before she left. "Fancy nice? Or sundress nice, or shorts and a blouse in the daytime?" She hardly ever shopped, had never gone without Lucy, and until now didn't need fancy clothes, but she forced herself to visit the shops in the town near the stables and bought herself a few simple things that looked like good basics to her. She showed them to Anthony and he approved.

"Why not wear something sexy?" he suggested. She had a great figure she never took advantage of to show off. "You're a girl." He had never known a woman like her, so totally without artifice or vanity.

"Until now I only owned one dress, to wear to church on Christmas. All I need is riding gear, and I can't wear that to dinner," she said, still nervous about her wardrobe even with the new additions.

And Lucy had never been helpful in that department either. She was used to wearing her housekeeper's black dresses, and housedresses and slippers on her days off when she sat in front of the TV watching her favorite shows. Annie still missed her, and her unconditional love, and Jonathan said that he and the boys missed her terribly too. She'd been gone for less than a year, and so much had changed. Everything had, for all of them, especially in Annie's life.

She had an allowance to spend now, which the cabinet had approved. It seemed extremely generous to her, and was put in an account for her every month, but she had no expenses living at the queen's stables, and she'd never been extravagant. She did wish she'd had time to shop more when she packed her meager summer wardrobe for Balmoral. She saw Anthony briefly the morning she left. He was rushing to the airport for his flight to Nice, and what he referred to as Sodom and Gomorrah with French subtitles in Saint Tropez, on his friend's yacht. He couldn't wait.

"Good luck!" he called over his shoulder as he hurried down the stairs. She left a few minutes later, and Lord Hatton had one of the grooms drive her to the train station, where she boarded with her single battered suitcase, feeling like an orphan again, and not a royal princess.

The trip to Aberdeenshire in Scotland took eight hours, changing several times, and the scenery was beautiful along the way. The area around the castle was very rural, which was what the queen and Queen Mother loved about it. She had already spent most of the summer there, and was now at Sandringham in Norfolk with friends. And she was leaving this time in August to the young people. Annie knew that the family usually spent Christmas there, and only went to Balmoral in the summer, for a proper holiday. Of all of them, Balmoral was the queen's favorite castle. It had a romantic history. Victoria and Albert had rented it in 1848, and had liked it so much, they continued to lease it for four years, until Prince Albert bought it as a gift for Queen Victoria in 1852. They had built an entirely new castle there, and it remained their favorite holiday home. The rest of the time, they used Windsor Castle as their main residence, and preferred it with their nine children when they were growing up. They lived at Buckingham Palace for part of the time, but Windsor was the main seat of the monarchy during Victoria's reign.

Balmoral was on the bank of the River Dee, near the village of Crathie, and the queen's private secretary picked Annie up at the station, and was surprised to see she had come with only one very small bag, which he carried for her, and put in the queen's Rolls for the short drive to the castle.

"Did you have an easy journey, Your Royal Highness?" Sir Malcolm asked pleasantly. He was happy to see her again, and she was relieved to see a familiar face.

"The scenery was beautiful." She had brought a picnic lunch to eat on the train, prepared by the excellent chef at the stables.

"Dinner will be at eight o'clock," he informed her. "Family in the drawing room at seven." A wave of panic washed over her as he said it.

"Is it formal dress?"

"Never at Balmoral. Her Majesty prefers to keep things informal here. A simple dress will do nicely. There's a picnic lunch planned tomorrow, and a barbecue the day after. Her Majesty's children love barbecues. They visited a ranch in America last summer, and the queen enjoys barbecues too." He smiled at her, and a few minutes later they reached the castle. It was more of a large estate house, and was less daunting than Buckingham Palace, or the other residences like Windsor, which was a real palace, and one of the oldest castles in the world, and rivaled Versailles in France. Balmoral was far more human scale.

A flock of corgis greeted them when they got out of the car, and the queen herself appeared a few minutes later to welcome her, and escort her inside. She hugged Annie when she saw her. Annie was wearing a navy blue linen skirt, which was sadly crumpled from the trip, a white blouse, a blazer, and sandals, and looked like a schoolgirl as she followed her aunt into the house.

There was a striking redheaded woman playing the piano and singing, with a crowd of young people around her, and Annie recognized her immediately. It was Her Royal Highness Princess Victoria, her other aunt. She waved from the piano with a broad smile, and three handsome young boys glanced at the new arrival and went on singing. They were singing American show tunes, and knew all the words, as Annie approached cautiously, the queen went outside with the dogs, and the head stewardess took Annie's bag from the secretary, who followed Her Majesty outside for a brief conversation before he left.

The song ended a few minutes later, and Princess Victoria stood up and came around the piano, observing her niece closely, and looking deeply moved. Annie looked so much like her mother that there were tears in Victoria's eyes when she hugged her.

"At last! I was in India for a month when you met my mother and sister. I've felt quite cheated not to meet you before this. Do you sing? We do a lot of it here," she said, and the boys laughed. "I have no voice at all, but that never stops me," she said easily and laughed. But she played the piano beautifully, and sang better than she admitted. She did a lot of it at parties. "I'm your naughty aunt," she said happily. "The queen is the good one. And these are your cousins, my dear." She introduced her to the queen's three sons, who were eighteen, seventeen, and fourteen, close to the ages the three princesses had been during the war. They were Princes George, Albert, and William and were good-looking boys. They had the Teutonic blond looks of their father, who appeared a few minutes later to welcome her as well. He was Prince Edward. He had renounced his German nationality when he married Alexandra and exchanged his German title for a British one.

They all went out on the terrace after that, and half an hour later, Princess Victoria offered to show Annie to her room.

"You're a brave girl to come and meet all of us at once. I hear you're a smashing rider. Your mother was as well, dangerously so, I fear. She was about your size, and fearless on a horse. Our father was always afraid she would break her neck and kill herself riding." She looked wistful as she said it. "I'm afraid I was the wicked older sister who always scolded her. Jealous, I suppose. It seems so stupid now. I'm so glad you're here." She didn't say it, but it had occurred to her that Annie gave her the chance to do things better now, and make up for how mean she had been to Charlotte in their youth. "You look just like her, you know," she said softly as they reached the top of the stairs and she walked Annie into a splendid room, all decorated in yellow satin, and floral silks, and filled with antiques. "This is my favorite guest room of all," she said, as Annie caught her breath and looked around. She had never seen a bedroom as beautiful in her entire life. There was a portrait of Queen Victoria in her youth on one wall, and a huge canopied bed. "This was her favorite house," Victoria said, pointing to the painting. "Prince Albert bought the original house for her as a gift and then built her a new one. They were a very romantic couple, and madly in love. I suppose all those children were testimony to that," she said and laughed. She had a very light spirit and seemed like a lot of fun, as Anthony had said. She was much more frivolous than her older sister, although they were only a year apart. Princess Victoria was forty-two but didn't look it. She seemed very young, in white linen slacks, with a starched white shirt and silver sandals. The queen had been wearing a linen skirt and pale blue twin set, and her traditional double strand of pearls, which she wore every day, wherever she was. "And don't worry about dressing for dinner. We don't bother here. It's all very casual," she added.

"I didn't really know what to bring," Annie said in a soft voice, feeling nervous with this dazzlingly attractive woman who seemed so at ease in her own skin and so full of life. It had shocked her how much Annie looked like her late mother, they were almost identical, but she tried not to let it show. It was a knife in her heart, and almost as though her younger sister, Charlotte, had returned to them in the form of this shy, pretty young girl.

She could see why her mother and sister liked her. She was so unassuming, and so sweet and direct, with no artifice or pretense. Her manner was like Charlotte's too, and even the way she moved. "Don't let us overwhelm you, my dear," she added before she left the room. "There are a lot of us, but we mean you no harm, and your cousins are wonderful boys. We're all going fishing tomorrow. And you can ride if you like. Alexandra keeps some very nice horses here. I hope you'll enjoy it." She smiled and left the room, closing the door behind her, and Annie lay down on the huge bed and looked around, smiling. Everything was so beautiful, and they were all so nice. She still couldn't understand how all of this had happened to her. She wished Jonathan was with her, so he could see it all too. She would tell him all about it after the weekend.

She bathed before dinner. The bathroom was old-fashioned and had an enormous tub. She wore a plain black skirt and a white silk blouse, one of her few choices. She made up with youth and beauty for what she lacked in fashion, and the queen looked as though she approved when Annie entered the room in her simple skirt and blouse and black high heels that were new too, and hard to walk in, but looked pretty on her. Victoria came downstairs a few minutes later in a Pucci dress she'd bought in Rome, which the queen thought was too loud and too short, in a bright paisley pattern in turquoise, yellow, shocking pink, and black with shoes to match. Victoria had famously great legs and liked to show them off, although the queen disapproved. Annie looked like a schoolgirl in comparison, but a very proper one, and resolved to go shopping soon with her new allowance, for future family occasions. She had almost nothing to wear, and they all looked so fashionable to her. She wouldn't have dared to wear a dress like Victoria's, but it looked like fun, and molded her fabulous figure. It all went well with her flaming red hair, which she wore loose down her back, and made her look even younger. Annie could easily see how she'd had an affair with one of Anthony's thirty-year-old friends. She looked barely older than that herself.

The queen had seated Annie next to her at dinner, and they talked about horses all through the meal, which suited them both, and put Annie at ease. She knew little about anything else, but a great deal about horses. And the queen invited her to go riding with her the next morning, before the planned fishing expedition. Annie accepted with delight, and after dinner they all gathered around the piano again, and sang all their favorite songs. Annie even knew the words to some of them and sang along. It was a fun evening, and they all went to bed early.

Annie had agreed to meet the queen at the stables at seven, was up at five and watched the sun come up over the hills. She arrived punctually at the stables. The queen was already there, and had chosen a mount she thought Annie would enjoy. He was a very lively horse, and she'd brought him to Balmoral for the summer to see how she liked him. Victoria had already said he was too nervous and hard to manage, and she preferred one of the older mares. She wasn't quite as horse mad as her sister, although she was an excellent rider.

They all were, but Victoria didn't enjoy a challenge as much as the queen had heard Annie did.

Annie got in the saddle with ease, and calmed the big horse quickly. She had him well in hand by the time they left the stable yard a few minutes later, and headed along a path that led into the hills, and crossed a stream, which Annie and her mount jumped with ease.

"Do you hunt?" the queen asked her, and Annie shook her head.

"I never have, but I'd like to."

"We'll arrange that for you this winter. You'll enjoy it. Lord Hatton tells me that you dream of being a professional jockey. It will happen one of these days. They can't keep women out forever," she said calmly.

"I hope so, ma'am. It doesn't seem fair. We're only eligible for amateur events, and most of them aren't very good. I'd give anything to be in a real race," Annie said.

"I believe it will happen one day," she said. "Dangerous though. Be careful, my dear. Lord Hatton said you're a fearless rider. That's not always a good thing. Never forget these are powerful beasts, and we don't control them as thoroughly as we believe. They have a voice in the matter too." Annie smiled. She believed the same thing.

"I respect the horses I ride." She knew the ones that were dangerous, although she had a penchant for those, which Lord Hatton had spotted, and reported to the queen. He had said that it would make her an excellent jockey if she ever got the chance.

They rode for an hour, and then went back to the stables. Before they left to go back to the house, the queen showed her the Shetland ponies she bred there. She was very proud of them. And then they returned to the house for breakfast with the others. The whole group went fishing after that. The queen stayed back to attend to her official boxes and diplomatic pouches that were brought to her even here. Annie caught two fish and squealed with delight when she did. Her oldest cousin, Prince George, took them off the hooks for her. He was four years younger than Annie, and a very serious, polite young man. He was next in line to the throne and would be king one day, which always had a sobering effect on the next in line. Prince Albert was a year younger and full of mischief, and at one point, jumped into the lake fully dressed and climbed dripping back into the boat while everyone complained. He shook the water off himself and onto his relatives like a big dog, but the weather was warm. Prince William at fourteen was very studious and shy and still at Eton and more introverted than his two older brothers. His gentleness touched Annie and she chatted with him.

At lunchtime, they had the picnic that the cooks had packed for them in wicker baskets. Stewards arrived in a van to serve it at folding tables with linens and china. Everything was easy and fun and prettily done, and the following day, they had the American-style barbecue that the queen's sons had requested. Everyone loved it, hot dogs and hamburgers and corn on the cob, apple pie and ice cream.

"I want to work on a dude ranch next summer," Prince Albert announced at lunch. It sounded like fun to all of them. He'd been talking to his mother recently about transferring to an American university, and she hadn't agreed to it yet, but he was adamant. He was fascinated by all things American. He told Annie all about a rodeo he'd gone to when they vacationed in Wyoming. "I hear you're a bruising rider," he commented, and Annie smiled, surprised.

"How did you hear that?"

"My mother told me. She said you'd be a professional jockey if women were allowed to."

"I'd love that," Annie admitted. "I doubt it will ever happen here. Maybe in America one day. They're much more open-minded."

"About everything," Prince Albert confirmed. "I'd love to live there one day. My brother had better never abdicate. I want to be a cowboy when I grow up, not a king." It struck her then that it was a serious concern for all of them, the reality that one of them would be king or queen one day, although she was too far down the line to worry about it. But it was a heavy responsibility for Queen Alexandra's sons, particularly the two oldest. Her own father had become king reluctantly, when his brother had abdicated. So it did happen.

The end of the weekend came too quickly. The others were staying on for a few more days, although Princess Victoria was leaving for London the next day, and the queen was planning to spend another week there. She urged Annie to come again, now that she had met everyone in the family, other than distant cousins who were scattered all over Europe, many of them on other thrones.

"You're a true Windsor," she said to Annie when she left. They all hugged her and hoped to see her again soon. She had another month of work ahead of her at the queen's stables, and Prince George and Prince Albert promised to come and see her before they went back to university, and Prince William before he started the new term at Eton.

The queen touched on the subject of where Annie would live after she finished her internship at the stables. There were apartments available at Kensington Palace, if that appealed to her. Annie had been planning to go back to Jonathan to help him with the twins. She said she'd like to think about the queen's offer of an apartment.

It hadn't occurred to her that they would do that and she was pleasantly surprised.

She was far more relaxed on the trip back on the train than she had been on the way to Scotland. She had managed to stretch her meager wardrobe to its limits. She had been impressed by how fashionable Princess Victoria was, and she was so lively and stylish at everything she did. She lightened the mood wherever she was, but unlike the queen, she had few responsibilities, not even a husband and children. She had been very warm and welcoming to her newest cousin and gave her little snippets of advice throughout the weekend. Publicly, she had a reputation for being flighty and a party girl, but Annie could tell that she was intelligent and much less superficial than she pretended to be. It was simply the style she had chosen for herself when she didn't marry. She jokingly referred to herself as the family spinster, which was not the image Annie had of her at all. She was a very glamorous, beautiful woman.

In contrast, the queen was actually more lighthearted than she seemed publicly. She was a warm wife and mother, and enjoyed the time she spent with her family at Balmoral. She was already regretting that the summer was almost over. From Annie's perspective it had been a very successful weekend, and she had gotten to know a little bit about all of them, and genuinely liked her new family.

She didn't see Anthony until the following evening, when he came back from the South of France a day late, and looked a little worse for wear but said he had had a fabulous time. He had stayed on his friend's yacht, had lunch at the Club 55, danced at all the discotheques, picked up numerous women of assorted nationalities, which he didn't tell Annie, but she could guess. When he asked about her weekend at Balmoral, she said she'd had a fantastic time. He smiled at her enthusiasm.

"It's more your cup of tea than mine," he said. "My father loves it too. I always find it incredibly boring. It's a little too rural and family for me. Did Princess Victoria sing?"

"Every night," Annie said as she smiled at him, "and we had a barbecue." He didn't tell her the details of what he'd been doing in Saint Tropez, but a family barbecue with teenage boys present had not been on their agenda, much to his relief. But Annie had loved it. She was at a very different point in her life than he was and family-style weekends didn't thrill him, even with the royal family. He wanted racier diversions and couldn't see himself ever content with a life like that. And he knew that Princess Victoria was far more like him. But Annie's innocent enthusiasm seemed sweet to him.

She was already busy with the horses by the time he got there. His father was annoyed with him for returning a day late, but Anthony was used to it, and the lecture he got didn't impress him or bother him at all. He'd had a lifetime of them, about responsibility, his least favorite word.

Annie hardly saw Anthony all week, and the following weekend she went home to Kent for the twins' birthday. She had promised to be there, and wouldn't miss it. It was a very different weekend from the previous one at Balmoral. They went out to dinner at an Italian restaurant, and bowling afterward, and the Markhams let them use their pool because they were away. Annie spent hours in the pool with her brothers, and had given one a camera, and the other a stereo for their birthday. She was happy spending the weekend with them, with their father looking on. She had two families now, one royal, and the other, the one she had grown up with, as the daughter of employees on a big estate. The two lives were entirely different, and yet she was at home in both of them. She had adapted surprisingly well to the new one, as the niece of the queen, and the cousin of the future King of England. She was both people now, the simple girl she'd grown up as and a royal princess by birth. The boys teased her about it when she went bowling with them, and they asked if the queen had her own bowling alley at Buckingham Palace. Annie said she didn't, and Jonathan laughed.

"If I were king, I'd have my own bowling alley, a pinball machine, a jukebox, my own movie theater, and an Aston Martin," Blake said, imagining it, and his older sister grinned at him.

"Why an Aston Martin?" she asked him, thinking of Anthony Hatton's Ferrari, which seemed more glamorous to her.

Her brother gave her a look that implied she didn't know anything. "James Bond drives an Aston Martin," he said with a supercilious look, and she laughed again.

"Of course! Silly of me," she said, kissed him on the cheek, and went to buy popcorn for all of them. She was still smiling at the image of Blake as king with his own movie theater, jukebox, pinball machine, and bowling alley. She wondered if her new cousin George had those on his list too. More likely on Albert's, or maybe William's. There was something universal about teenage boys that was very sweet, even if they grew up to be king one day.

Chapter 14

The month of September went by too quickly for Annie. She loved her duties at the queen's stables, and her internship had only been for two months. She was sorry to see it come to an end. Anthony's had been for a shorter time, and he left in the middle of September. He was starting a new job at a public relations firm in London, which sounded interesting to her. He said it would be mostly organizing parties and special events for VIPs, and using his connections to get wealthy new industrialists introduced into society, and helping them get into the right circles. It didn't sound like a serious job, but it sounded amusing and right up his alley, since it involved parties.

"They pay dearly for that kind of service," he explained to her during dinner at their favorite pub the night before he left. She had enjoyed their friendship of the last month and a half, more than she'd ever expected to. He was deeper than he looked, although he never set the bar high for himself, and having fun was always the top priority to him. It sounded like he had found a job that met that criterion and he got paid for it. It was the best of all possible worlds for him. "What about you? What are you going to do when you leave here in two weeks?" he asked her.

"I'm going to travel for a month, to Australia. I've been dying to see it," she said innocently, and he looked at her with suspicion. It was the first time she had mentioned it to him.

"Why is it that I don't believe you? What do you have up your sleeve? Something to do with horses undoubtedly. Amateur races perhaps?" He grinned at her and she laughed.

"You know me too well. Don't tell your father. He wouldn't approve. He and the queen think that the amateur races in Australia aren't worth bothering with. But it's good experience if they ever change the rules here. I could ride in the Newmarket Town Plate. But I didn't have a mount for it. So, I'm off to Australia."

"And after that?"

"I don't know. I could go home to my father for a bit, and give him a hand in the stables. He hurt his knee and could use the help."

"Why don't you buy yourself a decent dress and come to London. You could come to some of the parties I organize. I can put you on the list as Her Royal Highness, and you could impress my crude clients with the important people I know."

"It sounds a bit awkward to me." She looked hesitant.

"It's not. They're actually very nice, and I could use some more royals on my list. Victoria will come to any party. But it's a bit slim pickings after that. I need another Royal Highness. Hell, I'll buy you the dress," he teased her. "Something shocking and naked and sexy." He liked the vision of it and she laughed.

"I'd look like a ten-year-old who ran away from a brothel," she said. "Why couldn't I come in my riding clothes?"

"On horseback preferably. You can always join the circus if you're bored."

"Thank you," she said primly.

"Just don't get yourself killed in those second-rate amateur races in Australia. Be careful, Annie. I know you won't be, but I'll worry about you."

"No, you won't." She laughed at him. "You'll be too busy giving parties to think about me."

He looked serious when he answered. "That's not true. I think about you a lot. And I do worry about you. You need someone to take care of you."

"No, I don't," she said stubbornly, jutting out her chin. "I'm tougher than I look."

"And more vulnerable and innocent than you think. I don't want anyone taking advantage of you." He felt protective of her, which was new for him.

"I'll be fine," she assured him. He remembered all too easily how terrified he had been when he thought she was dead when she fell off the horse during their second race. They had never raced again. She was like his little sister now. She was unfamiliar with the world she had been catapulted into, and the people in it, who would have liked to take advantage of her in countless ways. Anthony was well versed with that world, she wasn't.

"Just be careful." They went to his room after dinner that night, for the first time. But she knew she had nothing to fear from him now. He wasn't a masher, there were more than enough women who were desperate for him, and they had genuinely become friends.

He poured her a short glass of gin, and she made a face when she drank it. He drank a malt whiskey, neat, and they sat talking for a while, and then she got up to leave.

"We got a new horse today. I'm exercising him tomorrow to get a feeling for him," she said as she stood up. "I'm going to miss this place."

"They should hire you. You're better than any of the trainers they've got." He meant it, and walked her to the door, and she looked up at him with a smile. She seemed so tiny standing in front of him as she looked into his eyes, and for the first time, he wanted desperately to kiss her, but didn't dare. There was a long awkward moment as she looked up at him and felt something too. She thought it was the gin, but he knew it wasn't the whiskey, it was her. But the last thing he needed was a royal princess, and to have his life run by the queen and the Crown and the cabinet, who would have to give their permission for every move he made if they ever got serious. He couldn't think of anything worse or more restrictive. He liked being a free man. He bent down toward Annie then, and kissed her gently on the cheek, with greater tenderness than she had expected, or he had intended to show her. He wanted desperately to put his arms around her, but resisted the urge, and she scampered back to her room with a wave and closed the door.

"No!" he said to himself out loud as he closed his own door. "Never! Don't be ridiculous. She's a child." But she wasn't a child, she was a woman, and there was something so damn enchanting about her. He poured himself another whiskey, and lay down on his bed and fell asleep. He woke when he heard her leave for the stables at six o'clock the next morning, right on schedule. But he had come to his senses by then, and the moment had passed.

He left for London that morning to start his new job, and two weeks later, as she packed to leave, Annie had two surprises. One from Lord Hatton, and the other from the queen.

Lord Hatton offered her a job at the queen's stables as an assistant trainer, and she was thrilled. He asked what her plans were, and she said she was traveling for the next few weeks. He invited her to return when she got back, and move into the trainers' quarters and start her job. He was as pleased as she was, and delighted when she accepted, and he said the queen would be too.

The second surprise she got in a letter from the queen's secretary. Her Majesty wanted Her Royal Highness to be the first to know. Mr. Jonathan Baker was to be knighted. The queen had several discretionary titles that were in her gift, and knighted certain subjects when she deemed it appropriate. For being responsible for returning Her Royal Highness Anne Louise to her royal family, and asking for nothing in return, but doing it merely for honorable reasons, the queen was proposing to knight him at the end of October, as Sir Jonathan Baker. Annie was even more excited about that, and couldn't wait to tell him when she got home to Kent that night. She was staying with him and the boys for a few days before leaving for Australia for three weeks, to see if she could ride in any of the amateur races open to women there, even as a substitute. Annie had always wanted to go there and try out.

She waited until the end of dinner that night to tell him the big news about his knighthood. The boys were restless and wanted to leave the table, but she told them to wait. Jonathan stared at her when she told him he was going to be knighted, and he had tears in his eyes.

"*Sir* Jonathan? Are you joking?" She handed him the letter from the queen's secretary. "But I didn't do anything," he protested. "At first I was afraid they might put me in jail when I tried to reach the queen," he smiled.

"You did everything, Papa. You found a way to reach the queen. None of this would have happened if you'd stayed silent or lost your nerve. I have two families now, thanks to you, and I'm a princess." She told him about the job at the stables too. Something wonderful had happened for both of them. She was to be paid a salary for her work, and was pleased. And she didn't need an apartment in London now.

"What are you doing in Australia?" He always worried about her.

"Just looking around," she said. He didn't believe her.

"Don't do anything foolish."

"I won't. And I'll be back in time for your ceremony." The twins had been impressed too.

When he told John Markham the next day, he responded with a promotion and a raise. He invented a fancy new title for him, since he was already stable master, and the raise was appropriate. Jonathan had promised to invite him to the ceremony too. And Annie learned while she was home that Annabelle Markham had a new secretary and Jonathan had just started dating her. The twins said she was very nice, and good-looking. Annie was happy for him. He deserved it. He had done so much for her, and always had. He was going to bring his new date to the knighting ceremony too. He still got tears in his eyes whenever he thought about it. He had never expected anything like it to happen to him. He was going to be a knight!

Annie left for Sydney after a week at home. She only stayed two weeks in the end, and was disappointed in the amateur races. She thought they were poorly organized and unprofessional. She was able to sign up for two of them and didn't like her mount in either case. The women were rough and the organizers seemed crude to her. It wasn't what she had hoped for, and she was happy to come home, although she thought the country was interesting.

She was happy to be back in England, and had dinner with Anthony when she returned. He was having one of his first events in the new job that weekend, and wanted her to come. It was to introduce a well-known American into British social circles. He'd rented a fabulous house in Mayfair for the weekend to give the party.

"I feel a bit like a pimp doing this kind of thing," Anthony admitted to her. "These guys want to meet women, mostly hookers in the end, and be seen with respectable women. I draw the line at drugs, but they expect me to do everything for them. And they're powerful men. They don't take no for an answer. Will you come?" he asked her hopefully.

"I'm not going to impress anyone, Anthony. And I have nothing to wear."

"Go to Harrods or Hardy Amies, your aunt Victoria shops there. I need you on my team," he said, nearly begging her.

"I am on your team. Why do I have to be there?"

"To impress them."

"Will Victoria be there?"

"She's going to some ball in Venice. I need *you*."

"All right, all right," she said grudgingly. "What kind of dress?"

"Sexy, slinky, half naked," he said without hesitating.

"That's not me."

"All right. As sexy as you dare."

"Now I feel like a hooker," she grumbled.

"That makes two of us. I feel like a pimp," he said and she laughed.

She went to Harrods the next day and bought a simple black velvet strapless dress and a fake diamond necklace that looked real, black satin high heels and an evening bag. The night of the party, she pulled her blond hair into a neat-looking bun, put on a little makeup, and looked surprisingly regal when she arrived in Mayfair at the address of the house he had rented for the event. He took her aside immediately, and took a leather box out of a drawer. He opened it and held out a beautiful small antique tiara and placed it on her head as she looked at him in surprise.

"I borrowed it from Garrard's. It was Queen Victoria's. Now you look like a princess," he said, looking pleased, and she was startled when she looked in the mirror.

"It's gorgeous."

"You can't keep it. But you can say it was your great-great-great-grandmother's." He was perfect in the role of PR man, and she was impressed when she saw him in operation that night. The party went off seamlessly and his client was delighted. The press was there and took a photograph of her with the host, who was an oilman from Texas, who had just invested a fortune in aeronautics in England, and wanted to make a big splash. He had wanted to meet the queen, which Anthony told him wasn't possible, so Her Royal Highness Princess Anne Louise was second best and an adequate consolation prize for the Texan, who invited her to visit him in Dallas. She looked beautiful that night and every inch a princess, and Anthony thanked her and kissed her cheek when she left and handed him the tiara.

"I thought you did a great job," she complimented him. "You make an excellent pimp."

"And you make an excellent princess, Your Royal Highness." He was glad they were friends now and so was she. "I'm keeping you on my list. And I like the dress by the way."

"I only spent a hundred pounds on it. I can't ride in it, so I didn't want to go nuts," she said, laughing.

His client was beckoning to him then, and he rushed off and she left. She was surprised that she had had fun, but she had. And Anthony looked very handsome in black tie. It had been a glamorous evening, and she liked wearing the tiara. She felt like a real princess in it.

There was a photograph of her with Anthony in the papers the next day. And her aunt Victoria called her when she got back from Venice and saw it.

"Be careful, my darling," she warned her. "Anthony Hatton is charming, but he's a player. Don't lose your heart to that one." She was a woman of the world and wise about men.

"I'm not. We're just friends. He needed a princess to impress his client," she told her aunt.

"Oh God, he'll whore us all out if we let him." She laughed at the thought. "I was at a very amusing ball in Venice so I couldn't be there. You'll have to come with me some time. The Italians are so sexy and handsome. They're all broke but so charming. Everyone is a prince there. It was a divine party. And you looked very pretty with Anthony in the photo. I just worried when I saw it."

"His father is my new boss. He just gave me a job as an assistant trainer at the stables."

"Excellent." They talked for a few more minutes and hung up. The call didn't really surprise her. She knew that Anthony had a reputation as a playboy in London, but he was harmless, and there was no romance between them. They were just friends. He sent her red roses to thank her for coming to the party, which was very nice of him.

After that she turned her attention to the ceremony for her stepfather. The queen did it herself at Buckingham Palace in a small receiving room. It was all very official, with a saber she used to tap him on each shoulder and declare him a knight of the British Empire, and he would be known as Sir Jonathan Baker hereafter. Tears rolled down his cheeks as she pronounced it, and Annie cried too, and was so proud of him. The boys had new suits, their first, for the occasion, and Jonathan did too and looked very proper. His mother was there and was bursting with pride, and she was happy to see Annie. It made Annie miss Lucy too, who would have been ecstatic at the knighting ceremony. The Markhams attended, and the woman Jonathan was dating, who was very polite and nice to Annie, and seemed very smitten with him. There were several officials and the lord chamberlain of the queen's household and her secretary. A round of champagne was served, and then Jonathan treated his family and the Markhams to dinner at Rules, the oldest restaurant in London. At Annie's request, Anthony arranged to have them go to Annabel's to dance afterward. It was a perfect evening. Annie couldn't help thinking how her life had changed in a short time. Her stepfather was a knight now, and she was a royal princess. The headwaiters and manager at Annabel's fawned over her, and she danced with Jonathan. He smiled at her, and she called him Sir Jonathan, and he called her Your Royal Highness . . . but whatever the titles, she knew she would always be just Annie to him, and the daughter of his heart, which was the best part.

Chapter 15

At the end of October, Annie returned from Kent to the queen's stables to start her job as assistant trainer. She'd been staying with Jonathan and the boys and enjoyed it. It felt almost like old times, except for Lucy's absence. Annie still missed her.

As a trainer, she had more responsibilities than she'd had as an intern, and was assigned to the three barns on a rotating schedule. She learned a great deal about their breeding program, which she discussed with Jonathan whenever she visited with them. The process of selection of matching up the horses to be bred was fascinating, and as much art as science. Lord Hatton consulted with the queen about almost every choice.

Annie loved her job, although it was all-consuming and she had no time for anything else. She didn't mind.

In November, she received the queen's invitation to spend Christmas with them at Sandringham, which meant that she couldn't spend it with Jonathan and the twins if she accepted, but he understood, and thought she should spend it with her royal family this year. She was sorry not to be with him in Kent, but Christmas with her royal aunts, uncle, cousins, and grandmother, was appealing too. She didn't know who else would be there, but had the impression it was only family. And this time, she would have to buy some clothes. The only proper dress she had was the one she had bought for Anthony's party for the Texas oilman. She was sorry she didn't have the tiara to wear with it again. It had been the perfect look, and she smiled when she thought of it. It seemed particularly appropriate because people were always comparing her to her own mother and Queen Victoria, since both of them had also been small. The rest of the family seemed to take after the German side and were much taller than she. All of Queen Alexandra's sons were tall like their father, and the queen was tall too.

Sandringham was in Norfolk, much closer to London than Balmoral Castle, and it was where the royal family usually spent Christmas. She shopped for some dresses, most of them black or navy, and a deep red velvet one for Christmas Eve. She bought gifts for everyone when she had a day off. She bought Jonathan a beautiful set of antique leather-bound books and a pinball machine for the twins, which was delivered the morning of Christmas Eve. When she called, Jonathan said they had gone nuts and invited all their friends from school to come over and play.

And she had sent a beautiful warm black coat to Jonathan's mother, her other grandmother. She had seen too little of her since going to work at the royal stables, but she wrote to her whenever she had time. Her new allowance enabled her to make generous gifts to all of them, and she was sorry not to see them over Christmas. She knew they understood that she had new responsibilities now, and two families. It was going to be her first royal Christmas.

Annie was shown to a beautiful bedroom at Sandringham when she arrived, and several footmen carried her bags and all her packages to her room. She was directing them about where to put everything when a familiar face walked past her room, and she saw Anthony Hatton standing in the doorway, smiling at her. His father was there too, and she remembered that the Hattons spent Christmas with the queen's family every year. She was embarrassed not to have brought something for him. She had given Lord Hatton a bottle of Dom Perignon champagne before she left the stables. She was genuinely surprised to see Anthony. She hadn't seen him since his party for the oilman. They had both been busy with their new jobs.

"I hoped I'd see you here." He smiled at her as he crossed the room to kiss her. "I meant to call you, but my life has been insane. The PR firm I'm working for has really taken off. I've been running parties for them every week with a list of VIP clients an arm long. What about you? Is my father working your tail off?"

"Yes, and I love it." She smiled at him.

"Are you behaving?" he asked her.

"Of course." She wasn't sure what he meant by it, but she had no time to do otherwise. He noticed but didn't mention that she looked suddenly more grown up, and more sophisticated than she had when he met her. She was wearing a red wool suit with a fashionably short skirt, which was part of her recent haul from Harrods when she was buying gifts. She thought it would come in handy at Sandringham. He was admiring her legs with the short skirt. She was small but well proportioned, and he'd never noticed her legs before in her riding clothes, or her evening gown at his party.

"My room is just down the hall if you need anything," he said, as he left to check on his own bags.

Christmas at Sandringham was more formal than the family gatherings at Balmoral in the summer. There were no picnics or barbecues, and the queen's secretary had called to tell her that dinner would be black tie, which was why she'd gone shopping, so she was prepared. She had bought three long dresses, and had brought the strapless velvet one, which was the only one she'd owned. She'd bought a kilt, the red suit she was wearing, a black velvet suit, and a white wool dress by a French designer for Christmas Day. She had a full wardrobe and she could fill in with some skirts and sweaters she had brought from Kent the last time she went there. As always, when she went downstairs for cocktails before dinner, Princess Victoria was wearing a very chic French designer black cocktail dress and looked sexy and fashionable, and the queen was wearing a black velvet evening suit with a long skirt, with her pearls, diamond earrings, and a very handsome tiara.

Annie was seated next to Anthony at dinner, and he leaned over and whispered, "I should have brought the tiara from Garrard's that you wore to the party. I meant to give it to you for Christmas, and I must have forgotten it at home." She grinned at his comment, and remembered how much she liked it. "It suited you very well. You should wear tiaras all the time."

During dinner she told him how lovely her father's knighting ceremony had been and how much it meant to him, and Anthony was touched. Somehow, despite everything that had happened to her in a short time, it hadn't gone to her head, and she had managed to stay real.

"What about you? Do you still like the job?" she asked.

"It's a hell of a lot of work, and some of their clients are real jerks, but some are very nice. The Americans mostly. There's kind of a sweet innocence to them. They all want to meet the queen, and think they should. They don't really get how it all works, the protocol, and all the rest. We should get a stand-in that looks like her. They'd never know the difference." Annie laughed. It was fun sitting next to him, he always had something interesting to say and he always made her laugh. "What about you, how does it all feel? Has the protocol gotten to you yet? I know Victoria gets fed up with it."

"I'm not the queen's sister," she reminded him. "I'm only her niece. No one worries about what I do. I'm kind of below the radar and I like it that way."

"Until you put a foot wrong, and then they'll come down on you like bricks, if you go out with the wrong man, or say the wrong thing." That was Victoria's specialty. She was always dating men that her sister and the cabinet didn't approve of, or being too outspoken or critical about the government, the prime minister, or her sister.

"I don't do anything they can object to," Annie said easily.

"You will one day," he assured her, "and then there will be hell to pay." It was why he had never gone out romantically with Victoria, or anyone royal. He didn't care that she was older, nor did she. But he confined his love life to commoners, socialites, debutantes, models, and starlets, which caused comment too, and had won him the reputation of being a playboy, as Victoria had warned her. But Annie was in no danger of falling prey to his charms. She knew him too well now and still only liked him as a brother.

Her cousin Albert was seated on her other side at dinner the first night, on Christmas Eve, and he was talking about college, and a ski trip to France he was planning after Christmas. She had seen in the press that he was dating a beautiful girl, who was a duke's daughter, but there was no evidence of her there. None of them brought their dates to the queen's home for Christmas, not even her sons. It was strictly family, and the Hattons. Lord Hatton was seated next to the queen on one side, and her oldest son, the heir apparent, on the other. She was deep in conversation with Lord Hatton about a horse she wanted to buy, to use for stud services. Horses were her main topic of conversation in private. The prince consort was seated next to his sister-in-law Victoria, and she was making him laugh as she always did, with irreverent stories. She brought out the best in him. Men loved her.

The ladies left the table at the end of dinner, and waited in the drawing room for the gentlemen to join them shortly after, and then they played charades over coffee and brandy, followed by card games. At midnight they all went upstairs. Gifts were to be exchanged the next day before lunch, which would be a sumptuous meal in the main dining room. They followed the same traditions every year.

When Annie went to her room at the end of the evening, there was a fire burning brightly. The room was warm and cozy, and she was relaxing in a chair thinking of what a nice time she'd had, when there was a knock on the door. She went to open it, and was surprised to see Anthony standing there with a bottle of champagne in his hand and two glasses.

"A bit of bubbly before bedtime?" he offered. She wasn't tired and she let him come in, and he sat down across from her in front of the fire and stretched his legs out as he filled two glasses with champagne, and handed one to her.

"I'm glad you're here," he said, looking relaxed. "It's all a bit serious for me, and a little formal. But staying home alone on Christmas would be depressing. So I let my father talk me into it. And to be honest, I hoped you'd be here. I wasn't sure if you'd be in Kent instead."

"I thought I should be here this year."

"Be careful. The royal life is a web you'll never escape."

"You make it sound ominous," she said as she sipped the champagne.

"Not ominous, insidious. After a while, nothing compares to it and you get trapped. Like Victoria. I'm sure there are a dozen places she'd rather be. But she's still here."

"It's home to her," Annie said.

"She'll wind up an old maid if she's not careful. Men are afraid of this, and she won't be young and beautiful forever. She's already forty-two, and I don't think any of the men she's been in love with wanted to take this on."

"Why not?" Annie looked surprised, as he finished his glass and poured himself another. She wondered if he was a little tipsy, but he didn't look it.

"Because the queen makes the rules, my dear, for the entire family. *And* the cabinet. *And* the prime minister. *And* the archbishop. And all the rules and traditions that have existed for hundreds of years. You can't escape that. It's a prison of sorts, a golden one, but nonetheless the walls are thick and the doors are barred, and they let very few people in. Queen Alexandra is a stickler. It will happen to you too if you're not careful. You can't just marry whoever you choose now. They have to approve."

"Are they still that strict?" Annie looked surprised. These were modern times, and the queen was young.

"They are," he answered. "You're far enough down the line, so they may not be as tough on you. But poor George and Albert will have to marry the girls their mother approves of. No go-go dancers for them," he said, and she laughed.

"Well, they don't need to worry about me. I don't want to get married. I just want to be a jockey one day, if they ever relax the rules and let women into the inner sanctum of racing."

"You can't wait for that forever."

"Yes, I can," she said confidently. "That's my only goal for the moment."

"Then God help the racing committee. I get the feeling that you always get what you want."

"Not always, but I'm willing to wait and be patient."

"You'll probably marry and have ten children before that," he said lightly.

"I hope not. I'm not sure I want any," Annie responded seriously. "It certainly didn't work out well for my mother," she said quietly, and he looked at her gently.

"Are you afraid of that happening to you?" he asked, and she nodded. It was her worst fear, dying in childbirth. He had his own demons.

"That was a long time ago, during the war. She was young, and you probably weren't born in a hospital," he said sensibly to reassure her.

"No, I wasn't, but it still happens even now."

"Think of Queen Victoria. She was as small as you are, and she had nine children, all at home, and she was fine. I suppose we all have our terrors. I'm afraid of the woman I love leaving me, the way my mother walked out on my father. It nearly broke him. I don't

think he ever recovered. I don't think he's loved a woman since."
Although he had dated many, and had a reputation as a ladies' man.

"It's odd how the things in our childhood mark us forever," Annie
said. "Once I knew about my mother, I decided I didn't want children. It seems safer not to try." And yet she never played it safe on
horseback, and had no fears there. But she guarded her heart. And
so did Anthony and his father.

"It's not too late for you to change your mind about having babies.
You're young. It will be fine, if you fall in love with the right man.
Finding a woman who won't fall in love with someone else and leave
you is harder," he said, expressing his own fears.

"Maybe you don't know the right women," she said, and he stared
into the fire as he thought about it and then looked at her.

"Probably not. The ones that sparkle like diamonds in the snow
are always the most dangerous. I don't trust them, but they're always
so damn tempting. I think my mother was like that. She was the
daughter of a marquess, and she was a famous beauty. My father was
dazzled by her. But she left him for another man, as you know."

"Love seems complicated," Annie said softly, and he nodded.

"It does, doesn't it? It shouldn't. It should be so simple between
two good, honorable people. The trouble is, so few people are honorable. And the ones who are can be damn boring," he said and then
laughed. "Like your aunt Alexandra. She's a woman of duty and
honor, and a profoundly good person, but I don't imagine she's much
fun to live with and must be rather dull. Victoria is a great deal more
amusing, but I wouldn't trust her. I suspect she can be very naughty,
and even wicked. Her love affairs never last and they're never with
suitable people. She prefers the high-risk ones, but when you do

that, you wind up alone like her." He was in a serious contemplative mood, but Annie suspected that his analyses were correct. "Who knows, maybe your mother would have left your father by now, if they'd survived."

"I don't know much about her. No one likes to talk about her. It makes them too sad. She was so young when she died."

"I can understand that. And one thing I do know," he said, looking seriously at her, as he slid out of his chair across from her and came to sit on the floor next to the low chair where she was sitting. "I know you're an honorable woman, Annie, and you're not boring. I always have fun with you, that's a rare combination." She smiled down at him, and always felt comfortable with him.

"Thank you. I have fun with you too, except for the time I nearly killed myself racing with you."

He winced. "Christ, I thought you were dead. I've never been so frightened in my life."

"Well, I wasn't," she said. "I was lucky."

"We both were." He leaned forward and the next thing she knew he was kissing her, not violently or passionately, but tenderly, as though he meant it. She was shocked and hadn't seen it coming.

"What are you doing?" she said in a whisper, and he kissed her again, and this time she kissed him back. She hadn't expected anything like this from him.

"I'm kissing you." He answered and smiled at her, and did it one more time. "Every time I see you, something happens to me. You're everything I want in a woman, Annie. But I'm scared."

"Of what?"

"Of ruining what we have. Of you leaving me one day. Of the royal rules squeezing the life out of both of us. It terrifies me, but I know I want to be with you one day, and be married to you, and have babies with you, and I won't let it kill you, I promise." He sounded frighteningly serious about all of it.

"You don't know that it wouldn't kill me," she said, remembering her mother.

"I don't want anything bad to ever happen to you. I hate the idea of your being a jockey. You could break your neck and die, a lot easier than in childbirth. What I can never figure out is how we get from here to there. I've thought about it. How do we get from where we are now to a grown-up married life with children and dogs and all the good things that go with it?" He looked genuinely worried.

"Maybe we just wait till we're ready." He had opened new doors and windows to a vista she had never even considered, but she liked it. He put his arms around her and held her close as the fire crackled and she felt the warmth of him around her and on her lips when he kissed her. She had never felt anything like it for any man, until now.

"I don't want to wait," he whispered to her, and then pulled away slightly to look at her, "and this isn't just a clever plot to get you into bed on Christmas Eve and walk away the next day. I'm in love with you. I knew it the day I nearly killed you when we were racing. I just haven't figured out what to do about it. And you're too young to get married, maybe we both are. I still have some growing up to do too, but I don't want to lose you while we wait. And I sure don't want to lose you to some stupid horse race."

"You won't." But he knew he could if she got her wish and was able to become a jockey. "So what do we do?" she asked softly.

"I don't know. Let's spend time together when we can. I can come to the stables when I have free time, and you can come to London to see me."

"Should we tell people?"

"Eventually. Not yet. They'll figure it out. And there will be lots of people telling you I'm a player and not to take me seriously." She laughed at that.

"Victoria already has, after she saw the photo of us in the newspaper at your party for the Texan."

"She should talk." He rolled his eyes. "She's slept with half of Europe. I'm an amateur compared to her. And in the past she would have been right about me. I feel differently about you, Annie. You're different, and I'm different when I'm with you."

"And when you're not?" She wasn't entirely oblivious to his reputation.

"Leave that to me." He kissed her again then, with mounting passion, their champagne forgotten, all he wanted were her lips and to feel her in his arms. He derived strength from her, and he trusted her, and knew he could. She was a good woman. "Would you go away with me?" he asked her when he pulled away to catch his breath. And she was out of breath too, as she thought about it.

"Maybe. Not yet. It's too soon." He nodded and didn't argue with her. "I don't want to get pregnant. My mother did that. I don't want to start out that way, in a panic, and doing the wrong thing."

"There's a pill you can take now, not to get pregnant. They have it in the States."

"Oh." She didn't know about it, and had no reason to. She was entirely innocent. "I would do that. I don't want us to make any mistakes." He nodded, neither did he. He wanted this to be right, for both of them. It was a first for him, but he'd been thinking of her that way for a while, since the party.

"I'd love to go to Venice with you," he said, "or somewhere in

France." She nodded, carried away with the images he was sharing with her, and eventually he carried her to the bed and lay down next to her and just held her. "I love you, Annie," he said peacefully, and she had never felt so safe in her life. He didn't try to do anything he shouldn't. Eventually when the fire died down and the room got chilly, he got up regretfully, and stood and smiled down at her. "My beautiful angel. I don't know why you dropped into my life. I don't deserve you, but I'll try. I promise you that." She smiled up at him, got off the bed, and followed him to the door of her room. He peeked out to make sure there was no one in the hall, and he didn't have far to go to his own room. He kissed her one last time. It had been an important night for both of them. Life-changing, if they stuck to it and all went well.

"I love you," she whispered to him. "Happy Christmas."

"Happy Christmas," he whispered back and then sped down the hall to his room and disappeared. She softly closed the door, wondering what would happen and if he really meant it. If he did, she had never been happier in her life. She was still smiling when she went to bed and burrowed under the covers. In his room, Anthony was standing at the window, looking at the snow on the ground, and thinking of his mother, hoping he would be luckier than his father had been. But with Annie, for the first time in his life, he thought he had a chance. He had opened his heart to her, and all he could do now was pray that he was right. She was the first woman he had trusted in his entire life. It was even more important than loving her.

Chapter 16

Everything about Christmas changed from the moment Anthony told Annie he loved her. It was the most beautiful Christmas of her life. They met at breakfast the next day, and all appeared to be normal. They sat next to each other and held conversations with the other people at the table as though nothing had changed. But their entire universe had altered overnight. Annie felt as though she was floating.

She called Jonathan and the twins to wish them a Happy Christmas.

Anthony snuck into her room that afternoon to kiss her, and again when she was changing for dinner. He could hardly keep his hands off her. She didn't want to do anything foolish, and he wanted to be responsible. After dinner on Christmas night, he stayed with her for hours and they talked about the future. It sounded magical to her. He lay on her bed and held her and they kissed endlessly, but they didn't make love. That was new for him. Any woman who hadn't slept with him before, he had lost interest in immediately. With Annie, it was all different, and he didn't want to do anything to hurt her or put her at risk.

They managed to avoid the scrutiny of the entire group by being discreet and appearing casual with each other. And no one suspected anything by the time they all disbanded on Boxing Day, the day after Christmas. The queen had to get back to Buckingham Palace, Victoria was going skiing with friends in Saint Moritz, and Cortina after that. Anthony's father had business to attend to. The young princes had to go back to school, and the prince consort was going hunting in Spain with the king. They all had their roles to play and their lives to pursue. He hated to let Annie go back alone on the train for the long trip back to Newmarket, but it was how she had come, and he had to drive his car back from Sandringham. He couldn't leave it there. His father had come in his own car, so he couldn't drive Anthony's back for him. And he was stopping to see people on the way back so couldn't offer Annie a ride.

The head steward put Annie on the train, and she felt as though she were in a dream all the way back to Newmarket, and in a cab back to the stables. It had been the most magical Christmas of her life. Anthony couldn't even call her at the stables, without everyone knowing. Instead he showed up three days later for the weekend. His father was away, and he had dinner at the pub with Annie, and the next day they rode out together on a trail that was muddy but not icy, and they were cautious so the horses didn't fall. He smiled at her as the horses walked along side by side.

"When are you coming to London?" he asked her.

"I have three days off in two weeks. I could come then."

"It's going to be so hard having you here," he said, impatient to spend time with her. "I'll get you a room at the Ritz," he said and she nodded. He came to her room that night, when the other trainers were out for dinner, and they lay on her bed for a while.

"How would I get that pill you mentioned?" she asked him shyly and he smiled. He didn't think she was ready and he was surprised. "I don't think I trust us," she said wisely.

"I'll take care of it," he promised. "I have an American friend who can mail them to me. They're easier to get there." He didn't want to make any mistakes either and spoil everything. She was too important to him.

He left the trainers' quarters before the others got back, and stayed in his father's house. She visited him there the next day, but they were circumspect, with a great deal of kissing and touching and fondling, but nothing more dangerous than that.

He hated to leave her on Sunday night, but she promised to come to London in two weeks on her time off. He wrote her short funny letters which made her laugh, and told her how much he loved her. She got a steady stream of mail from him, and had to force herself to concentrate on her work. And at the end of two weeks, she took the train to London, he met her at the station, and drove her to the Ritz. He hadn't intended to stay with her, or he would have taken her to his apartment. But in the end, he couldn't leave her, and she didn't want him to. He had come prepared just in case. He didn't want to risk an accident the first time.

He was as gentle as he could be with her, and made it as painless as possible, knowing she was a virgin. But she was a willing, exuberant lover and surprised him. They hardly got out of bed all weekend. It was raining and cold, and they were cozy in the suite. He had brought the birth control pills as promised, and warned her that they would take a week or so to be effective, so they were careful.

They slept and talked and ordered meals, and went for a few walks around the neighborhood of the hotel, and by the end of the weekend, they belonged to each other, and Annie felt like a woman of the world.

She felt as though everyone would notice how changed she was when she went back to the stables, and she could hardly pull herself away when he took her to the station and put her on the train.

"I love you, remember that," he whispered to her and they waved to each other, until the train pulled away and entered a tunnel, and then she sat dreaming of the weekend all the way back to Newmarket. He threw caution to the winds and called her that night. There was an open phone in the trainers' quarters, so she couldn't say much, but he told her again and again how much he loved her and she said she did too.

She almost wanted to tell Jonathan about Anthony, but she didn't dare. And remarkably, they managed to keep their affair a secret for the next several months. She stayed at his apartment in Knightsbridge the next time, and thereafter, and they cooked breakfast together, and at night he took her to dinner at his favorite restaurants. Miraculously, they never ran into anyone they knew, and never got caught on their weekends together. She got two weekends off a month.

All she had done since Christmas was work and see Anthony. It was like living in a bubble, and in March, the queen's secretary called her to invite her to attend the Cheltenham Festival in Gloucestershire. It was a three-day event for chasers and hurdlers, with the Champion Hurdle, the Champion Chase, the World Hurdle, and the highlight of the jump season, the Cheltenham Gold Cup. She was thrilled to be asked. They had a horse running in the Champion

Chase, and the secretary said she was welcome to invite her father as well if she liked. She didn't dare ask if she could bring Anthony too, but she knew he could ask to go with his father, since he would be in the royal box too.

Annie had seen the queen several times at the stables, but she hadn't seen her socially since Christmas at Sandringham. Lord Hatton and the trainers kept her running at work. She was familiar with the horse they'd have in the race and had exercised him several times. He was young and considered a long shot in the race, but the queen had a great deal of faith in him, and the jockey who would be riding him. He had won some impressive victories for them before.

Annie told Anthony about the race as soon as she accepted, and he said he'd arrange with his father to be there, and no one would find it unusual. They both wanted to remain discreet for now, or the queen and cabinet might start to interfere, and then the press and public opinion. Neither of them wanted to face that yet.

She invited her father and he was delighted. When the day of the race came, the queen and Lord Hatton invited her to the paddock before the race. The horse seemed tense, as though he sensed what was coming, and the jockey was calm. He was the same size as Annie, but powerfully built, with strong shoulders and arms, and a rider's legs. If they won, the odds were twenty to one.

When she went back to the royal box, Anthony had arrived. Victoria was there in a glamorous outfit with a dashing looking new man. She kissed Annie's cheek and was happy to see her. They kept promising to lunch with each other, but they hadn't yet. They all watched intensely as the horse took off, slowly and steadily at first and then stronger and stronger, as none of them dared to breathe or speak. Then with a powerful surge, driven forward by the jockey, their horse shot ahead gathering incredible speed, and finished four lengths ahead of the horse behind him. Everyone in the royal box gave a scream. Victoria and Annie were jumping up and down. The queen hugged Lord Hatton, Jonathan pumped his hand to congratulate him, and Anthony grabbed Annie and held her and they smiled at each other. The horse had won, at twenty-to-one odds. They all went to congratulate the jockey, who was covered in mud and wreathed in smiles. The queen hugged him and had mud on her face afterward and they all laughed. Her sons had come down from school for it, and there was jubilation in the royal box. The purse was a good one, and they had all bet on him.

Annie's eyes were alight afterward and Lord Hatton laughed at her. "You can taste it, can't you?" He could see how badly she wanted to be a jockey and win a race. "One day. It will happen," he assured her.

"I'll be an old woman by then," she said, looking discouraged.

"You're still a baby, you have time," Anthony's father said. She saw Anthony look unhappy and he said something afterward, when he gave her a ride to the restaurant. The queen had invited them all to dinner to celebrate.

"You still want to race as badly as that?" Anthony asked her, worried. He had heard the exchange with her father and saw the look on her face.

"Yes, if I could. But I don't think they'll ever let women race here in my lifetime."

"And if they do?"

"I'd like to try it," she said softly. It wasn't worth arguing about, since it wasn't a possibility.

"What if we're married and have children by then?" he asked pointedly.

"I suppose it would be too late then. Please don't worry about it. It's not happening."

"But it could, and you could break your neck out there." He looked anxious and upset. He was willing to think about settling down now. She wasn't. Racing was in her blood. She wanted that more than any man. He could see it in her eyes every time the subject came up.

"Thompson didn't break his neck today," she said quietly.

"He's been doing it for years, and one day he might. I don't want my wife and the mother of my children dead on a racetrack," he said, looking angry. But more than angry, he was afraid for her.

"It's been my dream all my life," she said quietly. "If I had the chance I'd do it." She was always honest with him. "But I don't have the chance."

"I hope it stays that way." He didn't speak again until they got to the restaurant and then he relaxed, and she noticed the queen watching them once or twice, and wondered if she suspected anything. But she had no reason to object. She'd known Anthony all his life, and there was nothing she could object to. His father was a lord, he was well educated, well brought up, and a gentleman. She might object to their having an affair, but they were both single, and it was 1967, not 1910. And thanks to Anthony and his friend in New York, she was on the pill, so she wasn't going to get pregnant and cause a scandal with a child out of wedlock. And they intended to get married. Someday. Although neither of them was in a rush. They had everything they wanted now. The queen didn't ask any questions, or comment, nor did Victoria, who was there that night too.

In May, on Annie's birthday, Anthony took her to dinner at Harry's Bar, and dancing at Annabel's afterward, since he was a member of both clubs. They ran into Victoria, who arrived at Annabel's shortly after they did, with a married American she'd been dating less than discreetly, which the queen wasn't pleased about. Victoria took one look at them, and could see what had happened. She sent over a bottle of champagne after wishing Annie a happy birthday, and in return, they toasted her and her handsome friend. He was a well-known actor, married to a movie star, and wanted to divorce his wife for Victoria. It had been all over the tabloids.

By coincidence, they left the club at the same time, and the paparazzi were waiting for Victoria and her movie star. They got photographs of Annie and Anthony too, and recognized both of them. It was a bonus for the paparazzi, and the tabloids were full of both couples the next day, with the headline over Annie and Anthony's photograph, ROYAL WEDDING BELLS? GOOD JOB, ANTHONY!

The queen called Annie that morning from Buckingham Palace and discreetly asked if the rumor was true. Were she and Anthony planning to get married?

"We're seeing each other," Annie admitted with nothing to hide, "but we have no plans to marry at the moment. It still seems too soon, to both of us." It was the truth.

"I have no objection, as long as he's sown the last of his wild oats. He was a bit of a playboy for a few years, I believe. But he's the right age to settle down, *if* he has." He had just turned thirty-one, and she was twenty-three now. "He's a lovely young man. I've known his family all my life. Just don't wait too long, if that's what you want to do. You don't want to become fodder for the tabloids, and have the paparazzi following you around all the time. Once you're married, they'll lose interest." Annie didn't want to marry just to get rid of the paparazzi, but the queen had made herself clear. She had conservative values and she preferred marriage to dating. "You're old enough now, dear." But Annie didn't feel old enough at twenty-three, and she was still getting used to the royal life. It was her first taste of what Anthony disliked so much, pressure from the Crown.

She reported the conversation to Anthony when he called her, and he was annoyed.

"That was my point earlier. I don't want the House of Windsor telling us what to do. We should get married when we want to. We're just getting started. What's the hurry?"

"I'd rather wait awhile too. Twenty-three seems so young to get married. I kind of thought twenty-five or -six," Annie said thoughtfully.

"Thirty-one seems young to me too. I used to think thirty-five was the right age for a man. We'll know when it's right. But it should be up to us. She's going to put the heat on now. And can you imagine what she must have said to Victoria today? She must be having a fit over that." She was, and had told her sister to break it off immediately before she disgraced herself again. Victoria was used to it by now. She'd been battling with her family over who she dated for twenty years, and seemed to take pleasure in shocking them, the public, and the press. Annie and Anthony didn't want to be part of that.

Lord Hatton called Anthony for confirmation too, and said he was delighted about Annie. He couldn't have made a better choice, and when were they getting married. He hoped it would be soon. Like the queen, he thought they should get out of the public eye and the press quickly, and marriage was the fastest way to do that. It seemed like the wrong reason to marry, to both of them.

Jonathan called to tell her he was thrilled, he liked Anthony immensely, and to do whatever she wanted. But the palace and even Anthony's father were pushing for a fast marriage, which felt rushed to them. They refused to be pushed, much to the queen's chagrin, but she had bigger problems with her sister.

Annie went to Saint Tropez with Anthony that summer for her holiday, and they were beleaguered by the paparazzi and followed everywhere and had to take refuge on a friend's yacht, and sailed for Sardinia, where it happened all over again. It was endless. Whenever they went out, in London or any other city, even if they went to the grocery store, they wound up all over the tabloids, kissing, not kissing, holding hands, having an argument in the park once. Anthony was seriously annoyed about it.

"I don't want them rushing us into marriage. And even if we get married, they'll follow us around now. If we have a baby, have kids, get pregnant, go skiing. Whatever we do, they're going to pursue us. I hate this." He looked furious, and she didn't like it either. "Do you want to get married now?" he asked her bluntly. "I'll do whatever you want." But it took the fun out of it, getting married because they were being pressured into it, by the queen or the tabloids.

"Not really," she said honestly. "Why don't we just call a moratorium on it, and make the decision in two years when I turn twenty-five. I'll be ready then. You'll be thirty-three. And screw what the tabloids think, or anyone else."

"Sounds perfect to me," he agreed. "Two years, and then we'll jump in. Done." He kissed her to seal the deal. It seemed like an unromantic decision, but the right one for them.

The press continued to follow them around after that. But not as avidly. They got bored with it without an engagement or a wedding date. And the queen continued to drop hints whenever she saw them, but she was much more upset about her sister, who seemed to enjoy creating scandals. She always had.

Annie and Anthony were happy as they were. She stayed with him when she was in London, and he stayed in her room at the stables now, since everyone knew about them anyway. His father lent him his house frequently. So everything calmed down, and their relationship continued. In their minds, they figured they'd get married, or at least engaged, in two years when Annie turned twenty-five. It seemed the right age to both of them. And to satisfy her longing to race, Anthony's father convinced her to enter the Newmarket Town Plate that fall. It was the only women's race under jockey club rules. She placed second and was jubilant. But it only made her hunger to race against men more acute. She entered again the following year and placed first. Shortly before her twenty-fifth birthday, before they could revisit their marriage plans, Annie got a call from a famous trainer in Lexington, Kentucky. He invited her to race for the stable he worked for, in the Blue Grass Stakes Thoroughbred race at Keeneland racecourse in Lexington. She would be competing against male jockeys for a million-dollar purse. It was a pari-mutuel race, the opportunity she'd longed for all her life. They had heard of her, and seen her race at the Newmarket Town Plate. She would be the first female jockey registered for the race in Kentucky, and her heart was pounding when she hung up after the call. She was so excited she could taste it. She had waited for this moment for years, and she knew she was ready. She had accepted on the phone, and now she had to tell Anthony. She hoped he'd be reasonable about it. She knew Lord Hatton would be excited for her, and Jonathan would too.

She waited until Anthony came up for the weekend, and didn't say anything to him about it before that. They were paying her a fortune to do it. But she wasn't doing it for the money, although that was nice too. She was doing it because it was her dream, and she knew she had to do it. And she expected Anthony to know that too.

There was no avoiding the subject. He could tell that she was hiding something, and she didn't want to conceal it from him. She told him about the call an hour after he got there.

"You turned them down, I hope?" he said, looking tense, his eyes never leaving hers.

"I couldn't. I've waited all my life for this, and you know it. I have to do it."

"And risk your life as a jockey? Competing against men?" He looked horrified.

"I'm not going to die, Anthony. This is my dream," she said quietly.

"I thought we were your dream, you and I. If I ask you not to do it, will you turn it down?" He was turning it into a proving ground, and a test, which wasn't fair. She didn't answer for a moment, and then shook her head. It was a crucial moment in their relationship, and she knew it. But she couldn't give up the race for him.

"I can't. Don't ask me to do that. It's not right. I've wanted to be a jockey as long as I've been riding."

"What about us?"

"Why can't we do both? I'm not going to race forever. But give me a year. There's talk that they'll allow women to race in the Kentucky Derby next year. It would be the high point of my life."

"I don't want to be married to a jockey. What do you want, Annie? Me? Us? Or to be a jockey? You can't have both." His eyes were like steel as he looked at her. He had dug his heels in. He had never said it as clearly before. She was twenty-five and didn't want to give up her dreams or lose them.

"Why not? Why do I have to give up my dreams to marry you?"

"Because I don't want to be married to a woman who could die any day of the week, or break her neck and be paralyzed, just because she wants the thrill of winning and can't give it up. It's not compatible with marriage and having babies, and you know it."

"So we wait a year. Let me race for a year, and then I'll quit. I promise." After the Kentucky Derby if the rumors were true and she could compete in it in a year.

"I don't believe you. You won't quit. It's in your blood. You have a decision to make," he said in a voice that was pure ice. "If you go to Kentucky and ride in this race, it's over with us. I'm finished. If you want to be married to me, turn the race down. Once you start riding as a jockey in legitimate races against men, you'll never give it up. I know you." She knew he was right, and she was willing to make the sacrifice for him, but not just yet. She wanted to live her dreams first. This was her chance. He gave her a hard look that left no room for argument. "Let me know what you decide," he said, and slammed out of his father's house, where they'd been discussing it. His father was in his office and had left them the house. She heard Anthony's car drive away.

She was heartbroken over his decision, but she thought he was being unreasonable, and there was no way she was going to give up this race for him. It was a huge deal and the beginning of a whole new chapter of her life. She had waited all her life to be a jockey, legally, in the big leagues, not some second-rate amateur race. She had waited two and a half years to get engaged and become his wife. There was no choice in her mind. She was going to the States, and if he couldn't live with it, then he wasn't the right man for her. She was *not* going to give up her dreams for him. And if he loved her, he wouldn't ask her to.

She didn't call Anthony and he didn't call her. Three weeks later, she was on the plane to Kentucky. Her dreams with Anthony were over. Her dreams of being a jockey just meant too much to her to give up, even for him, and she truly loved him. She expected him to understand how much the race meant to her. He did, which was why he had left her and hadn't called. The race meant more to her than he did.

Chapter 17

The race in Kentucky in June was the most exciting event of her
life. It lived up to all her expectations. The horse she was hired
to ride was spectacular. She had heard about the breeder for years
but never met him. Lord Hatton knew him, and had guessed that
they would give her a fabulous horse to ride and he'd been right. The
queen had called to wish her luck. Victoria had sent a telegram, and
Jonathan had called and told her she could do it, to focus and think
of nothing else.

Anthony was heavy on her mind, and her heart, but she couldn't
allow herself that now. She couldn't think of anything except the
race. She would talk to him afterward, and try to make peace with
him. But for now there was only the track she'd be running, the race,
and the horse she'd be riding. Nothing else in the world mattered.
She spoke to no one in the last week except the breeder, the trainer,
and the owner. And she trained on the horse all week, getting to
know him.

She slept two hours the night before the race, and woke up at four in the morning. She took a long hot shower and went for a run to try to relax, and was in the horse's stall and had a long conversation with him. She knew he could carry her to victory. The odds were thirty to one against her. No one thought a woman could do it in a race like this. It was a historic moment. There was one other woman registered to ride. She was riding a horse that had won numerous races in the States. He was a sure thing, and an easier ride than the horse Annie would be riding. Hers was named Ginger Boy, and no one was sure what he could do. Except Annie, who believed in him, and knew he could win.

She stood quietly stroking him, and talking to him. "We can do it, you know. I know I can, and so can you. Don't let them spook you, Boy. Just take it nice and easy at first." They weighed her, and she put on the colors of the owner she was riding for. Her helmet was secure, and the owner and trainer watched her as she mounted Ginger Boy. Her small white face was serious and her blue eyes looked huge.

"Good luck, Your Royal Highness," the owner said, hoping he had done the right thing hiring her. She looked so delicate, and her hands looked so small compared to the huge horse she was riding. He was a powerful beast.

"Annie will do," she said to the owner, and went to line up, as they watched her, and then the owner went to his box to watch the race. It was being televised around the world on sports channels everywhere. There were news crews all around the racetrack. Annie saw nothing as she lined up, except the track and the horse she was riding. She thought of nothing except what they had to do.

They got a slow start as she intended, and ran steadily, gathering momentum and speed as they went, passing horses, flying like the wind, pressing harder, going faster, and in the final stretch she pushed him as hard as she could, knowing what she needed from him, and Ginger Boy knew it too. "Give it to me now, come on, Boy, you can do it. We can do it!" He ran faster and harder than any other horse she'd ever been on. He flew over the ground, and she felt as though they were running above the ground in slow motion. She heard nothing except his breathing and her own, faster and faster. She heard people screaming and the roar of the crowd. She flew through the finish line with no sense of who or what was around her, or where the other horses were. All she knew and felt was Ginger Boy. She galloped him for a few minutes after the finish line to slow him down, and patted his neck with all her strength. "Good Boy, you did it! I'm proud of you," she said and finally looked up. She had no idea how they had finished, and she saw the trainer running toward them, he was crying and waving his hands as she slowed Ginger Boy, and the trainer reached up and hugged her.

"You did it! Oh my God, you did it!"

"How did we do?" she asked him, as Ginger Boy danced and she gently led him in a walk off the track. She could still hear the crowd screaming and see people waving.

"Are you serious?" The trainer looked at her as though she had just landed from outer space. "You came in first, by five lengths. You made history." She jumped down and he hugged her, and she led Ginger Boy off the track toward the winner's circle. Her legs were shaking and she was in a daze, as the grooms took his lead away from her, and people hugged her and lifted her off the ground. Camera crews were in her face, and then the owner was hugging her and his wife was crying. The other female jockey had come in eighth.

"You were the most beautiful sight I've ever seen," the owner said to her with tears running down his cheeks. At that moment, she wished she could share it with Anthony and Jonathan and all the people she loved. She couldn't wait to see the footage of the race. But for that one moment in time, it had been just her and Ginger Boy, and nothing else in the world mattered. She was a born jockey and she knew it. She knew she had done the right thing coming to Kentucky. She couldn't have given this up, and was glad she hadn't. This was her moment. She wanted Anthony to be part of it, but he wasn't.

She gave two TV interviews and one to the BBC before she left the racetrack in the owner's Rolls. Her legs felt like rubber and her head was pounding. She had gone to see Ginger Boy and thanked him before she left.

She went back to the hotel and watched it all on TV on the replays. Jonathan called her, and the queen, and Anthony's father, and told her how incredible she had been. Anthony didn't call, and she realized now that it probably was over, but she wasn't sorry, even though she loved him. She hadn't given up her dream.

She flew back to England the next day, and had a hero's welcome at the stables when she got back to Newmarket.

The queen had sent a car and driver for her to take her back to the stables, and she came to see her the next day. She hugged Annie when she saw her, and told her how proud she was of her. She was as excited as Annie, and knew how proud Charlotte would have been of her.

"How's Anthony?" the queen asked with a worried look.

"He's not," Annie said quietly. "He said that if I went, it was over with us. So I guess it is." She looked sad about it, but she didn't regret it, and her aunt nodded.

"He might get over it," she said gently.

"Maybe not," Annie said. "But I couldn't give it up for him. I waited too long for this."

"I'm glad you didn't," Alexandra said quietly. "You'd have regretted it all your life, and resented him for it." The owner had accepted the trophy for her. No one could take away the records she'd broken, or the victory she'd had with Ginger Boy. Winning first place had been incredible.

After the queen left, Annie got a call from the owner of a horse farm in Virginia. He wanted her to ride his horse in the Kentucky Derby next year if female jockeys were admitted, and it looked as though they would be. She accepted on the spot.

She called Jonathan and told him that night and asked him to go with her, if she rode in the Derby next year. She was on a high now, and Anthony was still lodged in her heart like a glass splinter, but she didn't have to give any of it up now, and she couldn't. He was right.

She called Anthony the day after she got back from Kentucky, but he didn't pick up, and he didn't call her. She called him at his office, and they said he was in a meeting. And he didn't return that call either. So she had her answer. She had won a major female racing victory in horseracing history, but lost her man. He had said it would be that way, and he was sticking to it. He knew what he wanted and so did she. But she couldn't let him control her or force her to give up her dreams. It would have been so wrong. In the end, her being a princess hadn't done them in, but her being a jockey had.

*   *   *

She saw him in the paper the next day, at a party with a famous model. She was wrapped around him like a snake. So he had gone back to his old life. And she had too. The life where the only thing that mattered was the horses, and now the victories. It hurt seeing him in the papers, but not as much as giving up the race would have. She couldn't let him cheat her of this, and she hadn't.

She saw him in the papers again a week later with a different girl. The owner who had asked her to ride for him next year in the Kentucky Derby flew to London to meet her. She saw Anthony in the papers again with a Hollywood starlet in London to promote her new movie. They'd gone dancing at Annabel's. Somehow the thrill of the women he was presumably sleeping with didn't seem equal to the race she had won, or racing in the Kentucky Derby, whether she won or lost next year. She hoped he was happy, but doubted that he was. His were hollow victories. She still loved him, and she missed him. She had wanted to share this with him, but not in a million years would she give this up for him. She couldn't.

She had dinner with Anthony's father at his house two weeks after she got home. He congratulated her and they talked about the race for half an hour, and then he told her how sorry he was about her and Anthony.

"So am I," she said sadly. "I just couldn't give it up for him, and he wouldn't settle for anything less. It was all or nothing."

"That's how life is sometimes," he said. "You did the right thing. There are some things you can't compromise and shouldn't. This was one of them. My son is a stubborn man, and a fool sometimes. We all are, I suppose. You're worth a million of these idiots he runs around with, or used to. I'm sorry to see him go back to that." Not as sorry as she was. But not sorry enough to back down and give it up.

"So am I," she said softly.

"He'll regret it," his father said. It was small consolation.

"Maybe not. Maybe we just weren't meant to be."

"What would you rather be? One of the most famous jockeys in history, the first woman to win a race like that, or his wife after you gave all that up?"

"I wanted both," she said honestly.

"It doesn't always work that way."

"I guess not."

A month later, in July, she flew to Virginia to meet the horse she hoped to ride the following year in the Derby. It wasn't sure yet. She and the owner had dinner, and discussed the race and his horse's history. He was an interesting choice for the Derby, and had won some big races before, but he had an irregular record at others.

"My boy will like the Derby," the owner said and smiled at her.

"So will I, Mr. MacPherson." She smiled back at him.

She rode him before flying back to England, and he was incredible. He responded to the lightest touch, voice commands, and almost to her thought processes as though he was psychic. The competition in the Derby would be stiff, and she would train with him before the race and study the other horses' histories too. She spoke to Lord Hatton about it, and he gave her some advice without ever having seen Aswan, the horse she'd be riding. He knew his bloodline, the trainer, and the owner.

She went to spend two weeks in Kent with Jonathan and the boys then, and spent August at Balmoral with her royal family. It was peaceful and relaxing, with barbecues and picnics and family dinners. George, Albert, and William had grown up even more, and she felt at home with all of them.

She had heard that Anthony was in Saint Tropez for the month and tried not to think about it. Her heart still ached when someone said his name.

The queen brought up her spectacular win in Kentucky again.

"Your mother would have been proud of you, and green with envy," she said, and Annie laughed. "She would have given anything to do what you just did. We're all proud of you, Annie."

"Thank you, ma'am," her niece said respectfully.

"Lord Hatton and I have a question to ask you. Will you ride for us in the Gold Cup Race at the Royal Ascot Meeting next June? We'd be honored to have you race for us. We'd like you to ride Starlight." He was a beautiful white horse, but he was young, and hadn't been in many races. "Not an obvious choice, but we think he's ready for his first big race, and a strong showing, and if anyone can make it happen, you've proven that you can. Will you do it?" she asked, as Annie looked at her in amazement.

"Are you serious, ma'am? I'd be honored. I'd like to start working with him soon. I haven't ridden him much." She loved the idea of riding on home turf, in England, on one of their horses, for her queen and aunt. It didn't get better than that. She thought the horse was ready too. He was at Lord Hatton's stables in Newmarket, so she could work with him anytime. And Royal Ascot was in June, and the Kentucky Derby in May, so she could ride in both races.

The Gold Cup was the highlight of the four-day Royal Ascot Meeting. At two miles and four furlongs, it was one of the longest races of the flat season, and a real test of stamina for horse and rider. Annie couldn't think of a greater thrill than riding in that race for the queen. The Ascot racecourse was in Berkshire, six miles from Windsor Castle, so Annie assumed the whole family would stay there. She was so excited she could hardly speak, she just beamed. And the queen was equally pleased she'd accepted.

Her aunt Victoria called her that night from the South of France. She was due at Balmoral any day.

"Well, you're certainly giving us some dignity, dear girl. I'm so proud of you, I could burst. George called me at midnight the night you won the race in Kentucky. He stayed up to watch you. Actually, half of England did. I won a thousand pounds on a wager, so thank you for that. I'll take you to lunch with my winnings when you come to London."

"Aunt Alexandra just asked me to ride for her in the Ascot Gold Cup next year."

"Fantastic!" Victoria said enthusiastically.

She hesitated for an instant then, and decided to tell her. "I saw Anthony the other night, at a party down here." She knew it was a delicate subject.

"How is he?" Annie tried to sound neutral about it, but she wasn't. It still hurt terribly, and Victoria could hear it. But she didn't want to keep it secret that she'd seen him, in case Annie heard it from someone else.

"Actually, he's a mess. He looks terrible. He looks like he's been drunk since you left for Kentucky. I saw him before that. I think he got sacked from his job, but I'm not sure of it. He didn't tell me, someone else did. You know how London is, a hotbed of gossip. He didn't mention you, but I suspect he misses you terribly. He's a fool if he doesn't. But he's probably too proud to admit it."

"I called him a few times, but he didn't pick up or call me back. It's just as well. There's nothing much to say now. I did exactly what he forbade me to."

"'Sorry I was an idiot' is always refreshing, but they never say that, do they? They paint themselves into a corner, and then go up in smoke. He had some dreadful woman with him. He looked like he was ready to kill her. Maybe he will, and go to prison. Suitable punishment for leaving you. He should at least apologize for that."

"It was a point of pride for both of us," Annie said in a subdued voice. They had been apart for three months by then instead of getting engaged. And she was booked for two major races next year, which he would never tolerate.

"It always is with men, darling girl. It always is. Well, I'll see you at the races, as they say. I'm glad Alexandra asked you to ride for us. You might as well instead of winning for the Americans. Give us some of that magic dust." Annie was happy talking to her, and she liked hearing about Anthony, even if he was unhappy and hated her for putting her dreams ahead of everything else, for a while anyway. She doubted that she'd do it forever, but for a while. She could pick and choose which races she'd do now, which was a nice position to be in. She hadn't expected it to happen this quickly. No one had. And she least of all. Anthony had predicted it.

She lay in bed and thought about him after she and Victoria hung up. She wondered if he was as unhappy as Victoria thought he was, or if he also felt he had done the right thing. He probably wouldn't admit it to anybody, and she'd never know. She doubted that he'd ever speak to her again, or not for a long time. Their paths would cross inevitably at some point. They had gone out for almost three years, but that meant nothing in the end, and certainly not now.

Whatever they had shared was dead and buried. He wanted nothing to do with her. He hadn't even congratulated her for her victory in Kentucky. He was history in her life now.

She went back to Newmarket at the end of August, and began training with Starlight for the Gold Cup race at Ascot, which was still nine months away. She had gotten confirmation that she could ride in the Kentucky Derby in May, and planned to spend March and April in Virginia, training with Aswan for the Derby.

She spent the next six months working hard for Anthony's father, training new horses and working with Starlight. She worked diligently with Starlight for Ascot and was pleased to find that the horse was both high-strung and receptive and easy to work with. Within a month, Annie felt in harmony with him, and was able to direct him with the slightest touch, and when she gave him his head, he flew over the terrain and was steady and sure-footed. His size and strength were in his favor, and even though he lacked age and experience, she could sense that he would be a great racehorse one day. What she needed to do was move him ahead quickly to a level of training he hadn't achieved yet when they started.

"How's he doing?" Lord Hatton asked her when he came out to the field where she was working with him, and watched him for a while. She had a remarkable, almost psychic sense of the horses she worked with, and he was impressed by the results she had gotten. Starlight was unpredictable and sometimes uneven in his progress, but she was able to get from him what no one else had yet, and she could see that the giant animal trusted her completely. He was a different horse than when she'd started working with him.

She spent Christmas at Sandringham with the royal family and New Year's with Jonathan and the boys in Kent.

Jonathan accompanied her to Virginia in March and stayed with her while she trained with Aswan. It had been an arduous year, nothing but work, and her skills were stronger than ever.

Jonathan was there when she came in second at the Kentucky Derby. It was an extraordinary win and made headlines worldwide. She returned to a hero's welcome in London, and celebrated her birthday with the family at Windsor Castle two weeks after she returned. She had just turned twenty-six.

It had been exactly a year since her breakup with Anthony. She was surprised when he sent her a note congratulating her for her heroic win at the Derby, and wishing her a happy birthday. She hadn't heard from him in a year. She thanked him, and was completely focused on training for Ascot. She was staying at Windsor Castle until the race in June. Their paths hadn't crossed in a year.

The day before the race, she let Starlight rest, so he'd be fresh and anxious to perform on the day of the big event. He was nervous and excited when they got him into his stall at the racetrack, and she took him out to exercise him briefly. They had brought two grooms and one of the trainers with them. That night, Annie went out to check on him and spoke to him soothingly.

The morning of the race, she could see he was aching to run. It was what he wanted to do with her now.

The royal party arrived in horse-drawn landaus and paraded along the track in front of the crowd.

The entire family entered the royal box. Everyone had come. The queen and Prince Edward were there, Victoria, and Alexandra's three boys had come from school. Jonathan and the Markhams were there, he'd brought the twins, and Penny, the woman Jonathan had been dating for some time now. Lord Hatton was seated next to the queen, and when Annie checked the box with binoculars, she gave a start when she saw Anthony standing just outside the box. She assumed he had come for his father, but she felt odd seeing him and wondered if their paths would cross after the race. She hoped not, and was sorry she'd seen him now. She watched him take a seat between Victoria and William, who was nearly hopping up and down he was so excited. She smiled when she watched him. They had brought him home from Eton. He had just turned sixteen, and the other boys nineteen and twenty. It was a major event, and one of the most important races in England. She never thought she'd see the day when she'd be racing in it. She was the first female jockey, and the only woman racing that day. There were very few who were ready for the transition, but the queen was setting the example in England after the Kentucky Derby. Annie had been one of two women at the Blue Grass Stakes and the Kentucky Derby. And in future, she knew that eventually there would be others, but not many yet.

She let Starlight walk a little, but he was too anxious to leave him out for long. She spoke to him soothingly, and then it was time to take their places. Annie was wearing the queen's royal colors of purple with gold braid, scarlet sleeves, and black velvet helmet with gold fringe. It was the greatest honor of her life. She was satisfied with the order for the race, and avoided looking for familiar faces as they rode to the start. She kept her mind and her eyes on Starlight, and nothing else. She praised him as they waited and then they were off. She gave him his head quickly because she knew him well now, and it was how he liked to run. He began strong and then settled into his pace, as she edged him forward and kept him steady on course, and then she urged him to increase his speed, pushing him harder and harder to his limits, using his strength and his size to gain momentum, and then she forced him on past what he wanted, but using his trust in her to push him beyond anything reasonable. He pounded and pounded and pounded the ground, faster and faster until his hooves barely seemed to touch the earth. If someone had asked, they would have thought she was flying, and then she pushed him for the final furlong, and she could see the others slip away as she and Starlight moved ahead, and with a final burst of agony and insanity, she asked his utmost from him, and drove him even harder, and they crossed the finish line alone. They kept going until she could slow him down without his getting injured, and came back, and looked toward the royal box with a broad grin. They had done it. Starlight had come through for his owners, his queen, and his jockey.

She had no doubt this time. They had finished in first place. And the announcer declared the winner, Her Majesty Queen Alexandra's horse Starlight, ridden by the queen's niece, Her Royal Highness Princess Anne Louise Windsor. It was the proudest moment of Annie's life, and one of the queen's best too. Annie could see them jumping up and down in the box, and could almost hear them screaming. The roar of the crowd had been tremendous, and Starlight looked startled by the noise, but Annie kept him in control. The queen and Lord Hatton came down from the royal box to accept the trophy with her, and the queen reached up and patted Annie's arm and thanked her. They were both crying and didn't even know it.

"What a wonderful race you ran, Annie," she said happily.

"It was all Starlight," she said modestly, and Lord Hatton was grinning broadly, as he thanked her, and she rode Starlight back to his stall. She stayed with Starlight for a few minutes until he started to calm down, and then she left him to the grooms and trainer, and walked toward the royal box to find her family. She was still feeling dazed herself and unsteady on her feet. She didn't even bother to clean up. She was covered with mud, and had splashes of it on her face and all over her helmet, when she walked straight into Anthony coming toward her. She stopped when she saw him and didn't know what to say.

"You were fantastic!" he said, and then folded her into his arms without caring about the mud all over her, still wet from the race.

"I'm filthy, don't . . ." He kissed her before she could stop him and it reminded her of the first time in Sandringham when he had surprised her and told her he loved her. When he finally stopped, she was even more breathless than she'd been from the race. And just as surprised as she'd been the first time he kissed her.

"I'm sorry I was such a fool. I wanted to tell you before the race, but I didn't want to throw you off. My God, you were incredible. You were a blur on the racetrack." Anthony was smiling at her as she looked up at him in amazement.

"Why did you come?" she asked him, rubber-legged from the ride. She imagined that he was there for his father.

"Why do you think? To tell you I love you and that I'm sorry. I was wrong, and you were right. This is what you were born to do. I was wrong to try and stop you. Thank God you didn't listen. It's a damn fine dream, and if we wait ten years to have children, then so be it." She was only twenty-six.

"I just wanted one year, not ten," she said softly. "I've already done what I wanted. This race was my dream, to do it here, for England, and for Alexandra. I won't do it forever, I promise," she said, and he stopped her and kissed her again.

"Don't make promises you can't keep. You're the best jockey I've ever seen. My father thinks so too. And to think I damn near killed you racing to a tree. Lucky I didn't," he said, and she laughed as she fell into step with him and he tucked her hand into his arm. She wanted to see the others now too.

"Why didn't you call me back?" she asked as they walked around the racetrack to the royal box.

"Because I wanted to be right, and I knew I wasn't. I got sacked, by the way. I was drunk for three weeks and screwed up all their events. I want to work with my father, and help him manage the farm. I belong there, and so do you," he said softly, and then stopped her for a minute before they reached the others. "Will you marry me, Annie, even though I was a fool?"

"Yes," she said in a voice so soft that only he could hear it.

"Do I have to ask your aunt?"

"Probably. And the prime minister, and the cabinet, and the lord chamberlain, and a million other people, and my father." They were both laughing as he followed her up the stairs to where they were all milling around and congratulating each other. The queen smiled when she saw them. Things had improved immeasurably in the last few minutes, and she wasn't sure if Annie was smiling because she'd won, or because Anthony had just kissed her. The queen had seen it through her binoculars and was pleased.

"I have a question to ask you later, ma'am," he said softly, and her smile widened.

"The answer is yes," she said, and he hugged her.

"Thank you, ma'am." They all stayed in the box for another half hour, and then left. They were having dinner at Windsor Castle that night, and there was much to celebrate. Annie left the box with them, with an arm around each of her brothers, and her three young cousins right behind them. Her face was still splattered with mud, and she'd never looked happier. And before they got into the van the queen had brought for them, Anthony stopped Annie and kissed her again. "You are one hell of an amazing rider," he said with a look of awe on his face. "Thank God you didn't let me bully you. I'm sorry I did," he said after the others were in the van.

"It doesn't matter. I didn't listen to you. I couldn't. But I love you and always will. I never stopped loving you all this year." But it had been a long, lonely year without him.

"I hope our children ride like you do. You made history today, Annie." And they both knew she would again. Possibly many times, and then one day she'd retire, but she would always have the memory of what she'd accomplished. No one could ever take that from her now. Anthony knew better than anyone that no one ever should. This moment, and this day, and this achievement belonged to her, and rightfully so.

"Are you two coming, or are we going to die of old age waiting?" Victoria shouted out of the van at them.

"Sorry," Anthony said, helped Annie into the van, and hopped in behind her. They took off for the castle with everyone laughing and talking about what a great and utterly unforgettable day it had been.

Chapter 18

Jonathan and Annie were waiting in a small room at St. Margaret's Church on the grounds of Westminster Abbey, the Anglican parish church near the Palace of Westminster. It had been built in the eleventh century. She had chosen a simple white lace gown with long sleeves and a tiny waist, and she looked more than ever like a fairy or a very young girl. She was wearing a veil, and the gown had a train which stretched behind her as she stood nervously with her stepfather, waiting for their cue to start down the aisle.

Sir Malcolm Harding, the queen's secretary, came in holding a leather box and handed it to Annie as she looked at him in surprise. Her grandmother, the Queen Mother, had given her a double strand of her own pearls that morning as a wedding gift, and said they had been a gift from her grandmother, Queen Alexandra, on her wedding day. The queen had given Annie a heart-shaped brooch by Carl Fabergé encrusted with diamonds and pearls on pale pink enamel, which she had worn at her wedding, and she had no daughters to pass it on to, so she was giving it to her sister's child. And even more meaningful to her, Annie was wearing the gold bracelet with the gold heart charm that had been her mother's and Alexandra had given her.

"Who's this from?" Annie asked Sir Malcolm about the antique leather box she took from him, and he smiled.

"Your husband, ma'am. He wanted you to have it immediately." She opened it in haste and smiled when she saw it. It was the tiara he had borrowed from Garrard's for her, that had been given to Queen Victoria by her husband, Prince Albert. Theirs was one of the great love stories of the British monarchy. "He was hoping you could wear it with your veil. It's your wedding gift, ma'am." It fit perfectly over it, and was just the right proportion, as though it had been made for her. Annie had loved it when she'd seen it, when Anthony borrowed it for her for the party. She had remembered it, and apparently so had Anthony. It was back in the right hands, with Queen Victoria's great-great-great-granddaughter. Sir Malcolm took the box and disappeared with it. Annie looked up at the man who had been her father for most of her life.

"You look like a queen, not just a princess," Jonathan said, in awe of the moment. She had chosen to have no attendants, only him walking her to her husband in the small chapel.

"I love you, Papa," she whispered.

"I love you too, Annie," he said as the music started, the door opened, and they headed toward the aisle. When they reached it, she saw Anthony waiting for her at the altar. It was meant to be, just as everything that had happened was. Being brought back to the Windsors, where she belonged, learning about her mother, meeting Anthony, winning the races, and now this moment when nothing else mattered. She had lost him for a year and found him again, or he had found her. She knew she would love him forever, like Victoria and Albert.

They walked slowly down the aisle, and she stopped next to Anthony, who was beaming at her. They had already been through so much, and knew each other so well, their fears and their dreams, their hopes for the future. Her dreams had already come true, and now she had him, and hopefully one day their children.

Jonathan took his place in the pew next to Penny and the twins, and across the aisle, the prince consort sat next to the queen, as Alexandra and her sister Victoria held hands, watching Annie, and remembering when there were three of them so long ago. The Queen Mother sat next to them, with tears in her eyes, remembering Charlotte too, and all three of them were struck by how much Annie looked like her. She was the image of the mother she had never known.

"She looks just like her, doesn't she?" Victoria whispered to Alexandra, and the Queen Mother took Victoria's other hand and held it. They were all there now, with their history and their stories, their loves and their losses, and George the future king sat right behind his mother, with his brothers beside him. Just as the past stood behind them, the future lay ahead with George and his brothers, and Annie wore the tiara their great-great-great-grandmother Queen Victoria had been given by her husband. It was all woven together like a never-ending chain of love stories and people and monarchs, as Annie looked into the eyes of the man she loved and was about to marry.

"Thank you," she whispered to him, and pointed to the tiara.

"I love you," Anthony whispered back, as Jonathan watched the little girl he had loved and taught to ride and had become a princess.

They all stood together, as Alexandra and Victoria thought of Charlotte, and seeing their niece standing there in her image, it was almost as if Charlotte had come home at last.

As Anthony and Annie exchanged their vows, the past and the present, and the future, blended into one shining moment which united them all in memory forever.

Danielle Steel

Have you liked Danielle Steel on Facebook?

Be the first to know about Danielle's latest books,
access exclusive competitions and stay in touch
with news about Danielle.

www.facebook.com/DanielleSteelOfficial

EXPECT A MIRACLE

'The right words can bring you back to reality or make you dream, can comfort you when you're in despair or make you laugh out loud. The right words can open your mind or give you hope.'

Danielle Steel is the author of more than 140 novels and has sold 800 million copies of her books across the world. She is one of our best-loved and most influential modern writers.

As a young girl, Danielle began collecting quotations that had special meaning to her. In *Expect a Miracle*, Danielle has compiled some of her favourite quotations, proverbs and sayings to live and love by. These are words to comfort you, to move you, to inspire you, and to make you laugh.

With a heartfelt introduction by Danielle, *Expect a Miracle* is a perfect companion to her much-treasured books.

Coming soon

PURE STEEL. PURE HEART.

Pin Down

Pin Down

ONE GIRL'S HARROWING AND DISTURBING
TALE OF INSTITUTIONALISED ABUSE

—

TERESA COOPER

Dedication

To Deborah, who touched the hearts of those who
knew her and to my three children, who bring me
such happiness.

———

First published in Great Britain in 2007 by Orion Books
an imprint of the Orion Publishing Group Ltd
Orion House, 5 Upper St Martin's Lane,

:d,
h
se
of

ISBN: 9780 75288 611 8

Printed in Great Britain by Clays Ltd, St Ives plc

To protect the innocent, some of the names and details in this book
have been changed. All the events described actually occurred.

www.orionbooks.co.uk

Acknowledgements

I would like to thank my children, who have seen me through difficult times and kept me strong. Their love and support has been paramount to the mother and person I am today. They are my life and the air that I breathe and I am so very proud of the people they have become. My love is forever with them every step of the way and I wouldn't be here if it were not for their love and direction.

I would like to say thank you to my sister, whom I love dearly, and my brother, and may the future bring them much happiness.

I need to mention my eighteen pets that make my home and life complete in so many ways and fill the house with love and companionship. Not to mention all the antics they get up to, which have been the source of many magical moments for me and my children. Thank you to our vet, who does a great job.

I would like to say thank you to Clare, Amanda, Angela and Lorraine at Orion Publishing, who have been a tower of strength and support, but also for being wonderful to work with and know. Thank you to Orion for their support in bringing my book to you.

In April 2006 I also met Eve White, my fantastic agent, who has been there for me every step of the way including my highs and lows. Your support and amazing character have been exceptional.

A very special thank you to Rebecca, who has worked very closely with me on the book and our friendship is one I treasure. It has been an emotional journey for both of us and one that will not be forgotten. So much emotion went into *Pin Down*, going through the files and documents, and I couldn't have done it without her.

Acknowledgements

Jules, my best friend at Kendall House, was there for me not only at Kendall House but also since our recent reunion, supporting me, mothering me, keeping me strong and being my rock.

My warmest thank you and love to the late Mr and Mrs Whattler, who showed me the most sincere kindness and courage during the most traumatic time of my life, and to their family for all their support and care. The love I received from this special family was paramount in my life and one I will always hold dear. I will always be so grateful that the Whattlers came into my life when I was at Kendall House. Many children in the care system never have the opportunity to experience the love and care I received from the Whattlers. I know there are people out there who can give children from broken homes the support they need and work patiently with them to develop their true personality and bring out the best in them.

Much love to all my friends including Chris, Dave, Julie, Helen, Roger, Anwer, Paul, Angela and Jennifer, who have seen me through and been there for me every step of the way.

Thanks also to Church in Society, especially Adrian and David for providing information, files, listening to me when I needed someone to talk to and for their support.

To Rob, my webmaster, who has made the website **no2abuse** possible and for his continued friendship.

To John Lord for his website www.about-gravesend.co.uk, and for his support, research skills and providing me with photos and information.

To Richard Lord at Gravesend Library, who has been an asset to his profession and contributed his expertise, research and support.

Barnet Local Studies & Archives for providing photos.

To Steve at Chelmsford Library for providing information.

To the Salvation Army for their support and The Benevolent Fund for providing photos.

A special thank you to everyone who has given me support and to survivors of abuse who fight hard to help make changes.

Teresa Cooper
April 2007

CHAPTER ONE

June 1971

'Hurry up!' Mum yelled.

She grabbed my arm and dragged me up a gravel path leading to a big, old-fashioned house. On each side of the entrance there was a tall stone pillar with a stone ball on top. The house was surrounded by trees and enclosed by a high grey wall.

Clutching my favourite doll with one hand and pushing my toy pram with the other, I tried to keep up as Mum rushed towards the front door. But she was going too fast for me. I stumbled and fell, yelping with pain as the gravel cut into my knees.

'Hush, or they'll hear us!' Mum said in a forced whisper. Picking myself up, I gulped back my tears and tried to be brave.

At the entrance to the house, she took a piece of paper out of her bag and pinned it to my chest. She gave me a sad half-smile and tears welled up in her eyes. 'Make sure you're a good girl for your mum,' she said. 'I love you. Always remember that.'

I watched in bewilderment as she walked away, leaving me behind on the doorstep. She picked up her pace and started hurrying towards a car by the side of the road. I could just about make out the driver. He had a wrinkled brown face and wiry grey hair. I'd never seen him before.

I felt a lump rise up the back of my throat. 'Mum!' I called out, tears streaming down my face. Without turning back, she disappeared into the car and it pulled away, out of sight.

I didn't know what to do. I was used to Mum's erratic ways, but she'd never left me alone like this before. When would she be coming back? I sat on the doorstep and began to wait, but waiting was boring, so I started playing with the new doll that Mum had given me for my fourth birthday the week before. She was beautiful. I loved her long golden hair and gleaming blue eyes.

I noticed that Mum had left behind a black bin liner she'd been carrying. Curious, I peeped inside. It was stuffed with all my toys and clothes. I pulled a few things out and lined them up. At least I'd have plenty to play with until she came back. I was used to amusing myself and there was a lot here to distract me.

An hour passed. I wondered how much longer I'd have to wait. Suddenly the front door of the house swung open and I heard a voice behind me. Turning round, I froze at the sight of an old lady in the doorway.

'Hello, what have we got here, then?' she said in a calm, gentle tone.

I put my doll in front of my face. 'Fuck off,' I muttered.

The old lady reached down and unpinned the note from my chest. 'Now then, we don't tolerate bad language here,' she said. She took a firm grasp of my hand and led me inside the house. Within moments several children had gathered in the hallway. They stared at me, saying nothing. My legs began to tremble.

Another lady appeared. 'Who's this?' she asked brightly.

'It appears to be Derek's daughter,' the old lady said, scanning my mum's note. 'Can you stay here with her for a minute while I make a phone call?'

Holding on to my doll for dear life, I tried to avoid the stares of the other children. One of the bigger girls stepped towards me and gave me a dirty look, as if she knew me. She had long mousey hair, just like mine. A skinny boy wearing wonky glasses came up beside her. His white-blond hair was cut into a basin shape and his front teeth were missing.

'You're Teresa,' the boy said. I told him to fuck off too.

The old lady came back and knelt beside me. 'Well, young lady, we're very glad to see you,' she said. 'You've been missing for quite a while now and we've all been worried about you.'

What did she mean? I hadn't been missing. I'd been with my mum. 'Fuck off, fuck off, fuck off!' I shouted.

The children around me laughed, but the old lady's face grew stern. I ran and hid behind a big white door, shaking with fear and confusion. She followed me. 'Don't be scared,' she said. 'I'm Miss Foley, a friend of your father's. You're safe now.'

'Leave me alone!' I screamed.

The doorbell rang. Miss Foley went to answer it. A man stepped into the hallway. The girl with long mousey hair and the boy in the wonky glasses ran up to him and clung to his legs.

'Where is she?' he said. I peeped out from behind the door. He turned and walked towards me, his expression eager.

Cowering, I looked up into his face as he reached down and gathered me into his arms. His eyes were full of warmth. Tears rolled down his cheeks as he held me tightly to him.

'Teresa! My little girl!' he sobbed. 'I'm your daddy. We're so glad to have you back. Remember David and Bernadette, your brother and sister? We've all missed you so much.'

'I knew immediately it was her,' Miss Foley said.

'It's her all right,' my dad replied. 'Where did you find her? Have the police been told?'

Dad's life was too chaotic to have us living with him, so he left me with Bernadette and David at Miss Foley's children's home in Putney, South West London. I soon settled in. Even though I was only four, I was used to adapting to new situations. My life was constantly changing. At six months old, I'd been put into care for a month while Mum had an operation. Two years later, when she was again admitted to hospital, Bernadette, David and I spent a couple of months at a children's home in Tooting. Not long after that, Mum ran off with one of her boyfriends and I didn't see her again until the day she sneaked back into our flat and snatched me away behind Dad's back.

After that I lived with her in a big house in the countryside, where she was employed as a housekeeper. But she had her work cut out looking after the house and keeping tabs on an inquisitive toddler. First I broke a mirror. Then I let the dog out. Finally Mum lost the job. Shortly after that she dumped me outside Miss Foley's children's home like a piece of lost baggage.

My mother, Georgina Cooper, had not had an easy life. Her father had died young and she had struggled to look after her younger sisters in a desperately unhappy household. Unbeknown to my dad when he married her, she'd fallen pregnant in her late teens and had been forced by her mother to give up the child for adoption, against her will. Afterwards she suffered from a combination of severe post-natal depression and repressed grief. I don't think she ever really recovered. She was always very affected by her hormones.

In the early 1960s post-natal depression was dismissed as 'baby blues' and went untreated. What's more, there was still a huge stigma attached to having an illegitimate child, so there would have been no sympathy for her loss. Shortly after her baby girl was adopted, she met my father, Derek Cooper, and six weeks later they were married.

Dad was always saying that Mum was mental and had lost her marbles, but it was more a case of not getting the help she needed at that crucial time after the adoption. She took the bereavement and depression with her into their relationship and as the years passed she became totally screwed up by it. I was the last of their three children. The oldest was Bernadette. Two years later came David, and two years after him, I was born, 'on the toilet in a nunnery', as my mum described my entry into the world at St Teresa's Hospital in Wimbledon.

My father was a good man with a strong work ethic and sound morals, but a weakness for drink. He had a large family full of interesting characters, but most of them cut him off after he married Mum. They absolutely hated her and told Dad that she had been a prostitute before he met her. I don't know if it was true or not. Either way, they never had a good word to say about her.

Mum and Dad were married for about eight years before Mum left for good, taking me with her. She was petrified of Dad by the end and claimed that he had beaten her senseless countless times. In turn, Dad accused her of having affairs and said that the real reason I'd gone into care so young was because Mum had tried to suffocate me when I was a baby.

They fought like cat and dog and were always blaming each other for something or other.

'I only just managed to stop her from smothering you,' Dad used to say. 'So I was frantic when she stole you and ran off. I didn't know if I'd ever see you alive again.' It was years before I heard Mum's side of the story.

After she dropped me off at Miss Foley's, I didn't see Mum again for what seemed like ages. I missed her desperately. Even though it was good to be around other children and I enjoyed going to nursery school, nothing can replace your mum. I saw quite a lot of Dad though. He used to come round at the end of the day when Bernadette and David finished school. Dad told us that he couldn't have us to live at home with him. He said he couldn't cope, what with work and everything. He was a trained army mechanic, but he never seemed to hold a job down for long and did all kinds of work, from gardening to helping out behind the bar at the local pub.

His flat was only a couple of streets away from Miss Foley's, but it seemed like another world. Situated on the second floor of a huge 1960s concrete council block, at the top of a dark, gloomy flight of stairs, it was a boxy three-bedroom maisonette with low ceilings. Since Dad couldn't be bothered with housework, it was always a tip.

I got on well with Miss Foley. She'd known my dad for a long time and they were good friends. Although I had a few run-ins with her over the next eighteen months, she seemed genuinely fond of me. She was strict but kind, like a matron in an old film. You always knew where you were with her.

I dreaded hearing the words, 'Your dad can't make it tonight.' The only time I really felt part of a family was when he visited. The rest of the time Bernadette and David acted as if I didn't exist. Bernadette, in particular, wasn't at all sisterly towards me. From the start I had the feeling that she disliked me, and she was always my dad's favourite.

One Saturday in July, Bernadette, David and I were playing in Miss Foley's dining room, where the toys were kept. It was really hot and the windows were open to let in fresh air. I was excited because Dad was due to arrive any minute and take us home for the weekend. I tried to fill the time until he came by playing with a toy train. Suddenly David snatched the train away from me. 'Give it back!' I shouted.

He pushed me away and I fell backwards onto the floor. 'He's older than you,' Bernadette said. 'If he wants the toy you have to give it to him.'

'No!' I protested. I got up and charged towards him, intent on getting the train back. The next thing I knew I was dangling upside down out of the window, hanging precariously between wall and fence, my face dragging through cobwebs and leaves. Bernadette and David held onto my ankles, threatening to drop me on my head. I screamed for dear life.

By the time Miss Foley came to investigate the noise, they had pulled me roughly back inside.

'What's wrong with Teresa?'

'Just another one of her silly tantrums, Miss,' Bernadette said, sweet as pie.

'Calm down and be quiet,' Miss Foley told me.

'Fuck off!' I shouted hysterically.

Miss Foley pursed her lips. Taking my hand, she led me to the laundry room. 'You've got a very dirty mouth,' she said. 'Let's wash it out.' With that she shoved a big red bar of Lifebuoy soap into my mouth.

I choked and retched several times, but she kept ramming it back into my mouth. Just when I thought I was going to vomit all over her, she finally pulled it out. 'Now rinse your mouth out,' she said. No matter how much water I sluiced around my mouth, I couldn't get rid of the taste. There was soap stuck to the back of my teeth all day.

A few minutes later, Dad arrived. 'What's wrong with you, Teresa?' he asked. 'You look like you've swallowed a lemon.'

'Miss Foley washed her mouth out for saying bad words,' Bernadette said.

'Mum says those words all the time,' I said in my defence.

'Yes, you're just like your mother,' Dad sighed. 'You look like her, you sound like her and you even swear like her.'

Dad had a pretty Irish girlfriend called Martha, who used to look after us while he was down the pub. She took us to the park with her three children and fed us piles of sandwiches. Sometimes it was better to stay at Martha's house, because Dad and his drinking pals would often stay up late into the night. I was often exhausted from lack of sleep when he dropped us back at Miss Foley's on a Sunday night.

That December our Christmas treat was a trip to see *The Three Little Pigs on Ice* in Wimbledon. I was really excited as we piled into the back of the van. There were nine of us children, plus Miss Foley and another lady. Best of all, Dad was driving us.

The brightly lit ice rink was packed with noisy, expectant kids and their parents. A few minutes after we'd found our seats, the lights dipped and the arena went quiet. I snuggled up to Dad, who was sitting beside me. He gave me a squeeze. I felt so happy.

Loud music started playing and dozens of multicoloured spots of light swirled around the arena. Then the three pigs appeared in the middle of the ice, skating in time to the music, bathed in spotlights. I was entranced. It was just like something off the telly, a dream come true. I'd never seen anything so magical. When the big bad wolf came on, we were encouraged to shout out a warning to the little pigs. I screamed myself hoarse. 'Behind you! Over there!'

When the show ended, I couldn't stop clapping. I was still so caught up in its fairytale dream that I didn't watch where I was going as we filed out of our seats. Thrilled to be handed a goodie bag full of Disney toys and sweets, I dawdled behind the others while I explored its contents.

When I next looked up, everyone was gone. My heart started thumping. Where was Dad? Where were Bernadette and David? The arena was practically empty. The only people I could see were a couple of cleaners moving methodically along the lines of seats.

I ran around frantically, calling out for Dad. Finally a security guard found me and took me to the stage manager's office. It was full of people. 'Where are your mummy and daddy?' someone asked. I burst into tears. I had no idea.

A policeman turned up to question me. He grabbed a handful of sweets off a nearby counter and pushed them into my small hands. But by now I was too distraught to answer his questions. I wasn't interested in eating sweets either. I just couldn't believe that Dad and the others had left without me. I was four and a half years old.

Suddenly the door of the office opened and in came the three little pigs! Everyone laughed as they sang and danced around the room. Soon I was laughing too, especially when my idols showered me with toys and sweets. They treated me like a princess and I got to meet the other characters and explore their dressing rooms.

Eventually Miss Foley came back to pick me up. She told me off for straying, but no one told her off for forgetting me.

It was only when the police rang that anyone realised I hadn't come home with them. They hadn't missed me at all. Young as I was, this thought festered inside me for weeks.

I found it hard to believe that Bernadette hadn't noticed I wasn't in the van, but I suppose it's possible that she was distracted by the excitement of seeing the show. I wondered if she had been secretly pleased that I'd been left behind. She never bothered much with me and we rarely played together. She preferred to sit on the stairs and watch the world go by through the gaps in the banister.

Like a lot of older sisters, she seemed to take pleasure in seeing me upset, or in trouble. Aware of how much I loved my long hair, she was all for it when Miss Foley decided that I needed a haircut. She laughed as one of Miss Foley's assistants chopped it off. 'Fuck off!' I shouted, enraged. I ended up having my mouth washed out three times that day. I must have eaten a whole bar of Lifebuoy by bedtime.

A couple of days later I came across a big pair of scissors in the bathroom. One of the staff had left them on a shelf after cutting a plaster strip for another child. I picked them up and headed for the landing, where there was a good view of Bernadette sitting halfway down the stairs. Tiptoeing towards her, focused on her hair, I opened the scissors in anticipation of my first snip.

Grabbing my chance, I lunged forward and hacked a great lump of hair from the back of her head. She howled and jumped on me, trying to wrestle the scissors out of my hand. 'Stop it now, girls!' snapped Miss Foley as she rushed up the stairs to separate us. It was a wonder neither of us was injured.

Some of the other children in the home were quite disturbed. There was a horrible kid called Kevin who seemed to get a kick out of biting people, and I was one of his main targets. The staff used to press coins on my bite wounds to stop them getting infected or inflamed. It was an old wives' remedy, but it seemed to work.

I got my own back on Kevin whenever we were served liver. Like most kids, I hated liver and would do anything to avoid eating it. I pretended to like it, but when no one was looking, I'd flick bits of it off my plate so that they landed under Kevin's chair. Then he'd get told off and the staff would give him another helping.

In October 1972, when I was five years old, we went back to live with Dad. I was thrilled to be going home. 'Come back and see us soon,' Miss Foley said, giving me a squeeze when Dad came to pick us up. I felt a tug in my heart. Little did I know how much I was going to miss her in the months to come.

Things went horribly wrong almost from the moment we moved back into Dad's. He was always drunk, always legless, always aggressive and always having parties at one and two o'clock in the morning. After they'd finished down the pub, he and his mates would come back to the maisonette and sit there getting drunk all night, playing music on the old-fashioned stereo, keeping us awake. No one looked after us while he was down the pub.

He didn't wash anything. He didn't clean up. There was rarely any food in the house. Occasionally we'd come back from school to find he'd tidied up a bit and then he'd do us egg and bacon, or beans on toast, but mostly we lived off biscuits and crisps. He sometimes made an effort on Saturday. David and I would watch *Dr Who* on the old black and white telly in the kitchen while Dad chopped potatoes. David used to make me laugh by saying, 'Gobble gobble, chop chop!' but Dad always told him to shut up.

I don't have many memories from that time. Mostly I remember Dad being drunk. After a year of chaos, he approached Wandsworth Social Services and requested that we be taken into care again. That's how we ended up at The Haven children's home in Crystal Palace Park Road in South East London. He was sad to let us go, but came to visit us there at least once a month and often telephoned.

Run by the Salvation Army and housed in a huge old Victorian mansion that had once been a hospital, The Haven was a home for children aged two to twelve from all over London. We spent three years there and I liked everything about it from day one. The kids were divided according to their age and assigned to one of four groups – Eisenhower, Churchill, Schweitzer and Kennedy – and each group had its own colour and identity. I was put in Kennedy (yellow) in the charge of Captain Drummond, a really nice middle-aged woman with sparkly blue eyes.

I could see right across London from my bedroom window. I used to sit and gaze for hours at the lights at the top of the Crystal Palace transmitter, which Captain Drummond called, 'our very own Eiffel Tower'. The staff called me a dreamer, but I was also known as 'Gabby-Abby' because I talked too much. I couldn't help it. I'm a Gemini and we chat for England.

The Haven staff seemed genuinely to care. When I fell off the roundabout in the back garden or was stung by a hornet or bitten by the cook's dog, they were full of sympathy and took me straight to the doctor. Punishments for bad behaviour never went beyond being sent to your room or made to sit on the equivalent of a 'naughty step'. I never saw any violence or abuse the whole time I was there.

There was a trampoline in one of the rooms and one day

I fell off it and landed on the floor right next to Captain Drummond, with a view directly up her skirt. 'I can see your knickers!' I shouted gleefully.

She didn't see the funny side. 'You mustn't say things like that,' she said sternly and sent me to my room.

We went on loads of trips. One year we bundled into a coach and went to the annual Policeman's Ball in Kent, a charity event that raised money for children's homes, among other causes. There was a long line of tables piled high with puddings and sweets, so we kids had a wail of a time. Dickie Davies was there, the sports presenter with bushy eyebrows. Bernadette thought he was lovely, so she wasn't best pleased when he picked me up and made a fuss of me.

Every September we'd go to a children's party at the Miss World contest in London, organised by Eric and Julia Morley. I loved it. It was like a fairytale adventure. The Morleys took a lot of interest in us and I think they donated money to various children's homes as well. We didn't actually watch the contest, although we did get to meet the contestants. They would come downstairs loaded with presents to watch us eat jelly and ice cream and play party games. They were stunning! David fell in love with one of them and she gave him a signed photograph.

I imagined Mum to be beautiful like the Miss World contestants. By now I was finding it hard to picture her, but in my dreams she was a long-lost princess. I was sure that one day she would arrive at The Haven, dressed in a beautiful gown and a tiara. Then she'd shower me with gifts and sweep me away to a life of luxury in a far-off palace.

One day she really did come to visit. Although she wasn't wearing a shimmering dress, she was even more beautiful than I had imagined her to be. She was tall and slim with short blonde hair and amazing blue eyes. She was very loving too, and wouldn't stop kissing and cuddling me. A lifelong fan of Avon products, she brought us a wonderful selection of shampoos and bubble bath, along with a ring with a ladybird on it for Bernadette and a Noddy ring for me. We went to the dinosaur section of Crystal Palace Park and spent a happy afternoon in the sunshine. Then, just as suddenly as she had arrived, she was gone. I can still remember how hollow I felt after she left.

At first I really missed her, but I was young and there were plenty of distractions. Next door to The Haven there was an old people's home and if we were good we were allowed to go and visit the residents. Bernadette hated it, but I'd have my hand up immediately when the staff asked us if we wanted to go. The old people were always pleased to see us. I had a great time moving from one old lady's lap to another, chatting away and eating the sweets they'd saved for me.

We were taught that God was love and He was everywhere. This made sense to me because there was a real atmosphere of love among the staff and children at The Haven. I definitely felt loved while I was there. We said grace before each meal and the Lord's Prayer every night before bed, and the staff often used to sing us to sleep. I always prayed for Mum to come back soon.

Every week we went to Sunday school, where we were taught Bible stories. Captain Drummond used to give me a coin to put in the collection box at church, but one day I kept it and spent it on gobstoppers and bubblegum on the way home instead. I buried my goodies at the foot of one of the tall fir trees that lined the pathway leading back to The Haven, but when I went back later to collect them they were gone. I was convinced that it was God's way of punishing me.

Once a year we held a fete in the back garden. We'd knock on doors all around Crystal Palace and ask people for their empty jam and coffee jars, which we soaked in a great big sink of water to get the labels off. Then we'd decorate the lids, stick new labels on, fill them with bath salts and sell them at the fete. We made all kinds of things to raise money for the home, and the locals would come along to support us.

At Easter some benefactor or other would donate a massive Easter egg covered with sugared flowers, as big as a person. The staff broke it up into huge thick pieces and divided it among us. One day I slipped into the room where the pieces were kept, took a great big piece and ran off with it. Coincidentally I went down with a horrific bout of gastric flu later that day, which I was convinced was another punishment from God. The vomiting and diarrhoea went on for days and days and throughout it all I prayed intensely for God's forgiveness. I vowed never to steal again.

Each year at Christmas an enormous fir tree was delivered on a big army truck – a present from the Queen, so the staff said. There were lots of beautifully wrapped presents for everyone, donated by various children's charities. The tree was always unbelievably tall, like something from the land of giants in a fairytale. The whole building exploded with excitement when it arrived. We all rushed into the hall to help decorate it.

One year I was hanging silver baubles on the tree's lower branches when Captain Drummond called me into her office. Bernadette and David were already standing in front of her desk.

'I've got some wonderful news for you, children,' she said. 'You're going home to your father's house for Christmas!

15

We'll be really sad to say goodbye to you, but won't it be lovely to be living as a family again?'

Two days later, Dad bundled us and our Christmas presents into a blue car. Captain Drummond and several other members of staff came to see us off. One of the staff – a woman named Katherine – was in tears as she waved goodbye. As the car drew away, she broke into sobs. I remember thinking how nice it was to feel loved.

CHAPTER TWO

January 1977

Dad hadn't paid the gas and electric bills, so the flat was freezing cold. The sitting room stank of booze and fags. The carpet was sticky, the atmosphere depressing.

Dad wasn't just drunk in the evenings anymore. He was drunk all day and all night, every day, for long stretches at a time. Almost every penny he got from the social and his jobs on the side went on getting pissed. He didn't think to go and buy food. The fridge was always empty. There was a constant rumbling in my belly. Birthdays and Christmas didn't figure at all. I don't remember even seeing Dad on my tenth birthday, let alone getting a card or present.

Dad's method of laundering our clothes was to throw them into a bucket to soak and then forget about them. Days, sometimes weeks later – whenever the smell of stale water became overpowering – he'd rinse them out in the sink. Everything I wore reeked of damp, mould or dirt. In the absence of hot water, I rarely bathed or washed my hair. Before long I was skinny, scruffy and filthy.

At fourteen, Bernadette was old enough to disappear off to her friends' houses, leaving David and me to fend for ourselves. Every morning we woke up hungry. If Dad was in a particularly good mood, he might go out and buy food for breakfast. The rest of the time we had to beg him for money for chips, and when he couldn't or wouldn't give us any, we had to improvise.

We did a lot of out-of-season carol singing, which yielded results even in the height of summer. People gave us money, socks, old jumpers and fruit. Mostly, all we could afford to buy was biscuits.

One day David took a chisel to the iced-up freezer compartment at the top of the fridge, but all he found was a packet of ancient sausages, so we fed them to the cats that roamed outside a little old lady's house next door to the flats. With her straggly silver hair and baby blue eyes, the old lady was very intriguing. She had the most unlikely son – a biker who wore tasselled leather jackets and looked like a member of Hell's Angels.

I loved her cats, especially the one I named Blackie. He purred a lot and was so silky to touch. He would come running to me every time I called him from outside the flats, and then he'd follow me along the wall and the fence to the base of a huge tree, where I'd sit and stroke him. He was my only real friend and I felt peaceful around him.

Dad didn't like me touching the cats because I kept getting ringworm from them, but I didn't care. I didn't get love from my dad. I didn't get it from my sister and the other kids in the flats were always taunting me. So I found my world in those cats, especially Blackie.

One day he stopped coming when I called. I never found out why. I felt very alone without him and kept going back to the wall to look for him, but he never appeared again. I cried for weeks over Blackie.

When we didn't have any money and Dad was down the pub, David would sit me on the photo booth outside the local Asian deli, which had a wall running along beside it. 'I'm going in the shop for something to eat,' he'd say. 'When I shout "run", run!'

Sure enough, a few moments later he'd come bolting out of the shop clutching a packet of biscuits, which were the easiest thing to snatch because they were closest to the door. I'd jump off the photo booth onto the wall and sprint around the corner to a nearby block of flats, where we'd eat the biscuits in a reeking stairwell. The shopkeepers always chased David, but they never caught him.

He didn't steal for the sake of stealing. He had to steal, to keep himself – and me – alive. But it definitely set him down the wrong path. One freezing cold winter's day when we were absolutely starving, he went through Dad's pockets while Dad was out cold on the sofa, pissed as a cricket. It was a dangerous game to be playing, because if Dad woke up there would be all hell to pay. But what was the alternative? Not realising that he was taking the biggest note of the lot, David tentatively pulled a twenty-pound note out of Dad's trouser pocket.

It was snowing as we trudged towards the chip shop opposite Dad's local, the Fox and Hounds. We bought a bag of chips each, which felt like luxury because we usually had to share a bag. I can still remember how delicious every mouthful tasted. It was the best meal ever. Next we went on the bumper cars at the little fairground next to the pub, something we'd always longed to do. I loved the crazy rush of adrenalin as I crashed around that little rink. We buried the rest of the money in the snow round the back of the pub, for safekeeping.

Back at home, Dad was shouting and crying, going mad about the missing note. 'What have you done with it?' he screamed at us. 'I need that money! Give it back now!'

After forcing a confession out of us, he marched us up to the Fox and Hounds and made us dig through the snow. We searched for ages but the money was either gone or lost. He gave us a hiding when we got back to the flat. Then he went back to the pub and got pissed again.

Dad hit us a lot. Not just the odd slap – he would really lay into us. Once he broke a tennis racquet over my head. Usually he'd start on me first. His excuse would be that I resembled Mum in some way: I sounded like Mum; I cried like she did; I looked like her. He hated being reminded of Mum. David often came to the rescue. He would stand in between us and take the blows that were meant for me. Dazed and distracted, Dad would then focus his drunken aggression on my brother instead.

A beating usually meant being smacked around the head, kicked, pushed and thrown against the wall, but occasionally Dad took it even further. When the police told him that David had stolen a bike, he threw him over the banisters, dragged him into the bathroom, grabbed him by his head and smacked his face into the sink. I looked on aghast as the skin on my brother's face split across his eye and started spurting blood. It was like a horror film. The blood went everywhere.

One particular time, Dad was beating me so hard and swearing so vehemently that his false teeth shot out and landed on the floor. It was totally unexpected. He stood stock still with a look of amazement on his face. I was really hurting, but I couldn't help laughing, and once I'd started I couldn't stop. Even Dad had to laugh, right in the middle of hitting me. For a change I was off the hook without David having to step in between us.

Dad had his good moments though. One happy incident can see you through twenty bad ones, which is why when I look back, the good outweighs the bad. At Easter he went into the sweet shop halfway down Putney Hill and bought us a Kinder Egg each. We sat for hours playing with the toys we found inside. In the early summer we went on a day trip to Brighton with his new girlfriend, Bella. He was happy that day, so we all had a really good time, even David.

My brother was a mass of contradictions. He stole for me and shielded me from Dad, but he could also be really mean to me, so it was sometimes hard to know where I stood with him, or what he was going to do next.

I loved all kinds of animals, so I was thrilled when we found a live newt at Kingsmere Pond on Wimbledon Common. Dad said we couldn't take it home, but unfortunately for the newt we smuggled it into the flat anyway. If I'd known what David had planned for it I would have thrown it back into the pond.

At home David moved the kitchen table into the sitting room, placed a bowl of hot water on the floor and spent the next hour knocking the poor animal off the table into the water. I begged him to stop – I was so upset that I became hysterical – but he just kept telling me to shut up. Eventually he got fed up because the newt had no life left in it. I tried to stroke it back to life. It twitched a bit and then died.

I buried it in an Altoids Mints tin in the gardens behind the flats. A few days later I noticed that its little grave had been disturbed and went to investigate. Suddenly my brother and his friend Paul appeared out of nowhere, brandishing the poor, dead, rotten, disinterred newt. They held me down and tried to force it into my mouth but I fought them off and ran away.

David was attracted to danger. He was always throwing himself off great heights, whether it was scaffolding or the top diving board at Putney Swimming Baths. One day he jumped off a high wall and broke his ankle severely. I was inside with Dad when the neighbours came to tell us that he'd been injured. Dad was too pissed to go and see what had happened, so I went instead. I found David lying on the ground, screaming in agony. 'Wait here, I'll get help,' I said, sprinting back to the flat.

Dad was still slumped in his chair, barely conscious. I tried to pull him up, but he was too heavy for me. 'David's really hurt,' I yelled. 'You've got to do something!' Dad was furious that he had to take my brother to hospital, because it meant less drinking time down the pub.

When they came home several hours later, David had a plaster cast on his leg. But the next day, while Dad was at the pub, he hacked it off with a pair of scissors. Dad went mad, whacked David and took him back to the hospital, where they put on another, thicker cast.

A week or so later, he cut it off again. This time the doctors were so annoyed that they put on a fibreglass cast. Undeterred, David borrowed a saw and sawed it off.

'Doesn't it hurt?' I asked.

'Does it matter?' he said. He just didn't care about anything.

Of the three siblings, I think David probably had it the hardest. We all knew that Bernadette was our dad's favourite. Dad didn't provide David and me with basic food, but he bought Bernadette clothes and dolls and paid for dancing and trumpet lessons. It was no secret that I was Mum's favourite. She constantly assured me – on the phone or during her occasional visits – that she was trying to get herself into a stable and settled position, so that she could have me to live with her. But both Mum and Dad rejected David, which must have been very difficult for him.

His reputation for being bad and wild didn't do me any favours with the kids on our block. Wearing shabby, unwashed clothes didn't help either. The other kids were wicked to us and called us every name under the sun. We were scum to them. They scared me because whenever they saw me they'd spit or shake their fists and threaten violence. Not one of them ever had a kind word for me – more likely I'd get a slap. So I'd sit on the stairs of the flats, paralysed by fear, unable to go up or down. No one ever wanted to play with me, not even the girls my own age.

Our next door neighbour always talked to me like I was dirt. I used to get scared walking past her door. Most of the adult neighbours were polite to me, but she wasn't. She would stand in the doorway and stare me out as I walked past, so I'd wait in the stairwell until she went inside before I ran into Dad's. She knew we were beaten at home and yet she was still horrible to us. I was terrified of her son. He used to chase David around and beat him up. Her daughter was always getting me into trouble with the other kids.

Down the stairs lived a girl called Susie. She was the same age as me and went to the same school. One day her mum Barbara told her to invite me out for the day. They also invited another girl called Jill. We took a picnic to Box Hill. It was a beautiful sunny day.

As soon as we arrived, Susie and Jill sent me to Coventry. It's a horrible feeling when someone won't say a word to you or even look at you. I spent most of the day talking to Barbara while Susie and Jill played badminton and styled each other's hair. Then a man wearing a black protective glove walked past. Perched on the glove was a huge, chained falcon. It fascinated me so much that I stopped caring that the girls weren't talking to me.

Towards the end of the afternoon I stood up and launched myself down the hill at breakneck speed. The feeling of freedom was exhilarating. I was intoxicated by the fresh air and sense of wide, open space. Except when Dad took us to visit our nan at Roehampton Vale, I rarely went further than the local high street and pub.

We had regular visits from a social worker from Wandsworth Social Services – a kind lady called Nicky Fletcher. She meant well, but I don't think she realised quite how bad things were for us at home. Dad always knew about her visits in advance, so he'd make sure he was sober – and the flat relatively tidy – when she came to see us. Still, she knew enough to realise that there was no chance of Dad taking us on holiday, so she arranged for Bernadette, David and me to join The Haven's annual holiday in Hastings.

It was the long hot summer of 1977 and I had just turned ten. We spent every day on the beach, building sandcastles and playing rounders. At night we camped in a church hall. I loved every minute of it. But on the last day the mood suddenly changed. I was happily playing a ball game near the cabin on the beachfront, where the staff were listening to the radio and making sandwiches and tea. A little boy started screaming that a dog had run off with his ice lolly, which I found hilarious. I turned round to tell Captain Drummond, but inexplicably she and the other staff had tears streaming down their faces.

'What's wrong?' I said, feeling alarmed as they began to bawl their eyes out.

'The King is dead!' Captain Drummond wailed.

'Oh,' I said. 'Come and play ball?'

They were all absolutely devastated. Everyone on the beach was. I couldn't understand it, because apparently none of them had actually known this Elvis bloke they called the King. A real sense of mourning descended on our group and the staff rounded us up and took us back to the church hall. To me, it just seemed a waste of a good afternoon on the beach.

Back at home, Dad was now getting so out of it that he could hardly make it back from the pub. He was constantly falling over and hurting himself. Worried that he might do himself an injury, I started waiting outside the pub doors at closing time until he staggered out. He'd hang on to me as we weaved our way up Putney Hill. It was a long, tiring walk and an embarrassing one, because everyone we passed stared at us. That's when I first realised what a spectacle we were to other people, the scrawny little girl and her drunken, lurching old dad. Bernadette wouldn't go near him in public.

Dad was loved by everyone at the Fox and Hounds, where he often helped out behind the bar. Dad's friends loved me too and sometimes I used to sneak into the pub and watch them playing cards. I was thrilled when Mary, the landlady, taught me how to knit. My first solo attempt was a baby's booty. When it was finished, I rushed to the pub to show everyone. To my dismay, Dad and his friends cracked up laughing. 'Wow!' Dad said, slipping it on his foot. 'When are you going to knit me the other one?' My beginner's lack of perspective meant that I hadn't calculated the dimensions very well.

Around this time, Nicky Fletcher went on maternity leave and was replaced by a new social worker, Elizabeth Pryde. Mrs Pryde definitely disapproved of my trips to the pub. I'll never forget the day I met her. Slim, with blonde bobbed hair, she turned up at the flat wearing a green skirt, a green top, green tights and green shoes. I took an instant dislike to her. Dad did too. He said she was the spitting image of the leader of 'the flaming Tory Party'. David called her 'the leprechaun'. I just thought she looked like a big bogey.

Mrs Pryde was always nice to us in front of her colleagues at the Social Services offices in Putney, but she was another person on home visits. David and I went to her office to ask for money for food a couple of times, but she told us to go away.

When Dad admitted that he was again finding it hard to cope with us, Mrs Pryde arranged for David and me to go into temporary care. I went to Westdean Close Children's Home in Wandsworth, and David went to Blackshaw Road in Tooting. Bernadette was allowed to stay at home because Dad said she wasn't any trouble.

The home at Westdean Close was a big modern building on two floors. I have no idea why I was sent there because it was totally wrong for me. The other kids were quite a bit older than I was and they were a rough, tough bunch. Luckily they decided to take me under their wing and treat me like a baby sister. I dread to think what might have happened if they'd turned against me.

The staff were OK, apart from Tony, a slightly creepy man of about thirty. Tony constantly gave the impression that he was sneering at me. He made a lot of snide remarks about my appearance and took pleasure in pointing out how immature I was for my age. He also seemed to enjoy telling people I was mad. I don't think he really meant it, but it upset me a lot because Dad was always saying that Mum was mad.

Everybody at Westdean smoked. Cigarettes were stolen moments of sophistication, rebellion and secret pleasure. Sharing a fag was a way of bonding. They called it 'two-sing'. Not long after I got there, a couple of girls pushed me up against a wall, put a cigarette in my mouth and lit it. Some of the other kids gathered round to watch me have my first smoke. 'Make sure she inhales!' one of the boys said.

Already pale with fear at being picked on, I went green as I choked on the cigarette's acrid fumes. Feeling panicked, I sucked in as much fresh air as I could before giving it another go. It was important to pass this initiation test. Smoking was cool and I really didn't want to come across as a loser. After a few more puffs, the smoke began to go down more easily. 'You're getting the hang of it,' one of the girls said approvingly. Before long I was totally addicted and spending my school lunch money on packs of ten Embassy.

The Westdean kids broke all the rules. They used to run off secretly at night and meet up with the kids from David's home, which was somehow connected to ours. One night they took me along with them to a park in Tooting. We had to climb over a really high wall to get in. Not having seen David for a few weeks, I was actually quite pleased to clap eyes on him for a change, but he didn't hang around. He and the rest of the gang ran off to another part of the park, leaving me on a bench with a couple of cigarettes and a guy called Bradley.

Bradley and I two-sed the cigs and then he tried to kiss me. 'Omigod,' I thought as his tongue emerged from his mouth and began probing my lips. 'What's he trying to do?' It wasn't anything like the scenes I'd watched between Scarlett O'Hara and Rhett Butler in *Gone with the Wind,* my favourite romantic film. I kept my lips pressed firmly together.

'What's wrong?' he asked.

I searched desperately for something to say, some way of distracting him. Just in time I saw a plane moving across the sky. 'Look! An aeroplane!' I said. I began to chatter about planes, airports, holidays, other countries – anything to delay another uncomfortable kissing moment. As I rambled on, I kept thinking, 'What am I doing here? Why did they leave me with him?' By the time the others came back, I think poor old Bradley was glad to get shot of me.

Around this time Elizabeth Pryde paid me another visit to say that she had arranged for me to be fostered. I was glad to get away from Westdean, but my time with the foster family was very brief. It was a loving family environment – a couple, their two daughters and another foster girl – but I felt uncomfortable. I just didn't fit in. They seemed to expect me to slot automatically into their routine. Suddenly I was supposed to go to a posh school, wearing a smart new uniform, and then come home, do my homework and go to bed. It was a life I'd never had, a life I wasn't used to, and I didn't know how to adapt.

One of the daughters secretly smoked and so did the other foster girl, who had been with them for some time. I shared a bedroom with her, and when she offered me a drag on the cigarette she was smoking out of the window, I accepted. Just after she'd put it out, the mother stormed into the room demanding to know which one of us had been smoking. I got the blame and was subsequently asked to leave. It seemed totally unfair, but I was actually quite glad to get out of there, even if it meant I had to go back to Westdean.

By now I'd moved to Mayfield secondary school in Wandsworth. Bernadette was there too, but a lot of the time she wouldn't acknowledge that I was her sister. The girls in my class didn't want to talk to me either. The only friend I made was a girl called Penny, who was quite scruffy as well, which is probably why we bonded.

Although I could be a real chatterbox, I was often quite withdrawn at school, especially if I'd been home for the weekend and had the bruises to show for it. It's hard to act normally when it hurts to sit down and I think the other kids picked up on that. I was always being bullied.

But on a good day, I really enjoyed some of the lessons. I loved all the practical subjects, like cookery, art and dress-making, and I liked writing essays and poems. My maths was above average and my French was actually quite good. 'Bonjour, Papa,' I used to say when I saw Dad. 'Ça va bien?'

I was proud of my ability to conduct basic conversations in French. I knew how to ask someone their name, what time it was and how to get to the nearest train station. I could chat about food, the weather, school and my family. I knew the words for all the colours, days of the week, months and most everyday household items. I dreamed of going to Paris and practising my new-found language skills. I imagined myself walking through the streets wearing a black beret. 'Je m'appelle Teresa,' I'd say to the people I met. 'Comment t'appelles-tu?'

There were some crucial gaps in my knowledge though. My ignorance of biology meant that I thought I was dying the day I started my period. Unfortunately, creepy Tony was on duty that day.

'I'm bleeding!' I told him, filled with panic. 'I need to go to hospital.'

'You're absolutely bonkers, aren't you?' he said. He loved saying it. He knew how much it upset me. 'Listen, everyone,

Teresa's becoming a woman!' he declared, with a horrible grin on his face. It sounded ominous. I hoped it didn't mean I'd suddenly turn into my mother.

It wasn't long before he had told everyone in the home about my transition to womanhood. Unlocking the supplies cupboard, he took out a couple of sanitary towels and threw them at me. 'Go and put one of these on,' he said, turning his back and walking away.

I gathered that I wasn't going to die, aged twelve. The opposite, in fact – I was growing up. But I still didn't know what to do with a sanitary towels. Back then they involved loops and belts and things – and I was too embarrassed to ask anyone. So the next day in school I just sat there and bled, doubled up with stomach cramps.

When I asked to be excused and got up from my seat, Mrs Brown, the Maths teacher, noticed the stain on my skirt and realised what was going on. She arranged for me to be taken to the medical room to be cleaned up. The school nurse gave me a fresh skirt and showed me how to use a sanitary towel. 'You're having a period,' she said. 'It's very normal.' What a relief it was to hear those words!

Back in class, the girl behind me prodded me. 'Why didn't you tell us you were in a children's home?' she said. Mrs Brown gave me a reassuring smile. She'd obviously told them a bit about my background while I was in the medical room. The girls in my class were much friendlier after that, which made life a bit easier.

One morning the fire alarm went off. We all had to evacuate the building and line up in the playground. After a few minutes, a rumour went down the lines that someone had set fire to the dining room. Then, sure enough, the fire engines arrived.

Next, everyone was speculating about the identity of the culprit. News travels fast in schools. Within a day we all knew who was responsible. 'Have you heard? It was Bridget.' At the time I couldn't put a face to the name. Little did I know that both would come to haunt me in the not too distant future.

At home, where I spent most weekends, Dad was more aggressive than ever, and the beatings he gave us more violent. When David and I sensed the onset of a ferocious mood we would run and hide in the junkyard opposite the flats. The only way in was through a corrugated iron fence, which Dad was never able to negotiate. Instead he would smash himself against it and scream, 'I'm going to kill you!' He was really scary. On the other side of the fence, we quivered with fear.

Amid the debris of metal sheets, broken glass, steel pipes and tools there was a rusty old wreck of a caravan. We took to spending our evenings inside it, with only a candle for a light. Later we progressed to sleeping there, even though it was freezing. Most of the time Dad didn't even notice we were gone.

He often threw us out in a drunken rage. Once we went to Nottingham to try to find Mum, who had written to us from a Nottingham address. With two pounds between us, we took the bus to St Pancras and got on the train, only to be met in Nottingham by the transport police. They tried tracing Mum, but she'd moved on without leaving a forwarding address, so they rang Dad. A social worker took us back to London the next day. We comforted ourselves with the thought that at least we'd got a bed for the night and some hot food, courtesy of Social Services.

Dad chucked us out one freezing cold November night.

We took refuge in the caravan, but after a couple of hours we were chilled to the bone. There was no choice but to brave Dad's moods and go back to the flat. We could see lights on, but there was no answer when we knocked on the door and the piece of string with the key hanging inside the letterbox had been removed. Assuming Dad was comatose, we lay down and fell asleep outside the front door, exhausted.

The next thing I knew I was being shaken awake by a policeman. 'All right, love?' he said. It was three in the morning. Apparently one of the neighbours had rung to report us. It took another hour to rouse Dad. For once I was glad to slip between the filthy, smelly sheets of my bunk bed.

As the situation at home spun out of control, life at Westdean took a sudden turn for the worse. Creepy Tony took to coming into my bedroom and sitting on my bed at night, which made me feel extremely uncomfortable. Something about his dark presence felt wrong. One night I woke up to find him there again and I freaked out, absolutely petrified. I started screaming at him to leave me alone.

'Be quiet!' he hissed, but he couldn't quieten me down. I began sobbing uncontrollably.

Sally, another member of staff, came to investigate the commotion. 'What's up with Teresa?' she asked.

'I have no idea,' Tony said. 'You know how mad she can be.'

'I am not mad!' I yelled. 'You scared me! I woke up and you were on my bed!'

Again I thought about all the times that Dad had described Mum as mad. He was always saying it. Since he constantly reminded me that I was just like Mum, and sometimes added that I was mad like Mum, Tony's comment had hit a nerve. I knew I wasn't mad, but there are only so many times you can be told you're insane before you start worrying about it. Images of Tony on my bed kept flashing through my mind. What had he been doing before I woke up? Had he even touched me? I couldn't remember. All I knew was that my instincts were on high alert.

In his report on the incident, Tony described me as 'a wicked child'. He no longer came to sit on my bed, but I never really felt safe from him or his nasty jibes. I begged Mrs Pryde to send me somewhere else, somewhere like The Haven or Miss Foley's, where I'd be happy again. Unmoved, she told me there was nowhere else for me to go.

CHAPTER THREE

When I did finally leave Westdean Close a couple of months later, I couldn't get out of there fast enough. I was ready and waiting by the front door with my suitcase before the staff even had a chance to tell me to pack. I didn't bother saying goodbye to anyone. I had no friends there.

Bernadette and David were back at the flat in Raynors Road, so I went home to the usual chaos. But this time Mrs Pryde pushed Dad into taking us to be evaluated at the Roehampton Child Guidance Clinic, where we had regular family therapy sessions with Dr Williams, a consultant psychiatrist. I didn't mind going, but the meetings always seemed to end the same way, with Dad and Bernadette ganging up against me and David, calling us mad.

'She's crazy like her mother,' Dad kept telling the doctor.

'And every bit as annoying,' Bernadette would add.

I hadn't seen Mum for more than four years and couldn't recall whether I resembled her or not. I could only assume they were right, and act accordingly, so when Dr Williams asked me awkward questions about the past, I babbled a load of rubbish to avoid giving a straight answer. I wasn't going to tell him about Dad's violence or Bernadette's indifference to me, especially not in front of them. So I just chatted away about the first thing that came into my head, just as I imagined my 'mad' mother would.

Although he tried not to show it, I think this tried Dr Williams's patience sorely. But what was he expecting? He was never going to get me to grass up my own family while we were all in the same room together. I knew that if I told him about Dad hitting us, I'd get a beating when we got home. David could easily turn on me too, so I didn't want to say anything about his behaviour. As for Bernadette, I couldn't help craving her love, even though she had never shown me any, so I wasn't going to complain about her either.

Dr Williams came to the conclusion that it would be better for David and me if we didn't live at home. David went to Dunstable Road Children's Home in Twickenham, but Dr Williams said he was finding it hard to settle on somewhere for me.

'You're an intelligent girl, Teresa, but not very easy to evaluate,' he sighed.

Finally, he arranged for me to make a visit to the adolescent unit at Long Grove Psychiatric Hospital in Epsom.

'But I'm not ill!' I said.

'It won't be forever. Just take a look round and see how you find it,' he suggested.

During this time Dad was going through a really dark phase. His drinking was getting worse, he wasn't earning any money and he was always in a bad mood. So when Mrs Pryde joined Dr Williams in pressuring me to go to the adolescent unit at Long Grove, I decided to give it a try. Anything was better than living at home.

The unit was located in the centre of the hospital. It wasn't a secure unit as such, but it was locked at night, probably to protect us as much as to keep us there. We were allowed into certain parts of the hospital grounds, but I didn't venture far. There were all these mental patients wandering around and I found it a bit scary.

There were about thirty of us in the unit. The other kids were really nice to me. I was twelve and they were all around fifteen and sixteen, so again I suppose I was a bit like a little sister to them. Certainly I seemed to bring out their protective instincts and no one picked on me too much.

The unit was T-shaped, with two dorms on opposite sides of a corridor, the boys' dorm on the right and the girls' dorm on the left. The beds in each dorm were partitioned off with curtains. Beyond the girls' dorm at the far end was a fire door marked 'exit'. To my horror there were also two padded cells hidden away in their own little corridor. Down the left side of the corridor were toilets, bathrooms and doctors' rooms. At the end of the corridor was a play area with a pool table in it, a dining room, a smoking room and a back door leading to the garden where we would sit and play on a makeshift tyre swing.

Every morning before breakfast there was a group meeting in the games area. I often took my knitting along with me, which annoyed some of the kids because all they could hear was the click-click of the needles. I was always hungry and my stomach used to make loud growling sounds too. In the end, I was told not to bring my knitting anymore, but they couldn't do anything about my rumbling tummy.

I made two good friends at the unit – Esther and Sally. Esther was stocky, with greasy shoulder-length hair, and looked a bit like a boy. I liked her from the moment I met her, even though she didn't utter one word in all the time I knew her. If she needed to give an answer she would either nod or write things down. I used to sit on a chair in her cubicle with my feet up and chit-chat away to her for hours. It was great for me, because I love talking! She'd just smile at me as if to say, I'm enjoying just listening to you.

Something awful must have happened to turn Esther mute, but I never found out what it was. A lot of the kids at Long Grove were severely traumatised. Some of them – boys included – had been violently raped or attacked at a very young age. In comparison to most of them, I was the lucky one, and it seemed odd that Dr Williams had wanted to place me there.

I remember asking Dr Staple, the consultant psychiatrist, why I had been sent to Long Grove.

'It's not ideal. It's just a temporary measure,' he told me. He was worried that I was too young to be mixing with the others and agreed that I did not have the same issues and problems.

'So why am I here?' I asked again.

'Good question!' he said, fiddling nervously with his moustache. I never did get a proper answer.

The staff were OK to me, but Esther was petrified of them. She had a phobia about grease, which they tried to cure by smearing butter and lard on her arms. It was awful to watch her being pinned to a chair and made to face her biggest fear. It was torture for her. Things got even worse when they started taking her over to the main hospital, where they gave her drugs and electric shock treatment. It was cruel of them to subject her to added trauma. She used to come back to the unit in a terrible state, crying hysterically. I hated the way they treated her.

They seemed to find Esther's silence very frustrating. One staff member in particular – a guy called Neil – was nastily aggressive in his attempts to force her to speak. One day I came across him shouting at her and another girl, Chrissie, over something they were supposed to have done wrong. He was threatening Esther with a spell in one of the padded cells if she didn't answer him. It looked as if he was about to hit her.

I launched myself at him. 'Don't you dare hurt her!' I yelled.

He turned and grabbed my face. As I pulled away from him, he dug his nails in and dragged them along one of my cheeks. I felt a burning sensation, but had no idea of the damage he had done until Chrissie screeched, 'Oh my God, your face!' There were huge raw stripes down my cheek. He had ripped off practically all the skin on one side.

The police were called in and they interviewed Esther, Chrissie and me. Neil was suspended and I went home for a few days. Dad was shocked to see me. My face looked really bad, all scratched up. It took weeks and weeks to heal properly.

In June we went on a camping trip to Dover. The weather wasn't great but we had a good laugh. On the morning of my thirteenth birthday, some of the lads dragged me out of bed and threw me into the sea. That was my birthday treat. They ripped my tent in the struggle, and of course that night it belted it down with rain. I woke up at 4 a.m. in a soaking wet sleeping bag in a drenched tent. Dripping with rainwater, I made my way over to the staff tent and slept the rest of the night there.

I was small for my age and very skinny, but at least I was officially a teenager. It was 1980, the Specials were big and Sally and I fancied ourselves as rude girls. I dyed my hair every colour under the sun and wore a pair of two-tone burgundy trousers with a white stripe down each side. Sally had a fantastic black and white checked skirt.

Like every other teenage girl, I dreamt of love and romance, and I started getting crushes on every other male I came into proximity with. When I confessed as much to Dr Staple, he told me not to worry. It was totally normal for a girl my age, he assured me.

I had a big crush on a skinhead boy called Kevin. He and his best friend Andy were kings of the castle at the unit. Kevin, especially, was everybody's idol. I was mad about Matt, one of the teachers, too. But my biggest crush was on Bill, one of the porters. Bill was probably in his early thirties, but he was very sweet and charming with me, so when he asked me if he could give me a kiss, I let him. I didn't understand the problem with the age difference. I just thought he was a really nice person. Since I didn't get any attention from the boys in the home because they were into the older girls, it felt good to have someone showing an interest in me. It made me feel special. Then one night a member of staff caught Bill tapping on the girls' dorm window, trying to attract my attention. I never saw him again after that. I think he might have been sacked.

Mum got in contact again and I was allowed to meet up with her. By now I hadn't seen her for five years. It was hard not to be nervous. She was very good-looking, my mum. I was dazzled by her appearance. She flung her arms around me and called me her 'darling girl'.

'Don't worry, I'll get you out of that place,' she told me. 'I want you to come and live with me when I'm settled. Would you like that?'

'Yes please, Mum, as soon as possible,' I said. I didn't see or hear from her again for months.

Dad was a regular visitor though. Sometimes he turned up smelling of booze and other times he only stayed half an hour, but I was always glad to see him. One day I had some exciting news for him.

'Dad, I'm in a show they're putting on!' I told him.

'Are you playing the back end of a donkey?' he joked.

'No, I'm the lead!'

Dad's face was a picture as I explained that a staff member had heard me singing alone in the games area one day. She had immediately complimented me on my voice. At first I hadn't known what the hell she was on about. I'd always thought my voice was terrible. But the next thing I knew I was learning lines and songs and dances – and two weeks later I was up on stage in front of an audience playing Pandora in a musical called *Pandora's Box*.

After the show, a lot of people came up to me and told me I had a wonderful voice. I didn't know how to react. I wasn't used to being told I was good at anything.

Although life wasn't too bad for me at Long Grove, I was restless and longed to be free. Sick of rules and regulations, I ran away one night with Esther and two other girls. It was spooky making our way through the hospital, listening to patients crying and moaning in their wards, knowing that some of them were really dangerous. We got out of a window and scurried over to the shrubbery on the other side of the lawns. I was so tense as we made our way through the bushes that I jumped at every tiny rustle, creak or twig snapping. I kept expecting one of the mental patients to leap out of nowhere and murder me, which the others found hilarious.

It took ages to get out of the grounds. Well, it felt like ages, but perhaps it was only about fifteen minutes. Once we were beyond the gates, we set off in the direction of Epsom train station. It was a very long walk along dark roads and unlit alleyways. It seemed to last forever. But finally we got there, only to find that the station was closed for the night. It was pitch black and deserted.

'We'll have to sleep here and get the first train that comes in the morning,' I said, looking around for a timetable.

Esther nodded and made signs to the effect that we weren't bloody well going back to the unit! It didn't matter that we had no money and no plans to go anywhere particular. We just wanted to jump on a train and get away, even if it meant bunking the fares.

I saw a car approaching. 'Quick! It might be the police,' I whispered. We had already discussed what we would do if a police car passed us. Because Esther looked like a boy, we'd decided to try and pass ourselves off as a drunk couple out late. We put our arms round each other and pretended to kiss. The other two did the same. The police car drove straight past us.

'We fooled them!' I said, laughing.

A few minutes later the car returned for a second look. Busted! The policemen took us straight back to the unit. The staff weren't too bad with us and as I went off to sleep, back in my narrow bed in the girls' dorm with the curtains drawn around me, I couldn't help giggling about Esther's sudden sex change.

At Christmas I was permitted to go and stay with Mum for a few days in Brighton, where she was working as a housekeeper. Bernadette, David and I took the coach from Victoria. I sat next to David. Bernadette found a seat at the back of the coach and pretended not to know us. Mum met us at the other end. She was so happy to see us. It was the first time she'd had us all together since we were small and she was determined to enjoy every minute.

Mum's joy was infectious and we had a lot of fun. On

Christmas Day we wore paper crowns and pulled crackers. There were lots of presents too. After a proper traditional turkey lunch, Mum and Bernadette dressed David up as a girl in a dress and a fur coat. They even did his make-up. He looked ridiculous by the time they'd finished with him. I laughed until the tears streamed down my cheeks. Later on I got legless on sweet wine and threw up all over the bathroom floor. I was mortified, but nothing could dent Mum's good mood. As she helped me to clear up, she told me that she was going to apply for custody of me.

'I want you home with me,' she said, giving me a hug.

On Boxing Day we went to visit some of her friends. They were Indian and gave us a fantastic Indian meal. In the afternoon David and I walked down to the seafront and watched the waves. It was great to spend time with my brother again. He had put me through hell on many occasions, but I loved him all the same.

The following day we returned to London by coach and I reported back to the unit at Long Grove. After such a lovely time with Mum, I really resented being in an institution again. I took to tattooing myself with Quick Ink, a needle and a matchstick, and joined up with a gang of kids to raid the staff bar beer supply.

In late January, Sally heard that her brother had committed suicide by taking an overdose. She was devastated.

'I've got to get home and see my parents. Will you help me get out of this place?' she sobbed.

'I'll come with you, if you like,' I offered. We sneaked out of the unit later that evening and caught the train to London.

There was a heavy atmosphere at Sally's parents' house when we got there. Her mother looked almost mad with grief and shock. Her father sat pale and staring at the wall in the sitting room for hours on end. I wanted to get away, but I felt bad about leaving Sally, so I agreed to stay the night.

When we got back to Long Grove the following day, Dr Staple called me into his office. 'In view of your latest attempt to abscond from the unit, I have written to Wandsworth Social Services to say that it's time for you to leave us,' he said. He went on to explain that I didn't have the kind of problems that the unit specialised in dealing with and he had decided to exclude me. He said that the unit was geared towards helping children with severe trauma and mental health issues, which was not how he would describe me. In his opinion I had coped pretty well with a difficult child-hood. There was nothing wrong with my mental health and I did not need psychiatric help.

According to Dr Staple, my problems were social, in which case it was recommended that I go out into the world and live as normal life as possible, going to a normal school and making friends.

'I have suggested to Social Services that they look into the possibility of sending you to a state-run boarding school if you can't live at home. Either way, we are going to have to say goodbye to you.'

After ten months at Long Grove, I was finally moving on. Although it was hard saying goodbye to poor Esther and Sally, I was hugely relieved to be leaving, not least because I didn't want to risk getting the same kind of treatment they were doling out to Esther. She wasn't the only one either. During my time at the unit I saw other kids being punished and given drugs, so I had every reason to want to go. Or so I thought.

Less than a week later I was in court to answer Wandsworth Social Services' application for a full care order. I didn't want to be there. I didn't think it was right. I hadn't done anything wrong and I couldn't understand why it was happening.

The judge explained what a full care order was and asked me if I was happy about it. I wasn't happy about it at all and said so. It just seemed weird. Wandsworth had stripped my mum of her custody rights and handed me to my dad, knowing that he was violent and a drinker, so what did they care?

In the end I didn't have a choice. The judge read out some sort of section and told me that Wandsworth Social Services would now be my full carers instead of my dad. He didn't say that this gave them the right to do what the bloody hell they liked and I didn't realise that I was now completely in their power.

At first I was placed with Miss Foley, at her new children's home in Briar Walk, Putney. It was nice to be back under her wing. She was always very kind to me and trusted me with the little kids. I used to walk them down to the local shop to buy sweets.

It was lovely to be near Dad again too. He was working at the Fox and Hounds and I'd wander down there to play dominoes and rummy with him and his friends. Dad and I used to sit at the piano and sing 'Blue Moon' together. I played the melody and he played the low part. I also helped him to collect up the glasses and clean the mirrors with vinegar. We had such a lovely time. His friends were always very nice to me, even when I thrashed them at cards. I started thinking that I was quite a fun person, someone whose company people might enjoy. It was a real boost to my self-esteem.

Occasionally Dad took me to the working men's club balls

in the function room at Putney Swimming Baths, and to dances at the Conservative Club (even though he voted Labour religiously). He and his friends taught me to waltz and fox trot and a little cha cha cha. I loved it. I wasn't a bad dancer. I would even go so far as to say I was quite graceful.

Social Services were not happy about me going to see Dad at the pub. 'It's a bad influence,' my social worker told him with a frown.

She kept on at me about going to boarding school. 'But I like the way things are,' I told her. Dad and I were bonding finally. He didn't hit me anymore. Life was better than it had been for a long while.

'You can't stay at Miss Foley's forever. It's only a temporary option, and you know it.'

She told me about a small, specialised boarding school in the middle of the Kent countryside that took girls aged thirteen to sixteen. It was run by something called the Council of Social Responsibility.

'There is so much more space and greenery than there is in London, and it's near the sea,' she said. 'I've got a girl who is doing really well there. It's a very relaxed, happy place and there are no more than fifteen girls, so everyone gets lots of attention.'

It sounded good. I had always craved attention. I pictured long walks on the beach and through fields. I imagined myself sitting in the middle of a happy, laughing group, playing cards and telling jokes and stories. I told her I'd think about it.

Meanwhile Mum sent me a note telling me to meet her outside Miss Foley's. I wasn't supposed to see her without permission, so I had to sneak away without telling anyone where I was going. That day she wasn't the happy manic person we'd spent Christmas with. She seemed very nervous and distressed and kept clutching my arm as she spoke.

'Are those bastards getting you down?' she asked.

'Who do you mean, Mum?'

She shook her head sadly. 'There's no hope for you, Teresa. I'm sorry to say it, but it's true. I know what's going to happen to you. No one will ever want you. You're going to spend your life being shunted from pillar to post like an unwanted piece of baggage. You're just no good.'

Her words really upset me. I began to cry. 'I don't understand. Why are you saying this?'

'It's all over,' she went on. 'Nobody is ever going to love you. You're very ugly, you know. I can hardly bear to look at you sometimes. Ugly, ugly girl! I don't want you to suffer any more. No one cares about you, so I've come to give you something that will help you. If you don't do as I tell you then you will suffer. Promise me you'll do as I say. Promise me!'

'I promise, Mum,' I replied through my tears. She was still my princess on a pedestal and I believed every word she said. I would have done anything for her.

She rifled through her handbag and pulled out a box of pills, which she pressed into my hand. Staring intensely into my eyes, she said, 'In the medicine cabinet at Raynors Road you will find a brown bottle of pills with a white label. Your dad is never without them. I want you to swallow them along with the pills I've just given you.' She took hold of my shoulders and gently shook me. 'Listen to me, Teresa, it's for the best. You'll be better off. And it's not a bad way to go.'

She went on and on, begging me to take the pills and end my life, until I was distressed to the point that I could no longer think clearly. Eventually we said goodbye. Drying my tears, I headed off to the Fox and Hounds to ask Dad for the key to the flat. I didn't mention that I'd just seen Mum.

'What do you want?' he said, handing over a bunch of keys.

I tried to seem casual. 'Oh, just some clothes.'

At the flat I headed straight to the medicine cabinet. It was funny – I'd never really noticed it before and I'd certainly never opened it. I took all three of the tablets in the bottle Mum had described, plus the ones she had given me. Then I sat down and wrote a note to Bernadette, telling her that I was going to die.

I dropped the keys off with Dad on my way back to Miss Foley's. I also gave him the note addressed to Bernadette, telling him not to read it. He was honourable like that; I knew he wouldn't open it. He gave it to Bernadette when she passed by the pub.

Back at Miss Foley's, I went into my room and lay down. Some time later, a member of staff called Mark came into my bedroom and asked if I was all right.

'Not really,' I said. I felt woozy and had stomach ache.

'Bernadette has rung and she's very concerned about you. She thinks you might have taken some tablets. Have you?'

'Yes, but I'm OK though.'

'You don't look OK. What have you taken? Show me. They could kill you.'

I didn't understand the permanence of death. I just knew that my mum wanted me dead and I was trying to please her by doing what I'd been told to do. I thought it would please both Mum and Dad.

Mark took me to hospital, where the doctors concluded that what I'd taken was not enough to do any real damage, mainly because the pills Mum had given me were laxatives. The pills in Dad's medicine cabinet were tranquillisers though, so it was lucky there had only been three in the bottle.

I went to sleep at the hospital and woke up amazed that I hadn't died. Seeing a nurse, I thought, 'Hang about, this isn't heaven!' The whole incident had given me a bit of a fright as well as a bad tummy. I asked for my mum but she wasn't there, even though Miss Foley had rung and told her what had happened. I didn't see her for a while after that. It was hard not to hate her.

What was her motive for persuading me to commit suicide? I've often wondered. Perhaps she felt that if she couldn't have me, why should anyone else? Or maybe she wanted to save me from the same mental health system that had let her down so badly and destroyed her soul? It's impossible to know. She was a sick woman who had been in and out of hospital for nearly two decades.

I told Miss Foley the truth of what had happened. I'm not sure if she believed me that Mum had told me to do it, but we had a good talk in the sitting room and she gave me a lovely cuddle.

'There are to be no more secret meetings with your mum,' she chided gently.

At our next meeting, Mrs Pride my social worker informed me that it was time to make a decision about boarding school.

'What are my choices?' I asked.

It was Kendall House – the wonderful haven in Gravesend, Kent – or nothing, she said. 'There's a space for you now and I believe you will be happy there.'

Miss Foley seemed less certain that it was the right place for me. 'Are you sure?' she asked. She was frowning. She seemed anxious.

'I need to be around other girls my age, and it will be good for me to be in the countryside,' I explained, parroting the official Social Services line. 'You know how much I love animals and nature.'

It was only later, when it was too late to change my mind, that David warned me not to trust Social Services. 'I wouldn't believe one word they say,' he said. My heart began to thump. He was right, of course. They had only started being nice to me when the business of boarding school had come up.

The day before I left for Kendall House I received a letter from Mum. Inside it, she had enclosed a St Christopher pendant on a silver chain. 'St Christopher is the patron saint of travellers,' she'd written. 'He will protect you on your journey.' I was wearing it as I got into Mrs Pryde's car. Mark loaded my bags into the boot and we set off. Miss Foley waved until the car was out of sight.

CHAPTER FOUR

25 June 1981

The journey seemed to go on for ages. I was gasping for a cigarette to calm my nerves, but Mrs Pryde had made me put my packet of JPS in the boot. I kept asking her to pull over.

'Not much further now,' she said in the singsong tone she always used with David and me in front of her colleagues at the Putney Social Services office.

'I'm thirsty,' I said. 'Please can we stop for a drink?'

'Hang on, we're nearly there!' she chirped.

Something didn't feel right. She was being too cheery, too pleasant. I began to tense up. What if Kendall House wasn't as nice as everyone had made out? My heart pounded as we sped out of London through the suburbs and into Kent, passing towns and fields along the way. Finally, we drove along a tree-lined street and pulled up outside a big detached red-brick Victorian house. It had a grey slate roof and huge bay windows above and on either side of an arched doorway. The windows were hung with drab net curtains. It wasn't a bit like I had imagined and didn't even remotely resemble an idyllic mansion in the countryside.

'Here we are! Kendall House!' Mrs Pryde was still speaking in that false tra-la-la voice, as if we were friends on a lovely day out.

She got out of the car. I stayed put. Feeling really uptight, I said I wasn't going anywhere until I'd had a fag. She went up to the front door and knocked.

'Come along, Teresa,' she coaxed. 'You can have a cigarette the moment we're inside, I promise.' She took my bags out of the boot and dumped them on the doorstep. Reluctantly, I got out of the car.

I could hear the clink of keys and locks turning as we waited outside the double doors at the entrance to the building. 'This isn't how you described it,' I said. She said nothing.

Eventually the doors swung open and a middle-aged woman appeared in the doorway. 'Welcome to Kendall House,' she said. 'I'm Kate.'

'Hi,' I mumbled, trying to force a smile. I'd been in and out of homes all of my life, but this was different. I had a very bad feeling about it. My heart was racing as we stepped inside.

Kate briskly locked the front door behind us. Directly in front of us was another door, also locked. For the moment we were trapped. She sorted through a big bunch of keys, found the one she was looking for and skewered the keyhole. We entered a long hall with several doors leading off it.

'Teresa, you come with me,' Kate said. 'Mrs Pryde will log you in and go through the necessary paperwork in the office.'

Mrs Pryde halted outside the first door on the right, and knocked. A key turned. The door opened. Kate led me down the hall and through a heavy wooden door, which creaked as she pushed it open. We came to another door. She jabbed it with a key. 'Here we are,' she said. 'The staffroom.'

'Why are so many doors locked? Is there a problem with burglaries in this area?' I asked.

'Let's start getting you organised now, shall we?' she said brightly, totally ignoring the question.

'Can I have a cigarette, please?' I said. 'I was promised I could have one as soon as we got here.'

She smiled. 'I'm sorry, but girls are not allowed to smoke on the premises.'

My heart sank as she told me that cigarettes were a privilege that had to be earned. 'Kendall House has a system of rewards and punishments to encourage good behaviour in the girls,' she explained, going on to list some of the other so-called privileges, which ranged from walks to family visits.

'You can't stop my dad coming to see me!' I protested. 'He'll bust his way in if you try.'

Her eyes narrowed. 'In the beginning, nobody is allowed visitors or phone calls,' she said. 'You'll need time to settle in. But after that, if you behave well, you'll be able to ring him and arrange a visit.'

My head swam. I couldn't bear the idea of not seeing my dad, let alone not speaking to him. He wasn't the greatest father, but I loved him all the same.

'He said he'd come with my sister Bernadette next weekend,' I said, hoping that this would somehow change her mind. 'Mrs Pryde said it would be fine.'

'Well, I can assure you that it's not going to happen,' Kate said sternly.

Tears pricked my eyes. 'Why not?' I asked. 'He's my dad. I should be able to see him, and my sister too.'

She smiled. 'It's one of the rules. It's the same for everybody. All the girls have to obey them, not only you.'

A lump rose in my throat. The urge to talk to Dad was overwhelming. 'Can I just ring him and give him the number here, then?'

'No, sorry, that's not allowed. I'll drop him a line later with all the necessary information.'

The door opened and another woman entered the room. 'Ah, Mrs Kale,' said Kate. 'This is Teresa, the new girl. Will you stay here with her while I go and find Benita?' She turned to me. 'Mrs Kale is one of the staff here.'

Mrs Kale took a packet of cigarettes out of her bag. I watched avidly as she lit up. 'Please let me have one,' I begged. 'It's my first day and my social worker promised I could have a fag when we got here. She promised!'

She smiled kindly. 'Girls are not allowed to smoke on the premises, but on this occasion I'll make an exception,' she said, offering me one of her Bensons.

Finally, a cigarette! I puffed it gratefully.

'It won't take you long to learn the ropes,' said Mrs Kale. 'But there are certain things you should know straight off. Firstly, you have to put your coat and shoes in the coat cupboard around the corner.'

'I see,' I said, although I didn't see at all.

She extended her arms as if to take my long navy coat. I shrugged it off my shoulders and gave it to her. She gestured to my feet. 'What?' I said.

'Your shoes.'

'Yes?'

'Take them off.'

I stared down at my scuffed black court shoes. 'But they're the only ones I've got.'

'You're not allowed to wear shoes in the house and all coats and shoes are locked in the coat cupboard. I'll find you a pair of slippers once you've taken those off.'

Reluctantly, I stepped out of my shoes. 'Why aren't we allowed them?' I asked.

'Oh, lots of reasons, but mostly because of noise and dirt,' she replied.

'I'll need them when I go out.'

'Yes, but only when you've earned the privilege of going out.'

Again, that word 'privilege'. I didn't understand the way it was being used. To me, a privilege was something special, something good, not a basic right like wearing shoes, or going to the corner shop. But before I could argue, she was telling me more about the rules at Kendall House. She seemed to enjoy it.

Girls were banned from discussing their lives before Kendall House, she told me. This made it easier for everyone to make a new start, with a clean slate. 'No one can judge you on your past if they don't know anything about it,' she said. I wasn't sure what she meant. Why would anyone judge me on my past? I hadn't done anything wrong.

'One moment, Teresa,' she said. She left the room, taking my coat and shoes with her. When she returned she was clutching a pair of old-biddy slippers with plastic bottoms. She began to recite a litany of rules. Phone calls from family members were only allowed on Fridays. The laundry room and kitchen were out of bounds, as was the dining room, except at meal times. No eating between meals. No food allowed in the dorms, schoolrooms or sitting room. On and on she went. I found it impossible to take everything in.

'Understood?' she asked, when she had finished explaining bath times and restrictions. I nodded dumbly, trying to hold back the tears. 'Don't worry, you're not the only new one,' she said. 'Another girl arrived yesterday, so perhaps you can help each other to settle in.'

Kate returned with Benita, a grim-faced Asian woman of

around twenty-five wearing drainpipe jeans and high heels. Benita told me to open my bags and show her what was in them. I watched as this complete stranger rummaged through my clothes, fingered my underwear and inspected the contents of my sponge bag. She confiscated my cigarettes, matches, money and aspirins, before reciting another bunch of rules.

'At the end of the day, you must hand in your knickers for laundering to the member of staff on duty,' she said. 'When you come on your period, just let a member of staff know and you'll be given a sanitary towel.'

Soon it was back to 'privileges' again. Watching television, listening to music, reading books and magazines, using pens, paper or drawing materials, even attending lessons – these were all concessions that could be given and taken away. Punishments included being made to wear our nightclothes during the day. After a while I stopped listening. I couldn't digest any more rules.

A wave of tiredness washed over me. 'Would it be all right if I went and lay down for a bit?' I asked.

'Of course not, don't be a baby,' Benita said. 'You're not allowed into the dorms until bedtime. Now come with me.'

She showed me around the ground floor, repeating Mrs Kale's warnings about the rooms that were out of bounds. The front room and dining room doubled up as school-rooms, she explained. The bathroom was next to the laundry. She stopped in front of the only unlocked door we'd come to so far. 'And this is the girls' sitting room.'

Hesitantly, I stepped through the doorway. With its plastic, foam-filled chairs and old cheap carpet, the girls' sitting room reminded me of a hospital waiting room. There were about seven girls gathered around the television, and one girl was sitting in the corner, rocking and staring into space. Benita came up behind me and introduced me. 'Hello,' I said shyly. There was a tremor in my voice.

'Yeah, hi,' someone said. The atmosphere seemed heavy with unspoken tensions. Only a couple of girls bothered to look away from the TV. One of them wrinkled her nose and then turned back to the screen.

'Sit down and watch some television, Teresa,' Benita said, walking away. She looked at her watch. 'Tea is in just over half an hour. I expect you're hungry after your journey.'

My stomach churned. Food was the last thing I wanted. 'What are you watching?' I nervously asked the group.

'Telly, thicko. What does it look like?' said a small dark-haired girl, raising a couple of half-hearted laughs from the others.

Fighting the urge to run out of the room, I went to sit down. As I walked towards a spare seat, a leg shot out and smashed into my shins. I tripped and pawed the air, just catching myself before I fell.

A heavy-set, muscular girl in a nearby seat screamed with laughter. 'Watch your step, new girl,' she said. 'You don't want to go arse over tit, now.' Sucking air in through her teeth, she turned to face me. 'Not that you've got much in the way of arse or tits,' she added, looking me up and down disdainfully.

She flicked a glance at the thin black girl sitting next to her. The girl gazed at me, saying nothing. There was a hardness in her expression that chilled me to the bone. I made a mental note to stay out of her way.

Feeling totally unwelcome, I slipped out of the room. I was unsure of where to go next or what to do, so I climbed the stairs leading to the next floor and sat halfway up, watching the goings on below through the bars in the banister. A couple of girls passed me on their way downstairs, staring me out as they went by. Whispering and giggling, they headed towards the sitting room.

I heard someone say, 'Look what the cat's dragged in,' but I wasn't sure if it was me they were talking about.

Resting my elbows on my knees, I covered my face with my hands. Tears trickled through my fingers. I wasn't good at making friends at the best of times, but it looked like it was going to be virtually impossible at Kendall House. The girls were all so hostile. So much for my dreams of cosy chats and walks on the beach. I longed to be back at Miss Foley's where the staff were caring and the kids were nice.

Suddenly I was aware of someone standing at the bottom of the stairs. I peeped through my fingers. My heart thumped. It was the stocky girl from the sitting room.

'Aw, diddums,' she said, her voice dripping with sarcasm. 'Don't you like your new home? Missing your mummy and daddy, are you? Well you'd better get used to it!' The last part was shouted, like the punchline of a rowdy pub joke. She scrunched her face into an ugly grimace.

I buried my face in my lap and tried to pretend she wasn't there.

'It's teatime, crybaby,' she snarled.

'I'm not hungry,' I said.

'Think you've got a choice, do you?' she laughed. 'Haven't they told you what they do to you if you don't behave? You've got a big shock coming then. This place is your worst nightmare. If you break the rules they drug you and lock you up.' She paused.

'I don't care,' I said, even though her words had made me shiver. I thought about Esther at Long Grove, and how badly affected she was by her sessions in the hospital. I remembered the change in some of the other kids too.

'And guess what?' she went on. 'I'm even worse than your worst nightmare. So you'd better come down and eat your tea. You need to keep your strength up, because I'm going to get you later.' She punched the air with her fist and began to beckon me downstairs, laughing like some demented witch.

Just then, someone called out, 'Bridget!'

She froze, mid-cackle. 'Yes?'

The scary black girl was standing in the hall. 'Leave her alone,' she said.

Bridget raised her thick arms as if she had a gun pointed at her. Suddenly she didn't look so tough. 'I'm not doing anything! I'm just calling her for tea,' she said defensively.

The black girl said nothing more, but watched stonily as Bridget turned away from the staircase and sauntered in the direction of the dining room. 'Thank you,' I said softly, but she didn't respond. I waited until she had gone into the dining room before I left my safe place on the stairs.

Tea was a miserable affair. Desperately trying not to cry, I silently pushed piles of stewed meat and veg around my plate, feeling dazed. No one made conversation with me, not even Bridget, who was too busy trading insults and threats across the room with the others to pay me much attention. Once I caught the other girl – Maya – staring at me. Although she didn't say a lot, I sensed that Maya was top dog among the girls. They were nervous around her, jumpy. When she made a joke, everyone laughed. When she offered an opinion in her soft low voice, everyone agreed with her.

Halfway through the meal, a girl on the same table as me abruptly pushed back her chair. 'I can't stop shaking,' she moaned, staring down at her hands. They were trembling like mad.

'Shut your gob, Jane, you drama queen,' someone said.

'No, but look!' she wailed. She appeared to be transfixed by the sight of her shaking hands. She tried to stand up, but collapsed back onto her chair. 'I feel so weak, so weak . . .' Her voice trailed off.

I didn't know what to do. The girl was obviously ill, but no one seemed to care. 'Are you OK?' I asked.

'I feel like I'm dying,' she whispered feebly. 'They're killing me. Kendall House is killing me.'

'Hurry up and die, then!' Bridget shouted. The rest of the girls laughed.

I was shocked by their callousness, but didn't feel brave enough to speak out. Moments later, Benita came in and hustled Jane out of the room. I noticed that she had trouble walking and had to lean on Benita for support.

As soon as tea was over, I went back to my place on the stairs. A couple of girls shoved past me on their way up to the first floor. One of them flicked my face. 'You're in trouble,' she said with a sneer. 'Bridget's got it in for you.'

I heard Benita calling me. It was time to show me around the rest of the house, she said. I asked if Jane was feeling any better. Fine, she replied matter-of-factly. She led me upstairs, her bunch of keys jangling. On the first floor landing, she unlocked a door on the left – a schoolroom. Straight ahead was the washroom and toilets, also locked. Next to the washroom was Miss Woods's office. Miss Woods was the superintendent of Kendall House. I would meet her in the morning.

On the right, next to Miss Woods's office, I noticed a wooden door with a small window in it. It looked like a police cell door. I asked Benita about it.

'Oh, that's the detention room,' she said breezily. 'Hopefully you won't be spending much time in there!'

We went up some more stairs. The higher we got, the shabbier the decor was. Downstairs everything was polished and spick and span, but up here the paint on the walls was chipped and there were patches of threadbare carpet. We came to a thick fire door. As Benita unlocked it, I heard the sound of a baby crying. I jumped. It was so unexpected. 'What's that?'

Benita explained that Deborah, one of the girls, had just had a child. For the moment, mother and baby were staying in the room known as Sick Bay, which was on the right as you came up the stairs. A group of girls was fussing over them in a big way, especially Maya, who I later learned was good friends with Deborah. I noticed that Sick Bay also had a wooden door with a peephole window in it.

To the left there was a toilet, which was locked, and a bedroom where the night staff slept. There was also a nurse's room, another staffroom and a girls' dormitory. Up a few more stairs, on the top floor – the shabbiest floor – there were two more dorms, a fire escape and a staff bedroom. The rooms all had to be unlocked in order for me to see inside them. Every window was nailed shut. There was no fresh air. Most of the rooms smelled of stale bodies.

'Is this some kind of prison?' I said. 'Because if it is, I think there must have been a mistake. I haven't done anything wrong. I'm not supposed to be locked up.'

'I'm sure it's for your own good, Teresa,' Benita said. 'Just wait until you settle in. You'll find it's not so bad.'

I shook my head. She was wrong. I knew I'd never get used to being trapped inside this building, nor would I be able to accept it.

Then, on the way downstairs, she started talking about how some of the girls were allowed to keep hamsters and rabbits. My heart soared. It was a ray of hope. I told her about how much I loved animals.

'Will I be allowed to have a pet?' I asked. I thought about Blackie, the old lady's cat that had meant so much to me at the flat in Putney. I knew that having a pet to love could make all the difference.

'You're a real little softie at heart, aren't you?' she said with a note of dislike in her voice.

I flashed back to Bridget's raised fist. The girls at Kendall House were obviously a bunch of hard nuts, so perhaps I'd better start giving the impression that I had a tough side too. 'I can be quite hard too,' I said, but it sounded feeble. I had never been the aggressive type and I had a feeling I never would be. Still, something told me I wasn't going to survive very long if I didn't try to stand up for myself. I'd better save my soft side for the hamsters and rabbits.

I made my way to the girls' sitting room, telling myself to be brave. Just then, Bridget came rushing past. She collided with me and punched me hard on the arm. Bursting into tears, I retreated to my place on the stairs.

I cried myself to sleep that night. Staring through the darkness at the only photograph I possessed, a framed picture of Dad, David, Bernadette and me, I thought about how much I missed them. 'Please don't leave me here,' I prayed. 'Someone, please, please, rescue me.'

'Shut up or you'll get a slap,' said Zara, the girl in the bed next to mine. I buried my face into my pillow and tried to muffle my sobs.

CHAPTER FIVE

'Get up, you lot,' Benita growled. She yanked open the curtains next to my bed. Sunlight streamed into my eyes. I was already awake. I'd hardly slept. My head was throbbing.

'You'd better not snivel and cry like that again tonight, or I'll strangle you while you're asleep,' Zara threatened from her bed. I said nothing. I couldn't tell if she was serious or not. She got up and put on a dressing gown. 'Come on, it's time for morning wash.' She aimed a kick at my bed on her way out of the room.

Eyes still puffy from crying through the night, I followed her to the washroom on the first floor, where some of the girls were lined up in front of the basins along the wall, washing themselves down. I was horrified by the lack of privacy. There was no way I was going to strip off and scrub my privates in front of everyone.

When the first lot of girls had finished at the basins, the next lot stepped forward. Keeping my eyes averted from the girls on either side of me as they pulled their nightdresses off, I washed my hands, cleaned my teeth and splashed water on my face.

Turning to leave, I came face to face with Bridget, who was standing behind me, her broad, muscly arms crossed over her massive bust. 'And where do you think you're going, smelly?' she said, grinning nastily.

'To get dressed,' I said, trying to pass her.

She took a step to the side and blocked me. 'But you haven't finished washing.'

'I have,' I said firmly.

'Suit yourself then, you dirty bitch.' She pinched her nose and scrunched up her face. 'No one's going to want to sit next to you in class!'

I got dressed and walked miserably down to breakfast, tummy rumbling. In the dining room there were boxes of cereal lined up on the counter near the hatch. Plates piled with cold toast sat uninvitingly on the table, with another plate covered in small squares of butter alongside it.

'Is this it?' I asked Zara, pointing at the plates of toast.

'Yeah,' she said despondently. 'Don't eat it all at once.'

After breakfast I was called into the office and introduced to Miss Woods, the elderly superintendent of Kendall House. With her fluffy, scarecrow-style grey hair and thin, pursed lips, she reminded me of an uptight matron in the *Carry On* films.

'Can you tell me why I've been sent here?' I asked. 'I'm not violent. I've never broken the law. I really shouldn't be in a lock-up.' My voice cracked with emotion.

'I expect it all seems a bit strange just now, but you'll soon settle in,' she said, handing me a brown envelope with my name written on it. 'Here's your medication. Get yourself a glass of water from the tray over there.'

'What's it for?' I said, opening the envelope. Inside were four tablets, two blue and two white.

'Just swallow them down.'

'I don't understand. I'm not ill. I don't need any medicine.'

She sighed. 'It's for your own good, Teresa. Hurry up, now. Dr Peri's here and he wants to see you.' She picked up a tray holding a teapot and tea things, a plate of biscuits and two dinky cups.

Reluctantly I swallowed the pills and followed her up to her office, where a fat, smartly dressed man with dark skin was sitting in a comfortable armchair. Miss Woods set the tray of tea down on a small table in front of him. I hovered in the doorway, not wanting to go any further. There was something about this man that made me feel very uncomfortable.

'You must be Teresa,' he said, his chin wobbling as he spoke. 'I'm Dr Perinpanayagam – Dr Peri to you. Come in and sit down.'

I disliked him immediately. Everything about him struck me as repulsive, from his beady little eyes and fleshy lips to his enormous Buddha-like belly. The hairs on the back of my neck stood up as he beckoned me inside the room. I took a small step forwards. Again he told me to sit down. I refused. I definitely wanted to remain standing.

Miss Woods pulled up a chair and sat down right next to Dr Peri, her legs spread so wide that I could see right up her skirt. I looked away, shocked.

Dr Peri asked if I was settling in. I told him I hadn't slept all night. 'I'm not supposed to be here, but no one will listen to me,' I said. 'Why have I been given pills? I'm not ill. I don't need medicine.'

He raised one eyebrow. 'If you are not supposed to be here, why did Social Services send you here?' he asked.

'God knows,' I burst out. 'I didn't know it was like this or I would never have come anywhere near it.' He shook his head, as if in disbelief.

I listed my objections to the rules and restrictions. 'I want my shoes back,' I said, tears streaming down my cheeks. Getting more and more worked up, I complained about the other girls, the lack of privacy and the attitude of the staff. 'Please let me out of here!' I begged. 'I'm not a criminal and I'm not aggressive like the others.'

Dr Peri raised the palms of his hands. 'Now calm down, young lady,' he said in an infuriating tone of voice. He was so smug, so patronising. 'I have read your medical and social history and I know all about you, so obviously I am in a position to tell you what is best for you. Firstly, I can assure you that everyone is here to help. What is more, the rules were made to make life easier for you, so you had better start cooperating.'

'No,' I wailed. 'You don't understand! There's been a terrible mistake. I shouldn't be here. I'm used to being free. I've never been locked up before.'

He glanced at the file on his lap and started wagging his finger at me. 'Do not try all this pretending, because it will not work with me. It is all very well to act the poor little innocent girl, except that I happen to know that you were excluded from the adolescent unit at Long Grove Hospital. So you are not so innocent after all.'

'I am! Why are you trying to twist everything? ' I sobbed. 'I got excluded because there was nothing wrong with my mental health. It was the wrong place for me, like Kendall House is the wrong place for me!'

He gave me a menacing look and told me to keep my voice down. 'If you keep up these hysterics I will have no hesitation in admitting you to one of my beds in the psychological unit at Stone House Hospital,' he said. 'And you do not want that, do you?'

I immediately fell silent. There was no point in arguing,

especially if he had the power to make things even worse for me. Clearly I was never going to get a straight answer out of him. He didn't care about me. No one cared about me. Trying to talk to the staff at Kendall House was like banging my head against a brick wall. They weren't going to let me go. I was stuck here until they sent me somewhere else, or I escaped.

'In the meantime, I am prescribing you a mild sedative to help you sleep at night,' Dr Peri went on. 'You seem extremely excitable.'

'I don't want your medicine,' I said.

He leaned back in his chair and rubbed his blubbery stomach. 'The sedative will help you. You will feel a lot better when you are sleeping properly.'

'I don't want it. I won't take it.'

His eyes flickered with reptilian indifference. 'You do not have a choice,' he said. He waved an arm at me. 'You can go now. You are dismissed.'

As I turned and left the room, I heard him sneer, 'Believe me, Doris, she will show her true colours in time.'

A few moments later, Miss Woods followed me out of the room. 'Now hurry along and get to school. You're due in RE with Mrs Petsworth downstairs,' she said. I glared at her, my eyes welling up again, but she took no notice.

Brushing away the tears, I made my way down to the classroom at the front of the house. As I opened the door, I locked eyes with Bridget, who was sitting in the back row. In a repeat of the pantomime that she'd acted out in the bathroom earlier, she screwed up her face and pinched her nose.

'Ah, come in, Teresa,' Mrs Petsworth said warmly, gesturing to a spare seat. 'We were just talking about the origins of Christianity.'

I sat down and tried to focus on the class. Having spent three years at a children's home run by the Salvation Army I knew a little bit about the struggles of the early Christians, and Mrs Petsworth seemed impressed by my knowledge. But she was an uninspiring teacher and it wasn't long before my concentration began to wander. I still wasn't feeling fully awake and my mind was fuzzy, which I put down to my sleepless night.

At break time I wandered back to my spot halfway up the stairs. As I sat there with my head against the banisters, I became aware of a presence at the bottom of the staircase. I looked up fearfully, expecting to see Bridget. To my relief it wasn't her, but a girl I hadn't noticed before. She had a sweet face and lovely almond-shaped eyes. 'I'm Emma,' she said with a friendly smile. 'Why do you keep going up there? Come down and chat to me.'

I was so grateful for those few friendly words that I could have hugged her. I stood up and followed her into the girls' sitting room. Within a few minutes of talking to her, I had a much clearer idea of how things worked at Kendall House, including the rules that could be bent and those that couldn't. She warned me against a few of the staff members, especially a nurse called Harriet, who could be really mean, and the biology teacher, Mrs Tarwin.

When I mentioned my run-in with Bridget in the washroom, she told me not to worry too much. 'That's just talk,' she said. 'Don't get me wrong. Bridget's a scary bitch. But she won't do anything bad without Maya's permission. Maya's the queen bee here. If she hasn't taken against you, then you're safe.'

She went on to repeat some of the rumours about Maya and the things she'd done in her time at Kendall House, which included beating up several girls and sexually abusing at least one. When I thought about Maya's cold staring eyes, the stories weren't hard to believe, even though she didn't exactly have an overpowering physique. 'She may be thin but she's vicious,' Emma warned. 'Whatever you do, don't get on the wrong side of her.' Even the thought of it made my blood run cold.

As for Bridget, she was a big bully and best avoided. Everyone was convinced she was a lesbian. 'The staff love her, especially Janice, one of the nurses,' Emma said. 'Know what I mean?' She nudged me and gave me a knowing look.

'So do Bridget and Maya . . . ?'

'I don't think so. They're not friends,' she said, grimacing.

Emma didn't seem to care that we weren't supposed to discuss our lives before Kendall House. She gave me a brief run-through of the other girls' histories. One of them had been sent there for arson, another for assault. There was a compulsive thief, a mugger and a girl who was so promiscuous that her parents had given up on trying to control her. Someone else had made repeated attempts to kill herself.

'And Bridget?' I asked.

'She set fire to a school in Wandsworth.'

I thought back to Mayfield School and the day we all drilled into the playground because a girl called Bridget had set the dining room ablaze. It had to be the same girl.

'What about you?' Emma asked.

I shook my head. 'I just can't understand why I'm here. I've never broken the law or stolen anything. I've never hit anyone, never even had a boyfriend. I took a sort of overdose a few months back, but the pills were mostly laxatives, so they didn't do any harm. So I have no idea what I'm doing here.'

68

She beckoned over a girl who had just come into the sitting room. 'This is Jules. She's new too.'

I liked Jules on sight. She was smaller than I was, with curly brown hair and kind brown eyes that twinkled with humour. Jules was as bemused as I was about being sent to Kendall House. She had arrived there the day before me and hated it as much as I did. 'I'm not like the other girls, either!' she assured me.

I glanced over to the far corner of the room, where a petite girl with curly, bright ginger hair was sitting in a chair, rocking and making moaning noises. 'We're nothing like her, that's for sure,' I said. 'She was there yesterday too. What's wrong with her?'

'Georgie?' said Emma. 'She's harmless, but she's not all there, if you get my meaning. She's a lot older than the rest of us, at least twenty. Sophie says she was sent here because she kept trying to have sex with strangers and there was nowhere else for her to go.' She tapped her forehead. 'She shouldn't be here. But none of us should. It's a hellhole.'

I thought about the girl with the trembling hands in the dining room the previous evening. 'What about Jane?'

Emma mimed giving herself an injection. 'Drugged up,' she said.

Just before lunch, I was called in to see Mrs Ryfield, the head teacher. Slim and extremely tall, with a beehive hairstyle that exaggerated her height, Mrs Ryfield wore old-fashioned glasses with winged frames. To me she looked like a towering, elongated version of 1960s pop singer Mary Wilson.

'I thought it would be good to have a little heart-to-heart,' she said. She asked how I was finding Kendall House.

'At last!' I thought. 'Someone who is going to listen.' I let loose a torrent of questions and complaints. 'What was I doing here? Why were they giving me pills? Who was Dr Peri? Why were all the doors locked?'

Her kindly expression disappeared and she raised her hand. 'That's enough. Everyone has to go through the privilege system. By taking this attitude you're not helping yourself and you're certainly not helping anyone else.'

I bowed my head, hopes dashed. No sympathetic ear here then.

After lunch I was called into the downstairs office by a mixed race member of staff named Harriet, whose light-skinned face was sprinkled with freckles. There was a line of girls in front of me, and Harriet was handing each of them a brown envelope and a glass of water. 'Drink them down quickly,' she said when it came to my turn. 'You don't want to be late for lessons.'

Although I remembered that Emma had warned me not to tangle with Harriet, I couldn't help saying, 'Why am I being given these pills? I don't want them.'

'Hurry up, I said!' Her dark eyes flashed and another cold shiver ran through me. I gulped down the pills and went upstairs to the maths class.

I was good at Maths, even though I didn't particularly enjoy it, and at first Mrs Connolly seemed pleased with my contributions to class. 'Well, at least someone knows their long multiplication!' she said approvingly.

Then, about half an hour into the lesson, thick waves of tiredness began to flow through me. My eyelids started drooping and my vision blurred. 'Teresa?' Mrs Connolly said, waiting for the answer to a simple equation.

I shook my head in an attempt to clear my mind. 'Sorry, I'm feeling exhausted all of a sudden,' I explained. 'I didn't sleep much last night. It must be catching up with me.'

'Try a bit harder. It's an easy one.'

I did my best to concentrate on the equation, but the symbols in my exercise book were wobbling in front of my eyes. 'I can't do it,' I said weakly. I was sorely tempted to lay my head on the desk and go to sleep right then and there.

The next lesson was needlework, also taught by Mrs Connolly. I loved making things – needlework was one of my favourite subjects – but I could hardly keep my eyes open as I practised my cross stitch on a piece of square cotton. I was also beginning to feel a bit sick.

Towards the end of the afternoon I started to brighten up and managed to tune back in to what Mrs Connolly was saying. It was a relief to feel the sharpness returning to my brain, to be able to think straight again.

I sat next to Emma and Jules at tea. Jules was really upset. She kept bursting into tears and saying, 'I can't stand it here. I've got to get out.'

'Are they giving you tablets?' I asked.

'Yes. They're making me feel bloody awful.'

On our way to the girls' sitting room I heard my name being called. 'Not again,' I thought. 'Please, no more pills.' Pretending I hadn't heard, I sat down in front of the TV with the others. Adam Ant was on *Top of the Pops*. Jules's sadness melted away and a soppy look appeared on her face.

'He's revolting! You can't like him,' I teased.

'I love him. Don't you say a word against him!'

A figure appeared at the door. It was Harriet. 'Teresa! Jules!' she barked. 'Come into the office now.' Jules left the room. I stayed put.

Emma nudged me. 'You'd better go,' she whispered. 'Harriet can be a real bastard when she wants to be.'

I traipsed along to the office, where Harriet handed me another brown envelope with my name on it. 'How much longer am I going to have to take these tablets for?' I asked.

'Just do as you're told and you won't have any trouble.' She turned away to busy herself with paperwork.

Half an hour later, back in the sitting room, the intense waves of tiredness returned. My hearing kept zoning in and out and I started nodding off in front of the television. I couldn't keep up with what was happening on screen. The other girls broke into laughter, but I didn't get the joke.

'Are you OK?' Jules asked.

'I feel really weird,' I said. The words came out slurred. My mouth was dry; my tongue felt fat.

I stood up and walked up and down the hall outside, shaking my head from side to side. It felt like someone had taken out half my brain and stuffed rags in its place. My neck was floppy. My limbs felt heavy. I desperately wanted to lie down. Instead I staggered to my place on the stairs, where I sat, slumped, with my head resting against the banisters. I hardly noticed when Bridget walked past and gave me a kick. It didn't even hurt.

Sometime later – maybe an hour or two – my head began to clear again. I got up and went to look for a member of staff. That night a woman called Maggie was on duty. She was slim, with blonde bobbed hair and a kind face. I found her in the sitting room. 'The pills they're giving me are making me feel really ill,' I told her. 'I shouldn't be taking them. They're sending me to sleep.'

Maggie said I'd get used to the effects in time. 'You're a bit of a fusspot, aren't you?' she said.

I shook my head. 'I was fine until I started taking the tablets. Now I feel terrible.'

She told me to take it easy. After all, she said, it was only my second day at Kendall House. 'That's what's worrying me,' I told Jules later. 'If I feel like this now, how will I be in a week's time?'

'I'll go mad if I don't get out of here soon,' she whispered. 'Will you come with me if I find a way to escape?'

I didn't hesitate. 'Yes! Don't go without me.'

'I won't.' She squeezed my arm. 'We're in this together.'

At nine o'clock, after we had been given hot milk drinks and a piece of fruit, I was called into the office and given another brown envelope. Harriet watched carefully as I swallowed four pills, plus the extra one that Dr Peri had prescribed to help me sleep. Half an hour later I dragged myself up to the top floor and collapsed on my bed. I don't remember drifting off. In the morning I awoke from a dreamless oblivion to the sound of Zara shouting that some bitch had stolen her hairbrush.

CHAPTER SIX

I still felt really woozy. I told Harriet that I didn't want to take any more tablets. She was unsympathetic, so I threatened to starve myself unless I was taken off them.

'If you don't cooperate, you will be punished,' she warned. I tried keeping the pills on my tongue so that I could spit them out later, but she forced me to swallow them while she watched.

The house had emptied out. It was a Saturday and most of the girls had gone to their parents or to foster placements for the weekend. Bridget and Maya were still lurking around though, so I kept a low profile. Bridget had made it clear that she was going to beat me up at the first opportunity and although Maya appeared not to have a problem with me, I didn't want to take any chances. All I could do was hope that Jules came up with an escape plan sometime soon.

When I caught up with her, she said that she had checked all the windows in the house and that every single one was nailed shut. 'Don't worry though, I'll find another way to get out of here,' she said.

She sauntered over to talk to Paula, the member of staff on duty in the sitting room. Soon they were laughing and chatting away, much to my amazement. So far I had only seen Jules being rude or sullen with the staff. I moved closer so that I could listen in. First, they discussed various Kendall House rules and privileges. Then Jules casually asked if any of the girls had ever tried to escape. Paula said that it wasn't unknown for girls to run away, but they were always caught, brought back again and punished.

'So, how do they get out and where do they go?' Jules said. She caught my eye and quickly looked away.

'What does it matter? They never get far,' Paula replied. She cocked her head and wagged a finger at Jules. 'Don't even think about trying anything silly unless you want to spend a week in your nightclothes.'

After lunch, Bridget and Maya were allowed out for a walk and a cigarette. This really annoyed us. 'It's not fair! I'm dying for a fag. I haven't had one for days,' I said.

We confronted Brenda, another member of staff. 'We haven't been allowed out since we got here,' Jules complained. I backed her up, arguing that it was unhealthy to stay inside all the time.

Brenda smiled. 'You know that newcomers aren't allowed out,' she said, adding that if we were good girls we would eventually earn the privilege of a walk.

At this, Jules started to get really worked up. She swore at Brenda and said she'd smash a window if she didn't get permission to go out soon. For the second time that day I threatened to go on hunger strike. Brenda reacted coldly and threatened Jules with the detention room if she continued using bad language. Jules swore under her breath and said she couldn't give a fuck where she was sent. Brenda must have heard her because she grabbed her by the arm and yanked her towards the door.

'Get off!' Jules yelled, pulling away.

Brenda stumbled. Surprise flickered in her eyes. 'Why, you little . . . ! You'll soon find out what we do with nasty little rebels like you.' She pulled Jules roughly out of the door and marched her off. Within a few minutes she was under lock and key on the first floor. I felt so sorry for her.

I mooched around for the rest of the day, experiencing intermittent patches of drowsiness, just like the day before. They wouldn't let me see Jules. I kept asking, but the answer was always no. Eventually I managed to sneak upstairs just before tea. From the landing, I could hear her crying and banging on the door. She was begging to be let out. I tiptoed forward and knocked softly on the door. 'It's me. Teresa,' I whispered.

'Teresa!'

I sat on the floor and began talking to her, reassuring her that nothing she'd done deserved such bad treatment. Not even liking Adam Ant! That made her laugh and by the time Benita found me and sent me downstairs, she'd started to calm down.

After tea, my nose clogged up and I felt like I was going down with flu or a bad cold. Harriet smeared my throat and nose with Vick's Vapour Rub and took me up to my dorm, unlocking and locking doors as we went.

'It's the medicine. I'm sure it's making me ill,' I told her.

'What nonsense. It's just a summer cold.'

The next morning Jules was visibly shaken after a night spent in the detention room. Her eyes were really swollen. She said she'd cried for most of the night. 'It was horrible, like being in a prison cell. But I don't care how much they try to break me, they won't stop me from getting out,' she kept saying.

My flu symptoms had improved slightly, but I was feeling

very run down. Every time I had another dose of medicine, my head and limbs felt slower and heavier. I wondered whether eventually I'd come to a complete halt, like a wind-up toy that's lost its key.

Bridget was spending the rest of the weekend at Janice's house – Janice was the nurse that Emma had told me about – and Maya was out with another member of staff, so there were only three girls left in the house: Jules, Georgie and me. We spent the morning in the sitting room, listening to records. Georgie hogged the record player, playing her Culture Club records over and over again until I felt like snatching them from her and breaking them over my knee. She was totally obsessed with Boy George and rocked and dribbled more than ever while she listened to him.

My moods were all over the place. One minute I was calm and the next I felt like slashing my wrists or throwing myself out of a window. 'This place is going to drive me around the bend,' I told Jules.

'I'll already be there when you get there,' she said with a sigh.

The next few days went by in a blur of pills, lessons and rules, punctuated by terrifying encounters with the other girls. Some of them could be really scary. Every time Bridget passed me in the corridor she'd start on me, and she was always hissing threats about knocking my teeth in and beating me up. A girl called Sophie K said she'd rip my tongue out if I complained about any of her favourite teachers or staff members, and Zara kept taunting me that I was a baby. But Zara could also be unexpectedly nice, so I never knew where I was with her.

One morning, about a week after I'd arrived at Kendall House, I woke up in floods of tears. I couldn't stop crying. It was weird. It felt more like a physical than an emotional reaction. I went on weeping all through the morning wash and was still crying at breakfast.

'Shut up, for God's sake!' Zara yelled at me. 'You're always crying. What's wrong with you?'

'I don't know,' I wailed. 'I can't stop.'

'Have they got you on them blue and white pills?' she asked.

'Yes,' I said, going into another heaving round of sobs.

'It's a side effect of them pills,' she said. 'It'll wear off by this afternoon.'

What she said made sense, but it didn't stop me bursting into tears at unexpected moments. I was all over the place. Of course I had plenty to cry about, but this felt as though it wasn't really me crying, rather a distant, shell-like version of me. I felt so weak too. The more tears I shed, the more it seemed as if my life was draining out of me.

By lunchtime when the mood finally lifted, I felt knocked out. 'You were right about it wearing off,' I told Zara in between yawns. 'How did you know?'

'I've been on bloody pills for a year and a half. I hate them.'

I shuddered. The thought of spending years feeling floppy, emotional and fuzzy-headed frightened me. I felt I'd rather die than endure that.

'Why are some girls on pills and others not?' I asked. She couldn't say.

The favouritism at Kendall House was obvious for all to see. Maya was always being asked into the staffroom for tea, or to have a cigarette. The staff seemed to dote on her. Bridget was another of their pets. They weren't drugging her. In fact, she seemed to be more on their side than ours. Every morning she stood on self-appointed inspection duty in the washroom, arms crossed, eyes trained on the girls. She had no shame about stripping off and making a meal of washing herself with a flannel down below, sound effects included, and she made no attempt to disguise how much she enjoyed watching us undressing and washing our privates.

I was so uncomfortable with the way she stared that I just cleaned my teeth and splashed water on my face. When she reported me for being unhygienic, I was given several lectures on cleanliness by Shirley. Shirley was one of the nicer members of staff, but she was strict as well.

I refused to obey the rule that said you had to give your dirty knickers to a member of staff at the end of every day. Instead I washed them myself and put them to dry on the radiator, hidden under my towel. Jules did the same. It just didn't feel right to give them to the staff, especially when there were men on duty. Of course, Bridget reported me for this as well, and when Shirley asked me about it, I felt totally tongue-tied. It was degrading to be questioned about such personal things.

Humiliation was an everyday part of life at Kendall House. Since we weren't allowed to keep a store of our own sanitary towels, I had to tell a member of staff when my period started. Unfortunately, the only person available that night was a tall, greasy-haired man called Philip.

'I need a sanitary towel,' I mumbled.

'On your period, are you?' he said.

No, I want to wear it as a hat, you idiot!

'Yes,' I said, cringing.

'Come back to me with some proof and I'll give you an ST.'

'Proof?' I couldn't even begin to imagine what he meant.

'Stains on your knickers, for instance.'

'No way!' I protested.

We got into an argument and I angrily stood my ground. Finally Benita turned up and took me into the staffroom, where the sanitary products were locked away in a cupboard.

'This time I'll let you off. Next month you will be required to prove that you are menstruating,' she said.

'No.'

'Fine. Bleed all over the place, then; it's your choice.'

'But why?'

Her reply was mystifying. 'The girls are known for abusing certain hygienic products like STs,' she said. 'They ask for more than they need and then they misuse them, which is a terrible waste of money. They're not cheap, you know!'

She handed over a thick Dr Whites towel with loops on each end. I wasn't sure how you secured them to your knickers and asked if the loops were supposed to attach to something. She said that the belts that held them in place were prohibited and I'd have to improvise.

'Has anyone ever tried to hang themselves with a sanitary towel belt?' I asked. 'I suppose there's a first time for everything!'

I asked how she expected me to 'improvise'. 'I'll leave that up to you,' she snapped.

Inevitably the sanitary towel kept riding down my knickers and I ended up leaking. Just as inevitably, Bridget noticed the red marks on my clothes and made endless nasty comments about my standards of hygiene. Even though I had frequent baths, she held her nose and screwed up her face every time I entered a room. I began to hate her for it.

After two long weeks at Kendall House, they let me phone Mum and Dad. I tried the Fox and Hounds number first, hoping Dad would be there, as there was no phone at home. It rang and rang, but no one picked up.

Next I tried Mum. 'Hello, love,' she said. 'How are you doing?'

A lump formed in my throat and for a moment I wasn't sure if I'd be able to speak. 'Oh, Mum!' I croaked.

She instantly picked up on my distress. 'What is it, Teresa? What's wrong?'

Suddenly it all came flooding out. 'Mum, I hate it here!' I told her about Bridget, Dr Peri, the locked doors, the pills – everything.

'I knew it! I knew they were going to lock you up,' she said angrily. 'Find a way to escape and once you're out, ring me and I'll tell you how to find me.'

'I will, Mum,' I'd said, my heart leaping with hope.

Two days later, I was finally allowed out through the kitchen into the back garden. Having been cooped up inside for so long, the garden felt like another country, another planet. I kept taking in long, deep breaths of fresh summer air. It felt so good to be out in the open, even though the garden was enclosed by a huge metal fence, about twelve feet high. Turning my face up to the sky, I forgot my troubles for a few moments and relished the warming sensation of sunshine on my face. I stretched out my arms and twirled in a circle, enjoying the sense of space and freedom. As I spun around, I kept hearing Mum's voice urging me to run away.

Harriet doped me up again after lunch. Then Kate sent for me. 'Janice says you behaved very well in the garden this morning, so I'm going to let you come out and spend your pocket money with us this afternoon.' She looked at me expectantly.

I took the hint. 'Thank you!' I said, perking up at the thought of a change of scene.

My weekly pocket money allowance had been set at seventy-five pence. Out of that I had to buy some personal products, including soap, shampoo and deodorant from the Kendall House supply. The shampoo came in Sunsilk sachets that cost five pence each. The deodorant was called Mum, somewhat ironically. Although it didn't work very well, we all loved it because it came in pretty pastel pink or blue and had a lovely scent.

I'd already spent most of my first two weeks' money, but I just about had enough left for a packet of cigarettes, or almost. Zara and Sophie C agreed to chip in so we could buy a pack of twenty.

We went into town and wandered around the shops in the local high street, waiting for a chance to sneak off and have a smoke. Kate kept her beady eye on us though. I thought we'd never be able to give her the slip. Finally, she was distracted by a discussion with a shop assistant about whether stripes or plain material worked better for curtains. As she eyed up several bolts of cloth, Sophie C nudged me and nodded towards the shop door. I nudged Zara and raised my eyebrows, but Zara shook her head and motioned to us to leave without her. We tiptoed out of the door. As soon as we reached the pavement outside, Sophie C broke into a run. I sprinted after her with no idea of where I was going, nor did I care.

I'd hardly had any exercise for weeks and was quickly out of breath. 'Where are we going?' I asked, panting.

'Fags first, then my mum's.' She disappeared into a sweet shop and came out with twenty Embassy.

We got a train and a bus to her mum's house, where her mother welcomed us with open arms and gave us a slap-up meal. I rang my mum on the number she had given me, my heart thumping. But Mum sounded flustered and told me to stay at Sophie's for now. She was changing jobs again, she said. 'So it may take me a little while to get settled and ready for you.' I felt sick with disappointment, but tried not to let it show.

Towards evening, my mind started feeling a lot clearer than it had been for the previous fortnight. 'Give me another fag,' I said to Sophie C. 'They're making me feel much better.'

'You'll have to go back tomorrow or the next day, girls,' Mrs C said, sighing. 'They'll definitely come looking for you here.'

'Can't you hide us somewhere?' I pleaded. I hated the idea of being locked up again.

'I'm afraid not, love,' she said with regret.

We stayed up late watching telly and larking around. It was wonderful to be able to do and say what we wanted, even if it was only giggling at a silly joke as we drifted off to sleep in Sophie's bedroom. For once I didn't feel totally conked out, just pleasantly, naturally tired.

I woke up in the middle of the night to the sound of loud knocking. Someone was at the front door. A couple of minutes later I heard the rumble of low male voices and Mrs C saying, 'Not at this time of night, surely?'

Heavy footsteps pounded up the stairs. Sophie's bedroom light snapped on. Two burly policemen dragged us out of bed and took us downstairs into a waiting police car. Mrs C came outside with a carrier bag. It had our clothes in it. 'Aren't you even going to let them get dressed?' she said.

'No point,' one of the policemen said. 'They're going straight back to bed.'

I thought this meant they were going to take us back to

Kendall House. I begged them not to. 'They're drugging me,' I said. 'They're turning me into a zombie!' Neither of the policemen replied.

They put us in a dirty holding cell at Bromley Police Station. It stank of vomit. No one checked up on us all night. In the morning they sent a policewoman to let us out. We told her about being forced to take medicine at Kendall House. She seemed to take a keen interest and I began to hope that she might follow up on our complaints. But when she came back she said that she'd been told we were psychiatric patients, so it made sense that drugs were being used on us.

'I'm not a psychiatric patient!' I said.

'Me neither!' said Sophie.

The policewoman shrugged. 'Sorry, girls, I'm afraid I can't help you.'

Some hours later, Kate drove us back to Kendall House in silence. Tears dripped down my cheeks at the thought of being forced to take more pills. Finally I said, 'Why did you tell the police we were psychiatric patients? You more or less said we were mental, didn't you?'

Kate sighed. 'Teresa, were you or were you not a patient at the Long Grove Adolescent Unit?'

'But they chucked me out because it was the wrong place for me! I'm not mad. Dr Staple said I wasn't mad. I shouldn't be on pills. There's nothing wrong with me.'

'Pipe down, for goodness' sake,' she said. She turned on the radio and hummed along to an old 1950s track.

Miss Woods gave us a right telling off when we arrived. We were ordered to bathe and get into our nightclothes again. 'Am I supposed to go to lessons in my nightie?' I said.

'You're not going to lessons. Oh no, you're coming with

me.' She grasped me by the wrist and led me upstairs to the first floor.

It wasn't until we reached the top of the stairs that I realised where she was taking me. 'Don't lock me up. No!' I pleaded, trying to pull away from her and run back downstairs. Remembering how Jules had looked after a night in the detention room, I dreaded having to go through the same experience.

'Did you think you weren't going to be punished? What a very stupid girl you are, then. Now don't go kicking up a stink and making my job harder. You know it won't do any good.'

Harriet appeared on the landing and stood with her arms crossed as Miss Woods unlocked the door to the detention room. 'In you go, then.'

'No, please!'

Harriet stepped forward and gave me a violent push. 'Get in there!' she ordered.

I took a couple of steps forward, even though every part of my body was silently screaming at me to make a run for it. Harriet pushed me again and suddenly I was through the doorway. The door flew shut and the lock immediately turned. I was trapped.

The detention room was tiny and claustrophobic, with minuscule plastic windows high up on the wall. It contained nothing but a built-in wooden cabin bed. Miss Woods told me to bang on the door to attract the attention of a staff member when I needed the toilet. The rest of the time I was supposed to keep quiet and stare into space, except when they brought me more tablets to take. Books and writing material were banned. A little later, I asked if I could work on my sewing. The answer was no.

'Have you locked Sophie up too?' I said.

'Sophie is being dealt with,' Harriet replied tersely. She refused to elaborate further.

I cried myself to sleep and woke up in the early afternoon feeling alone and sorry for myself. I hadn't heard from my dad or Bernadette since I'd arrived at Kendall House. David was in a new home and couldn't be contacted. My mum was going God knows where. Nobody cared about me.

I was allowed downstairs to eat tea before being taken back up again. Kate came in for 'a chat'. I told her how scared I was of some of the girls and said I was going to tell Elizabeth Pryde about all the threats Bridget had made.

'Mrs Pryde is Bridget's social worker as well, didn't you know?' Kate said.

I bit my lip. Just my luck.

I spent a fitful night in the detention room, obsessed with the thought that the door was locked and I couldn't get out. What if there was a fire? Would I be forgotten in the scramble to evacuate the building? I kept turning the possibilities over and over in my mind, and when I did sleep, I had vivid nightmares about being trapped in a coffin or underwater. At one point I woke up and sat bolt upright. The walls of the already cramped room felt as if they were closing in on me. I got out of bed and banged on the door. 'Help! Let me out!' I shouted. No one heard. No one came. I started screaming, but nothing made a difference.

I woke up feeling groggier than ever. I wasn't allowed to get dressed. That 'privilege' had been taken away from me, so I went downstairs in my nightdress once the staff had unlocked the door. After breakfast, I had to line up and swallow the usual dose of tablets, even though I complained that they were making me ill. I had a constantly runny nose and was getting a lot of headaches.

In Mrs Nuttall's drama class, my head began to throb again. Mrs Nuttall had given me a good part in the play reading, but I kept stumbling over the words.

'Come on, Teresa, you can do better than this!' she said.

I threw my copy of the play on the floor. 'I can't do anything on these pills!' I howled. 'I can't think straight. Everything's blurry. It's horrible. I think they're trying to drive me mad.'

My head was swirling and my thoughts were jumbled. 'I hate it here,' I went on, desperate to make her understand what I was going through. 'The staff think I'm crazy. The girls want to beat me up. No one likes me because I'm new. My dad doesn't want to know. My mother has disappeared again. My brother's locked away. My sister doesn't care. All I want to do is kill myself!'

My legs began to feel wobbly. I sat down. I rested my head on the desk and drifted off to sleep.

After lunch, and more pills, I went to the bathroom and splashed water on my face in an attempt to wake myself up. But crushing tiredness overcame me during that afternoon's cookery lesson and I lost my sense of coordination, spilling stewed prunes all down my nightdress.

I expected Mrs Ryfield to be cross, but she said, 'Don't worry, let's get it in to soak before it stains.' She led me down the hall, unlocked a door and handed me over to Dot, who was in charge of the laundry.

'Dear oh dear,' Dot said kindly, inspecting my nightdress. 'Were you trying to drown yourself in prunes?'

I laughed weakly. She helped me to get cleaned up and gave me another apron. Just then, I heard a miaow. I scanned the room eagerly and spotted a cat poking its head through a hole in the wall, a plump tabby with a really pretty face.

'There's Buttercup,' Dot said. 'That's odd. She usually hides from strangers, but she doesn't seem to be so scared of you.'

'Perhaps she can tell how much I love cats,' I said. I knelt down and called her over, but she just watched me warily.

Buttercup lived in the laundry with the other Kendall House cats, but she was special. Like me, she was scared of everyone apart from Dot. It took me ages to gain her trust. She was incredibly shy. At first she would just peer through the hole in the wall when I called her name. She watched nervously as I knelt and talked to her, and resisted all my attempts to coax her to come nearer.

As time went on, she grew braver and crept closer and closer to me, until one day she finally sat on my lap. I felt immense happiness in that moment. She was very loving, and would purr and rub her head against my face. She gave me love in a place that was cold and cruel. But the moment another girl came into the laundry, she'd be gone. She was as lonely and scared as I was.

I told Dot about my love for animals and she asked whether I had a hamster yet. 'I'm getting one next week, if I'm good,' I said, smiling for the first time since I'd been brought back to Kendall House. I was thrilled when she said I could come back and see Buttercup soon.

My euphoria was short-lived. There was a strange atmosphere in the sitting room after school and when I asked Zara what was going on, she ignored me. Neither Emma nor Sophie C would talk to me either. I noticed that they were sucking up to Bridget more than usual, telling her how nice she looked and asking what she wanted to watch on TV.

'Bad news: Maya's gone,' Jules whispered a few minutes later. 'She's left Kendall House for good. Bridget is queen bee now.'

My heart fluttered with fear. Now I understood why none of the other girls were talking to me – Bridget would have told them not to. Jules said she'd stick by me though. I was so grateful. Having a friend by my side made all the difference.

As the evening wore on, it became clear that we'd both been sent to Coventry. We tried not to take any notice and settled down to do a jigsaw puzzle, but it was hard to pretend we didn't care. I kept worrying that the girls in Jules's dorm would turn her against me during the night. She said I was being silly, but I knew how hard it was to stand up to that kind of pressure. If she were anywhere near as scared of Bridget as I was, then she wouldn't hesitate to do what Bridget told her to.

For the second night in a row I was forced to sleep in the detention room. I tossed and turned in the thin, hard bed, unable to calm my anxiety. Now that there was no one to stop Bridget bullying me, there was no telling what she would do.

My fears were confirmed in the washroom the next morning. 'Smelly cow!' she shouted as I cleaned my teeth. 'I'm in charge here and I'll beat you senseless if you don't wash yourself properly today. Get undressed right now.'

'I've already washed myself,' I said.

She stepped forward and slapped the back of my head. 'Don't you fucking talk back to me, you little bitch!' she yelled. 'You'll do as I say or I'll kill you.'

I believed her. There was something so twisted and thuggish about Bridget that I wouldn't have put anything past her, not even murder. I took off my nightdress and wrapped a towel around me in an attempt to stay partially covered up while I washed my body.

'What are you trying to hide?' she crowed. 'Do you think anyone wants to look at your ugly, scrawny body?' She went into a rant: I was mad, I was ugly and no one liked me. I was thick. I stank. If I didn't hurry up she was going to smash my head against the wall. I left the bathroom in tears, dreading the rest of the day.

Next I was summoned to Miss Woods's office, where Dr Peri delivered a lecture on obedience from his usual comfy armchair. Wearing nothing but my nightdress, I stood before him as he explained the consequences of breaking the rules. He shook a fat finger at me. 'I will permit you to get dressed today, but only because this is the first time you have absconded,' he said. 'If you do it again you will be punished a great deal more severely.'

Something told me that I was supposed to be grateful and express my thanks. But I wasn't, so I didn't. He waved me away when I asked if I'd be allowed to stop taking tablets four times a day.

No one spoke to Jules and me at breakfast. It was a horrible feeling having ten girls stare through you as if you weren't there. Jules tried to reassure me. 'It won't go on forever. They'll pick on someone else in time,' she said. I wasn't so sure. The glint in Bridget's eyes had been there from the moment I'd first met her. I couldn't see it disappearing any time soon.

CHAPTER SEVEN

Dad was given permission to visit the following Sunday. 'Teresa, what's happened to you? You're so thin and pale. You look awful!' he said.

'Oh Dad,' I said, breaking into uncontrollable tears. 'This place is terrible. Can't you get me out of here?'

He was appalled to hear about the pills they were giving me. 'I'll ring Social Services and give them a piece of my mind,' he promised. 'They've no right to be drugging my daughter.'

When he left an hour later, he was full of assurances that he would also be phoning Miss Woods to complain about the way I was being treated. 'See you soon,' he said. 'Hang on in there. I'll sort them out.'

I didn't have a lot of faith in Dad's ability to change the situation, but it was the only hope I had, tiny as it was, and like a drowning man clinging to a matchstick, I hung on to it for dear life. Then, less than a week later, the matchstick floated away when he rang to say that he was being evicted from the flat. He sounded really low. 'I've got my own battles to fight for now,' he said dejectedly, 'so you'll have to look after yourself for the time being.'

I wasn't sure how long I could go on. Life was getting worse every day. Bridget's grip on the other girls was so powerful that they ignored me most of the time. Even Jules was finding it tough to stand up to them, just as I'd predicted. I didn't hold it against her. When you've got a gang of girls constantly pushing you one way, it's very hard to keep going in the other direction.

I never knew when or where to expect some kind of assault, whether verbal or physical. Violence could erupt at any time, often at totally random moments. It wasn't only directed at me. There was constant in-fighting among the girls. It seemed as if there was always someone punching or kicking someone else, and scraps would start at dinner time, bath time or bedtime – even first thing in the morning. On more than one occasion Zara slapped me as I got out of bed. 'I've just about had enough of your bloody crying,' she'd say.

One afternoon I was last in line for my pills behind Sophie K, who was in a foul mood. She told Harriet that she was not going to take her tablets. 'I won't take mine either,' I said, hoping that Sophie would appreciate the back up, even though I found her a bit intimidating. She was blonde and of medium build, with a great big scar on her face that she got in a car accident before she came to Kendall House.

'Shut up, Teresa!' she shouted. The next thing I knew she had leapt at me and was ferociously pulling my hair, trying to rip it from my scalp.

Harriet separated us, with the help of Ivy and Benita, who took me upstairs and made me change into my nightclothes. 'Why isn't Sophie being punished?' I asked. Surely they had noticed that she'd started it.

'If you make trouble, you get trouble,' Benita said cryptically.

My stomach twisted. I didn't bother to argue. Even the staff seemed to be turning against me.

Although it was a struggle to keep myself alert when I was being drugged four times a day, the fear-fuelled adrenalin that constantly pumped through me seemed to run counter to the effects of the pills. I became nervy and jumpy and hypersensitive to the slightest noise or movement, even when I was really drowsy. I could always sense when someone was coming up behind me; I didn't have to hear them first.

When two new girls arrived – Nicole and Tina – I half-hoped that Bridget and the others would forget about me and start picking on them instead. Unfortunately, it didn't work out that way. Nicole was very, very pretty and Bridget seemed to be enchanted by her from the start. Her eyes lit up when Nicole first appeared in the girls' sitting room and I noticed how she would stare at her whenever she was near, greedily taking in the girl's cute symmetrical features and glossy dark blonde hair.

As for Tina, she was small and thin and looked like she couldn't hurt a flea, but in her case appearances were definitely deceptive. Word soon spread that she'd been sent to Kendall House for attacking a girl with a hot iron. According to the rumour, she'd held the girl down and pressed the iron against her cheek, scarring her for life. Nobody dared to ask her about it, but from the start it was obvious that she was a hard nut, despite her tiny frame. She seemed OK at first, but she soon developed a habit of creeping up behind me and launching herself onto my back, clinging on like a crab, biting and pulling my hair. She did it to everyone.

In the end, it got to the point where every time I walked away from her, Tina was hanging off my back. She was that bad. You could beat the shit out of her – you could probably take the head off her body – and she would still hang onto your back. Small as she was, she was frighteningly disturbed. Nothing and no one seemed to scare her, not even Bridget.

Two days after Sophie K attacked me, Harriet ordered me to get out of my nightie and get dressed. 'Ever been to Dover?' she asked.

I thought back to the old songs Dad and his friends had sung around the piano at the Fox and Hounds. 'No. Are the cliffs really white?'

'Well, you'll soon find out, won't you?'

Sure enough, after lunch several girls plus Harriet and Brenda piled into Fred's van and drove along roads signposted with pictures of ferries.

'Let's stow away to France,' I whispered to Jules. 'They've got great beaches and je parle bien français.'

She laughed. 'I'd rather go to Holland and cycle through fields of tulips.'

As we drew into Dover, chattering about our dreams of escape, Fred started making suggestive jokes about running away with sailors. Sophie K rolled her eyes. I remembered hearing that Fred was known for making innuendoes about sex. Harriet and Brenda laughed though. They seemed to find him funny.

Fred was engaged to Janine, one of the staff at Kendall House, and I'd already seen him a few times. He was very unattractive. With his thin lips, weak chin and greasy black hair, he looked like Dracula on a bad day. To add to that impression, he often wore sunglasses, even when the weather was dreary.

The van pulled up in a car park near the docks. Before we got out, Harriet laid down the law. 'We stick together. Any funny business and we go straight back to the house.'

'We'll be as good as gold, don't you worry,' Sophie K said, sounding like butter wouldn't melt in her mouth.

But the instant we got out of the van, Sophie made a bolt for it, sprinting out of the car park at full pelt. I watched her go, amazed. She was running fast enough to win an Olympic medal. Brenda and Fred pursued her, leaving the rest of us with Harriet, who made us get back in the van and wait until they caught up with Sophie. We ended up playing I spy for the next hour. Some trip that turned out to be. I didn't even get to see the white cliffs.

Sophie was picked up trying to hitch a lift at the ferry exit. 'I nearly made it,' she said under her breath, as Fred and Brenda bundled her back into the van.

'Better luck next time,' we commiserated.

On the drive back to Gravesend we silently hatched another plan to escape, this time involving the whole group. Pulling up outside Kendall House, Sophie C gave everyone a discreet thumbs up. I drew in a deep breath and got ready to run.

As Fred let us out of the back of the van, we burst out onto the pavement and hightailed it off in different directions. 'Go, go, go!' shouted Sophie K.

I lost sight of her and Jules, but Sophie C and I linked up and legged it as fast as we could towards town, with Brenda following hot on our heels. Adrenalin pumped through me as my feet pounded on the pavement, and although the unused muscles in my thighs soon began to ache, my legs went on pumping away, fuelled by desperation. But then, as we raced down Cobham Street, Sophie stumbled over a small pile of bricks on the pavement. I tried to steady her, but lost my footing and tripped, landing painfully on my knees. Thirty seconds later Brenda had us firmly in her grip.

'You'll be in your nightclothes for a week this time,' she gasped angrily.

Back in the dorm at Kendall House I heard that Sophie K and Jules were still missing. A wave of depression swept over me at the thought that Jules might get away for good. Of course I would be glad for her if she managed to escape, but how would I survive without my only true friend? As I changed into my nightie and tried to prepare myself for another tortured night in the detention room, I was over-whelmed by a sense of hopelessness. What was the point in going on?

I picked up the framed photo by my bed and stared at the smiling faces of my family. Why had everything gone wrong for us? It seemed so unfair that other girls my age were living happy, settled lives within loving homes, while I was shut away in a lock-up for delinquent girls – for no other reason than that there had been nowhere else to send me long term. A surge of bleak fury went through me and I threw the photo to the floor. The frame cracked and shards of glass flew everywhere. I burst out crying.

In a jumble of self-pity and anger, some kind of hazy logic told me that perhaps it would just be easier to end things now. After all, anything was better than being stuck in Kendall House, and I was sure that nobody would miss me when I was gone. I reached down and picked up a sliver of glass. It felt sharp and lethal against the tips of my fingers. I jabbed my wrist with it. Tiny droplets of blood formed on my pale skin.

Suddenly something snapped inside me and I began to slash my arm, all the way up to the elbow and biceps. Soon the whole arm was running with blood and my hands were covered in cuts and grazes. I hardly felt any pain; my nerves seemed totally numb. Instead it felt a little as though I had lanced a boil, releasing a build-up of misery and tension. It was a relief to express how much I was hurting inside, even if it meant turning my pain and anger in on myself.

Harriet found me lying on the bed in a daze. 'Teresa!' she shouted. 'What have you done, you stupid girl?'

She cleaned me up, using cotton wool and witch hazel, while Miss Woods swept up the glass. 'Here, drink this,' Harriet said, passing me a glass of cloudy hot water.

'What's in it? I don't want any more medicine.'

'It's a vitamin drink. It'll stop you feeling so weak.'

I took a sip. It tasted very odd, like a mixture of cough syrup and almonds. 'It won't knock me out, will it?' I asked, but she wouldn't say. Thirsty from the exertions of the afternoon, I drank the rest down in one, and twenty minutes later, I fell into a state that wasn't so much a sleep as a coma. I was dead to the world for the next fourteen hours. Annette – another member of staff – had to shake me awake the next morning.

My eyelids felt heavy; my limbs were like lead. I dragged myself down to breakfast but kept dropping my knife as I tried to spread butter on my toast.

'You don't look well,' Jules said. Neither did she. They'd grabbed her and Sophie K about an hour after they'd caught up with Sophie C and me. She had spent the night in the hated detention room, drugged up to the eyeballs.

'I feel like I've been hit with a sledgehammer. God knows what was in that drink Harriet gave me!' I said.

'Me too,' she added wearily.

I shambled along to the music class in my nightdress. I got on well with Miss Shilling, the music teacher. She knew how much I enjoyed the subject, so she usually gave me a certain amount of leeway when I grew sleepy in class. But today she seemed surprised by my inability to join in with recorder practice. The most I could do when she asked me a question was smile stupidly at her, and I kept nodding off.

Art with Mrs Nuttall was no better. My painting skills were reduced to toddler level and I tipped over two tumblers of water. In the end Mrs Nuttall suggested that I sit quietly with a book. I didn't care one way or the other. Nothing seemed to matter.

Later in the day my mood switched from dopey to jittery and I went up onto a nervous high. I'd lost my appetite and hadn't eaten all day, so I was already buzzing from lack of food, as well as the after-effects of the previous night's medicine.

Jules was my partner for the afternoon disco and ballroom dancing class in the front room. Our attempts to rumba were a complete disaster; it was the drugged leading the drugged. She went one way and I went the other and we kept bumping into each other and treading on each other's toes, much to the chagrin of Mr and Mrs Harding, the older couple taking the class. Worse still, because I was feeling so jumpy, I kept missing beats and jigging around to try and make up the rhythm. In the end, Jules took over and yanked me around the cramped dance floor, taking care not to hurt my bandaged arm.

Dad and his friends had taught me to waltz and foxtrot at the working men's club balls, but my fogged brain could scarcely recall the steps. I looked over Jules's shoulder to try to get some tips from the other girls. They were no help. We were like a bunch of elephants and one-legged giraffes.

But catching sight of Bridget's huge backside swinging from side to side under her grey skirt, I couldn't help giggling. There was something absurd in the way she danced. For one, it's impossible to look tough doing the cha cha cha. What's more, she was a really rubbish mover.

I wasn't the only one who found Bridget's dancing funny. Every time she swung her backside, the room rippled with suppressed laughter. She could sense it too. If she caught anyone looking at her, she would get a right cob on. 'What you staring at?' she'd hiss. It was so hard not to laugh in her face.

I thought Jules and I looked rather glamorous waltzing in our brushed cotton pink nighties and dressing gowns, but the floaty look didn't suit the next stage of the class, which was disco dancing. Every week, Mr and Mrs Harding brought along the same record – the cheesy 1980s track, D.I.S.C.O by Ottawan – and played it over and over again. We were supposed to perform a routine with arm movements that spelt out the word 'disco'. It was like the YMCA routine, and I could never get it right.

Jules constantly had to nudge me and shove me in the right direction, which had us in fits of laughter. Added to that, I couldn't help watching Bridget out of the corner of my eye. For some reason it was important to her to suck up to Mr and Mrs Harding and she tried diligently to get her moves right, even though she had not one ounce of dancing talent.

'Watch this!' Sophie K whispered to Jules and me about halfway through the lesson. She stood behind Bridget and imitated her, exaggerating her clumsy movements. Everyone laughed. Suddenly Bridget whipped round to face her and pushed her backwards, screaming obscenities.

'Stop that now!' Mrs Harding said, putting out a frail arm to restrain Bridget.

''You can fuck off too, you daft old bitch,' Bridget shouted, totally forgetting to suck up. Mrs Harding recoiled in horror.

'Don't speak to my wife like that!' Mr Harding protested. 'And don't ruin the class for the rest of the girls. Everyone else is having a lovely time, aren't they?'

'No, we hate it! Why do you make us do the same stupid dance every single week?' yelled Sophie C. Mrs Harding started saying something, but Sophie told her to shut up, 'you old bag'.

Soon most of the girls had joined in, subjecting the couple to a barrage of shocking insults and bad language. They quickly fled the room and reported us to Mrs Nuttall, and for the rest of the afternoon we were made to sit in silence. By then I was feeling sleepy again, so I was glad of the break, and anything was better than hearing that damn D.I.S.C.O. track on repeat. It was like some horrific form of torture. Even to this day I could recite the lyrics in my sleep.

That evening Mrs Pryde rang and left a message to say that David was being sent to Feltham Borstal for burglary. I was devastated for him. Everyone knew how rough borstal was. As the tears flowed, I knew I was crying for myself too, because this meant that David wouldn't be able to visit me now. We probably wouldn't see each other for ages.

Even though my brother was often mean to me, we had been through a lot together and I missed him. I couldn't understand why he hadn't written to me as he'd promised he would. (I found out later that Kate was withholding his letters. Her excuse was that she thought they would distress me.) Harriet found me sobbing in the dorm and I told her how worried I was about him. The more I talked about him and the rest of the family, the more upset I became. Eventually she forced me to drink down another glass of hot vitamin drink. I went out like a light again, back into the same dreamless, lifeless sleep as the night before.

I woke up at dawn, feeling on edge. The sky was orange and pink through the cracks in the curtains. I got up and started to pace the dorm, but five minutes later a wave of tiredness swept through me and I slept again. My jaw ached when I finally got up for good. 'You were grinding your teeth,' Zara said when she saw me rubbing my jaw. 'We all do it. It's the pills.'

The contents of the brown envelopes Harriet was giving me had begun to vary. Along with the blue and white tablets there was sometimes a yellow one and other white and orange pills of varying sizes. I asked Harriet repeatedly, but she wouldn't tell me what they were for, or why I was supposed to take more of them some days than others.

I started getting rashes and dry patches on different parts of my body. My right ear was constantly itchy and flaky. My hair lost its sheen and my mouth filled up with ulcers. Worst of all, I began suffering from what felt like period pains – but all through the month, not just when I was menstruating. They would start as a dull ache in my lower back and then gradually encircle me, creeping across my stomach until I had a ring of pain around me. Sometimes the pain in my kidney area would get so bad that I'd be doubled up, unable to go on with what I was doing.

The staff and teachers were totally unsympathetic. 'Always moaning and groaning, aren't you?' Mrs Petsworth used to say, tutting away.

One morning Mrs Macdonald flashed up a card with 'hypochondria' written on it. She asked the class if they knew what it meant. 'Teresa's a good example of a hypochondriac,' she said with a superior smile. It didn't seem fair. My symptoms were very real – and very worrying – to me. I knew I wasn't being paranoid.

Harriet made me take more and more of her lethal hot water concoctions. It didn't matter how hard I tried not to drink them – spitting, dribbling and spilling them were just some of my avoidance tactics – she always made sure that enough went down to zonk me out.

Increasingly I didn't make it to breakfast. One of the staff would come into the detention room or my dorm and rouse me around lunchtime. Even then it would be hard to wake me. I started falling asleep in class and my crying fits became more frequent and intense. I kept picturing David trying to tough it out at Feltham Borstal. It upset me to imagine how unhappy he would be there and I guessed he was probably be feeling suicidal, like me. I hated to think of Dad being evicted from the flat too. Where would he go? And what about Mum?

I had a fantasy that one day soon the family would come together again and we'd all live happily ever after. Dad would go to work and Mum would cook delicious meals. Bernadette and I would swap clothes and make-up and then we'd all sit around the telly in the evenings, laughing and joking. David would get a job and a girlfriend, and on Saturdays they'd take me skating, or to the cinema. I'd have lots of friends and Mum would make them welcome in our house, cooking them meals and fussing over them, and me.

Apart from when I was lost in my dream world, life was bearable only when I was in the laundry with Buttercup the cat, or helping to clean out the other girls' hamsters. I was always begging Miss Woods to let me have a hamster of my own. 'I'll look after it so well! I'll feed it and make sure its cage is always clean!'

'You have to earn that privilege, as you well know,' she'd say primly. 'You won't be getting one unless your behaviour improves considerably.'

She kept dangling it like a carrot, and then telling me that I'd ruined my chances. She didn't seem to understand that a lot of the time it felt as though I didn't have much control over the way I behaved or reacted. I didn't want to fall asleep in class any more than I wanted to slur my words or forget what I was saying mid-sentence, and yet I kept being told off for all three. However hard I struggled to be normal, my mood swings were becoming more extreme, and I could swoop from a state of deep sadness to hysterical laughter in the blink of an eye. I started harming myself with whatever I could get my hands on, from plastic and glass to the edges of pieces of paper.

I constantly thought about suicide. I couldn't see any point in living through this hell, without an end in sight. I pictured death as a blissful escape. It seemed as if things just couldn't get any worse. How wrong I was. In fact things were about to get a lot, lot worse, beyond my darkest imaginings.

CHAPTER EIGHT

I began to forget my French. Just over a month into my time at Kendall House, I could no longer recall words that had come easily to me before, or translate basic sentences like, 'The book is on the table.' To me, this was proof that the daily cocktail of pills was affecting me in a very harmful way.

'The tablets are making me stupid!' I complained to Mrs Nuttall. 'Don't you remember how good my French used to be?'

'I just don't think you're trying,' she said condescendingly.

Nothing I said made a difference. It was like living among Martians. I was trapped in a twilight zone where I could not make myself heard, or believed. I felt totally helpless. There was nowhere to turn, and no one willing to listen. I couldn't see the point in going on.

In despair, I grabbed a plastic pen, snapped it in half and plunged it into my arm. Blood dribbled down my skin, but I didn't care. I didn't feel any pain.

'Stop that at once!' Mrs Nuttall cried out, rushing towards me. 'Where did you get that pen?' She tried to snatch it from me. I pushed her away.

'Leave me alone,' I said. 'It's my pen. I can do what I want with it.' I jabbed my arm again. The pen began to splinter.

'Teresa, don't!' She left the room, swiftly returning with Harriet.

'Give me the pen,' Harriet ordered.

'No. Don't come near me.'

Harriet lunged at me and tried to grab the pen, but I shoved her back. Her dark eyes flashed with anger. She pressed her lips together into an uneven grimace.

'Go away! I've had enough of being controlled,' I said.

I slashed at my arm with a piece of jagged plastic, fast and furious. Soon there was a criss-cross pattern from the top of my left arm right down to my wrist. Thin streams of blood dripped into my hand. Watching them, I felt a temporary sense of peace, beyond pain.

I wanted to stop, but I was scared of lashing out. I knew it was wrong to hurt other people. It was far better to take it all out on myself. I felt desperately unhappy and lonely, and so small and insignificant that it was almost as if I didn't exist. I had no mind of my own anymore. I was nothing.

Shirley entered the room. 'Now, Teresa, please . . .' she said in a placatory voice. Harriet lunged towards me again and I screamed loud and hard, drowning out whatever it was that Shirley said next.

Harriet wouldn't give up. I could see she wanted to fight. Now Shirley came for me too, grabbing for my arms and trying to pull them behind my back. But I wouldn't give in. The fear of being restrained gave me unexpected strength and I struggled furiously, punching and kicking in every direction. Mrs Macdonald appeared out of nowhere and tried to pounce on me, and at some point Mrs Petsworth joined the fray. Her long thin arms kept reaching out to grasp me, but I slapped them away.

Miss Woods and Matthew, who was the part-time book keeper at Kendall House, burst into the room and rushed at me. Matthew was thin and wiry, but very muscular. He punched me hard in the back, winding me. I fell forwards, face down, with my arms outstretched and flailing. 'Pin her down!' Miss Woods shouted. 'Quick, Harriet, inject her.'

I was still kicking and yelling as they yanked my arms behind me. Matthew took hold of my hands and pressed them against my lower back. A heavy weight landed on my left leg, squashing it. I realised that someone was sitting on me to keep me down. Someone else sat on the other leg. A hand kept pressing my head down. I heard my jaw crack as they pushed my face hard against the ground. I tried to resist and push up with my neck, scared that my face would smash into the floor again. Someone grabbed my hair and jerked my head upwards. A fist thumped into the middle of my back. My chest felt like it was caving in. I couldn't breathe or swallow. I was terrified.

I didn't want to live, but if I was going to die it would be at my own hands, not theirs. An even heavier weight pressed down on me. My ribs were hurting badly. I screamed out but they kept on pressing me down. I felt sick. Vomit rose up my throat and I started to choke. My hair stuck to my face. It was drenched in tears. I begged them to get off me. I screamed out that I would do anything they wanted me to.

'It's a bit late for that now!' Harriet said gleefully. She seemed to be enjoying the drama.

I heard Ivy's voice, and then Miss Woods's. Someone pulled my nightie up to waist level, exposing my legs and bottom. A rough hand started fumbling with my knickers. Terrified, I struggled harder, jerking and wriggling as much as I could. I was desperate to get away, out of their clutches.

My knickers tore as they were violently pulled down. 'No!' I cried out. 'Get off! Help me, someone!'

'Stay still,' Harriet ordered. 'Just lie back and think of England. What's the point in struggling? There!'

A sudden, searing pain shot through my bum down my legs and up through my back. I screamed with every last bit of energy I had, petrified that they were trying to kill me. For a brief moment my body vibrated with the most intense pain and fear I'd ever experienced. Then I felt a potent mixture of drugs pumping through my system, immobilising me, shutting me down on all levels. My scream floated away into thin air, no longer loud or powerful. I heard myself whimper a couple of times.

They got hold of me as I went limp and dragged me like a rag doll through the corridor, not caring when my head knocked against a door. I could see and feel what was going on, but at the same time it felt as if I wasn't in my body. I saw several girls watching with wide, horrified eyes as they yanked me through the hall and up the stairs, like a pig to slaughter. My last thoughts were a jumbled mixture of confusion and hatred. And then I was out, dead to the world.

I woke up in the detention room, with Shirley standing over me. At first I couldn't think who she was. Petite, with plain, open features and short, curly, fair hair, she brought to mind a farmer's wife I had once seen interviewed on TV. Her arm was in a sling. 'You're a very naughty girl, aren't you?' she said.

I shook my head, unable to remember how I'd ended up in the room, or why. I tried to speak, but my mouth was as dry as a desert and my throat was sore. My body felt tender and bruised all over, as if I'd just gone ten rounds in a boxing ring. My arm was bandaged. A nerve in one of my eyelids kept flickering. I had a really bad headache and my brain was barely functioning.

With great effort, I managed to swallow. 'What happened?' I asked in a small, ragged voice.

'Come off it, Teresa, are you trying to tell me that you don't recall punching Harriet in the ribs, or hurting my elbow?'

I frowned and slowly shook my head again. 'No. I don't.'

'Well, I am in a lot of pain because of you. Every time I move my arm it hurts, and it looks like I'm going to be wearing this sling for at least a fortnight. So, what have you got to say for yourself?'

A surge of guilt overcame me. I hated the idea of causing anyone pain. It had never been in my nature to hurt anything. I loved animals. I loved people. I loved kids. I was that way inclined. To hurt someone was a major thing. 'Is it broken?' I asked.

'As it happens, it's not, but that's no thanks to you, madam!'

'I'm so sorry,' I croaked. 'I can't remember anything, but I'm sure I didn't mean to do it.'

'Sorry is better than nothing, I suppose,' she said. 'But it's not going to make my elbow better, is it? And it's not going to heal poor old Harriet's bruised ribs either.' She tapped her temple, as if pointing to her brain. 'You are just going to have to think harder about the consequences of your actions in future, aren't you? Perhaps this will teach you not to misbehave, eh?'

Hot tears welled up in my eyes. 'I'm sorry. I didn't realise I'd done it.'

'So will you promise me that we won't have hysterical scenes like that again? No more slashing your arms with pens, no more fighting with members of staff. If you want to stay friends with me, you're going to have to be a good girl from now on. Do you understand?'

I nodded, still unsure which hysterical scenes she was referring to. My mind was a haze and I was feeling incredibly small and weak and powerless. Right then I would have agreed to anything in order to get a bit of comfort or care. But suddenly I flashed back to the memory of someone pulling down my knickers. A mishmash of images crowded into my mind and I began to piece together what had gone on. Shuddering, I reached out and touched Shirley's arm. 'They hurt me,' I said. 'You hurt me.' As the full horror of what had happened came back to me, I shrank away from her, reliving my fear.

'No, Teresa,' she scolded. 'We simply stopped you from harming yourself.'

'But I ache all over.' I pulled up my nightdress to inspect my legs. My knees were black and blue. There was a hand-shaped bruise on my thigh.

'I'm not at all surprised. You wouldn't let us help you, so we had to use a certain amount of force. It was only for your own good, you know.'

Again those words: 'for your own good'. It was the catch-all reason for everything they were doing, from drugging me to locking me up, from taking away my shoes to pinning me down. But there wasn't any good in it. Everything was getting worse. I'd never self-harmed before Kendall House. I hadn't experienced all-day crying fits. I'd been a healthy girl with a good appetite and a clear complexion. I may have been messed up by my family situation, but I'd still managed to be happy and chatty most of the time. Yet now I had slash marks and scars up and down my arms. I was always in tears.

My appetite was tiny, my skin was covered in rashes and I was miserable most of the time. I told Shirley how unhappy I was feeling.

'Well, how do you think I feel?' she said with a poor-me smile, looking down at her trussed up arm.

I felt another pang of guilt. 'I'm so sorry, sorry, sorry! I'll never do it again, I promise.'

'That's what I like to hear,' she said, beaming. 'Now, if you're good I'll pop back later and give your hair a brush and tidy you up a bit. Would you like that?'

'Yes, please,' I said, my voice choking. More than anything, I wanted to be looked after.

I was alone for the next few hours, drifting in and out of sleep. I felt increasingly guilty about Shirley and hoped she believed me that I hadn't meant to hurt her. On the other hand, it confused me that she had joined the others to help pin me to the ground and inject me. What's more, she hadn't shown any sympathy for what I had been through. I was literally covered in bruises, from head to toe, but she hadn't batted an eyelid when I showed her the marks that she and the others had left.

Miss Woods came in for a chat. I tried to sit up, but my back was stiff and ached terribly. 'It really hurts. I think I need a doctor,' I said.

'There you go again, attention-seeking at every opportunity!' she tutted. 'You're unbelievable, you are, and after hurting Shirley like that too!'

'I didn't mean to! I said I was sorry.'

All the guilt trips they were throwing at me just made me feel worse about myself. I wanted to self-harm even more than before. I was useless. No good. Bad.

I fell back onto my hard pillow and stared at the ceiling

while she lectured me about my behaviour. She finished up by saying, 'I will be confiscating your pens and we will be monitoring all of your personal possessions. You have forfeited the right to be responsible for them yourself.'

'But I need pens to do my homework,' I said.

'Don't concern yourself with school for the time being. Far more important is learning how to get the best out of Kendall House, and you can do that by going right back to basics. So, no school tomorrow – I've told the teachers that you can have a few days off. We don't want you getting upset over your failures again.'

I thought back to Mrs Nuttall's class. 'I've forgotten how to speak French,' I said. 'I used to be really good, but I can't remember a thing anymore.'

Miss Woods pursed her lips. 'We can't all be clever, you know. But Mrs Connolly tells me that your needlework is excellent, so why don't you concentrate on the practical subjects when you get back to school?'

She just didn't understand. I tried to explain that the medicine was affecting my learning abilities, but suddenly I felt very tired and couldn't remember what I wanted to say. I tried to speak, but all that came out was a burble of mixed up French and English. My brain felt as if it had been liquefied. My thoughts were a swirling mass.

Finally I was able to say something coherent. 'I'm so scared. What's happening to me?'

Miss Woods stood up. She looked down at me with hard eyes. 'You are learning some of life's most important lessons, including how to cooperate,' she said. 'Yes, it can be difficult to adjust, but life will be impossible for you here if you don't learn how to live peacefully.'

A little later, Harriet came in with a handful of tablets.

She too was full of recriminations. 'How could you treat Shirley like that? Have you seen her poor arm? What disgusting behaviour! You should be ashamed.'

I burst into tears. 'I've said I'm sorry, and I am, I really am. I didn't mean to hurt her.'

After she had left I fell into a deep sleep. In my dreams, I was pursued by monsters wielding enormous hypodermic needles. As they got closer to me, I realised that Matthew and Harriet were among them, their features distended and distorted. Matthew was waving a pair of blue knickers. 'Lie back and think of England!' Harriet kept shouting. I woke up shivering and drenched in sweat.

When Harriet woke me up the next day, I was still feeling very groggy. 'Chop chop!' she said, throwing some of my clothes down on the bed. 'Get dressed. We're going out for a walk.'

'Is Shirley's arm better?'

'It's still extremely painful. She had to go to hospital to have it X-rayed in case it was broken. Honestly, how could you have done such a nasty thing?'

Once again I said how sorry I was. I still felt really bad about it. My stomach made a growling sound. I rubbed it. 'I think I'm hungry.'

Harriet gave me a slanted look. 'You do pick your moments, don't you? Shirley tried waking you for breakfast and for lunch, but she couldn't rouse you. Go and get a snack from the kitchen, but hurry up. I haven't got a lot of time for our little outing.'

'Where are we going?'

'You'll see when we get there.'

It took me ages to put on my clothes. I was a fumbling wreck – all fingers and thumbs, as my nan would have said –

and by the time I was ready to go out I had lost my appetite. My mind kept zoning in and out and I forgot what I was supposed to be doing half the time. Harriet became very impatient and rushed me along on our way into town. It was hard to keep up with her.

First we went to the chemist. I gazed longingly at the lipstick samples while Harriet discussed something with the pharmacist. Next we went to a hardware shop to pick up a couple of things. I began to wonder why Harriet had brought me with her. It wasn't as if she needed someone to help her with the few things she'd bought.

As if sensing my confusion, she said, 'Didn't you say you wanted a hamster?' She pointed at the pet shop on Philip Street.

Had I heard right? At first I couldn't believe it. But sure enough, she took me into the pet shop and told me to pick out a hamster. I went straight for the loudest and liveliest, a gorgeous little thing with light ginger fur and beautiful dark eyes. He was squealing like a nutter, full of energy, and running maniacally around his cage. I was even more impressed when I put my finger in the cage and he bit me. A true fighter, he wasn't content with just one bite. He sank his teeth in and hung on for dear life. I was determined to get him to like me.

'Isn't it sweet?' Harriet said. 'You should call it Ginger.'

She had to be joking. 'No, I'm going to call him Dynamutt. Yes, Dynamutt.' I laughed. It was thrilling to have my own pet. 'Because he's like a teeny, weeny explosive miniature dog!'

Harriet looked puzzled. 'Dynamutt? No, that's no good. Call it Ginger. That's a much better name.'

'Is he my hamster?'

'Yes, it's yours for as long as you tend to it and treat it well.'

'Then I get to choose the name. And it's Dynamutt.'

She pressed her lips together. How could she argue? She paid the shop assistant and we took Dynamutt back to Kendall House. He shrieked all the way. Perhaps he sensed what was in store for us both in the coming weeks.

Back inside the house, Harriet told me to put Dynamutt with the other hamsters on the bottom shelf of a built-in wall unit in the sitting room, and then to get back into my nightclothes. 'Please don't put me back in the detention room!' I said.

'Miss Woods says you can sleep in the dorm tonight, but only if you're good and take your pills.'

I groaned, although anything was better than being cooped up in that claustrophobic hellhole. But, as it turned out, I wouldn't have known much about it either way. The medication Harriet gave me after tea put me out like a light. I slept for fourteen straight hours and woke up at eight thirty the next morning with what felt like a head full of sand.

I didn't feel well enough to go with the other girls on their trip to the Isle of Grain that afternoon, but when they came back, I joined them in the sitting room to watch a film. Tina and Bridget kept interrupting the TV to say nasty things. 'I'm going to get a hamster,' Bridget said. 'I'm going to train it to fight your hamster and sink its teeth into your hamster's neck and suck out all its blood.'

I shuddered at the thought of my lovely Dynamutt being in danger. 'You're not coming anywhere near him,' I said. 'Only Jules is allowed to feed him when I'm not there.'

Bridget switched channels on the television. 'Hey! I was watching that,' Sophie K said.

'Ya boo sucks,' Bridget spat at her. Turning to me again,

she said, 'First I'm going to kill your hamster and then I'm going to kill you. Ha!'

I shut my eyes and clapped my hands over my ears, unable to bear the cruelty in her gaze, the sadistic satisfaction in her voice. 'Fuck off, fuck off, fuck off!' I mumbled, returning to my childhood mantra. I spent the rest of the evening sitting halfway up the hall stairs.

Two days later I was called into Miss Woods's office. Mrs Pryde was sitting in the leather armchair that Dr Peri favoured, with Bridget opposite her. Bridget was drinking from one of Miss Woods's dinky cups. There was a tea tray between them and they were laughing together about something. It was a very cosy, intimate scene, unlike any meeting with Mrs Pryde that I could ever imagine. I stood at the doorway wondering when they would notice me.

Just then Bridget looked up. 'Uh-oh, here's trouble.'

Mrs Pryde looked at her watch. 'Time's up now, Bridget. See you next time,' she said. Bridget scowled at me as she left the room.

'So, Teresa,' my social worker said, barely smiling. 'How are you getting on, then?' Looking vaguely bored, she settled back into the chair to hear what I had to say.

I begged her to take me away from Kendall House. 'I'm being drugged and bullied. I'm losing my mind!' I told her.

About five minutes into the conversation, she held a hand up to silence me. 'It's going to take time to settle in. Let's review things in a couple of months,' she said. She wrote a brief scribble in her notepad.

My heart thumped. 'No!' I protested. 'I'll be dead by then. I'm dying, Mrs Pryde. I'm sure of it. I can't think anymore. I'm battered and bruised and I feel ill almost all of the time. You've got to get me out of here now!'

She rapped her fingers on the arm of the chair and gave me one of her disapproving smiles. Glancing at her wrist again, she said, 'At least let's leave it until my next visit. I'm very pressed for time. I've got another appointment.'

'But you have to save me! I am being drugged to death.'

She sighed. 'Always so dramatic! Teresa, this is all in your head. Dr Peri is a highly respected psychiatrist who knows what he is doing. You must do whatever he says is best for you, for your own good. Whatever he says is right. Just remember that. Now hurry along and get back to school.'

'But I've only ever seen Dr Peri twice, for about five minutes in total!' I protested. 'He can't see what the drugs are doing to me. He doesn't bother visiting to evaluate me. How can he know what's best or isn't?'

I told her about how I had forgotten my French and most of my Maths. She rolled her eyes and assured me that I was in expert hands.

'Trust those who are older and wiser than you are,' she said, putting away her notepad. 'Time to go.'

I eyed the tea tray. 'Don't I get any tea?'

She gave me a tight smile. 'Too late, I'm afraid! Goodbye.'

That night I lacerated my left arm with a tiny shard of glass I found on the floor. As I slashed at my skin, I realised that I hated what I was becoming. It was almost second nature to hurt myself in moments of despair. It was like the next step on from crying – a release, but something I would rather not do.

Ivy dressed the wounds with Savlon cream and a crepe bandage. 'This is very silly behaviour, Teresa. If you're not careful you will scar your arms, which you will regret when you have a nice boyfriend one day.'

I had no idea what she was going on about. Boyfriend?

She was talking about a world I didn't inhabit, a place where mums baked cakes for their kids and boys asked girls to the cinema. Later Harriet made me sleep in the detention room, 'for my own good', although I saw it as a punishment. I banged the walls and shouted for ages, hoping someone would come and let me out, but no one did. I was desperate to go to the toilet and had to hold it in all night, which was very uncomfortable.

The next morning my head felt full of fog. My hands shook as I washed. I kept missing my teeth and cut my gum open with my toothbrush. A member of staff called Trinny was on duty, a very overweight older lady with white hair. I showed her my shaking hands and told her how bad I was feeling.

'Have you been glue sniffing?' she asked.

'No!' I said. The idea was almost laughable. Why would I want to get high on solvents when I was already out of my head on the drugs they were giving me? It didn't make sense.

Trinny dismissed my worries and told me to go to school. Feeling weak and dizzy, I stumbled into Mrs Macdonald's class and slumped in a chair. 'Why do I feel ill all the time?' I asked. Mrs Macdonald ignored me.

I began picking at the bandage on my arm. It felt uncomfortable. I wanted to take it off. A wave of tiredness swept over me. I put my head on the desk and went to sleep. When I woke up, I went to complain to Mrs Ryfield.

'I'm being over-drugged.'

'That can't possibly be the case. Dr Peri does the prescribing and he knows what's most suitable for you.'

My vision blurred. I found myself squinting at her. 'I'm not myself on these tablets. They are turning me into a zombie,' I said.

'Let's just wait and see, shall we? It's all for the best. Now go and get that bandage on your arm re-dressed.'

Kate took me to the nurse's station on the second floor, where Miss Woods changed my bandage. 'No more of this, Teresa! You've only got two arms and they've got to last you a long time,' she scolded.

That night I pulled off the bandage and re-opened the wounds with a piece of paper, adding a thousand tiny cuts to the pattern of despair on my arms. I wished I were dead.

Over the following weeks, my aches and pains got worse. My head throbbed and my eyes became highly sensitive to light. My stomach pains were excruciating at times; I frequently felt sick and feverish. My hands shook, my knees felt weak and often I didn't have the strength to walk even a few paces. I was always hitting tired patches, forgetting what I was saying mid-sentence or simply losing the energy to go on with whatever I was doing. I started to hallucinate and every movement I made was in slow motion. I trembled with cold a lot of the time. My nose was constantly runny and my eyes watery.

'It's hell, Dad!' I said, the next time he came to visit.

'Don't you worry, I'm going to write to our MP about it, get you off the drugs,' he promised.

I wanted to believe him, but he reeked of alcohol and I figured that he was unlikely even to remember the visit when he got home, let alone his promise to help.

I hated saying goodbye to Dad. I often wondered if we would both manage to survive until the next time we met. His life seemed so precarious, what with all the drinking, and I felt close to death a lot of the time. But at least he had his freedom. At least he could walk out of Kendall House and go where he pleased. I had no independence whatsoever.

I couldn't even go to the toilet without asking a member of staff to unlock the door for me.

We went on occasional trips and outings, but they were carefully monitored and restricted. The staff would bring along our medication and feed it to us in the most unlikely places, and they were always barking orders and shouting at us, so we rarely had any fun.

In early September, Fred and Maggie took Emma and me to Camber Sands in Kent. The weather was still good and it was fantastic to be able to stare at the wide horizon, dreaming of escape from Kendall House. My eyes were so unused to seeing beyond the walls of the building that it took a bit of time for my focus to adjust, but soon they were greedily taking in the open space.

My mood changed when I put on my swimming costume though. I could feel Fred's vampire dark eyes on me, his gaze lingering for far too long on certain parts of my body.

'Teresa may be skinny, but she'll soon get her curves in all the right places,' he said as I came out of the sea.

'Yes, it won't be long now,' Maggie agreed.

A little later, I spotted an ice cream van. 'Can I have an ice lolly?' I asked.

'Fancy licking something long and wet, do you?' Fred joked.

I laughed, not really understanding. His tone of voice made me feel uncomfortable. Maggie was having a swim. Something told me that he wouldn't have spoken like that while she was in earshot.

'Teresa wants to get her lips around something. How about you, Emma? Are you dying for a suck?' he went on.

Emma blushed and mumbled something. 'What?' Fred said, cupping his ear.

Emma said that she would prefer a cone to a lolly. 'I bet you would,' he laughed. 'You'd rather have something white and soft and creamy in your mouth. But Teresa wants something hard, don't you, girl?'

Bile rose up the back of my throat. 'I don't want anything,' I said, wrapping a towel around me to shield my body from his greedy gaze. 'You're just an ugly pervert and I wish you'd shut up.'

When Maggie came out of the sea, she announced that it was time for teatime medication. She took various bottles of pills out of her bag and sorted them into two batches, one for me and one for Emma. As usual, we complained that we didn't want them.

'If you do what you're told, you can have some money for the ice cream van,' she said. She couldn't understand it when we said we didn't feel like eating any ice cream today.

Back at Kendall House, Bridget was in a foul mood, picking on anybody who came within her field of vision – except her darling Nicole, of course. First in the line of fire was Jules, whose new haircut was not to her taste. 'No one would have called you pretty before, but now you look bloody ugly!' she shouted at Jules across the sitting room.

'She does not,' I said.

'How would you know, you ugly bitch?'

'Jules, your hair looks great,' I said.

Bridget's dark eyes burned with rage. 'You think that straggly mop of rats' tails looks good? You stupid crazy cow! You definitely deserve the beating I'm going to give you later. I'm going to stamp on your pathetic head and watch your brains ooze out all over the floor.'

She said it with such conviction, and the expression on her face was so vicious and brutal, that I felt compelled to back down. She was a hulking mass of muscle, fat and malice, truly frightening, the stuff of nightmares. I was absolutely petrified of her.

'Let's go, Jules. We don't need this,' I said. The sound of Bridget's terrifying cackle trailed after us as we left the room.

CHAPTER NINE

I was terrified of being injected again, so for a short while I took my pills without arguing. I thought that perhaps if I toed the line and made them think I was happy at Kendall House, they would treat me better, maybe even reduce the amount of tablets they were giving me. It didn't work, though. Nothing I did made a difference.

I tried to endure the mood swings and sleepy patches in silence, but it was hard. I just couldn't understand why I was being so heavily drugged, and none of the staff would give me a straight answer. I spent my days shuffling around the house trying to make sense out of chaos. All I knew was that what they were doing to me was very, very wrong.

The only time my life felt like it had any meaning was when I was tending Dynamutt, or playing with Buttercup in the laundry. I had some nice times with Jules too. But things were getting more difficult with the other girls every day.

Bridget always seemed to be behind me, whispering threats in my ear, enjoying the sound of her own sadistic fantasies. She made a real effort to turn the others against me, not just during an argument, or for an afternoon, but for good. Day in day out she drummed into them that I was unhygienic, mad, stupid and ugly, and the constant repetition seemed to work a spell on them. I probably was quite annoying at times, because I was half off my head and didn't know what I was doing, but I didn't deserve the treatment Bridget dished out. She went on and on about how I had no tits or bum and nicknamed me Titsalina Bumsquirt, which the others found hilarious. I felt increasingly isolated from the group.

Everyone was frightened of Bridget so they did as they were told, except Tina, who had a lot of fight in her. Tina was probably harder than all of us. You could not turn your back on that girl. Sophie K had a vicious streak. Zara was nice at times but weak at others.

Emma and Sophie C sometimes tried to protect me from Bridget, but it was hard for them. The only person I could really trust was Jules. Although her fear of Bridget meant that sometimes she ganged up against me with the others, when we were on our own it felt like we were soul mates – best friends for life – so I always forgave her.

My dad had made several requests to have me home for the weekend, but so far the answer had been no. So I was glad to hear Jules had a new escape plan. There was a trip scheduled to Oaklands Park, near Clacton-on-Sea, the following Thursday and she knew the area well. 'We'll get away quick and easy, through the woods,' she assured me.

Our only problem was to make sure we earned the privilege of going out that day, and that was never going to be a straightforward process. The privilege system, for all its supposed rules and regulations, often seemed to depend on the moods and whims of the staff. I never saw Bridget get carted off to the detention room, for instance, and hardly any of the staff told her off for doing things that would get me put in my nightclothes immediately. She wasn't on any drugs either, nor was Nicole. I did not once see them in the queue for medication.

I wondered whether Nicole got preferential treatment because she was so pretty, or because she was Bridget's best friend. It couldn't have been because she was well behaved, because she wasn't. She talked back to the staff, mucked around in lessons and joined in with Bridget's bullying. But like Bridget, she could also be a sneak, informing on the other girls to the staff, so maybe that's why she had it easy. I didn't trust her an inch.

Thursday arrived and by some miracle Jules and I were both allowed on the trip to Oaklands Park. Before we left, Jules told me to slip into the laundry when Dot wasn't looking. 'Grab some clothes. We'll want to change out of our track suits when we get away,' she whispered.

I had just finished stuffing a couple of clean skirts under my sweatshirt when Nicole came in. I dropped to my knees and pretended to be looking for Buttercup.

'You and that cat!' she sneered. 'It don't surprise me that the only friends you've got are dumb animals. They're the only ones that can stand you.'

'Go away, Nicole. Buttercup won't come out if you're around. She hates bad smells.'

'Cheeky bitch,' Nicole said.

Still on my knees, I rammed my head into her stomach. Leaving her doubled up in pain and winded, I went off to find Jules.

Nicole reappeared while we were queuing up at the shoe cupboard, waiting for Janice to come along and open it. She whispered something to Bridget, who pushed up behind me and kicked me twice, and then jerked her knee forcefully into my side. I drew in a sharp breath and tried to swallow the pain, not wanting to attract the attention of the staff. I regretted reacting to Nicole's taunt in the laundry and was determined not to do anything else that could come in the way of our escape plan.

Bridget clasped my shoulders with her fat fingers. I tried to shake her off. 'If you ever go near Nicole again I will come into your dorm while you are sleeping and suffocate you with a pillow,' she hissed at me. Her mouth was so close to my ear that she sprayed it with spittle. Suddenly she gave a terrifying roar.

I jumped. A violent shiver went through me. 'I won't go near her,' I whimpered.

The shoe cupboard stank when Janice finally opened it. Our coats and jackets were in there too, and they reeked of sweaty feet and leather. It was disgusting. By now my slippers were badly smelly as well. It didn't make any difference how often I washed my feet, they smelt horrible after five minutes in those slippers.

Oaklands Park consisted of a large open field area surrounded by thick woods. Jules and I played ball games with the others, biding our time until the right moment came to slip away. Although I was hot from jumping around, I said I was cold and put on my jacket. Jules did the same. 'You can't be cold!' Dot said. We assured her that we were.

'Can we explore the rest of the park?' Jules asked Janice.

'Only if you stay within sight. Don't go into the woods, will you?'

'No,' we chorused.

We sauntered off towards the end of the field, followed by Sophie C, and then Bridget and Nicole. 'Fuck off, Bridget,' I called behind me.

'Turn round and say that again!' she shouted.

'Come on, run for it,' Jules said as we reached the edge of the copse. We slipped in between a couple of trees and broke into a sprint.

'Wait for me!' Sophie called from way behind, but there was no time to lose. We went on running until we were out the other side of the trees and onto an adjoining road, where we made our way to the nearest bus stop. A couple of agonisingly long minutes later, a bus came along. We flagged it down and got on it, not caring where it was headed.

Two bus trips later we arrived at the nearest train station, where we took the first train to London. It was a cramped journey. Because we had spent the last of our money on the bus, we had to lock ourselves in the toilet to avoid the ticket inspector. In London, we jumped over the barrier on the underground and took the tube to Putney Bridge. From there we walked to my dad's flat in Raynors Road.

Dad was chuffed to see us. 'What a surprise! Come on in!' he said.

Jules's face fell when we got inside. Even I was horrified. The flat was an absolute tip, the worst I'd seen it, and that was saying a lot. Everywhere you looked there were fag ends, empty cans and bottles, dirty plates, glasses and clothes. I peeped into my old bedroom. It looked like a bomb had gone off.

I asked where Bernadette was. Dad said she was staying with friends. I wasn't surprised. How anybody could live like this was beyond me. Bernadette would have hated it. I felt really embarrassed in front of Jules.

'Sorry about the mess,' Dad said, coughing nervously. 'I was just about to give it a good old clear out. But let's get out of here and go and celebrate, eh? They'll be glad to see you at the Fox and Hounds.'

As if sensing my discomfort, Jules nudged me. 'We don't care about the mess. It's just great to be away from Kendall House,' she said, grinning.

She was right. We were free. This was our time to enjoy ourselves and, as it turned out, Mary the landlady at the Fox and Hounds let us sleep in a little box room at the top of the stairs. We spent the evening drinking Fanta and playing cards and snooker. It was really nice to see Dad outside of Kendall House. He got pissed, as usual, but he was in a good mood all night and we had a happy singsong round the piano.

Jules and I got up early and went to see him in the morning, taking tea bags and a pint of milk. It took ages to wake him up, but finally he answered the door. We washed up some mouldy cups and boiled the kettle. I told Dad about all the drugs they were giving me at Kendall House, and recounted the horror of being pinned down and injected. Jules described what it was like to be locked in the detention room. Her eyes filled with tears as she recalled the nights she had spent in that dreadful, tiny room.

Dad looked really upset. 'I'd like to have you back home, but you can't stay here,' he said. His future was very uncertain. Work was patchy and he had no idea when he was going to be evicted from the flat. 'It could be any day,' he sighed.

I suppose we had known all along that we would have to go back to Kendall House, unless we wanted to go on the run and sleep rough. It just wouldn't have worked out at Dad's, even if Wandsworth Social Services had allowed me to stay there, and Jules's family couldn't have us. We tried phoning my mum, but she was living with a man called Peter who wouldn't let me speak to her. I hated how he sounded. I could tell he was violent and controlling.

In the end Dad gave us the money to get the train to Gravesend. I felt suicidal at the thought of going back to

Kendall House, but there was no alternative. The police would have picked us up later that day anyway. Dad's flat wasn't exactly a subtle hiding place.

We found an empty carriage on the train. 'Look what I've got,' Jules said, giggling and taking a tube of Evo Stick and a plastic bag out of her pocket.

I had never sniffed glue before. Although I'd seen other kids do it at Westdean and Long Grove, I had never wanted to join in.

'It numbs everything. It will help you forget that we're going back,' Jules said.

At that moment I would have done anything to block out where we were headed, if only for a few minutes. 'Go on then,' I said.

We sniffed it in our seats. A low humming sound started up in my ears. Opposite me, Jules was laughing hysterically. Her eyes were red and she kept coughing. 'Isn't it great?' she said.

It definitely wasn't great for me. My head felt like it was caving in and the weird humming noise grew louder. Feeling sick, I crossed my arms over my belly and began to rock backwards and forwards. I vowed never to touch glue again.

We got off the train and wandered down to the banks of the River Thames, to a little wooden jetty next to a disused warehouse. It was cold and windy. The sky was grey and swollen with rain clouds. My ears were still buzzing. I felt unbelievably depressed, and my mood kept swooping lower and lower. Crying miserably, I told Jules that I'd rather die than go back to Kendall House. I took off my coat. 'I've had enough,' I said. 'I'm sorry! I can't take it anymore.' I ran to the end of the jetty.

'No!' Jules screamed. She grabbed hold of me just in time to pull me back from the edge. I tried to shake her off, but she clung on to me and pushed me onto the ground. Straddling me, she shook me by the shoulders and yelled, 'You can't die! You're my only friend.'

'I can't live either, not in that place!' I moaned. 'Let me go. I can't go on.'

She started crying too. 'It's the glue making you feel like this. Pull yourself together. One day we'll be free, Teresa. We've got to hang on until we are. You've got to get through this! We've both got to get through it, and the only way to do it is together.'

She begged me not to do anything stupid, but it was at least half an hour before she trusted me not to throw myself in the river. Finally, cold and exhausted, we walked slowly back through the drizzle in the direction of Kendall House.

A man with a dog was walking behind us. I jumped every time the dog barked. It was a scary-looking German Shepherd-mix, dark and ferocious, like something out of a horror movie. 'Don't look now. There's a bloody big mutt following behind us,' I whispered to Jules.

She peeped over her shoulder. 'You must be seeing things. It's a tiny little pooch!' she giggled. I looked again. Sure enough, it was only a yapping little lapdog.

Half an hour later we were back in our nightclothes, back in hell, and the next day Dr Peri changed my medication. There were more pills than ever in the brown envelopes Harriet doled out morning, noon and night, and I was even more zombified than before. I experienced a lot of giddy spells and numbness in my limbs. My stomach pains became more intense and frequent. Most mornings I wondered whether it was worth getting out of bed and trying to face the day. Something always laid me low, whether it was dizziness, a throbbing headache, tummy ache, nausea or faintness. I had a lot of trouble passing urine, which left me with horrible aches in my back.

I really was like the living dead. My reactions slowed. I couldn't keep up with what people were saying. My vision kept blurring and my coordination got worse and worse. I spilled my food down me when I was eating and couldn't keep it in my mouth while I was chewing.

Bridget had every excuse to taunt me now. 'You're turning into bloody Georgie!' she crowed. And to some degree she was right. I was becoming mentally and physically disabled. I just had to hope it was only temporary.

Jules tried to keep my spirits up. A few weeks after we got back from our latest escape, we were finally allowed a walk to Woodlands Park with Janice. As we made our way there, Jules started chanting, 'Kendall House is hell on earth', thrusting her fist into the air repeatedly. I tried to join in, but my arm wouldn't move properly and my tongue kept tripping on the words. I sounded like someone with a severe speech impediment.

On our way back I stepped out into a road without looking. A car screeched to a halt in front of me, missing me by inches, at which point I collapsed on to the ground. Jules dragged me out of the road and Janice slapped my cheeks to bring me round.

Back at Kendall House I was told off for attention-seeking and made to wear my nightclothes day and night for a week. 'Why did you do it, you stupid girl?' Dot asked.

'I don't know. I must have wanted to kill myself.'

'Don't be silly, Teresa. We all know how much you love a drama. And what would your hamster have done without you? You're always saying how much you love that little ball of fur.'

She was clever in that way, Dot. She knew how much I loved animals; her words gave me an instant guilt trip. I vowed to myself then that I would never leave Dynamutt. Along with Jules and Buttercup, he was part of my reason for living, and it wasn't his fault that I was having such a bad time.

If anything happened to me, I knew that Tina would claim Dynamutt. She was always bugging me to hold and feed him. She hadn't been at Kendall House long enough to have her own hamster, and sometimes I let her help with cleaning out his cage.

Every time I took him into the sitting room, Tina asked if she could put him away later. Normally I refused, but one night she looked so eager that I said she could hold him while I opened his cage.

She sat down next to me and watched as I played with him on my lap. 'Where are you going for Christmas?' she asked.

'I don't know. It seems a bit early to worry about it.' It was the middle of October.

'Most of the girls are going home, but I'm going to Miss Woods's house,' she said.

I wondered why Miss Woods hadn't asked me, and where I would go instead. It seemed unlikely they would let me go home.

'Come on, Dynamutt, time for bed,' I said, handing him to Tina. She cupped her hands around him.

As I leant down to unclasp the wire door, I heard her gasp, 'Oh no!'

'What is it?' I said, with a sudden sense of fear.

'There's something wrong with him.' She held out her hands. Dynamutt was lying floppy and lifeless across her palms.

Aghast, I took him from her. 'He was fine just now. What have you done to him?' I said. I sat down and laid him on my lap, tenderly trying to tickle him back to life. 'Someone get help!' I called. Sophie K ran off to find a staff member.

'I didn't do anything!' Tina screeched.

I glanced up at her. There was the barest hint of a smile beneath her apparent anguish. It dawned on me that she had deliberately tried to kill Dynamutt. I turned him over. His neck rolled at an unnatural angle. It was broken. I didn't want to believe it, but he was too obviously dead for me to delude myself that he wasn't.

Pulling my knees up towards my chin and wrapping my arms around them, I gently began to rock my darling hamster in my lap. Tears streamed silently down my cheeks.

'Why did you do it, Tina?' I asked. 'Surely you don't hate me that much.' But Tina was no longer there.

Janice bustled into the room, tutting. I told her what had happened. 'Tina loved your hamster, so why would she kill it?' she said. 'No, no, Teresa, these little creatures can die any time. It probably had a heart attack. Never mind, we'll get you a new one.'

I was hurt and angry at Janice's suggestion that you could replace something you loved so easily. I didn't want a new hamster; I wanted Dynamutt back. I cried all night and in the morning Zara told me she hated me for keeping her up.

I tried to get out of bed, but I had severe pains in my right side. Harriet came to see me. 'Stop messing around,' she ordered. 'This is nothing but attention-seeking.'

I tried to sit up straight, but the pain was overwhelming. 'I can't,' I gasped.

Harriet put her arm around me and pulled me roughly to my feet. 'You see? You can,' she said. She walked me to the detention room. 'Feeling better? If not, I'll have to leave you in there for the day.'

'OK, I feel better,' I said. Even though I was sure I was going to collapse at any minute, I couldn't bear the thought of being locked in that tiny room again.

'I told you it was all in your head.'

She took her arm away, leaving me unsupported. I dropped to my knees, creasing up in pain. My hands were shaking. Huge great shivers coursed through my body like crashing waves.

'You are being really pathetic. Stop faking. Get up.'

Mustering every ounce of energy I had, I staggered to my feet. 'I'll go to school now,' I mumbled, before falling into a dead faint. I spent the next two days in the detention room, in a state of tortured delirium, sweating and constantly thirsty. No one called in a doctor. I lay there having night-mares about Dynamutt's broken neck, wishing I were dead too.

When I got out, Jules introduced me to Danielle, the latest new girl. Like Jules, Danielle was in the morning and teatime queue for medication. Jules thought she was really nice. I reminded her that almost everyone was nice when they first arrived, until the drugs changed them.

As predicted, Danielle's personality began to alter as the days wore on. She went from being a normal, quiet girl to being hyper and rebellious. She slept in Sophie K's dorm along with Jules, and there were loads more fights at bedtime than there had been before she arrived. She and Jules used to spit at each other from their beds.

Danielle could be funny too. I was in their dorm the night she drew a huge red mouth on her face with lipstick, just before Benita came in to turn out the lights.

Benita screamed when she saw her. 'Wipe that off now! You look evil!'

'I am evil, bitch,' Danielle crowed. Benita dragged her off to the detention room.

When Benita came back, Sophie K told her to fuck off, so Sophie K spent the night locked in Sick Bay. It was a bad night for them, but a good night me because for once I got to sleep in Jules's dorm. We chatted for hours through the darkness about our dreams of life after Kendall House. Jules said she wanted to get married and have children. I said I wanted to run a cat shelter and breed hamsters.

'Don't you want a boyfriend?' she asked.

'No, just lots of baby hamsters.'

Benita came in and snapped on the light. 'If you two don't stop talking right now you will lose all your privileges for a month!' she shouted. Finally we drifted off.

It was around this time that I started having trouble getting to sleep at night. It was crazy – I felt dopey all day and then when it came to the evening I'd get hyped up with nervous energy. Thoughts whirled through my head like leaves in an autumn storm, and I could never quite catch hold of them. A lot of the time I felt utterly confused. Nothing made sense, except my desire to end the misery and turmoil. More and more I focused on finding ways to self-harm, scouring the floor for bits of glass and plastic, drawing pins, safety pins – basically anything with a sharp edge. If I couldn't find anything, I'd smash a light bulb. When someone deliberately left a pile of broken glass on my bed, I didn't question it. I just cut myself with it.

The patterns I made on my arms fascinated me. I spent whole days picking and probing the cuts, grazes and scabs on my skin. Walled in and locked up in Kendall House, with nothing to do and nowhere to go, my arms became my exploring ground, and I hacked out paths from elbow to wrist, creating new routes for the rivulets of blood to flow down.

Cutting myself became an important mode of expressing how I was feeling. When Bridget or one of the others was nasty to me, I took my fears and frustrations out on my arms. It went the other way too. One evening I carved Jules's name halfway up my forearm. The 'J' is still visible today, even after all these years. When Bridget saw what I'd done she accused me of being a lesbian, which was strange coming from her, considering how close she was to Janice. I protested that I loved Jules like a sister, but nobody seemed to believe me.

Sometimes Bridget was all right with me, but it never seemed to end well between us. When I got my new hamster, Vampire, she suggested mating it with her hamster Charlie. Of course I was thrilled at the idea of having some babies to play with.

Miss Woods was often warning us about putting the hamsters in the same cage. I think she was worried that they would breed out of control and overrun Kendall House. So we had to do it in secret. Every evening we let Charlie go in with Vampire for a few minutes. Charlie appeared to be very attached to Vampire. We watched him run up behind her, mount her and jiggle around. Never having seen anything mate before, I thought it was hilarious. Bridget was sure that there would be babies soon and so was I.

I noticed that Vampire was getting fatter. It was time to confess. I went up to Miss Woods's office and told her that Vampire was pregnant. She wasn't happy about it.

'What were you thinking? It will mean more vet's expenses, more trouble.'

'I'm sorry,' I said, but I didn't care that she was cross. The thought of looking after tiny, baby hamsters was just too exciting for words. We took Vampire to the vet's and when I got back I bragged about how I was going to be a grand-mother.

The next day Miss Woods called me up to her office again. 'I've seen the vet. Your hamster is back, safe and sound.'

'When are the babies due?' I asked eagerly.

'Teresa, I don't know how to tell you this, so I'll just come out with it. Your hamster is a boy. It's never going to have any babies.'

I went downstairs to the girls' sitting room and shouted, 'Vampire is a boy!'

'That means your Charlie must be gay,' Jules said to Bridget.

Bridget glowered at her. She strode over to me and slapped me round the head. 'Shut up about your fucking hamster,' she said.

'But I saw what Charlie was doing. He was having sex with him!' I laughed.

Some of the other girls made jokes about selling a story about the first ever pregnant boy hamster! Bridget's face was as black as thunder.

She punched me twice in the shoulder and once in the stomach, winding me. Then she grabbed me by the throat and pushed me up against the wall. 'I said shut up! Unless you want to die, that is.'

'Sorry,' I said, but inside I was laughing my head off.

After that, she was worse to me than ever. She and Nicole took to passing me nasty notes in class. They said things like 'We're going to get you' and 'Teresa must die!' At first I tried to ignore them, but after a while they began to scare me. Because I was so befuddled mentally, I became convinced that they really were planning to kill me. Bridget, particularly, looked at me with such hate and spite in her eyes that it was easy to believe that she wanted me dead.

Sometimes I couldn't get to sleep for worrying about whether I would survive the night. Although a huge part of me wanted to die, I was terrified of being murdered by Bridget while I slept. She was constantly telling me about all the ways she planned to kill me. I was sure that eventually she would be driven to act out her violent desires.

One evening as she passed me in the corridor she handed me a scrunched-up note that said, 'YOU ARE GOING TO DIE TONIGHT!' It was signed by several of the girls, including the Sophies, Nicole and Danielle. Scared stiff, I ran into my dorm and shut the door, wedging a chair up against the handle so that no one could come in. A few minutes later, Zara tried the handle. She called to me to let her in, but I shouted at her to go away, or I'd hurt her.

I sat down on my bed. I read the poison note again and started having trouble breathing. I began shaking and twitching as I gasped for air. My head was pounding. It felt as if it would burst. I tried to stand up, but I was too dizzy. I had the strangest sensation that my blood was freezing up in my veins. My skin became cold as ice. A massive pain spread through my chest and my breaths grew shorter and shallower. Panic consumed me. I was beside myself with fear. I clutched hold of the St Christopher's chain that Mum had given me. I must have gripped it too hard because the chain broke and it fell onto the floor.

Kate managed to push the door open. She made me put my head between my knees. Harriet brought me up one of her hot vitamin drinks. 'You are totally doolally, aren't you? Nothing but bloody trouble!' Harriet said.

'What does doolally mean?' I asked Shirley later.

She shrugged. 'Bonkers, barmy … why?'

'Mad, you mean?'

She frowned. 'Yes, mad.'

'Do you think I'm mad?' She smiled and said nothing.

Again, my blood ran cold. It was like they were brainwashing me, trying to make me believe that there was something wrong with my mental health, forcing pills down my throat, turning me into someone I wasn't.

'*I am not mad!*' I shouted.

'Calm down, or we'll have to put you back in the detention room,' she said.

My mum and dad in happier times, outside the registry office
on their wedding day.

The Haven, the home I was in from age six to nine. It was run by the Salvation Army and was one of the happier periods of my childhood.

Kendall House, photographed in 2006, has been turned into rooms for the homeless. It no longer has bars on the windows or reinforced front doors.

I was six years old when this photo was taken of me (on the left) with my brother and sister. This is one of the few photos taken of me as a child.

My most treasured memories are of Aunt Betty and Uncle Don (seen here holding their grandchild), who gave me love, a family and a home I was happy in.

10.10.31. ████ reports Teresa nursed in D.R. overnight checked hourly - has taken 2 mugs of water. Haloperidol 10 m.g. Valium 5 m.g. Sparine 100 m.g. Disipal 50 m.g. Aim to move from Valium and Sparine back to normal medication i.e. Haloperidol.

Fiona reports rang ████ - out until after 11 a.m. - message left asking her to ring K.H. - rang again 12.30 - they have definitely given S.W. message.

Mrs. Glenville reports Teresa came down during break - said ████ and ████ had thrown water over her in her bedroom.
Removed by housestaff. ████ tried to fight with Teresa but was held back by staff. ████ held Teresa to stop her fighting.

████ reports Teresa taken back to sick bay - hair wet also bedding, girls had thrown water over her. Pkt of biscuits found. Teresa said thats what girls were after. Asking why girls at her. I explained that as she reacted to everything this was to them a laugh and I had told her before she must try not to respond to their egging her on.
Dr. Peri - message left with Sec a.m. for an early D.V. as soon as he makes contact with hospital.

Fiona reports spoke to S.W. - brought her up to date with events and treatment. S.W. saw dad this a.m. and has told him Teresa very disturbed at present and talked to him about Teresa - I told S.W. re Teresa's feeling re Smallwood Rd - Dad apparently also feeding this to Teresa - agreed No way is Teresa fit for Smallwood and that I have told Teresa she would not be sent anywhere she did not want to go - Friend of dads and of Teresa's died Major Williams - Dad did not tell Teresa but S.W. thinks sister ████ may have done.

Jean reports 2 p.m. Medication given.
Haloperidol 10 m.g. Disipal 50 m.g. Valium 5 m.g. Sparine 100 m.g. orally.
Ate 4 slices toast and mug of milk - said this mornings fracaus with ████ and ████ did not upset her - used to being treated cruelly - sick of ████ - and ████ is only brave because Teresa too tired to cope ! Settled down and sleeping by 2.30.
6 p.m. Medication given:
Haloperidol 10 m.g. Disipal 50 m.g. Valium 5 m.g. orally taken withmilk.
Will have something to eat later.
May be removed to D.R. later - to sleep there and be observed. Toilet on the way please - has refused to 'go' for me today.

████ reports gradual reduction in medication Omit Sparine at 6 p.m. - a.m. give only Haloperidol 10 m.g. with Disipal 50 m.g. and continue reducing dose until back to normal over next few days. Keep Sparine and Valium for Crisis Intervention.
Aim to gradually bring Teresa back into circulation - but watch ████ who I feel will keep 'pot-boiling'

████ reports I checked Teresa every hour she slept all night. Has not been to toilet since I came on duty last night, has been given drink.

████ reports last night complained of back pain and is stillthis a.m. complaining her back is painful.

21.10.31. ████ reports URGENT. D.V. requested G.P. Teresa is reported not to have passed urine for 24 hrs. When I examined her - bladder appeared slightly distended. Teresa has her menstrual period - c/o pain in kidney region. Dr. visited 10.15 a.m. - bladder not distended though Teresa claims that she had not p.u. - c/o P.I.T pain on palpulation - 2 mugs sauschtaken a.m. At lunchtime Teresa had eaten toast and drunk tea said she still had not p.u. however, Jean reported Teresa had been to loo at 11's time. she had seen and

This is a page from my Kendall House files and shows just some of the drugs I was given and how I was bullied and locked in Sick Bay, which became my prison cell.

CANTERBURY and ROCHESTER DIOCESAN COUNCIL FOR SOCIAL RESPONSIBILITY
THAMES-SIDE BRANCH

Superintendent:

Telephone 0474 4125

Consultant Psychiatrist: Dr. M. S. Perinpanayagam

Kendall House,
46 Pelham Road,
Gravesend, Kent,
DA11 0HZ

23 February 1983.

Dr. B. █████████
█████████
GRAVESEND, Kent.

Dear Dr. ██████,

Teresa Cooper

I enclose copy of report on anal swab taken from the above
girl. It is likely that she has been sexually abused. At the
moment she is staying locally with her ████████████████████
if you would like to see her, we could arrange an appointment,
otherwise a prescription can be taken by one of our nurses to her.

I shall be on leave from Friday, 25th February until 15th March.
Mrs.   S.R.N., is my Deputy and will be in charge during my
absence.

Yours sincerely,

This letter was sent by Kendall House to my local GP. Not once did anyone act
upon the letter and I was left locked in Sick Bay, where the abuse continued.

CANTERBURY and ROCHESTER DIOCESAN COUNCIL FOR SOCIAL RESPONSIBILITY
THAMES-SIDE BRANCH

Superintendent:

Telephone 0474 4125

Consultant Psychiatrist: Dr. M. S. Perinpanayagam

Kendall House,
46 Pelham Road,
Gravesend, Kent,
DA11 0HZ

1 July 1983.

Dr. B. █████████,
█████████
GRAVESEND, Kent.

Dear Dr. ██████,

Teresa Cooper

Dr. Peri has today seen Teresa and suggested that she has
a course of Zelmid 100 mg. b.d. after meals.

Would you be kind enough to issue a prescription for this.

Many thanks,
Yours sincerely,

Zelmid was one of the few
registered drugs prescribed by my GP.
It was discontinued in September 1983, classified as dangerous.

My three beautiful children, photographed in 1993. We had a lot of fun having those photos taken (I was in the background pulling faces).

Christmas 1994. Christmas morning was always a great time for opening presents, dressing up and having fun. Sarah was exploring her vocals that morning in excitement at her new dress.

My beautiful daughter Sarah, who makes me smile every day; we share a lot of laughter and fun. She is a very strong person and is very talented, as are all my children.

Me and Sarah at a photo shoot in 2006. We had a great time having our make up and hair done together and shared some special moments.

I am now forty years old and I look forward to what
the future may bring for me and my children.

Chapter Ten

I woke up with throbbing temples. Every tiny noise sounded like a deafening crash. When Zara said good morning it felt like she was shouting inside my head. Searing pains shot through my stomach. My mouth was so dry that my lips kept sticking to my teeth.

'You are trying my patience severely,' Harriet said when I told her I needed to stay in bed. 'Get up and go to school now!'

After threatening me with the detention room again, she dragged me into Mrs Connolly's needlework class. But Mrs Connolly soon ushered me outside into the corridor. I heard her whispering to Harriet that I shouldn't be allowed around pins, needles or scissors.

I stumbled into the girls' sitting room, feeling lost and unwanted. Slumping onto a chair, I was overcome by despair. Why didn't Harriet believe me when I said I was ill? I had never felt worse in my life.

Frustration welled up inside me. Enough was enough. I was living in a crazy world where nothing made sense. In desperation, I looked around the room for something to slash my wrists with, but there was nothing. Suddenly I changed my mind and decided to go back into Mrs Connolly's class. I stood up, but my knees started trembling and I had to sit down again. I shook my head angrily. My mind felt so heavy and doped. I was sick of living in a haze. It was driving me mad. I couldn't stand it any more.

I hauled myself up onto a chair and tried to reach up to the ceiling light, hoping to take out the light bulb and smash it, then use it on my arms. One minute I was stretching upwards and the next I had lost my balance and toppled to the floor. I landed on my hip bone. The pain woke my brain up. Rage flooded through me. I started attacking the furniture, throwing chairs against the wall and screaming with fury.

Jules heard my screams. She rushed out of needlework into the sitting room. Stepping in front of me, she raised her hand. 'It's me, Teresa! Shhhh! Calm down, or they'll get nasty,' she warned.

Mrs Ryfield was right behind her. 'Go back to school this instant,' she told Jules. 'I will see to Teresa.'

I whirled round to face her. 'Don't talk to my friend like that!' I shouted. 'You fuck off right now!' I felt as if I might explode at any moment. Moving to the window, I banged my fists on the glass. 'Let me out of here!' I shrieked. 'Let me out before I die!'

By now I was frantic with fear, anger and confusion. My thoughts veered alarmingly from one extreme to the other, from feeling driven to harm myself to wanting to fight ferociously for survival. Either way, death seemed inevitable. I was emaciated and practically starving. I was being forced to take high doses of powerful drugs. I was getting weird, terrifying impulses telling me to kill myself. The other girls were always threatening me with violence. The staff had attacked me. Kendall House was having a hugely detrimental effect on my mental and physical wellbeing. I knew I had to get out, even if I died trying.

Jules tried again. 'Teresa . . .'

'It's no good, Jules! I don't want to live if I have to live here in hell. I can't go on anymore.' I threw myself at the window. The pane of glass vibrated in its frame. One more try and it would break, I reckoned. I stood back and prepared to launch myself at it again.

I heard a shout. Harriet was behind me. Kate was also there, and Shirley. A pair of long arms encircled me, strait-jacketing me. Someone wrestled me to the ground. I kicked out as hard as I could, jabbing randomly with my elbows and knees, struggling against three or four pairs of arms. A hand covered my face, squashing my nose. I tried to bite it. The hand pressed harder. I thought my nose would break. My cheek hit the floor. I heard my jaw crack. Another hand was up my skirt, fumbling with my knickers. I writhed and wriggled to stay out of its grasp, fuelled by panic and desperation.

Sensing a sudden prick at the top of my leg, I knew I'd lost the fight. 'You bastards,' I said just before the drugs took hold.

I woke up in Sick Bay. Someone was knocking at the door. It had to be one of the girls because when it was the staff they just barged in. 'Is that you, Jules?' I called out.

'No, it's Sophie C. Jules is in the detention room. She went mad after they carted you off. She overturned three tables at dinner! You've never seen anything like it: food and smashed plates all over the floor. Harriet and Miss Woods were furious. They injected her too. She told me to say, "Don't give up." OK? Bang on the door and she'll try to bang on the detention room door.'

'Thanks, Sophie,' I whispered.

Somehow it helped knowing Jules was in the same situation

as I was. Although it was upsetting to hear that they had injected her as well, I was touched that she had protested against what they'd done to me. She was a brave, loyal friend.

Her courage gave me courage. I got up from the narrow wooden bed and started banging on the door. Energy surged through me. I felt as if I'd been asleep for a hundred years and now had a century's worth of strength on tap. 'Jules! Jules! Don't let those bastards get you down,' I shouted. I heard a faint knocking from the floor below. She had heard me! I jumped up and down and kicked the door, shouting and yelling. Soon I could hear her banging away as well.

Some time later I went into a bit of a trance. My eyes felt glassy. I couldn't drag my eyes away from a biro mark on one of the walls. Harriet unlocked the door. In her hand was a small tray with a hypodermic needle resting on it. She sat me down on the bed. 'Make it easier on yourself. Lie back and think of England.'

'No!' I tried to push her away, but my strength was gone. I gave up resisting. In the past I had struggled and she'd missed my buttock and injected me in the small of my back or my leg, but she finally got me where she wanted in my bum, which was every bit as painful. However, this time I didn't keel over immediately. Either the drugs weren't strong enough to knock me out or I'd already slept so much that my body refused to sleep anymore.

She sat with me for another five minutes. 'After that much Valium and Sparine, you should be out by now,' she said, looking at her watch.

'Where am I going for Christmas?' I asked. 'Tina is going to Miss Woods. Can I go with Shirley?'

The question seemed to annoy her. 'Who told you that

Tina would be staying with Miss Woods? I know nothing about this.'

'I just heard,' I said. 'I want to know where I'm going.'

'Why aren't you asleep?'

'I don't know. Why aren't I dead? I should be after all the crap you've given me.'

I didn't fall asleep for another hour and a half. Two hours later, Harriet injected me again. Four hours after that, Janice injected me. In the evening they dragged me up to my dorm and put me to bed there. I didn't struggle. I had no reserves of energy left. The next day I was supposed to get up and return to school as normal, but I didn't make it downstairs until lunchtime.

'Morning, lazybones!' Shirley said as I wandered into the dining room on shaky legs.

'Morning,' I said, and immediately sank to the floor.

I came to with Harriet and Shirley bending over me. '. . . the biggest hypochondriac I've ever come across, and such a drama queen!' Harriet was saying.

'Are you . . .' I croaked. My head was spinning.

'Ah, Madam's awake,' she interrupted. 'Let's get her up to Sick Bay.'

I clutched at Shirley's arm. 'No, please, not Sick Bay again! I hate it in there. Just give me a few minutes to get myself together. I'll be fine, I promise.'

Although I didn't have much of an appetite, I ate as much lunch as I could in an effort to build my strength up. I mashed together the hot baked potato and crisps on my plate and added a load of salad cream, until it was one big soggy mix. I took tiny mouthfuls. It went down like baby food. I couldn't remember the last time I had eaten anything substantial. My legs were stick thin. My ribs showed through my skin. My collarbone was sharply pronounced. I was becoming weaker by the day.

My brain was in a constant whirl of conflicting thoughts and feelings. Part of me wanted to get stronger and fight to survive, but another part couldn't see the point in going on living. When I had eaten as much as I could, I pushed my plate off the table. It smashed into little pieces. 'I'm sorry! It was an accident,' I said, leaning down to clear it up.

'Don't touch it!' Trinny screeched. 'I'll get a broom.'

Too late! I had already slipped a couple of jagged pieces into my dressing gown pocket. Five minutes later, I excused myself to go to the toilet. Shirley escorted me. While I was in the cubicle, someone called her away and she left me alone.

I locked the door behind me and cut myself in the darkness. I did it without thinking – I couldn't have explained what was driving me. It was as if I had a destruct button and somebody else had pushed it.

Shirley came back and knocked on the door. 'Teresa?' she called.

I held my breath and said nothing, hoping she would think I'd left. Hearing her footsteps retreat along the corridor, I breathed a sigh of relief and went back to cutting my arm.

The footsteps returned – there was more than one person this time. I heard a scratching sound on the other side of the door, and then the lock turned. Janice, Harriet and Kate burst in. They injected me and dragged me up to the detention room, where I had another energy surge and banged on the door for three straight hours before collapsing in a heap on the floor.

I remember offering up a desperate prayer to God just before I passed out. 'Help me,' I whispered, my palms pressed together, my teeth chattering feverishly. 'Please God, save me from this place and the evil people here. I'm so scared, God! Please get me out of here before I die.' I fell asleep wondering if He had heard me. It was hard to believe that the loving god I had learned about as a child actually existed, but anything was worth a try.

When I woke up, I saw things another way. My zonked brain had gone into reverse and I realised that nothing could get me out of this hell, apart from dying. Death is my only escape, I thought, as I unwound the bandage on my arm and wrapped it around my neck. I pulled it tight. Choking and dizzy through lack of oxygen, I kept tugging it tighter and tighter, until I was on the verge of losing consciousness. Suddenly there was a commotion at the door. Kate and Miss Woods rushed in and caught me as I fell. 'Leave me to die,' I mumbled.

Kate tried to loosen the bandage, but pulled it tighter by mistake and I felt my eyes roll and my eyelids flutter. The next thing I knew I was being thumped on the back, causing me to cough and draw in long, deep breaths. In the distance I heard Harriet's voice saying, 'We'll have to cancel her father's visit tomorrow. He can't see her like this.' I felt the sharp pain of another injection and was asleep within seconds.

When I came to, it was morning. I knew this because Dot and Shirley brought me some tea and toast and referred to it as breakfast. My hand was shaking so much as I raised the mug to my lips that I spilt tea all down my front and over the bedclothes. I couldn't eat the toast. My appetite had gone again. They changed the sheets and I went back to sleep.

The next time I awoke, Dot was standing over me. 'Time

to get up,' she said. She hauled me out of bed and walked me upstairs to Sick Bay.

'Why am I changing rooms?' I asked.

'In case your father visits,' she said.

I didn't get it. The detention room and Sick Bay were almost identical, so what difference would it make where Dad saw me? It was only later that I worked out that because I was so thin and weak, they would have to tell Dad I was ill and confined to Sick Bay. Of course, the irony was that I really wasn't well, but it was their 'medicines' rather than nature that were making me ill.

The rest of the day went by in a blur. Janice brought me a glass of milk and some pills. Harriet brought me two roast potatoes, which I wolfed down greedily even though they were cold. A little later I vomited them back up. Ivy gave me more milk to drink. Harriet brought more pills. 'Is Dad here yet?' I kept asking. But Dad didn't come that day. Or if he did, I don't remember seeing him.

Sometime during the evening, Dot led me downstairs to the girls' sitting room, where I was greeted by a chorus of groans and catcalls. 'Titsalina Bumsquirt!' Bridget exclaimed. 'We were hoping you were dead.'

'You're not the only one,' I said, collapsing into a chair in front of the television. 'I'd rather be dead than sat here with you.'

'You look half dead, so with any luck it won't be long,' she fired back.

I caught Jules's eye. She was staring at me as if she hardly knew me. 'What is it?' I asked.

'Are you OK? You really do look ill,' she said. I was too tired to answer. I fell asleep in my chair a few seconds later.

Dot woke me. She wiped my face with a tissue. 'You were

dribbling,' she explained. 'Let's get you up to bed.'

'Yeah, get her out of here, the drooling spaz!' Bridget shouted. 'She's a fucking weirdo. We don't want her in here dribbling and mumbling rubbish.' I felt like punching her, but didn't have the energy.

Dot led me upstairs to the dorm. I got into bed and then got out again. 'Get into bed,' Dot said.

I got into bed and got out again. 'Let's not have any nonsense. Get back into bed now,' she said.

I got into bed and got out again. Then I did it again. 'What's going on? I don't understand,' I asked wearily. Every time I lay down, my brain signalled to me to get up. Then, when I was up, it told me to get back into bed. I struggled to keep my body from obeying the messages my brain was sending it, but I was like a puppet, a remote-controlled toy.

And so it continued. Against my will, I just kept on getting in and out of bed. It was scary and infuriating. Dot nagged at me to stop it. Harriet came in and shouted at me. I started to cry. I surveyed the room, looking to find a way out of my frustration. Why was this happening to me? Bridget's insults echoed in my head. I was mad. I was ugly. I was a weirdo.

I thought about my dad, David and Bernadette, and remembered a day earlier in the year when we had visited my nan. My mind lit up with flashes of the girl I had once been, not so many months before. A massive surge of anger rose inside me. '*What are you doing to me?*' I screamed at Harriet and Dot. Beside each bed was a locker containing each girl's personal things. I picked mine up and threw it across the room. Then I chucked Zara's locker after it.

'Stop this now or I will have to give you an injection,' Harriet said.

I whirled around and yelled at her, 'Why are you giving me drugs? Are you trying to kill me? Am I some kind of guinea pig in a weird scientific experiment?'

Harriet left the room without responding. In the meantime, Dot did not try to restrain me. It was obvious that it was going to take more than one person to keep me down.

When Harriet came back, I was waiting for her, senses alert. I pushed her away every time she tried to get near me with the syringe, jabbing out like a boxer. Dot made a few clumsy attempts to come closer; it was easy to dodge her. Neither of them were a match for me in my present mood; I could have fought off half a rugby team.

After a while they started calling for back-up. Soon a mix of staff and girls streamed into the room, maybe ten or twelve of them. Bridget was among them, of course. She loved to help out in a situation like this. They formed a semicircle and drove me into a corner of the dorm. In that moment I knew how a hunted fox must feel as the dogs close in.

'Ready; *now*!' Harriet shouted.

They leapt forward, shouting and screaming with savage ferocity. A mass of hands reached out and touched me all over, grabbing, pinching and slapping different parts of me. I struggled furiously while they pinned me down on my front and Harriet injected me – in the back of the neck this time – and I continued to struggle, kicking and punching, as they dragged me upstairs to Sick Bay. But the sheer number of attackers overwhelmed me. There was no way I could escape their clutches.

At one point I heard Harriet cry out. Her cry was followed by a clattering sound.

'You bitch!' Bridget yelled. 'You've knocked Harriet downstairs. I'll get you for that, you fucking cow.' She started slapping me around the face, really hard. The blows left my cheeks stinging with pain. I lunged and tried to bite her hand, but she was too quick for me and began to pummel the top of my head. Dot unlocked the Sick Bay door and I was thrown inside. I landed in a heap on the floor, like an old broken doll. I passed out.

I was vaguely aware of people coming in and out of the room during the night. I woke up around dawn to see Miss Woods standing over me. She seemed on edge and jumped when she saw that I was awake.

'What are you doing here?' I asked.

She held out a packed of biscuits. 'I brought you these. I thought you might be a little bit peckish.'

At the time I didn't question how truly odd this was. With an effort, I raised my arm and took them from her. 'Thank you. I'm not hungry now, but I might be later.' I tucked the packet under my pillow.

'Well, I'll leave you to rest. You've been sleeping like a log, haven't you?' She seemed to be seeking reassurance. 'No disturbances?'

'No,' I said.

'Good.' She left me in peace.

The next day the pains in my back returned with a vengeance. It felt like my lower back was on fire. I'd never experienced anything so agonising. I begged Harriet for some painkillers and she gave me some pills that I'd never seen before, but they didn't give any relief. So, despite my hatred of medication, I pleaded with her to give me some Normison sleeping pills, or some Valium to knock me out. By now I was getting to know the names of some of the medicines I was being given, although I still didn't know why I was taking them, or what most of them were supposed to do.

Finally she brought me a handful of pills. Normally I would have wanted to throw them back at her, but all I cared about was escaping from the pain, even if it meant losing myself in unconsciousness. I swallowed them down quickly and waited for oblivion to hit.

For the next two days I lay doubled up on the bed in Sick Bay. I began to have trouble urinating again. I kept thinking that I wanted to go to the toilet, but then when I got there I only managed to force out a small, agonising dribble. I was allowed to have the Sick Bay door open most of the time, so that I could go to the toilet without having to call a member of staff, but it reached the point where I was in too much pain to walk unaided.

Miss Woods came to see me on the third day. She looked alarmed when I told her I had not been to the toilet for at least twenty-four hours and said that she would call a doctor instantly. By now my bladder was obviously distended, pushing out my belly and giving me a malnourished appearance. My back felt sore and my kidney area hurt so much that my fists were constantly clenched. I found myself speaking through gritted teeth a lot of the time. I also started feeling very sore in my groin area, especially when I woke up.

The pain came in waves and I kept getting a feverish sensation in different parts of my body, as though there was a patch of hot blood chasing around my veins. One moment my cheeks would be burning, the next moment it would be my thighs, and the next my upper arms and shoulders were on fire. It was a really strange feeling. I told Miss Woods I would go mad unless it went away soon.

The doctor prescribed antibiotics, which began to work the next morning. The relief was incredible. I realised just how much energy I'd been using up simply coping with the pain of the previous few days. Finally I was able to urinate. I still felt very delicate, though, and slept the rest of the day away. When I woke up, Harriet forced me to take a handful of pills. Again I slept, still and dreamlessly, for a long stretch.

When I asked if I could start sleeping in the dorm again, Harriet told me no. Miss Woods also said it would be better if I stayed in Sick Bay for a while longer. I pleaded with her to change her mind, but she remained firm, without giving me a proper explanation.

With every day that passed in that horrible room, I felt my mood drop lower and lower. I couldn't understand why I was being kept in there, isolated from the other girls and dosed up to the eyeballs with injections and pills of every colour. I began to feel suicidal again and confessed as much to Shirley. As usual, she offered to brush my hair, something she knew I liked having done. She said that she could do me a home perm if I wanted. 'Yes, please!' I said. I was grateful for anything that would break the monotony of those long, boring days in the claustrophobic hell that was Sick Bay, even if I did look like a fright when she had finished with me.

Kate told me that both Harriet and Shirley had invited me for Christmas. I knew I would much rather go to Shirley's house, but was worried what Harriet would think if I chose Shirley over her. Harriet wielded much more power in Kendall House than Shirley did, especially when it came to the medication I was being given. I was terrified of her. On the other hand, I was desperate for a stable mother figure and Shirley was the nearest to maternal that I'd been able to find so far. I wanted to nurture our relationship and sensed that spending Christmas together would be an important landmark for us, a bonding event. I kept turning the pros and cons over in my mind, but found it impossible to make a decision.

Then suddenly Christmas wasn't important anymore. Just a week after I'd got rid of my waterworks infection, I woke up with a very sore groin, both inside and out. 'It's rebound pain,' Harriet said. 'It won't last.'

I assumed that she meant it was something to do with the urine infection, although I couldn't see how the two could be connected. When I asked her, she said, 'Why do you have to question everything? Shut up and it will go away.'

But it didn't go away. In fact, it got worse with each passing day. It always felt most painful during the night and in the mornings. I tried to describe how it felt to Shirley. 'It's like someone has smashed me down there with a hammer,' I said. The whole external area felt bruised, from the top line of my pubic hair right down to my genitals. My pubic bone was incredibly tender. My vagina felt sore and some days the whole area was swollen. I had no idea what could be causing these problems and became very scared that there was something seriously wrong with me.

Harriet and Shirley kept telling me that it was all in my head. When I told Miss Woods about it she said not to worry because I was being monitored by the staff and nurses. But no one actually gave me an examination, so how could they know what was really going on?

I began to fear going to sleep. I no longer had dreams, just nightmares filled with people and monsters. I started to associate them with the pain in my groin. Scary, distorted versions of Harriet and Miss Woods featured heavily – I had visions of them laughing demonically at me, egging on various members of staff to pin me down and inject me. An unfamiliar man kept cropping up. He was half-man, half-monster, with a mouth that opened so wide it could have swallowed me up. I kept waking up bathed in cold sweat, screaming silently, my groin throbbing with pain.

I asked Shirley if dreams could ever be powerful enough to make a person ill. She laughed and began to tease me about having an overactive imagination. 'No, really,' I insisted. I was desperate to be taken seriously. 'It's as if the monsters I'm dreaming about are real. It's as if they are actually doing what they're doing in my dreams in real life.'

'And what are they doing in your dreams?'

'Punching me. Bashing me down there. Hurting me. Pressing on me, and in me.'

She frowned. 'Dreams can be very vivid sometimes. It's probably just a phase you're going through.'

As time went on I became certain that there was a link between the pain in my groin and my recurring nightmares. No one would listen though. I started to wonder if Sick Bay was haunted by a violent poltergeist, or if Bridget had found some way of getting in during the night and hurting me. I begged to be allowed back to the dorm. Finally, after more than a week, Shirley said that I'd been given permission to leave Sick Bay.

I was hoping for a peaceful night's sleep at last, and went to bed early. But at around 9.30 p.m., Bridget, Sophie K, Sophie C, Jules, Danielle and Zara crept into the dorm and sat in a circle on the floor around a tiny keyring torch, whispering and giggling. I heard paper being ripped up and someone reciting the alphabet, then Bridget said, 'Is there anybody there?' Her voice was ghoul-like in the darkness. 'We call on you to speak to us.'

By now I was fully awake. 'Go away, I'm trying to sleep,' I said.

'Fuck off, or we'll set the spirits on you!' she said. The others laughed.

My heart began to pound. It didn't take a genius to work out that they were messing around with a ouija board – Jules had told me that a gang of them had been doing it for several nights in a row. 'Stop it! It's dangerous,' I said. I had always been scared of the supernatural.

'Shut up!' Bridget snapped. She started speaking in a ghostly voice again. 'Is there anybody there? Speak to us.'

After a few moments of silence, Danielle said, 'Look, the glass is moving! It's spelling out a word. D-I . . .'

I listened apprehensively as the next letter was disclosed. '. . . D . . . no, E! D-I-E, die!'

Lying stiffly in bed, frozen with fear, I heard Sophie C say, 'It's not funny like before. I don't like this, it's scary.' There was a muffled laugh, followed by several whispers.

'Shush, it's continuing! D-I-E-T-O-N-I . . .'

Fingering the broken St Christopher that my mother had given me, I tried to remember how the Lord's Prayer went. But it was no good; my mind was fogged with drugs. I could only recall the first few lines, and those only sketchily.

'. . . G-H-T . . . Die tonight!' Bridget said. Zara screamed.

'Stop it!' I shouted, leaping out of bed. I ran across the room and switched on the light.

Bridget jumped up and made as if to run at me, growling. I fled the dorm, calling for help. A member of staff called Paula appeared out of the staff dorm. 'What's wrong? You look like you've seen a ghost,' she said.

'Where's a Bible? I need a Bible to protect me. They're trying to bring dead people to life,' I stuttered, pointing towards the door of the dorm.

Ivy came hurrying up the stairs, her bunch of keys jangling

like ghoulish chains. 'Aaagh!' I shouted. Paula clamped her hands on my shoulders and told me to calm down. I went on insisting that I needed a Bible. I knew from films like *The Omen* and *The Exorcist* that a Bible could protect me from supernatural harm.

Bridget emerged from the dorm and told Ivy that they'd only been having a laugh. 'The glass was moving by itself, though, honest,' she said. 'Someone was trying to get a message to one of us. I wonder who?' She gave me a sideways glance. 'Wouldn't it be creepy if one of us died during the night?'

'Stop it!' I shouted. I couldn't bear it. I'd only just managed to get away from Sick Bay and my demon-filled nightmares. Now Bridget and the others had introduced ghostly spirits into the dorm. Nowhere felt safe. My knees started trembling.

'Stop scaring Teresa and go to bed,' Ivy told Bridget.

It struck me that perhaps the monsters in my Sick Bay dreams had been invoked by Bridget and the others. Maybe they had been sending them to torture me during the night. *'Get me a Bible!'* I yelled, over and over again, until I was nearly hysterical. Finally Paula went through my case and found the red, Revised Standard version that I had been given all those years ago at The Haven. I clutched it against my chest. 'God protect me,' I kept saying. 'Please don't let me die tonight.' I slept with the Bible under my pillow for several months after that.

Two days later, on Halloween night, Miss Woods organised a little party. We played blind man's buff, dunking apples and hunt the thimble. For once I actually enjoyed myself, because Bridget was staying the night at Janice's house, and in her absence the other girls were a lot friendlier than usual.

Even though I was feeling woozy from my daily dose of drugs, it brought back to me how it felt to be a normal fourteen-year-old girl having good old-fashioned fun. I forgot my troubles for a couple of hours and really let myself go. It was a welcome respite, but it was all too brief.

Chapter Eleven

Assembly was held every morning at 9 a.m. in the front schoolroom. It lasted anything up to an hour. I was usually too tired to register much of it, if I made it downstairs at all.

It was considered a privilege to choose which hymn or song we sang, so it was usually Bridget who got to decide. She always opted for a ridiculous kiddy song about a bear and a butterfly. It was about ugliness and beauty: the bear had fuzzy wuzzy hair; the butterfly grew wings and became beautiful. It was definitely a song to send you doolally and we were far too old to be singing it, but Bridget loved it. The rest of the assembly was taken up with a reading by one of the teachers or staff, followed by a boring lecture.

One morning in early November, while Miss Woods was reading out a particularly dull passage, Nicole yawned in a very loud and exaggerated way. Miss Woods looked up from her book and glared at her. I tried not to laugh, but the teacher's face was such a picture of outrage that I couldn't help letting out a quiet chuckle. On my right, Jules heard me laughing and snorted. Then Danielle giggled and let off a noisy fart. Blushing, she said, 'Whoops!' and the room erupted into muffled laughter.

Miss Woods paused for a few moments to shoot dirty looks at various girls, before continuing with the reading.

'Fuck me, Danielle, you smelly, stinky cow,' Bridget said under her breath, flapping her hand in front of her nose.

'Yeuch!' Nicole exclaimed.

'Don't pick on her. She couldn't help it,' I said.

'Shush!' said Mrs Petsworth.

'Have you got a dead animal stuck up your arse?' Nicole asked Danielle.

'Yeah, your hamster,' Danielle replied.

Jules started laughing.

'That's disgusting,' I said.

'Is that what you do for your kicks, you dirty bitch? Stuff animals up you?' Bridget hissed, her eyes glinting.

'Well it's better than sticking my head up the teachers' bums like you do,' Danielle said.

'If you say that again I'll make sure your head goes so far up your own arse that it comes out of your mouth, you arse-hole.'

Miss Woods stopped reading. 'Right, that's enough. Will Bridget, Nicole, Teresa, Jules and Danielle please leave the room now! I will speak to you later about your disruptive behaviour. All privileges are to be suspended as from this moment. No walks, no television.'

Mrs Petsworth led us to the schoolroom on the first floor. On our way up the stairs, Nicole sang a dirty version of 'What shall we do with the drunken sailor?'. This was apt, because her leg was in plaster after an accident in the garden and she was walking like a peg-legged pirate.

'Will you stop being so immature!' Mrs Petsworth barked.

'You treat us like babies, so why are you surprised that we behave like babies?' Nicole said.

'Goo-goo,' Jules said.

'Ga-ga,' I added, joining in the fun.

Mrs Petsworth handed out paper and crayons to keep us occupied. I scribbled like a child on my piece of paper. 'Look at da pwitty pitcha I drawed,' I said.

'Mine's better than yours,' Jules said, holding up her kiddy scrawl.

Bridget and Nicole started a babyish conversation about tits and fannies. Danielle soon joined in and it wasn't long before the three of them were singing another dirty song. Bridget started writing on the table with her crayons, and Nicole followed suit.

'Stop that now!' Mrs Petsworth shouted.

'Won't!' Bridget said petulantly.

Soon it came to that time of day when my breakfast medication started to kick in. Suddenly I felt tired, so I put my head down for a catnap. When I woke up, Bridget was cleaning off the crayon marks she'd made on the table. Meanwhile Nicole was shaking Ajax powder out of the window. 'Look, it's snowing!' she cooed.

'Shut that window, it's freezing!' Danielle said.

'Shut it yourself,' Nicole said.

Danielle moved towards the window. Bridget stood in front of it to block her. Danielle lunged at the window and pulled it shut. Bridget pushed her out of the way and opened it again. In the scuffle that followed, the handle got broken, which meant that the window could not be closed. The draught that came through it was icy.

Mrs Petsworth tried to settle us and handed out some Maths worksheets. 'No slacking, Teresa! Sit up straight and concentrate.'

'I can't. I'm too tired.'

'I see, we're in that kind of mood, are we? Well, I've just about had enough of your faking for today.' She glanced at her watch. 'I'm expecting you to have worked through at least one side of the page by the end of the lesson and believe me, I will not be happy if you haven't completed it.'

I wanted to please her but it was a struggle to keep my eyelids from closing. 'Please, Mrs Petsworth, just let me have five minutes' rest and I'll try again.' I looked at the sums on the page. They made no sense to me. I was no longer able to function at school, not on a normal wavelength. It was very upsetting.

'On no account will I allow sleeping in my lesson!' she snapped. 'Danielle!'

Danielle was snoring, her head resting in the crook of her elbow on the desk. She jerked awake at the sound of her name. 'Sorry, Miss!'

'Danielle's tired because she's been up all night having sex with hamsters,' Bridget said.

'That's enough, Bridget.'

'It's true! She told me it was,' Bridget whined.

'I said enough!'

Unable to keep my eyes open, I went back to sleep. The next time I awoke Danielle and Bridget were no longer in the room and Sophie K had joined us. Mrs Petsworth was at the door talking to Mrs Ryfield. 'Just keep them downstairs!' she was saying.

I heard Bridget's voice, and Danielle's, and then Mrs Petsworth stepped outside the door. Suddenly Bridget and Danielle stormed into the classroom. They slammed the door behind them and leant against it to keep it shut. 'Quick, help us keep her out!' they said.

In the heat of the moment we all helped to barricade the door. This wasn't difficult because it was a big heavy fire door that opened inwards, so it didn't take more than a couple of old chairs to wedge it shut. Mrs Petsworth and Mrs Ryfield knocked loudly and demanded to be let in, but Nicole told them to go away.

'Finally, some bloody peace and quiet!' she said, when the teachers had gone. 'I'm knackered.'

'Me too,' Danielle drawled sleepily. 'I hate these fucking drugs they keep giving me.'

I didn't care one way or the other what they did. I just wanted to go to sleep, so I pushed two desks together and lay down on top of them. Bridget and Danielle did the same. Nicole sat in a corner and dozed, while Sophie K doodled on a piece of paper.

'I'm going back outside. I don't like the feeling of being locked in,' Jules said. She pushed aside the chairs blocking the door and left. Sophie K replaced them.

About an hour later, Bridget and Nicole woke up and started looking around for something to do. By now I'd recovered from my morning slump and was feeling a lot more energetic. What's more, the rebellious spirit in the air was contagious and I felt like making a bit of mischief. 'Let's break open the art cupboards and do some painting,' I suggested.

Nicole's eyes lit up. She forced the locks on the cupboards and took out a load of paints and brushes. We used them lavishly. It was brilliant having free range of the art materials for once. At first we were constructively creative. I found a plaster bust of Alexander the Great in the cupboard and my artistic side ran riot as I decorated his bald, wreathed head in trippy psychedelic colours. Although I say it myself, Alexander the Great had never looked so good. He was a masterpiece by the time I'd finished with him.

Meanwhile, Sophie had noticed that some spanking new staffroom furniture was being carted outside into the back garden. Soon a load of stylish chairs and tables had been lined outside the back door while the staffroom was being cleaned.

Looking down from the window, I felt intensely irritated. 'Look at that!' I said. 'They get all that lovely fancy furniture while we have to sit on their rickety old cast-offs.' I flicked a glance over at the scruffy plastic chairs stacked up against the door.

'Yeah, it's totally unfair!' Nicole said. She grabbed hold of a squeezy bottle of red poster paint and squirted it out of the window, splattering the chairs and tables below.

'Let's have a go,' Bridget said eagerly, picking up a bottle of blue paint. Five minutes later we had all made an artistic contribution to the appearance of the staffroom furniture. The result was fairly appalling. Miss Woods was going to be hopping mad when she saw it. We went a bit paint-crazy after that, decorating the schoolroom in pretty colours. It looked a million times better than it had before, even though there were paint spills everywhere.

Nicole started skidding and sliding across the wet floor with her weight on her plaster cast, shouting, 'Whee, look at me!'

'Watch it, or you'll hurt yourself,' I warned. Sure enough, she slipped and fell awkwardly on her bad leg. Clutching it, she began to howl in pain. Bridget rushed over to comfort her.

There was more banging on the door. 'What's going on? Let us in!' several of the staff were shouting. For once they were powerless over us.

'No,' I shouted back. 'I'm not going to let you in, not by the hair on my chinny chin chin!'

For some reason this struck us all as hilariously funny and

the others started repeating it, even Nicole, who was still in pain. The more we said it, the funnier it became, and soon we were chanting away like demented little pigs.

When our laughter had died down I heard a man's voice coming from behind the door. He was telling people to get out of the way so that he could get through and force an entry. I froze. The voice belonged to Matthew, who had frequently featured in my Sick Bay nightmares. I began to feel dizzy and scared. It was weird: I really didn't want to see Matthew – the thought made me feel sick – but I didn't exactly know why. I couldn't understand why I kept dreaming about him, or why the dreams were still so vivid in my mind. Sitting down heavily, I held my head in my hands and tried to regulate my panicky breathing.

My energy drained away. I felt as if a huge concrete block had fallen inside my head and crushed my brain. I wondered again why I was being so heavily drugged. It just didn't make sense. Fear and confusion churned inside me. Frustrated, angry and shivering with cold, I picked up a block of hard paint and threw it at the open window. The window broke.

'Christ, you've done it now!' Sophie gasped.

Zombie-like, I stood up and went over to survey the damage. The middle of the pane had fallen out and there were huge long shards of glass sticking out of the frame. Because I'd developed a thing for self-harm, I couldn't help sizing them up for their arm-cutting potential. My eyes lighted on a really nice sliver that had fallen onto the windowsill. That's pretty, I thought, feeling oddly detached.

For some reason, hearing Matthew's voice again triggered the urge to cut myself. My mind was fogging up; I sensed that I had to do something dramatic to avoid whatever was going to happen when Matthew burst through the door. I picked up the sliver of glass and slashed my arms. Blood spurted everywhere.

Bridget screamed. The staff were now clamouring at the door, shouting and pleading with us to let them in.

'She's fucking cut herself!' Bridget shouted. She took off her blouse, soaked it in the sink, wrung it out and tied it around my wrist. I tried not to look at her great pendulous boobs as she tended to me. She was wearing a bra, but Bridget minus her shirt was still a disgusting sight.

'What the fuck did you go and do that for?' Sophie asked me.

'I don't know,' I said, feeling very faint. 'I just don't want to face that lot again.'

'Christ, look!' Bridget said, pointing at my arm. Her shirt was already soaked in my blood and the crimson stain was growing by the minute.

Sophie spotted a policeman in the back garden. 'We're in big trouble,' she said with a nervous giggle.

Soon there were policemen banging on the door. Then the fire brigade turned up.

'We'd better let them in,' Danielle said, gesturing towards the door.

'No!' I protested. I was quite happy to bleed to death. I think I must have been in shock.

But the others were worried not only about my arm, but also about Nicole's leg, which was still hurting from her fall. Bridget was desperate for her to have it seen to. So finally I gave in, mainly because Nicole really did appear to be in severe pain. What's more, I was beginning to feel really weak and didn't have the oomph to debate it any longer.

Bridget moved the chairs away from the door and pulled it open. All hell broke loose as a gang of staff rushed in shouting and yelling.

'I was trying to get us out!' Bridget told them. 'I didn't want to be here, but they wouldn't let me go.'

'That's a lie!' I mumbled.

'Teresa forced us to block the door – and then she hurt Nicole! I was scared to go against her. I didn't know what to do,' Bridget sobbed.

That woke me up. 'What a load of bullshit!' I screamed. 'I just wanted to go to sleep.'

Benita and Harriet dived on me, winding me in the process and smacking my head against the floor. They dragged me into the detention room, where at last I lost consciousness.

I was taken by ambulance to Joyce Green Hospital in Dartford, where I spent the next eight days on a psychiatric ward, as per Dr Peri's phoned instructions. Dr Peri didn't bother to put in a personal appearance, thankfully. I'd seen him a couple of times at Kendall House and that was enough to know that I didn't want him anywhere near me.

The first few days at Joyce Green went by in a haze of pain and medication hangover. Unbeknown to the nurses – because no one had told them – I was withdrawing from an extremely powerful combination of drugs and literally going cold turkey. My skin crawled; I became fluey and feverish. I kept begging for Valium, but was told that Valium was for adults. They would only administer it to someone of my age in an absolute emergency, they said.

'That can't be right!' I protested through chattering teeth. 'At Kendall House they give me at least four Valium a day, and sometimes they inject me with it as well.'

'Impossible,' the staff nurse told me. 'You must be muddling up the names.'

Dad and Bernadette visited a couple of times. Even though I was feeling awful, it was great to see them outside

Kendall House. Bernadette brought me some bubble bath, which was a surprise. She must have been feeling extremely sorry for me, because she'd never given me anything before in her life. I was touched.

I began to perk up. Although I was on a ward with a bunch of fairly unstable-looking characters, none of them tangled with me. Most days I watched telly, read magazines and chatted to the nurses. Physically, I began to feel better than I had in ages. My mind was gradually becoming clearer and, although I developed another uncomfortable urine infection, the pain in my groin had almost entirely disappeared.

Halfway through my stay I was given a gynaecological examination. The nurses seemed very concerned about the puncture marks in my bum and at the tops of my legs. I explained that this was where Harriet had injected me. They looked at me in disbelief when I said that sometimes I'd been injected three or four times in a day.

They took swabs from my vagina and rectum. 'It looks rather sore and inflamed around the anal area,' one of them said. 'I would say that you definitely had an infection. Have you been practising anal sex?'

'What's that?'

She raised an eyebrow. 'Anal penetration.'

'Sorry, I don't know what you mean.'

'Well, let's start with a simpler question then. When was the last time you had sexual intercourse?'

'I don't understand. Are you asking if I'm a virgin?'

'Not in the least! I'm asking when you last had sex.'

'I've never had sex. I'm only fourteen.'

She sighed. 'Are you sure? Well, if you say so. The results will be back from the lab in a few days, so then we'll all have a clearer picture, won't we?'

When the results came through I was informed that I had a Strep B infection, commonly associated with anal sex. The diagnosis confused me. I hardly knew what it meant. No one had ever sat me down and told me the facts of life; everything I knew about sex and procreation had been gleaned in snippets in the playground at school or from the older kids in the different homes I'd been at. As a result I was fairly clueless. I'd fallen for all the classic myths in the past, including the one about getting pregnant if a man put his hand on your knee. Once I'd even rushed off a bus before my stop, convinced I was pregnant after a man accidentally touched my leg with his hand.

The nurse gave me a course of powerful antibiotics, to be taken twice a day for a week. I took them without asking questions. I felt embarrassed, without really knowing why.

On my third or fourth day, a doctor appeared at my bedside. 'Your blood tests show traces of a surprising, if not alarming, variety of prescription drugs,' he said. 'Can you tell me why you're taking all these medicines?'

'You'd better ask Dr Peri. He's the one that prescribes them.'

'Indeed. Well, Dr Peri certainly knows his stuff, so far be it from me to question his methods. But I am amazed all the same.' He went away shaking his head.

When I saw him again a couple of days later, he asked me a lot of questions about my life. I explained that basically I had been sent to Kendall House because my dad was an alcoholic who couldn't get it together to pay the electricity.

'I haven't got a history of mental illness, or crime, so why are they giving me all those drugs? Do you think they should? Can you tell them not to? Can you tell Wandsworth Social Services that Kendall House is the wrong place for me?' Tears rolled down my cheeks. The thought of returning to Harriet's drugs regime horrified me.

'I can't promise anything, but I will certainly look into it,' he said, a look of grave concern on his face.

'Please do something,' I begged. 'Tell the police, tell Social Services! I'd rather die than go back there!'

Later that day he told me that he had contacted Wandsworth Social Services and the police to say that in his opinion it seemed inappropriate for me to return to Kendall House. 'I have written a report on you, and my conclusion is that there is nothing psychologically wrong with you,' he said. I don't know why no one listened to him. He was a doctor, an expert, but for some reason that counted for nothing.

On the day I left, Miss Woods tried to reassure him – and me – that Kendall House was the best place for me. I heard her say, 'It's a therapeutic environment for a disturbed girl like Teresa, and you cannot deny that she is very troubled. Don't overlook the fact that she was admitted here for cutting her wrists.'

'Of course not,' he said politely. 'But it seems to me that her desire to harm herself is a direct consequence of the drugs she is ingesting on a daily basis. I've seen the results of the blood tests. I cannot understand why . . .'

'It's not for us to question Dr Peri, is it?' she cut in. 'He is one of the most respected psychotherapists in the country.'

He tried again. 'All the same . . .'

Miss Woods held up a hand to stop him. 'I'm afraid I haven't time to discuss this any further. Goodbye. Thank you for looking after Teresa.'

'You're taking her straight back to Kendall House?' he asked.

She smiled primly. 'Indeed we are.' She hustled me out of the hospital and into her car, where Kate and Harriet were waiting.

On the drive back, I asked Miss Woods why neither Dr Peri nor Elizabeth Pryde had come to visit me at Joyce Green. She replied that neither of them had felt it necessary.

I pressed her further. 'Did you speak to Mrs Pryde? Is that what she said?'

Miss Woods hesitated. 'I didn't actually speak to her in person, but . . . she's a very busy social worker and it's not always possible to get hold of her at short notice.'

'You mean she doesn't really care about me,' I said.

'Not at all,' she replied brightly. 'But you're not her only responsibility!'

We drew up outside a set of tall buildings. I spotted a sign saying, New Stonehouse Psychiatric Hospital. 'What are we doing here?' I asked.

'Dr Peri felt that it would be helpful if you spent some time on his ward,' she said.

'Oh no,' I said, trying to get out of the car.

'Not so fast, young lady,' Harriet said, jumping out to block my escape. 'If Dr Peri says it's a good idea, then it is.'

My head swirled. What was going on? I was sure I had heard Miss Woods tell the doctor at Joyce Green that she was taking me straight back to Kendall House, but now I was at a mental hospital. Harriet and Kate walked me into the building and down miles of long gloomy corridors to the ward where Dr Peri had assigned me a bed. My heart sank as I took in my surroundings. The ward was filled with truly deranged-looking patients. They had mad eyes, and mouths that opened and closed like the mouths of suffocating fish. I felt as if I had entered a living nightmare.

'Can I have my own room?' I asked the nurse on duty.

'Not unless you want to sleep in a padded cell,' she laughed.

My first night at Stonehouse was incredibly scary. I was the only child on a ward of twelve patients, and the youngest by several decades. I felt like a rabbit that had been thrown to the wolves. Some of the other patients were severely schizophrenic. I was scared of them all, but one woman in particular gave me the creeps. She kept pointing at me and saying something that sounded like, 'I'll get you. I'll get you.'

One of the nurses tried to reassure me. 'No, Teresa, I think she's saying, 'Look at you,' because she thinks you're so pretty.'

I wasn't comforted. The woman had a crazy look in her eyes. There was a cruel curve to the shape of her mouth and she had a strangely flattened nose. I found it almost impossible to go to sleep in the same room as her, and even if she hadn't been there, it would have been hard to get any rest. Most of the other patients looked as if they were capable of violence or some kind of scary behaviour. One woman kept crying out all through the night; another would answer her every cry with a weird cat-like sound that made me shiver with fear. I lay in bed tense and alert, constantly on guard, my eyes darting around the room in search of any sudden movement. I relaxed only when it started to grow light, and finally I managed to snatch a couple of hours of sleep.

The woman with the flat nose continued to show a special interest in me. The next day she tried to sit next to me as I was watching TV and she kept following me around the dim, dingy day room. The more I saw of her, the more I wanted to get away from her, and the more she seemed to want to stick to me. There was something about her that gave me goose bumps and made the hairs at the back of my neck stand up.

In the evening I got talking to a very nice black nurse called Molly. I liked Molly because she treated me like an equal and talked to me as if I were an intelligent being, rather than an idiot, or a nutter. I was so used to being talked down to by the staff at Kendall House that it was quite uplifting to spend time with her, even if I was on a mental ward in a nuthouse. She invited me to sit with her and knit while she was on duty, and I really enjoyed our conversations, which were about everything and nothing.

The next time she was on duty I told her about my unease over the attentions of the flat-nosed madwoman. The woman had been especially troublesome that day, constantly trying to snatch my knitting needles away from me in the day room when the staff on duty weren't looking.

'Yes, I'd try and keep a distance, as much as you can,' Molly advised. 'That one can be dangerous.'

My eyes widened with fear. 'Why is she in here?' I asked, trying to keep my voice steady.

'I'm sure I don't know, but I've seen her in action and she can be difficult to contain. She's a strong one, a fighter.'

'I'm scared to go to sleep with her around,' I said.

'Don't worry, that's what I'm here for. I'll make sure you're safe.'

I found Molly's words reassuring, but didn't want to leave anything to chance, especially after one of the other patients told me that Flat Nose had murdered her entire family. 'Stabbed them in their beds,' the woman whispered. 'Husband, kids, the lot.'

Her words reduced me to a terrified wreck. Whether what she was saying was true or not, I was now even more petrified of sleeping on the ward. I pleaded with the staff to let me spend my nights alone in a padded cell, but it was out of the question. One night, however, Flat Nose got it into her head to jump out at me when I came back from cleaning my teeth. I screamed and ran to the end of the ward, looking wildly about for somewhere to hide. Seeing an open door, I slipped through it – and sure enough I found myself in a square white room with spongy, quilted walls. The door could only be locked from the outside, so I hid behind it, quaking. I stayed there for hours, until one of the male nurses discovered me and led me back to bed. Even then, I wouldn't allow myself to sleep. By morning I was strung out and exhausted.

'Why have I been put in with nutters and murderers?' I asked Molly.

'Dr Peri's orders!' she said. 'He's a very good doctor. I'm sure he must have his reasons.'

I soon discovered what those reasons were – not that I hadn't already suspected that this was some kind of sick punishment. On his one visit to the ward in my two weeks there, Dr Peri told me, 'This is what comes of talking nonsense to the staff at Joyce Green Hospital, Teresa. As usual, you have caused me unnecessary trouble.'

'I told the truth!' I protested.

'When are you going to learn to be obedient?' he snapped.

'Never,' I fired back. 'You will not break me.'

'We shall see about that,' he said with an ominous smirk. 'We shall see, indeed.'

I began to despair of ever getting away from Stonehouse. It wasn't that I wanted to go back to Kendall House, because of course I didn't want a return to the drugs, bullying, isolation and injections that characterised my life there. But the days and nights at Stonehouse were hair-raisingly bad. It was obvious that Dr Peri's intention was to frighten me into compliance to his rules and make an example of me to the other girls.

'I wish you could have me home again,' I said to Dad the next time he visited.

'You know I can't,' he sighed. 'I won't even have a home myself for much longer.'

It was Mum who got me out of there, believe it or not. I don't know how she got to know about it, but one day she just turned up and barged in, much against Miss Woods's wishes, apparently. The staff at Stonehouse had been instructed not to let my mum near me, on any account, but when it came to it they didn't try to stop her. She arrived with her best friend at the time – a big woman called Lisa – and she brought me lots of Avon goodies.

The first I knew about it, I heard shouting in the day room at around midday. The voice was familiar; suddenly I realised whose it was. I hurried towards the day room, my heart racing. Mum was going ape shit at Dr Peri, calling him every name under the sun.

'What the hell are you doing keeping my daughter here?' she yelled. 'You should be struck off for this! I'll see that every newspaper in the country knows what you're doing to that poor defenceless girl before I'm done with you, if you don't let her go *right now*. I'm telling you, and it's no idle threat! How dare you keep her here, you fat bastard? It's criminal to put a young girl in with this bunch of animals!'

For once, Dr Peri seemed not to know what to say. 'Madam, I would ask you to . . .'

'Don't you "madam" me! I know what goes on in these places. I've been locked up myself enough times. But now I'm telling you – and I'm only telling you once, mind – you had better discharge Teresa today, or you will pay the consequences. Are you listening to me? Mark my words, you fat fucker, or I'll bash the living daylights out of you.'

Mum was a champion that day; she really came through for me. Despite her pretty blonde, blue-eyed looks, she was hard as nails and could be very intimidating. Admittedly she didn't sweep me up and take me home – as I used to dream she would one day – but at least she saved me from mad murderous Flat Nose. She did what she could, within her own limitations. Within an hour I had left Stonehouse Hospital and was on my way back to Kendall House in Lisa's car.

Chapter Twelve

Mum stormed into Kendall House like a bloody hurricane. 'My daughter says that you've been drugging her and locking her up. On whose authority, I ask you?' she said, jabbing her index finger at Miss Woods. 'What right have you got to treat a fourteen-year-old girl in such a way? No wonder she hates it here!'

'Mum . . .' I said.

Shirley popped her head around the office door. 'Is that you, Teresa? Good to have you back!'

Miss Woods gave Mum one of her infuriating smiles. 'Please calm down and join me in my office for a cup of tea,' she said.

But Mum wasn't having any of it. 'Don't patronise me with your fake tea and sympathy! I intend to get some answers here today. I'm asking you again, why have you been drugging Teresa? She's just a girl. From what she's told me, you are putting her through total misery. Shame on you, you big bully!'

Harriet sidled up beside Miss Woods. She shot me a look of contempt. 'Is that right, Teresa? Have you been telling people that you hate it here and we treat you badly?'

A bolt of sheer terror went through me as I took in her spiteful expression. 'Er,' I said. It was all very well for Mum to make a fuss, but unless she could get me out of Kendall House, it was me who was going to reap the consequences of her outburst. 'Well, no, I don't hate it. I don't hate it exactly, Mum,' I stuttered.

I could see Mum was riled. 'Is that so? Have you been telling me lies?'

'No, Mum!' I frantically tried to signal my dilemma with my eyes, but she wouldn't look at me. I turned to her friend Lisa. 'Help!' I mouthed at her.

Lisa got the message, thankfully. She took hold of Mum's arm and hustled her towards the door. 'Let's get out of here. You've done what you can for today.'

On her way out, Mum turned around and shook her fist at Miss Woods. 'You keep your dirty hands off my daughter, or I'll smash your fucking face in!' she yelled. 'Stay strong, Teresa. I'll get you out of here by Christmas.'

The moment she had gone, Harriet ordered me into the ground floor office. 'So it seems that you've been telling all kinds of untruths while you've been away,' she said, handing me a brown envelope with my name on it. 'Well, your lies won't get you far at Kendall House. Now, take your medication and join Mrs Connolly's class immediately.'

I pushed the envelope away. 'I don't want it. I don't need it. The doctor at the hospital said so. He said there's nothing wrong with me.'

'Dr Peri, was it?' she said sharply.

'No, another doctor, a nice doctor! He said I shouldn't even be in here.'

Her eyes narrowed and her mouth twisted into an ugly grimace. For a second she looked absolutely evil. 'More lies!

You really are the limit. Now take your medicine!'

Her tone was so aggressive that I swallowed the pills as quickly as I could and left the room, heart thumping. Harriet could be incredibly nasty. Quite often she scared me half to death.

That evening, Charlie, a newer member of staff, made a point of coming to talk to me. Charlie was a nice man, a gentle giant over six feet tall with short ginger hair, glasses and a beard. He was a bit ugly, but he was kind and I liked him. He had been an undertaker in his previous job, which I found fascinating. He was always telling me stories about how dead bodies were prepared for funerals and burials with embalming fluids and the like. I think it was his way of trying to put me off trying to commit suicide, although I was only vaguely aware of it at the time.

I'll never forget one particular incident he told me about, when he went to work on a very old dead woman. He stitched her mouth up so that she was smiling in her coffin, but when her family came to view her, they were outraged. 'She never smiled once in her life!' they told him. He had to unstitch her mouth and redo it before they were satisfied. I loved that story. It made me laugh and laugh.

Charlie put a brotherly arm around me and tried to draw me out about why I had cut my arm in the schoolroom. I told him there was nothing to say. 'You'd want to kill yourself if you were me,' I said. 'Anyone would.'

Despite his best efforts to talk me round, I had already plunged back into what felt like an irreversible depression. The drugs were kicking in again, interfering with my thought patterns and slowing down my body. Once again I had almost zero control over my life, my mind or my physical functions. What's more, I'd been away for more than three weeks and felt isolated from the group. Bridget ignored me completely when she saw me, and Nicole and the Sophies followed her lead.

Jules didn't let me down though. Just before bedtime she gave me a big hug and told me not to lose hope. 'I've got another escape plan!' she said, brimming with excitement. She explained that every day for several weeks she had been gradually unscrewing the metal bar that restricted the opening of the large window in the front schoolroom. She had also been to work on the securing block that held it down, painstakingly unscrewing it with her fingernails when no one was watching.

'They don't call me Houdini for nothing!' she said gleefully, referring to the nickname she had picked up for her multiple escape attempts. 'We go tomorrow after tea,' she added, sounding like a prisoner out of *Escape From Colditz*. Her enthusiasm cheered me up no end.

The next day was Friday, the day we were allowed one phone call each. Dad called, furious that Mum had been to see me. They were still arch enemies, even after all this time, and Dad couldn't bear it when I saw Mum.

When I came back from speaking to him, Jules gave me a wink, and nodded towards the front schoolroom. 'We're leaving in a minute. Follow me or Bridget,' she whispered.

'Who else is going?'

'Danielle, Zara and Bridget.'

Just then, Jules was called away for a phone call and Janice called Ivy and Charlie into the staffroom, leaving the rest of us momentarily unsupervised.

'Christ, it's now or never! We've got to go right this minute,' Bridget said.

'We can't go without Jules. She did all the work to loosen the window,' I said.

'Suit yourself, Titsalina. The rest of us are going.'

I had to follow. The thought of getting out was too tempting to pass up. We slipped into the front schoolroom, climbed through the window and legged it. When poor Jules came back from her phone call, we were gone.

Less than two hours later, a police car picked us up in Dartford as we tried to hitch a lift to London. We were taken to Dartford police station, put in separate cells and told to wait until a member of staff turned up from Kendall House.

After what seemed like ages, a policeman came into my cell and told me to strip off my clothes, because he needed to check me for drugs and firearms. I refused.

'But I'm on my period!' I said, when I realised that he was deadly serious.

'A likely story, but it makes no difference. You still have to be searched.'

I felt totally sick and embarrassed about having to show him my body. Shakily, I began to take my clothes off.

'Get dressed!' he snapped when the search was over. He turned and left the room. The cell door slammed.

After about an hour, Mrs Tarwin arrived to pick us up. Mrs Tarwin was the biology teacher at Kendall House. She also had a hand in supervising our medication, perhaps because of her science background, or maybe just because she liked to put her oar in everything. By her side was Matthew, the part-time book keeper, dressed in his standard garb of brown suit and graying white shirt. The sight of him made my blood freeze. I hadn't seen him in person for some time, but he was still haunting my dreams, along with Fred, Harriet and Miss Woods.

I heard Mrs Tarwin telling a police officer that we girls were dangerous and mentally ill. 'That's a lie!' I shouted. 'I ran away because you're drugging me. And if you need proof of it, that policeman who strip searched me saw the bruises and injection marks.'

The policeman and Mrs Tarwin exchanged a knowing look. He obviously believed her side of the story. In his eyes we were a bunch of psychos.

'Come along, now,' Mrs Tarwin said, when she noticed that I was lagging behind the others. I felt like bursting into tears. Aside from the horror of having to go back to Kendall House, the thought of getting into a car with Matthew made me feel intensely uncomfortable. I felt sick as he drove us back, and tried not to look at his veiny, sinewy neck rising up from the seat in front of me. By the time we reached Kendall House, I was a nervous wreck. My hands were shaking and I was on the point of throwing up.

Miss Woods let us in and we went through the usual ritual of doors unlocking and locking as we entered the building. Suddenly I was overcome by claustrophobia. The fear of being trapped again, caged in like a helpless animal, appalled me. I hurled myself at the middle door in the hall, which had a glass pane in it. The glass wobbled. I went to punch it with my fist, but Matthew grabbed my arm. His touch made my skin crawl. 'Get your hands off me!' I shrieked. I began to scream hysterically.

Miss Woods scrabbled around with her keys and eventually turned the lock. I burst through the door into the main hall area looking for somewhere to run, but Matthew was too quick for me and clasped me around the waist from behind. He dragged me into the office, where he held me in a tight grip while Janice prepared an injection to 'quieten' me down. As I struggled to get away from Matthew, I heard her measuring out the doses. 'Haloperidol, 20; Valium, 20; Kemadrin, 10.'

Kemadrin was a new one on me. 'What are you giving me now?' I shouted. She ignored me.

Miss Woods came in and between the three of them they held me still for long enough for Janice to inject me. Feeling myself go limp in Matthew's arms, I pushed away from him and he let me fall to the floor. Then he lifted me up and carried me to the detention room, where I was locked up for the night, back in the land of nightmares.

I was in and out of the detention room for the next month, right up until Christmas. I was constantly made to wear my nightclothes and must have been injected at least five times during that period, if not many more, in addition to being given my daily dose of pills. They were using all kinds of drugs on me now. The names were totally meaningless to me, but I heard them so many times that I was able to recite them: Depixol, Disipal, Largactyl, Sernace, Haliperidol, Droleptan, Sparine, Normison, other drugs and lots and lots of Valium. Some came in tablet form, some were injected and some were given both orally and intravenously.

'We never see you in the dorm anymore,' Zara remarked one day over breakfast. 'That room's become your own private bedroom, you poor sod.'

'I've turned into the Kendall House dartboard too,' I said, thinking of the puncture marks on my legs and buttocks.

I developed another round of worrying symptoms, including facial twitches, persistent trembling in my left arm, pains in my back and sides, a tendency to go hot and cold, and horrific, brain-splitting headaches. I pleaded with the staff to let me see a doctor, but all they said was, 'You're not ill! It's all in your head.'

Although I knew that it was about as likely as snow in summer, I longed for a phone call from Mum to say that she had found a nice place for us both to live. I kept recalling how she had promised to get me out of Kendall House by Christmas. I wondered if she even remembered saying as much.

As it turned out, she did. But, as she explained on the phone one day in the middle of December, her situation was still too precarious to make room for me. She was now living with yet another bloke, somewhere near Petersfield in Hampshire, I think, and working as a housekeeper again. 'Just give me a few more months, Teresa,' she said.

'Yes, Mum,' I said dolefully.

All the other girls were getting excited about going to stay with their families over the Christmas break, but I had to make do with a visit from Dad and Bernadette on 23 December. It was great to see them though. My sister and I had a much closer relationship than we had done as children and I appreciated her regular visits. We went into Gravesend and wandered around the shops.

Before we left, Harriet had a word with Dad. 'I must emphasise that Teresa is not allowed cigarettes inside Kendall House. So please do not give her any to bring back here.'

Dad bought me a packet of Embassy just before we left Gravesend. 'Whatever you do, hide them from that miserable bint,' he laughed.

Christmas Eve arrived. The other girls left Kendall House – all except Bridget, that is. Like me, she had nowhere to go, and we were stuck with each other over the holiday. I had been dreading being left alone with her, but she was surprisingly friendly to me. I suppose she was just being pragmatic. Without me, she wouldn't have anyone to talk to apart from the staff. So for once she called a truce.

She was usually such a dark and scary figure in my life

that it was a relief to be on her good side for a change. I went along with whatever she wanted, just to keep her happy. On Christmas Eve, we played records and danced around the sitting room. The rest of the time we tended to the hamsters and rabbits. I now had two hamsters, Vampire and Nipper, and I loved them dearly.

On Christmas Day, we played a bit of a trick on Brenda, one of the members of staff. Brenda was okay, I suppose. She wasn't particularly sharp, so she was easy prey for hard types like Bridget.

Bridget's idea was to wrap up our Christmas dinner in pretty Christmas wrapping paper and give it to Brenda, as if it were a proper present. It sounds stupid, but it was actually such a silly trick that I couldn't help laughing. We wrapped up a couple of slices of turkey, roast potatoes, sprouts and gravy in some tin foil, wrapped that in another layer of tin foil, and then Sellotaped it up with a sheet of paper decorated with festive holly and ivy.

Brenda's face lit up when Bridget handed her our gift. 'Girls, how very kind of you!' she exclaimed.

'Well it's not much, but we really hope you like it,' Bridget said meekly. My stomach muscles ached from trying to hold in the laughter that was bubbling up inside me.

'Never mind, it's the thought that counts,' Brenda happily assured her, taking pains not to tear the paper as she unwrapped it. 'Ooh, shiny!' she said when she spied the tin foil. She started to finger it gently, evidently trying to guess its contents. By now I was rocking with suppressed laughter, and yet at the same time half-regretting what we'd done.

Brenda looked completely deflated when she finally got through the foil to the cold food and gravy, which dripped messily over her fingers. I felt a bit sorry for her, but the situation was so ridiculous that I had to laugh out loud. 'That's not very nice, is it?' she said crossly.

'Sorry, Brenda, it was just a joke,' we told her. She stalked off to wash her hands and we doubled up in hysterical giggles.

Later in the day, I went to Shirley's house and Bridget went off to Janice's. Shirley lived in a modern farmhouse building on a quiet lane. There was a big garden and a shed out the back, where Shirley tried to teach me to pluck a chicken. I couldn't do it. It made me feel sick. I was a lot happier playing with the poodle and the Labrador, or having a ride on Stan's tractor.

A couple of days later I went to Harriet's for the day. Hers was a fairly bog standard house, perhaps even a council house, on some kind of estate. Harriet's husband was white and very tall. She had two mixed race children. I don't remember much else about my time there because Harriet gave me a port and lemonade shortly after I arrived. This was not a very good idea, to say the least. Considering the cocktail of medication I was on, it's not surprising that I reacted badly to alcohol on top. I felt sick and woozy all afternoon and vomited twice when I got back to Kendall House.

New Year's Eve came and went, and the other girls returned to the house. Zara was one of the first back and we became quite close. I had hoped that Bridget might go on being nice to me beyond the holiday time, but it was not to be. Once Nicole and the Sophies were back, she reverted to her old ways. She seemed to get a lot of enjoyment out of manipulating the others, and I was always her target, whether directly or indirectly.

Bridget beat me up countless times, but she was scariest when she was playing mind games with me. When everything went quiet, I knew for sure that she was plotting some new torture. She totally controlled the others. If she told them to ignore me, no one would speak to me until she lifted the ban. If she told one of them to attack me, they did. It often got to the point where I'd be scared to walk from one room to another for fear of what or who was waiting around the corner. The not knowing used to terrify me. My life was dominated by fear.

I complained to the staff, but they seemed to think that it was my fault that the others treated me badly. Miss Woods used to lecture me about the compromises we needed to make to live harmoniously with each other. She called it, 'Living Together Syndrome'.

'If you're not pleasant to others, how can others be pleasant to you?' she'd say.

She was blind to the reality of the situation. How could I be pleasant when I was being beaten up every other minute and ignored the rest of the time – not to mention being drugged to high heaven?

The only chance I had to be pleasant was on the rare days when Bridget decided to be nice to me, usually after she'd had an argument with her darling Nicole. Suddenly, she would want to go out on a walk with me, or sit next to me in class or in the dining room. It always took me by surprise, but I never questioned it. Although I couldn't stand Bridget and had no real desire to be friends with her, when I was in her good books it simply meant that I had one less thing to worry about.

Towards the end of January, I started experiencing extreme stomach discomfort and sharp pains in my right side. I was also sick a lot. Harriet and Janice made the usual complaints about me being a hypochondriac and doled out extra Valium and sleeping pills. I tried not to swallow them – or any of the other medication they were giving me – because I was convinced that all the different tablets were making me worse, but Harriet caught on. 'Open your mouth!' she'd say after every dose, to check that I wasn't holding any pills on my tongue or in my cheeks.

I was certain I needed a doctor, but after two days of really bad stomach ache, Harriet still held the opinion that I was faking. 'I've heard it all before a thousand times, and you're not even a very good actor,' she sighed.

By the afternoon of the third day, I could barely walk. My stomach was distended and so sensitive to touch that I cried out in agony at the slightest brush of fingers or clothing. I began to feel feverish and extremely nauseous. My vision blurred. I couldn't focus on anything apart from the pain. Harriet told me to go and lie down in the detention room for an hour. 'I'll bring you something to help you sleep.'

'I don't want to sleep. I need a doctor,' I said.

'Of course you don't. It'll pass. It always does.'

Zara was allowed to come and see me. 'I brought you a Mars bar,' she said.

I was really touched, but I couldn't even look at it, let alone eat it. She tried tempting me to take a small bite, but I retched. 'I think I'll save it for later,' I said, slipping it under my pillow.

A little later, Shirley popped by to see how I was doing. 'Harriet says you've got your usual aches and pains,' she said.

Harriet had obviously made light of my symptoms, but I didn't have the energy to complain. Practically unconscious now, I pointed to my stomach. 'Don't touch it!' I croaked.

Shirley's face fell. 'Have you eaten anything?' She propped me up so that she could plump up my pillow. 'What's this doing here?' She pointed at the Mars bar. Knowing how much

I liked sweet things, she was surprised to hear that I didn't want it. 'I think Harriet ought to see you again,' she said anxiously.

Eventually Harriet took my temperature. She looked mildly perturbed as she read the results. Putting one hand on my forehead, she told me to show her where my stomach hurt. I screamed when she pressed it. The pain was horrific. I was sure I was dying.

'Shut up, you big baby.' She shook her head. 'If this turns out to be one of your attention-seeking exercises, I will be very angry.'

'I think we'd better call an ambulance,' Shirley said.

'That will not be necessary,' Harriet said firmly.

'This time she looks really ill,' Shirley insisted.

'She'll recover.'

In the end, Shirley dialled 999 against Harriet's wishes. I kept passing out in the ambulance, but at one point I heard Harriet say, 'If this girl is acting, then she deserves an Oscar.'

At West Hill Hospital I was given an emergency appendectomy. Four days later, when I got back to Kendall House, Harriet was the first person I saw.

'I've got a new name for you, Teresa, and it's Moaney. Because I have never known anyone moan as much as you do. So, are you feeling better now, Moaney? Or are you going to go on living up to your new name?'

'Well, I'm not dying of a burst appendix anymore,' I said. 'But if you go on drugging me, I expect I'll go on being ill – and complaining about it.'

Dad's next visit was in early February. While he was waiting to see me, he got talking to Nicole's dad. They got on so well that they decided to start coordinating their visits to Kendall House and take the train to Gravesend together. I was glad that they'd made friends, because Nicole was a bit nicer to me as a result – although only when Bridget allowed it, obviously.

Bernadette came to see me as often as she could and we began to get a lot closer. I didn't see Mum, but she rang quite regularly. One day I suggested that she come and see me with Dad. It was still my fantasy that they would get back together and make the family whole again. But Mum said that she had been told by various staff on the phone that she was no longer allowed to visit me.

I couldn't believe that they would try to stop me from seeing my own mother. Half-suspecting that she was making it up because she couldn't be bothered to make the trip, I asked Janice whether it was true.

'Yes, your mother's visiting rights have been suspended for now. Your father is adamant that she is a bad influence on you and has requested that she doesn't see you. What's more, she was very rude to Miss Woods the last time she was here. Such behaviour from visitors is unacceptable, I'm afraid. So she's only got herself to blame.'

My world was shrinking and I felt myself diminishing with it. I began to focus obsessively on trying to be good and earn the privilege of walks outside Kendall House. Walks were precious because we weren't allowed many, and they were our only little bit of freedom. Sometimes we were permitted fifteen minutes and sometimes half an hour; every second outside the house was a treat. But often we'd be promised a walk later, only to be told when the time came that the staff were too busy to bother with getting our shoes from the coat cupboard. It was incredibly frustrating. There was no consistency.

One day in early March, I was allowed to go out for a

walk at 3 p.m. – with Bridget, of all people. I sometimes wondered if the staff paired me up with her deliberately, because they knew how nasty she could be to me. Anyway, this particular day, Bridget decided to be nice, and Kate said that we could go out for a whole hour. For once, things felt like they were going my way, even though I had a streaming cold and the usual fluey symptoms that were a recurrent side effect of my medication.

As soon as we were out of the house, Bridget told me that she had stashed a bottle of wine behind a bush in the local park. 'I brought it back from my weekend away!' she said excitedly.

I'd had very little experience of drinking. Seeing Dad on the piss had put me off it, and after months on drugs at Kendall House I didn't like the idea of clouding up my brain any more than necessary. But this was a chance to bond with my deadly enemy and perhaps even disarm her by making friends, so I wasn't going to pass it up. When it came to Bridget, I lived in hope – pointlessly, as it turned out.

We rushed to the park and found the bottle in its hiding place next to the public toilets. Bridget was so happy that it was still there. But then her face dropped. 'I forgot to bring a bottle opener!' she said.

Fifteen long minutes passed as we tried to work out how to open the bottle. In vain we tried to dig the cork out using a twig. Extreme measures were called for. Finally I said, 'I've got an idea!' and whacked the neck of the bottle against the toilet wall. The bottle neck shattered and the cork flew out. Bingo! We had an open bottle of wine, albeit a lethally jagged one.

Bridget wasn't too keen on the idea of drinking from a broken bottle, but I tipped it up and poured wine in my mouth without the glass touching my lips. After a few moments, she did the same. We had to be really careful, because some of the jagged pieces had fallen into the wine, but we still managed to down about a quarter of the bottle each. Happily drunk, we strolled back to Kendall House.

As usual, Harriet was waiting to frisk us for hidden fags and matches on our return. However, she was so distracted by the smell of booze on our breath that she wasn't as thorough as she would have been normally, and I managed to smuggle in a fag, a match, and a strip of matchbox to strike it on.

'What have you been up to? I can tell you've been drinking!' Harriet said.

Bridget concocted some story about a man calling us into the pub and buying us a drink. I didn't dare speak, because I was so off my head. Harriet made us drink black coffee to sober us up, but it didn't really do the trick because I was on a wide variety of drugs as well as the booze, and no amount of coffee could counter their effects. My memory of what happened next is very patchy, but I do know that somehow I made my way upstairs and started chasing poor Georgie around, yelling abuse at her. A member of staff called Denise grabbed me and locked me in the detention room.

While I was banging on the detention room door shouting to be let out, Tina kicked off outside, yelling her head off like a mad woman and threatening Denise. What with Georgie running around like a headless chicken, Tina screaming and me banging, Denise certainly had her hands full.

I fell asleep, but it can't have been for long because when I came to, I still felt drunk. Remembering my hidden cigarette, I used my one match to light it. But it dropped out of my mouth, and the next thing I knew the covers on the bed had caught fire. I tried to get out of the room, but of course the door was locked, so there was nothing for it but to smoke the rest of my fag and go down with a smile on my face. Or that's how I saw it in my drunken state.

Suddenly, the door flew open and Denise pulled me outside. 'Quick! Where's a fire extinguisher?' she shouted.

I heard Sophie C say, 'I think there's one in Miss Woods's office, but the door is locked.'

'Well, find a member of staff to unlock it! This is an emergency!'

Feeling extremely lightheaded, I ran into the bathroom to finish my cigarette. Denise caught up with me a few minutes later, once the fire in the detention room was out. 'It's time for your teatime medication,' she said crossly.

'What? You've got to be joking! Considering all the wine I've drunk, more medication would probably kill me,' I protested. In a foul mood, I made my way to the downstairs toilet, which had been left open after someone else had used it. I locked myself in. I wanted to be alone.

Kate turned up and ordered me out of there. She fiddled with the lock and managed to get it undone from the outside, but I sat against the door so that she couldn't get in. To my surprise, it wasn't long before Bridget and Jules joined the quest to get me out of there. 'Go away,' I shouted. I was in floods of tears by now, convinced that the staff were waiting on the other side of the door to inject me – as a punishment for drinking wine and refusing my medication. 'You'll have to kill me before you get me out of here,' I said.

'Come on, Teresa,' Bridget coaxed. 'No one's going to hurt you. We're just worried about you.'

Although she had been nice to me earlier, I knew Bridget for the traitor she was and didn't trust her. She could turn against you quicker than you could say knife, so I wasn't taking any chances.

'If everyone else goes outside, I'm sure I can talk her round,' Jules said. I heard the sound of footsteps receding. 'Hey, it's just you and me now,' she added. 'What's wrong?'

I poured my heart out to her. I told her I wanted to die, and that I didn't think I could hold out much longer in this hell.

In a calming voice, she told me that she felt the same way. 'But I know I couldn't survive without you here, so please don't even think about dying. I couldn't bear it if anything happened to you.' She kept her voice to a whisper. Bridget was standing by the bathroom door and Jules didn't want her to hear what we were saying.

'Just imagine how great life will be when we get out of here,' she went on. 'We'll be free to do whatever we want. We can go to concerts together and . . .'

All of a sudden Kate rushed into the bathroom and ordered me out of the toilet. 'The house is on fire! Everyone needs to get out right this minute.'

'No way,' I replied, thinking it was just a ploy to get me out and inject me. I was staying firmly put. The fire in the detention room had already been extinguished, I hadn't heard the fire alarm and I couldn't smell any smoke. The big red alarm bells were situated right outside the office door, next to the bathroom, so I figured I would have been able to hear them if they'd gone off.

Just then, there was a lot of commotion outside the door and the next thing I knew a fireman's head had appeared over the toilet door. 'Teresa, is it? We need you to come out of the toilet because there is a fire. If you don't come out I will have to kick the door in and I don't want to do that because you might get hurt,' he said calmly.

Standing up took a lot of effort. My legs were like jelly and I was trembling all over. I opened the toilet door and fell into the fireman's arms. He led me through thick smoke in the direction of the back garden. I could see the smoke but still I couldn't smell it, because of my blocked nose.

Passing the sitting room, I saw huge flames licking the doorway. 'The hamsters!' I shrieked. Pulling away from the fireman, I dashed into the burning room and tried to grab at least one cage. But the metal bars had heated up and burnt my fingers as I touched them.

The fireman caught up with me and dragged me out of the room into the back garden. 'Please don't let my hamsters die,' I begged him.

'I'll do my best to get them out for you,' he replied, before running back to help the other firemen get control of the fire.

Meanwhile, there was another drama going on in the back garden. Bridget lunged at Tina like a lunatic and started to punch her. Then the other girls set upon her too. Everyone was shouting about the fire and the hamsters, and in my muddle-headed state it took me a few seconds to realise that Tina had started the blaze by holding a match to the curtains. I slapped my forehead. What an idiot she was! We had all joked about how great it would be if Kendall House burned down, but I'd never imagined anyone would actually try it.

A fireman walked into the back garden carrying Bridget's hamster cage. Panic surged through me. What if Nipper and Vampire hadn't made it? 'I will kill you if my hamsters are dead!' I shouted at Tina.

The fireman came back with another cage, this time containing Georgie's hamster. I was certain that my hamsters were dead now. In my rage and sadness, I went for Tina, but Jules held me back.

Then out of the blue – or out of the smoke, I should say – the fireman who had saved me appeared with my hamsters' cages.

'They were saved by the bedding in their little houses,' he said with a smile.

I had my babies back! I was so happy, even though the bottoms of their cages had melted.

Now the fire was out, we could breathe a sigh of relief. Or could we? A thought struck me. 'Why didn't the fire alarm go off?' I asked Miss Woods. 'What if one of us had been locked in the detention room, or Sick Bay, or we'd all been locked upstairs in our dorms at night?'

Miss Woods said nothing. She and the rest of the staff on duty stood apart from us, staring at the embers that continued to smoulder in the burnt-out sitting room.

Chapter Thirteen

I don't know whether they increased the dosage of my medication, or dramatically changed the combination of drugs they were giving me, but two days after the fire in the sitting room I woke up feeling very, very angry. My hackles were up. I was itching with rage.

Even Tina decided to give me a wide berth. I heard her telling Nicole, 'Teresa is in a really weird mood. Something's eating her. Stay away! She's a bit scary today.'

In class, I was rude to Mrs Petsworth, who wouldn't allow me to bring Vampire into the lesson. When she told me off for being a loudmouth I threatened to throw my books at her. Since I usually spent my time feeling doped up and sorry for myself, my new-found aggression was as much a mystery to me as it was to the others. It was strange and totally uncharacteristic behaviour.

Mrs Petsworth called for Harriet. Fearful of being injected, I agreed to settle down to work. But later in the day, the surges of rage returned. Heat kept rising up inside me like volcanic lava, threatening to erupt.

What happened next seemed such a relatively small incident – compared to some of the other stuff that went on – that in the months that followed I struggled to understand its significance, or why it might have triggered the unhappiest period of my life.

We were in the sitting room playing records after school and Bridget was dictating the playlist, as usual. Since I wasn't enjoying her choice in music, I got out my favourite Aswad twelve inch. When the track she had chosen came to an end, I went to put on my record.

'Hey! What do you think you're doing?' she asked.

'What does it look like?' I kept my voice light.

'I'm putting on the next one,' she said, swaggering over to the record player.

'Sorry, but this comes first.' I pressed my disc firmly down on the deck.

She looked around the group for support. 'I don't think so!' she sneered. 'Does anyone else here want to listen to Teresa's crappy reggae?'

The other girls said nothing. They were waiting for me to react. I didn't disappoint them. For once I wasn't going to give in to Bridget.

I placed the needle on the record and the Aswad song began to play. 'Come over here if you've got a problem with it.' I met her eye and held her gaze steadily.

A tiny hint of uncertainty flitted across her face. I had never challenged her so directly. In fact, since Maya had left, no one had. She seemed to hesitate, but there was no way she could let it go. Her position as queen bee of Kendall House was in jeopardy and she knew it. We all knew it.

She flew at me like a demon, spitting venom and abuse. I fought back angrily. Although she was a solid lump of lard and muscle, I had a feeling that I might be able to beat her just this one time. But the next moment someone was forcing us apart. I heard Harriet's voice, then Benita's, and felt the prick of a needle in my bum. I remember falling to the floor, face down, and then I blacked out.

I woke up in Sick Bay feeling woozy and disorientated. Whatever Harriet had put in the injection had totally cancelled out every last ounce of energy I had. I tried to get up, but could barely raise my head from the pillow. It felt floppy on my neck. My body was bruised and achy. I tried to call for help, but all that came out of my mouth was saliva. Instead of speaking, I was dribbling. My eyelids kept closing against my will. I had often thought I was dying before, but this time it had to be true. I couldn't even lift my arm up from the bed.

I'm paralysed, I thought. My heart raced in panic, but I found that I still couldn't move, not even with adrenalin pumping around my body. I tried to call out again. 'Help!' I mouthed the word but no sound came out. My head felt dizzy, as if I'd come to a sudden halt after spinning round and round in a circle.

My mouth filled up with saliva again, before overflowing with sour, creamy vomit. I turned my head and spewed it onto the pillow, coughing as it caught in my throat. Despite its acrid smell, I didn't bother trying to brush it away, or turn the pillow over. My eyelids started flickering; a muscle in my cheek twitched uncontrollably. I had an involuntary spasm in my leg. My foot flew towards the ceiling and fell heavily onto the bed again. So perhaps I wasn't paralysed after all? Thick waves of tiredness overcame me and I passed out.

The next thing I remember is that Janice was in the room. She made me take some pills. Finding that I could speak at last, albeit in slow, slurred tones, I asked what they were. 'Sparine and Valium,' she said matter-of-factly.

'What will it do?'

'Keep you sedated.'

'Why?'

'Dr Peri's orders.'

I inhaled a disgusting whiff of dried vomit. 'I've been sick.'

She smirked. 'You don't have to tell me. I can smell it.'

Tears welled up in my eyes. 'Can you change my pillow-case?'

She bristled. 'Let's make sure this medication goes down first.'

'When can I go back to the dorm?'

She took my pulse. 'Not yet. You stay here with the door locked and no visits from anyone, apart from staff.'

My heart sank. 'How long for?'

'However long it takes.'

'Why?'

'I think you know why.'

'I don't! What have I done wrong?'

'Well, for one, you deliberately started a fight with poor Bridget. She was very upset afterwards.'

'Poor Bridget? But she's the bully ...' It was incredible. I felt sure that Bridget hadn't been locked up for fighting with me. I didn't even bother to ask.

'Miss Woods has decided that you should be isolated from the group for the time being. Hence you stay here until such a time as she decides to reintroduce you to everyday life.'

'How long will it be?'

She pursed her lips. 'That's not for me to say.'

I slept a little after she had gone and woke up in a cold sweat, with red blotches all over my skin. My vision was blurry. The ceiling kept zoning in and out of focus. My stomach started cramping up. My groin was painful and I needed to go to the toilet, but I was locked in and didn't have the strength to get up and bang on the door. I called for help but my pronunciation was skewed and it came out sounding like 'Howrp'. I tried again to get my tongue around this simple word. This time it emerged in a throaty, unintelligible rasp.

Lying on the bed, repeatedly trying to call for help, I realised that the sounds I was making seemed barely human. I had no idea what was happening to me, or what I was becoming. It was terrifying.

Shirley came into the room. There were two of her. Both Shirleys enquired if I wanted a drink. I slowly shook my head. 'Tor-lay,' I said.

The Shirleys merged into one and then divided again. They cocked their heads. 'What's that, Teresa?'

With effort, I raised my voice. '*Tor-lay!*'

'Do you mean the toilet?'

I nodded as vigorously as I could.

'Can you get up?' she asked. There was only one of her again.

I tried to sit up, but instead my arm flew upwards and fell across my face. My legs played dead. It felt as if I had no control over my physical movements. I tried to explain. 'Can't, can't . . .'

She drew back my sheets and dragged my legs around until my feet fell to the floor. After helping me to sit up, she put her arms around me and heaved me into a standing position. My legs gave at the knee, but she managed to hold me up. Almost in slow motion, we shuffled out of Sick Bay to the toilet. Once there, she helped me to pull up my nightdress and sit down on the toilet seat. My head flopped forwards. I almost lost my balance and rolled off the seat.

I thought it would make me feel better to urinate, but at first nothing came out. Suddenly I felt a tremor of a contraction down there, followed by a needle-sharp pain. 'Aaah!' I screamed. A flush of intense heat swept through me and I collapsed onto the cool bathroom floor, where I lay half in relief and half in agony until Shirley hauled me up.

'Goodness me, you're like a dead weight!' she exclaimed. 'Have you finished with the toilet?'

Although my bladder still felt full, I was terrified of trying to urinate again. 'Infection,' I said, but my clumsy tongue and slurry voice made it sound like 'invasion'.

'Say again?' I pointed to my waterworks and repeated my attempt to say 'infection' about ten times.

Finally she got it. 'I'll ask Harriet to have a look,' she said in a reassuring voice.

'No!' I cried out. I had no confidence in Harriet after the burst appendix episode, which might have killed me had she continued to ignore my pleas for medical attention for very much longer.

I think Shirley understood my fears, because she said, 'I'll ask her to sort out some antibiotics immediately.'

Some time later, Harriet came in with a load of pills. Haltingly, I asked what they were. She wouldn't say. 'I haven't got time to sit around and chat with you. You're not the only girl in Kendall House!' she snapped.

Anger welled up inside me. I felt it flood into my brain like water gushing through the walls of a burst dam. 'I hate you!' I yelled.

'I can't understand what you're saying, nor do I much care to,' she said briskly.

She thrust a tumbler of water at me. The rim banged against my mouth. I went to drink, but couldn't coordinate my lips and the glass and liquid flew everywhere. 'I want my dad!' I wailed.

This she did appear to understand. 'You're getting no visits, oh no. You're staying in here until we can be sure you're not a threat to the staff.'

I didn't understand what she meant and asked her to explain. A threat to the staff? This was a new one. But she either didn't want to expand on her comment or couldn't make out what I was saying. Soon she was gone.

I lay back and tried to work out why I was being drugged and held in Sick Bay. It had to be a punishment for something, but surely it couldn't be the argument with Bridget. Most of the time that big bully never even got told off for beating me up, so it would be totally unfair of them to lock me up for starting an argument. It hadn't even been an argument. It was just a case of standing up for myself.

Hot tears dripped out of my eyes. Why was I even trying to think things through logically? Nothing made sense at Kendall House. Bridget had received preferential treatment from Day One, despite her vindictive ways. The staff knew she was malicious and ruthless, but instead of punishing her for it, they actively encouraged it. In return, I strongly suspected that she collaborated with them and their vicious regime, informing on the girls and stirring things up. Certainly, they seemed to like her. She was the one they invited into the staffroom for tea and the occasional cigarette, and she rarely – if ever – lost her privileges.

On the other hand, I was punished for the slightest wrongdoing. I was constantly being ordered into my nightclothes. I was more familiar with the detention room and Sick Bay than I was with the dorm. Apart from Shirley, the staff appeared to despise me. And I was being drugged to death. It was all so unfair, so wrong. Why didn't the staff like me? OK, I complained about being at Kendall House, but so did everyone else, including Bridget. So why was I the scapegoat? Overcome with self-pity, I sobbed myself to sleep.

The days and nights merged into one continuous long lonely torment punctuated by tea, pieces of toast and doses of medication. I was now being drugged more than four times a day. Sometimes I'd be given six envelopes – or more – within a twenty-four-hour period, and be forced to swallow their contents. If I kicked up a fuss, Harriet would inject me forcefully, leaving me with large black bruises.

For some reason I was still not permitted visits from any of the girls. I missed Jules the most, but would have made do with seeing any of them, apart from Bridget. Perhaps even Bridget; I felt so desperately isolated. I tried to make the staff stay and talk to me when they came to take me to the toilet, or give me medication, but they usually said something like, 'I've got work to get on with!' or 'Attention-seeking, as usual.' Most of them were so hard, so heartless. Couldn't they see how desolate I felt? Didn't they understand how cruel it was to place a fourteen-year old girl in solitary confinement for days on end?

'Please let me see the others. Please let me go back to the group,' I begged Harriet.

'I'm not sure that would be a good idea, even if Miss Woods allowed it,' she replied. 'Understandably, the girls aren't feeling very well disposed towards you at the moment.'

'What do you mean? Why?'

Harriet sighed. 'They weren't happy about your uncalled-for attack on Bridget – or the way you treated Mrs Petsworth.'

'But Bridget attacked me!' I didn't remember treating Mrs

Petsworth badly and so felt I couldn't answer that particular accusation.

I had often longed to get away from Kendall House, but all I cared about now was getting out of Sick Bay and down to the other girls. Of course I still wanted to escape entirely, but it was a case of one step at a time. I was in a prison within a prison. If I could only get out of my own private cell, I felt I could almost bear life in the main house. In reality, I would have felt suicidal either way, but being locked in a tiny cramped room for so long had shifted and warped my horizons. First and foremost my priority was to get the hell out of my tiny claustrophobic dungeon. I pleaded with every member of staff I saw, but they all said the same: in a word, no.

Shirley was the only one who was even a little bit kind to me. It was usually Shirley who took me to the bathroom and helped me wash. Depending on how drugged up I was, she had to guide, support or sometimes even half-carry me there. Although I was still extremely shy about showing anyone my body, I had to lose my inhibitions when it came to staying clean during this time. Sometimes I couldn't even get up, in which case Shirley gave me a bed bath. She was always very gentle and caring with me. When I was able to sit up, she'd brush my hair with soothing strokes and listen to my stories about life before Kendall House.

One day as she was helping me along to the bathroom, we passed the upstairs classroom while a lesson was going on. This was unusual, as my toilet and bathroom visits were normally timed so that I didn't have any contact with the other girls. The classroom door was open and I could just about make out a few faces through my fog of blurred vision and muzziness.

Suddenly I heard a shout. 'There's that fucking bitch! I'll fucking get her. Die, bitch, die! Don't even show your face around here no more.'

I recognised Bridget's voice. Her aggression was palpable, even to my confused mind. Shivers of fear ran through me like electric currents. I began to shake uncontrollably. Tears streamed down my cheeks.

Another shout went up. This time it was Zara, of all people. I thought we'd made friends, but apparently the connection had been severed by my absence from the group. 'Yer fucking uglier than ever, you scraggy cow,' she yelled. A burst of laughter followed this comment.

'Yeah, Titsalina Bumsquirt, you're wasting away!' Bridget added gleefully. 'You'd better hurry up and die, or we'll do it for you. How'd you like to be murdered in your bed tonight? Suffocated, or stabbed? Cos we're coming for you, bitch face! See ya later.'

'That's enough, girls!' Shirley said. She turned to me. 'Don't take any notice, Teresa. They don't mean it.'

I knew better. 'They do mean it. They hate me. Harriet told me so.'

Back in Sick Bay, I couldn't help dwelling on what Bridget had said. After all, I had nothing else to think about. 'They're going to kill me,' I told Janice when she came to give me my pills around 7.30 p.m.

'Nonsense! They can't get in here,' she said.

Just then there was a battering at the door. 'Are you in there, Titsalina?' Bridget shouted. 'We've come for you, just like we said we would. Are you ready to die? Are you? Have you made your peace with God? You'd better start praying, you bitch. You're going to need a guardian angel if you don't want to get killed tonight.'

There was more shouting from some of the other girls, along with various hissing and growling sounds. They sounded like a pack of wild animals. Bridget was obviously having a field day as the leader of the gang. I heard Zara's voice, and Nicole's. Tina was there too, and Sophie K. They banged and kicked the door some more. I started to tremble again. My mind felt like it was exploding with fear.

Janice stepped outside the door and tried to calm the group down. 'Go away! This is very silly behaviour,' she said.

There were gasps and a few muffled giggles. They had expected me to be alone. 'It's not you we're after, Janice, it's that titless squirt you've got locked up in there. I'm just itching to put a fist in her face,' Bridget said. Janice stood her ground and saw them off.

I burst into tears and began crying hysterically. 'Why are they like that? What have I done to them to deserve it?'

Janice seemed unsympathetic. 'I have no idea. You will just have to sort it out when you get up and rejoin the group.'

'When will that be?' Having been desperate to get out of Sick Bay and be with the others again, I was now feeling extremely apprehensive about what might happen when I did.

Janice seemed to have no idea of when I might be allowed out. She told me that Miss Woods was on holiday for the week – and obviously nothing would change until she was back.

'Why not?' I screamed.

Janice shrugged. 'Stop acting up. You really can be a pain, can't you?' Her words hit me like a slap in the face. Why didn't she care about me? Why couldn't she just have shown me a bit of sympathy?

'I'll stop forever if you want,' I said, clutching her arm. 'Just get a piece of glass and you won't have any more problems with me.'

She shook me off. 'Don't be silly.'

After she had gone, I worked myself up into a frenzy of worry. I was petrified that Bridget would return and somehow find a way in through the Sick Bay door. I had visions of her standing over me with a knife, laughing maniacally before she repeatedly stabbed me in the chest. I imagined her hands around my neck, pressing hard on my throat, strangling the life out of me.

There was a loud bang outside the room. I heard laughter and a scraping sound. A note slowly edged its way under the door. I reached out and grabbed it, hoping it was from Jules. To my dismay, it was signed by Zara.

'I DON'T WANT TO BE YOUR FRIEND ANYMORE. I HATE YOU. I'M GOING TO GET YOU KILLED. YOU DESERVE TO DIE. FROM Zara'

Ten minutes later, another note came through, expressing similar spiteful thoughts and threats. This time it was signed by all the girls. 'Stop it!' I shouted, suspecting that some of them were on the other side of the door, listening for a reaction.

I was right. I heard scuffling and whispering very nearby, and then Benita's voice rang out. 'You two! Get to bed this instant!' The sound of girlish giggles and running footsteps trailed away into the distance.

In a trance of fear and despair, I searched the room for something to cut myself with. But Janice had taken everything away, even the book that Mrs Connolly had brought me earlier in the day. My eyes lighted on Zara's note. Perhaps she had done me a favour by pushing it under the door, after all. I folded it into a point and dug the point into my arm. The skin of my forearm was still delicate from previous cutting; it wasn't long before I broke through it and released several drops of blood. I worked the paper edge into the cut, gently expanding it until a tiny stream of blood ran down to my elbow. I started to make another incision, but my weapon became soggy and I had to fold up the other note.

When Janice came back to give me a final dose of medication, she found me with scratches and small cuts all over my arms. 'And you wonder why you're in here!' she said with raised eyebrows, as if I were some kind of halfwit. 'I don't suppose it has occurred to you that you're just a little bit sick in the head?'

Her words made me snap back to reality. I looked down at my arms, aghast. 'I don't know why I do this! It's the pills. For some reason they make me want to cut myself.'

'What rubbish. Quite the opposite is true, in fact. Without the pills, things would be a good deal worse for you.'

She was wrong, but she wouldn't listen. The next day I took the light bulb out of its socket, smashed it and used the pieces to continue cutting myself. When Harriet came up with a tea tray in the late afternoon, she found me in darkness, my arms covered in blood. The sheets on the bed were also spattered. She was furious. Dragging me out of the room, she marched me down to the detention room and locked me in. She and Brenda complained heartily about having to change the Sick Bay sheets and hoover the floor.

Brenda escorted me back to Sick Bay. 'You've shot yourself in the foot with this latest escapade,' she said smugly. 'Miss Woods says that from now on you can do without a light bulb.'

I pretended that I didn't care. I told myself that the darkness in my room now matched the darkness in my soul. But in truth, those black hours of night terrified me. There was hissing and whispering outside the door at frequent intervals, along with banging fists. But at least I couldn't see to read the nasty notes the girls kept pushing through. Although what they wrote was still horribly mean, it definitely wasn't as scary in the light of day as it would have been in the dead of night.

As the days passed, my appetite diminished, until I stopped wanting to eat altogether. On the other hand, I was constantly thirsty and drank as much water and milk as I could persuade the staff to bring me. Often they left me dry-mouthed for hours, gasping for liquid like a dying man in the desert. They didn't care. 'You never stop, do you? No wonder they call you the moaner,' Trinny used to say when I complained about not having enough liquid.

Some days I slept fairly constantly, only managing to wake up for long enough to take the next batch of medication. Other days I would fidget for hours on end, unable to sit still. I had an invisible itch in my legs that drove me mad. I felt compelled to keep moving, because there was no way of scratching it. It wasn't on my skin, it was deep under the skin.

I had been suffering from rashes and dry patches of skin from the very beginning of my time at Kendall House, but these worsened considerably during my time in Sick Bay. I would flush hot and cold with fever or the sweats, and pink blush flames would appear on my legs, arms and stomach. The patches of dry skin on my arms and legs became red and inflamed, shedding flaky, silvery scales. They itched like crazy, and bled easily when scratched. Sometimes they cracked and bled without even being touched. Harriet said she thought it was psoriasis.

As time went on, the patches grew and spread and merged into each other, until my ears, arms and legs were thick with it, and my head was encrusted. On bad days, the pain was unbelievable. On better days it was merely a constant irritant.

Sometimes I had trouble breathing. I had no idea whether this was down to the stale Sick Bay air or my sense of claustrophobia or whether it was a side effect of one of the drugs they were giving me. I asked if I could go out for a walk every now and then, or even just spend some time in the garden.

'It would be nice, but Miss Woods says you can't be trusted quite yet,' Shirley told me.

'Does she think I'm going to steal the flowers?'

I hadn't talked to Miss Woods once since I had been locked up. She was either on holiday, on her day off, or 'out at a meeting' when I asked to see her. It was hugely frustrating. I needed her to explain why I was being isolated and sedated – and I was desperate for the chance to defend myself against whatever accusations she could throw at me.

Finally she agreed to see me. I was feeling really listless, so Brenda washed my hair for me and helped me clean myself up. As I was leaving the bathroom, I took a good look at my reflection in the mirror. My eyes were sunken and there were deep shadows under them. My face was thin and drawn. My hair was dull and lank, even though it had just been washed.

I shuffled into Miss Woods's office. 'I hear you wanted to speak to me, Well, speak away,' she said.

Earlier, in a rare moment of clarity, I had decided that it probably wouldn't be a good idea to go into this meeting with all guns blazing. Instead I told Miss Woods that all I wanted was to be liked by the staff and girls. From now on, I promised, I would do my best to get on with everyone. If she would let me out of Sick Bay, I would never be bolshy or answer back to the staff again.

She began to ask probing questions about what it was like to spend time in solitary confinement. It wasn't long before I broke down and told her how miserable and lonely my days and nights were. 'No one loves me. No one even likes me,' I went on weepily.

She guffawed. 'We all like you! We all love you, in fact. It's just that we don't like what you do – and we don't love the way you behave. Here at Kendall House we know you can grow into a nice person, Teresa, but you have to learn where you're going wrong. That is all that's going on here. We're teaching you right from wrong.'

'But I know right from wrong! I've never stolen anything or broken the law. I've never been violent . . .'

'Never been violent?' she said archly. 'Why do you think you're in Sick Bay at the moment?'

'But Bridget attacked me first!' I protested.

She frowned. 'Bridget? I'm not talking about Bridget. I'm referring to your unbridled attack on Mrs Petsworth.'

My head spun. Someone else had mentioned it, as I recalled, but I had no idea what she was talking about and said so.

Her lip curled in disbelief. 'Do you mean to say that you don't remember flying at Mrs Petsworth in a rage? Or that she tripped and fell as a result, bringing the blackboard down with her?'

I racked my brain, but had no recollection of anything like the scene she was describing, which seemed strange considering I could clearly recall the argument with Bridget. 'I don't remember it at all,' I said.

'Well, you are confined to Sick Bay as a result of the incident with Mrs Petsworth. And in Sick Bay you will stay until I'm fully convinced that you have learned right from wrong.' She waved a hand, as if the situation had started to bore her. 'That will be all now. Brenda will take you back upstairs.'

CHAPTER FOURTEEN

The days and nights in solitary confinement were long, lonely and desperate. There was nothing to do, no one to talk to, nowhere to look and no fresh air to breathe. Physically weak and getting weaker by the day, mentally confused and disorientated, I lay in bed, barely existing, as the hours, days and weeks of nothingness drifted by. Often the only sounds I heard were hissed insults and abuse through the Sick Bay door. Not a day went past when I didn't wish myself dead.

In the mornings I woke up wondering what would be wrong with me next. My nightdress always seemed to be stuck to me, glued to my skin with clammy sweat. I had headaches that mushroomed inside my head until I was sure that my brain would explode. Often I felt angry, agitated or nervous. Other times I was so sleepy and listless that my mind was a total blank.

My skin felt either cool and sweaty or hot and dry. The slightest irritation would cause it to flare up into a rash, and it was easily bruised. I suffered from tremors, twitches, shaking and convulsions. I had a lot of sore throats and it was often painful to swallow. Bitter flavours permeated my mouth, and I would spend whole days plagued by the taste of liquorice or mould or clay. My breathing went from rapid and shallow to scarily slow and deep. Sometimes there was a rattle in my chest. Walking was often a struggle. My sense of balance was all over the place, my coordination askew. My heartbeat would race or pound for no reason. I had frequent bowel problems, both constipation and diarrhoea.

I was still being forced to take medication at least four times a day. The number of pills they were giving me varied wildly, and for no apparent reason. Sometimes my night-time dose comprised up to nine or ten tablets, but no one would explain why. Whenever I had a crying fit, became angry or was rude to one of the staff, they'd give me 'crisis medication', which was just a bunch of extra pills, sometimes accompanied by something called Phenergan Syrup, which Harriet said would help with my waterworks, and also my rashes. The different tablets sent me from high to low and then knocked me sideways. As time went on, I could feel the various chemicals kicking in, usually within half an hour of being given my medication. I'd be swept away on one wave or another – to a place of drowsiness or restlessness, deepest sleep or tension and jitters.

One morning Shirley came up to Sick Bay with a cup of tea to find me cowering in the corner of the room, shaking with fear.

'What's wrong? What is it?' she asked.

I pointed at the bed. 'Can't you see them? Look at them all! They're revolting! Get rid of them now! Please, please get rid of them!'

She frowned. 'I don't see anything. There's nothing there apart from sheets and a bed.'

'No, look!' I screeched, leaping to my feet. 'Bugs, millions of them, pouring out from under the sheets, look at them, where are they going? Argh! Don't let them come near me, please, Shirley – stop them, save me, please, help me!'

'I'll go and call Harriet,' she said, hurriedly leaving the room.

'*Don't leave me!*' I called after her, hysterical with panic. 'They'll get me and kill me and crawl into my mouth!'

It seemed ages before she and Harriet appeared. Harriet was carrying a hypodermic syringe on a small tray. Filled with terror, I cried out, 'Don't inject me, please don't inject me! I need to stay awake, or they'll get me.'

Harriet's lip curled. 'You know what I always say, Teresa. This will be a lot easier for both of us if you lie back and think of England.'

Since the bed – to my eyes – was currently a seething mass of repellent creepy-crawlies, the last thing I intended to do was lie down. I pressed myself flat against one of the walls and resisted all attempts to pull me towards the bed.

'Go and get Janice and Benita,' Harriet told Shirley, who immediately scurried away. When Janice and Benita had been rounded up, the four of them held me face down on the bed – face down in imaginary wriggling bugs – and Harriet rammed the syringe into my buttock. I went out like a light.

The hallucinations got worse. There always seemed to be something creeping in or out of the bed. I started seeing little triangles with wings. They floated around the room. They followed me as I was accompanied to the toilet and they danced in front of my eyes, swooping over my head and fluttering in my peripheral vision. They were maddening, like nasty little faceless fairies sent from hell to tease and torment me.

I had one urine infection after another and was constantly uncomfortable. The old familiar pains returned to my groin area, which started to feel battered and bruised again. I experienced a burning sensation down there, as well as a sharp, prickly feeling that made me curl up in agony. My genitals were often sore, as if they had been rubbed raw.

I complained to the staff, but as usual they dismissed my worries as make-believe. Nothing made a difference. I could be howling in agonised torment, my face hot with fever, my body slippery with sweat, my hand tucked between my legs as if to shield my groin from further pain, and Harriet would simply say, 'Snap out of it, Teresa. I've had enough of your shenanigans today.'

'Help me, Harriet!' I would say through clenched teeth. But no matter how graphically I described what was going on down there, not one of the staff took me seriously or bothered to give me an examination.

Even Shirley, who was a lot more sympathetic than the rest of them, used to say, 'I expect it's hormones. You're at that age.' Or, 'It could be female growing pains.' Or, 'Perhaps it's a touch of thrush – don't worry, it's perfectly normal.'

I was ignorant, but not stupid. Was she trying to tell me that every teenage girl went through a phase of writhing in bed with her groin on fire, suffering from racking pain? It was just a part of growing up, was it? No need to call in a doctor? I couldn't believe it. I knew about periods, but no one had ever mentioned anything like this to me. It just couldn't be normal. Pain was your brain's way of telling you that you were ill – I knew that much.

My terrible nightmares returned. I was haunted by visions of scary men. A couple of their faces were familiar, but most of them were unrecognisable. They did unspeakable things to me. They hurt me. They enjoyed hurting me. They laughed as they hurt me. In the dreams I screamed for help, but my voice had no power and the screams came out silent.

I became intensely agitated during my waking moments. Harriet's way of dealing with this was to prick and pierce and puncture and stab my body with needle after needle, not caring if she left me covered in bruises. I was unconscious for most of the day and night, but the nightmares continued. The pain in my groin grew worse. Urination was often excruciating. I began to experience extreme discomfort when it came to my bowel movements. My back passage itched and ached and felt tender and sore. But still no one listened to me when I complained.

Then one evening I realised just how real my nightmares were. I woke up in a panicked haze. My brain was swirling; I couldn't see very well; everything felt dreamlike. There were two men in the room. One of them was pushing between my legs; the other was forcing himself in and out of my mouth. There was a belt tied around my neck. When they noticed that I was conscious, one of them tightened the belt. I fought for breath and passed out again.

The next time I woke up, they were gone. As I recalled what had happened, I vomited violently over the side of the bed. There were red marks on my neck. My lips were bruised and sore. My groin was tender and swollen. An unpleasant odour lingered in the air. It was familiar; I had smelled it before. In the past I had associated it with waking up from long stretches of drugged stupor. Thinking about it now, I realised that there was a link between the smell and my genital discomfort and pain.

In that moment I knew that this had happened before. Not once, but many times. Over and over again, these men and other men had violated my body while I slept, semi-comatose, under the influence of multiple prescription drugs, while I was oblivious to what they were doing to me.

My body started to convulse with shock at this realisation. My teeth chattered; my arms and legs shook uncontrollably. I threw up again and then dry-retched repeatedly. I searched my mind desperately for some way to contradict what I knew to be true. I didn't want to believe that these unspeakable things were being done to me. Surely it couldn't be possible. The Sick Bay door was locked day and night, so how could anyone get in?

I tried to reject the sickening knowledge that, for the men who worked in and around Kendall House, getting hold of a key to Sick Bay was probably kid's play.

But how did they get up the stairs without being seen? How did they do what they did to me without being heard? If my nightmares were in any way representative of reality, in the past they had laughed and joked as they abused me. So why had nobody heard them? Could I possibly have imagined the whole thing? Could it have been an hallucination?

By now my heart was pounding furiously. I was finding it increasingly difficult to breathe. Staring ahead into space, my eyes wide as saucers, my brain overloading with information I didn't want to absorb, I went into a full-blown panic attack. Triangles with wings crowded my vision. Bugs crawled all over my skin. As I tried to brush them off, I went into a frenzied bout of scratching.

I fell to the ground, shuddering. I rammed my head against the floor, frantically trying to smash the truth inside it to smithereens, desperate for this to be another dream or nightmare, just another hallucination. I yelled for help. I cried out to God. I begged the ground to swallow me up.

I couldn't cry enough. I couldn't scream enough. My mouth wouldn't open wide enough to express the enormity of my anguish. How could they do this to me? How! Why! The bastards! I felt my brain folding in on itself. Hate and fury surged through me. Self-pity flooded my mind. I pulled at my hair. I pummelled my fists into the floor.

I heard the clink of keys at the door. Harriet came into the room. 'Oh, look who's creating! Well, what a surprise. Having another one of your turns, are you? Dear oh dear.' Her voice dripped with disdain.

Her heartlessness blew me away. Lying on the floor in front of her, red-eyed, tear-stained, shaking, crying, and in obvious physical and emotional pain, was a fourteen-year-old girl. And yet all she could do was mock.

I pulled myself into a sitting position and tried to marshal my thoughts. 'I'm hurt, Harriet,' I said eventually, in a low, faltering voice. 'There were two men in here last night. They . . .' I couldn't go on. I began to retch again.

'Two men? In here? Oh, Teresa, really . . .' Her voice trailed off into a deep sigh of disbelief.

'It's true, Harriet. They hurt me down there. One of them, he, he, he . . .' I just couldn't say it.

'More nightmares,' she said matter-of-factly, passing me a handful of pills and a glass of water.

I shook my head. 'No, Harriet, it was real. They really hurt me. Two men. They were in here. In Sick Bay. On the bed. They shouldn't have been here.'

'Take your medication,' she said in her usual dictatorial way.

I looked down at the tablets in my hand. Orange. White. Blue. Yellow. Pills. Although I longed for oblivion, for an escape from the pain of what I now knew to be true, I was scared of going to sleep because of what might happen while I was unconscious. I threw the pills onto the floor and chucked the glass at the wall. 'I've been attacked!' I yelled at Harriet. 'Why won't you listen to me?'

Fifteen minutes later I was out cold again, and there was another great big pinprick hole in my bum.

I confided in the other members of staff. I pleaded with Shirley to believe me. I told Benita, Trinny and Ivy. No one took a blind bit of notice apart from Shirley, who tried to calm me down as she brushed my hair for me.

'I feel very sorry for you having such awful dreams, but you really don't have to worry. It's just not possible for anyone to get in here unauthorised,' she said soothingly.

I wanted to believe her. I wished it had been a dream. I started to question my sanity. Perhaps I'd gone mad. Maybe it had all just been an hallucination.

Fear overwhelmed me. Fear became my way of life. I was like a hunted animal, frightened all the time. I was scared to go to sleep, but it took so much energy to keep myself alert all the time that I was always dropping off, despite myself. I tried to stay awake, but it was so hard. I suspected that someone – Dr Peri, or even perhaps Harriet – had upped my nightly doses of sleeping pills. Such was my sensitivity to the different effects of drugs that I could feel them shutting me down more powerfully than before. It was like being hit on the head with an iron bar.

I became weaker and sleepier by the day. It felt as if the essence of life was draining out of me. Convinced that I was slowly dying, I dreaded the times when Shirley wasn't on duty. She was the only member of staff who showed any concern for me. She fed me when I was so out of it that I was physically unable to lift a knife or a fork to my mouth. She led me patiently to and from the bathroom, and never told me off for being slow, even when I could only shuffle at a snail's pace.

Eventually I was so frail that I didn't have the strength to chew my food. I couldn't hold it in my mouth. It would drop out and spill down my front. I was literally starving to death, so I was given soup for every meal. Shirley spooned it into my mouth. I wasn't eating much, but when she wasn't around I ate even less, because no one else could be bothered to take so much time and care over feeding me.

By now I was scarily thin. My ribcage was visible under my skin. My hip bones stuck out and my cheekbones were very prominent. When I looked in the mirror, I appeared to have aged dramatically. I looked like an old woman. My eyes were blank and empty. I was beginning to resemble a half-starved concentration camp victim.

The drugs profoundly affected my speech. A lot of the time I spoke so slowly that I sounded like I had severe learning difficulties, or a permanent disability. I began to forget how I normally spoke and became unsure about my accent. I tried to copy other people, but since there was a mix of regional and national accents among the staff at Kendall House, I found it hard to be consistent in my pronunciation. My mode of speech sounded very odd – I know it did, because people scrunched up their faces as if they couldn't make out what I was saying, or simply didn't like the way I was saying it. Communication was suddenly a lot harder. My identity was slipping away from me and I was helpless to do anything about it.

Who was I anyway? It was hard to recall that I was just a child whose parents had been unable to look after her, whose mother had persuaded her to make a suicide attempt and whose father couldn't get it together to pay the electricity bill. I could still just about remember the chatty, cheeky, card-playing schoolgirl who went to meet her dad in the Fox and Hounds, but I couldn't see how I could ever get back to being that person again. I was someone else now, a girl full of fear and rage, a child drowning in drugs and loneliness.

I started presenting symptoms of lockjaw, possibly caused by an infection picked up when cutting myself with something grubby. It began with stiffness in my muscles, and spasms in my jaw and neck. My speech deteriorated even more. I developed a high fever and suffered from convulsions and a persistent sore throat.

My psoriasis was horrific. Large areas of my body were disgustingly scabbed up. I only hoped that this would put off the men who had hurt me. Why anyone would want to touch someone with huge dry scabby patches all over their skin was beyond me. On the other hand, it didn't take a genius to realise that men who got their kicks raping an unconscious underage girl had to be totally sick in the head, and so couldn't be judged by normal standards.

The second time I was consciously aware of them in the room, I woke up to find myself being anally and orally assaulted. In the morning there was an agonising tenderness in my back passage area and blood on the sheets.

Benita was on duty that day. Now Benita was as hard as nails and not particularly nice, but although she might not take bullying or fighting very seriously, she was definitely not the kind of person to find sexual abuse acceptable. To her, it was a different matter altogether. She insisted that I be given a thorough medical examination.

She and Ivy were present when Harriet finally investigated my symptoms. Harriet took several swabs and cultures. It was an unpleasant, painful experience because the whole area was extremely tender. Benita looked shocked when Harriet said that there were tears in the fold of my rectum. I didn't know what this meant. Benita told me later that it was probably the result of a rash, or an infection.

Harriet sent the cultures off to a clinic for analysis. I was found to have thrush, a urine infection and a genital strep infection front and back. Harriet treated me with antibiotics and creams, but otherwise the symptoms – and my claims of being attacked – went uninvestigated. No one called in a doctor, or the police.

The staff were totally unsupportive. Benita wouldn't meet my eye for a long while afterwards, and didn't want to discuss my allegations. Harriet just tutted when I brought them up. Miss Woods told me I had an overactive imagination. Trinny rolled her eyes. Janice said it was all in my head. Most insulting of all, Dr Peri dismissed my claims as 'typical teenage fantasies'.

After that I had a long series of consecutive urine infections, each one worse than the last. The soreness in my rectal region healed and recurred, and healed and recurred, never fully going away. Antibiotics became a part of my daily dosages. As a result, I almost always had thrush. My discharge was foul-smelling, discoloured, and sometimes bloody. I had always suffered from bad period pains, but during my months in Sick Bay they became even more severe.

I began bleeding in my back passage. It became so bad that eventually Harriet took me to hospital, where the doctors treated me for rectal fissures. I also had a bowel stretch under anaesthetic, probably because they made the wrong assumptions about why I had anal tears. Unfortunately I was just too confused and out of it to question what was going on. All I knew was that I was a total mess physically.

Mentally, I was a paranoid wreck. I felt I could trust no one, not even Shirley. Although Shirley was becoming like a mother figure to me, and I was genuinely fond of her, I could not be a hundred per cent sure even of her. After all, if she couldn't put two and two together when the evidence was staring her in the face, how could she genuinely be on my side? A real mother would have believed her daughter. A real mother would have moved heaven and earth to save her child from further suffering. Or even forgetting the maternal side of things, a real friend would have felt compelled to speak up on my behalf. But Shirley did nothing apart from brush my hair and tell me nice stories. Perhaps she also felt helpless.

I felt so alone. I wasn't allowed to see the other girls. As spring became summer, they started going out for more trips to the beach and the park. I knew this because I was only allowed to come out of Sick Bay while they were out. 'They've all gone to Camber Sands,' Shirley would tell me. I longed for the chance to go with them, to see the sea and the horizon again.

Most of all, I missed Jules. I felt desperately lonely without her to talk to. I knew she would be worried about me. The feeling was mutual. I dearly hoped that she was taking care of herself, and that the staff weren't treating her badly.

As the weeks went by, enormous anger welled up inside me. It grew and grew out of all proportion until I was hardly able to contain it. I shouted at the staff, biting off their heads at the slightest incitement, growling, screaming and yelling at them, my mouth a cesspit of swear words and abuse. I self-harmed at every opportunity, taking my fury out on myself, slashing at my arms, scratching my scabs, drawing blood wherever I could, wanting to drown in my own blood.

I became incredibly sensitive to noise. My nights were tense and full of terror. I woke up at the slightest sound outside the Sick Bay door, convinced that it was the sound of the men returning to hurt me. It was like living through my own personal horror film. I badly needed rest, relaxation and proper sleep, but they were as far out of reach as Australia. Peace of mind was an alien concept. I longed for death, because I figured that dying was the only way to sleep without fear. No one could hurt me if I was dead. Finally I would be safe.

CHAPTER FIFTEEN

Time had very little meaning in Sick Bay. The days drifted and merged, the weeks stretched and contracted. An hour could last a week. A week felt like a year. The minutes dragged. The months bled into one another. There were moments when I even wondered if time had gone into reverse.

But then I would find that the days had suddenly zipped forwards. One morning I asked Harriet the date. She checked her watch. 'June the twentieth, why?'

'Oh,' I said. 'I've been fifteen for more than a week without knowing it.'

I had heard from the other girls that we were supposed to get a cake and a gift of fifteen pounds on our birthdays. But I got nothing. No one had even acknowledged the day, or thought to point it out to me. I asked if I could have the cake and money now.

'You should have mentioned it before. It's too late now,' Harriet said dismissively.

The summer months wore on. Locked in a tiny, airless room, stifled by its stale, unhealthy atmosphere, I lay slumped on the bed in a slick of sweat, motionless for hours on end. My days were a blur. I felt like a slug in slime. But at night, I took on a different incarnation. After sleeping all day, I'd be restless and agitated, banging on the door like a hyped up maniac, screaming to be set free.

Mrs Tarwin kept lecturing me about restoring normal sleeping patterns. 'How do you expect to get to sleep at night if you laze around all day?' she scolded.

'But what else is there to do, locked up in here?'

'Read, write, draw, knit, no end of constructive activities,' she said. 'You just have to be more disciplined with yourself.'

My muscles, unused, began to waste away. My legs trembled during visits to the bathroom. My skinny calves and thighs were barely able to hold me up. I developed bedsores, which were hardly distinguishable from my psoriasis scabs. It hurt to urinate. I had constant thrush. I begged Harriet to give me an overdose and kill me. She accused me of being melodramatic.

I pleaded with Mrs Tarwin to get a gun and shoot me.

'Oh dearie me,' she said absently. 'You really are in a bad way, aren't you?'

'I can't go on living in this hell. I want to die,' I told her, in floods of tears.

She turned to look at me, a frown on her face. For once she actually appeared to be seeing me for the person I was, rather than just a nuisance that had to be dealt with. I saw a flash of something in her eyes. 'Poor Teresa,' she said with what sounded like genuine compassion.

Whenever Bridget walked past the door she kicked it. She encouraged the others to do the same, so the door was constantly being thumped. She would whisper, 'We're going to kill you tonight. We've planned everything. First we're going to beat up the staff and steal the keys off them. Then we'll come in there and kill you.'

Lying in bed, drugged out of my head, I trembled at her

words. It got to the point where I stopped wanting to come out of Sick Bay because I couldn't face the thought of being bullied again. On the other hand, I was desperate to leave because of the men who came in to hurt me.

I hallucinated on and off, day in, day out, and it was truly scary to be seeing bugs and winged triangles that weren't there. I was petrified of being injected again. One way or another, I was terrified all of the time.

I was aware of very little that went on in the rest of the house, but the staff would give me snippets every now and then. I heard that Emma had left and a new girl called Estelle had arrived. I rejoiced for Emma and felt sorry for Estelle. Whoever she was and whatever she'd done, she didn't deserve to come to Kendall House.

Meanwhile, I watched the blue sky through the tiny window high up on the wall and imagined a world beyond my cell, where people lazed on park benches and kids splashed in fountains, where families packed picnics and towels into their cars and drove off to the seaside.

Teenage girls all over the country were falling in love for the first time. They were going to their first pop concerts, experimenting with make-up and jewellery, lying their way into nightclubs and sneaking into over-18's films. But these simple pleasures were denied me. I was trapped in a vacuum, learning nothing, experiencing nothing – except the dire consequences of mixing endless prescription drugs.

I cried for hours on end, unable to make sense of what was happening to me. I still hadn't been given a real explanation of what I was doing in Sick Bay, day in day out, or why I had been separated from the other girls. I still had no idea what the drugs were for – what they were or why I was being given them.

And what of the future? It was a huge black hole. I was given no incentives or goals, nothing to work towards or look forward to. No one seemed to know how long I was staying in Sick Bay, or what I had to do to get out. As usual, they trotted out that catch-all reason for everything – 'It's for your own good'. It was almost laughable, in a sick, dark, bleak way.

I had arrived at Kendall House healthy, lively and relatively happy. Yes, I'd had problems, but I had also been described as 'pleasant and charming' by a psychiatrist, and I'd always been able to see the brighter side of things. Well, most of the time, anyway. But now I was thin, ill and depressed. I was half dead. You only had to look at me to see how much I was suffering. So how could anyone say that anything good was being achieved during my time at Kendall House? They were either stupid, blind as bats – or consciously evil.

Mrs Tarwin started coming to see me more frequently. Tall, with blonde roller-curled hair, she was probably in her late forties or early fifties. She really seemed to feel sorry for me. Out of the blue, she said, 'I've got some friends who are interested in meeting you. I'm going to take you to their house. You'll like it there. They've got a swimming pool.'

I was only half-interested. Some days I didn't much care about anything except praying to God to let me die. Anyway, I was so out of my head that I wasn't sure if she was telling me a story, or talking directly to me. With all those drugs in my system, it was often hard to concentrate. 'That sounds nice,' I said, my eyelids closing. I drifted off to sleep.

A couple of hours later, she came back into the room holding an armful of clothes. 'Put these on, we're going out to tea,' she said, laying them on the bed.

It felt strange to change out of my nightdress, and even stranger when I put my shoes on downstairs. It was a long time since my feet had been out of slippers, and ages since I'd been down to the ground floor of Kendall House. The hall was eerily empty, because the other girls were all out at the local swimming baths. The staff were too afraid for my safety to risk another meeting. Bridget had turned the entire group against me. She was still furious with me for standing up to her and nothing could halt her bitter vengefulness towards me.

Outside the front door of Kendall House, I took a deep breath of fresh air and went into sensory overload. Fresh sights, sounds and smells assailed me: the sun on my face; a summer breeze in my hair; birds singing; a lorry passing by; my clumpy winter shoes crunching across the gravel drive; Mrs Tarwin's car starting up. It was hard to take it all in after so long inside.

I watched curiously out of the car window as Mrs Tarwin drove us along. I felt incredibly detached, as if the glass between me and the world was an extension of my body rather than the car's. I saw a young girl of about my age walking purposefully along the pavement, a large holdall slung over her shoulder. There was something buoyant in the way she walked that suggested confidence, happiness and freedom. I couldn't imagine strolling along like that, without a care in the world. I stared down at the contours of my bony legs, thin as broom handles beneath the dreadful flowery skirt that Mrs Tarwin had brought into Sick Bay for me. It struck me that I probably wouldn't be physically able to move like that girl moved, even if I wanted to.

We passed along several country lanes and through a village, before turning off a hill into a drive. At the end of the drive were two bungalows, one on each side, with a garage connecting them. We drew up next to the bungalow on the left, where there was a nice pond in the front garden.

A plump older lady with white hair and glasses answered the front door. She had a lovely smile. Mrs Tarwin introduced her as Mrs Whattler. 'Come in!' she said in a very friendly voice.

She led us into the sitting room, on the left of the hall. I noticed that she walked with a limp and her arm was disabled. I later found out that she had been paralysed down one side of her body as the result of a stroke she had suffered after the birth of one of her children. She motioned to a comfortable armchair and I sat down, eyeing the delicious spread that had been set on the coffee table in the middle of the room. My tummy rumbled at the sight of plates laid out with sandwiches, rolls and cakes.

A very tall older man with kindly eyes joined us. He had greying hair and striking dark eyelashes. He introduced himself as Mr Whattler. 'Nice to meet you, Teresa,' he said warmly. 'Are you hungry? Mrs Whattler's done a lovely tea for us.'

I instantly felt comfortable with Mr and Mrs Whattler. They were such nice people. Their kindness shone out of them. After tea they showed me around the house and out into the garden, where there was a porch with a swinging chair. There was also a shed and a swimming pool. The garden was blooming with flowers and there was a vegetable patch at the back, near the pool. To me, it looked like paradise after the dull, blank walls of Sick Bay.

Mr Whattler told me how much he loved gardening. Although I was dopey with drugs and didn't take in everything he or his wife said, I showed as much enthusiasm as I could muster and replied slowly and politely to every question they asked. I really wanted these wonderful people to like me.

They had a lovely kitchen. In one corner there was a basket for Henry, their dog. He was a gorgeous golden Labrador, a really gentle, soppy mutt. I loved him from the start.

When we left, Mrs Whattler said, 'It's been very nice meeting you, Teresa. We hope we'll see you soon. We'd very much like you to come and visit us again. Maybe you'd even like to come and stay the night in the spare bedroom?'

Her words touched me deeply, as did the soft, gentle way she spoke them. 'Yes, I would. I'd like that a lot,' I said, tears pricking my eyes.

She went on to suggest that I might like to go for a swim in the pool sometime. Hoping that she didn't detect the panic in my eyes, I made an excuse about not being a good swimmer. In actual fact, I was mortified by the thought of revealing my psoriasis. I felt like a leper under my clothes and was convinced that the sight of my legs, back or belly would repel her.

She must have sensed that my hesitation went beyond a fear of drowning, because she said, 'We'll just see how it goes next time, shall we? I just thought you might fancy a dip.'

As we left, she and Mr Whattler stood in the drive and waved us off. I waved back until long after they were out of sight. That night in Sick Bay I dreamed of Arctic Rolls and roses.

A few days later, I was summoned to Miss Woods's office by Dr Peri. 'How is life?' he asked. What a stupid question that was.

My words came out in a torrent. I told him how unhappy I was in Sick Bay. I asked why I was there, and what he was hoping to achieve by locking me up and isolating me. I demanded an explanation. I begged to be let out. I accused him and the other staff of cruelty.

He gave me the smug, superior smile that seemed to be reserved just for me. 'When we first met I knew it would only be a matter of time before you showed your true colours,' he said, his blubbery chin wobbling as he spoke. 'Hey presto, you went on to reveal yourself as disruptive, disturbed and aggressive.'

'That's not true! I'm not a troublemaker and I never have been,' I protested. 'I was fine before I came here. I was well behaved.'

'You may have thought you were fine, but I could tell that you were not. You have deep-seated problems and, as I say, it did not take long for you to reveal your true colours.

'It is a fact that you are known to bang on the door of Sick Bay for hours on end, to the extent that the staff are wary of entering for fear of being attacked. What's more, you have fought with the other girls and threatened violence towards a teacher. This is what I expected of you right from the start, and during these past months I have been treating you for your personality disorders.'

Hearing this, I was momentarily speechless. The thought of the staff being scared of me was ridiculous – and everybody knew that Bridget was a hundred times more aggressive than I could ever be. Tina, too. As usual, he was distorting everything.

'Your behaviour is erratic and you suffer from violent mood swings,' he continued. 'So what do you . . .'

'That's what your drugs have done to me!' I interrupted. 'I was never like that before.'

'So you admit that you are difficult and unpredictable,' he said, his eyes glinting.

'Not before I came to Kendall House, I wasn't. But what

do you expect when you're giving me all these pills? They make me feel weird! I'm not myself anymore.'

'My aim has always been to get to the root of your problems, in the hopes of calming your aggression and turning you into a normal, healthy girl. I feel that we have made some headway in this area. There is evidence to suggest that you are improving.'

Again, I had nothing to say. My physical and mental health had deteriorated to such an extent that no one could possibly call it an improvement. 'Are you going to keep me locked up?' I asked, finally.

'Well, the good news is that it will not be long before we reintroduce you to the group. After that, we will see about rehousing you in the dorms at night, but we will take it one step at a time.'

He pulled himself out of his comfortable chair with some effort, before stepping towards me. Taking my head in his hands, he planted a kiss on my forehead. I nearly puked on the spot. 'Get away from me!' I said, pushing him away.

He laughed. 'You are a tough girl, that is for sure. Almost too tough,' he said. He waved an arm. 'Take her to her room,' he told Harriet. For once I was almost relieved to get back to Sick Bay.

Later I thought long and hard about what he had said, and what his words actually meant. None of it made sense. What on earth could his motive be for turning a happy, healthy girl into a nervous wreck – and then smilingly pronouncing that she was getting better? The only explanation I could think of was that he had deliberately set out to mess with my brain so that he could treat me and then announce that he had 'cured' me. But why would anyone – especially a doctor – want to do that? It was crazy.

It wasn't long after that meeting that the number of pills in my daily doses began to be reduced. Very gradually my brain began to wake up. I felt like a patient coming out of a coma, slowly and agonisingly. But physically I felt no better. I started suffering from the worst itching I had ever experienced, along with the same kind of flu symptoms I remembered from my time at Joyce Green Hospital, when I was coming off the Kendall House drugs.

'It's perfectly normal,' Mrs Tarwin told me when I complained to her.

'In what way?' I asked miserably.

'Dr Peri is rebalancing your medication. You are bound to take some time getting used to the new doses,' she said.

One night as I was mercilessly scratching my skin from head to toe I heard the sound of a girl screaming. I strained to listen, wondering who it could be. The screams went on and on. They were unbearable. I wanted to cover my ears, but I was powerless over my hands, which wouldn't stop scratching. I heard shouting too. Who was it? I didn't recognise the voice. 'Stop! Stop!' she was crying. 'Help me!'

Are the men hurting her too? I thought. The noise went on for hours. I lay in bed and sobbed, sharing the girl's pain with every scream she let out. It was heartbreaking.

Mrs Tarwin took me to see the Whattlers again. On the way there, I asked her about the screaming girl. 'Oh, don't worry about Annie. She's just taking some time to settle in,' she said.

'What are you doing to her? She sounded like she was being attacked.'

'It's none of your business, is it? Don't put your nose in where it's not wanted. Annie is fine. She is getting the treatment she needs.'

'How can she be fine? She doesn't stop screaming.'

Mrs Tarwin clicked her tongue. 'If you go on with this, I will simply turn the car around and take you back to Kendall House.'

I didn't dare say any more. There was no way I was going to jeopardise my trip to the Whattlers' house. I couldn't wait to see them again.

This time, Mrs Tarwin left me with them for the whole day. I sat in the garden for most of the time, soaking up the lovely sunshine and talking to Mrs Whattler while Mr Whattler pottered around the garden. Again they suggested a swim. I refused. I was so conscious of my psoriasis and the self-harm scars on my arm that I wouldn't even roll my sleeves up in the heat, let alone change into a swimming costume.

We had cold meat and salad for lunch. I still didn't have much of an appetite, but I tried to eat as much as I could, so as not to seem rude. About five minutes into the meal, I became aware of Mr and Mrs Whattler watching me. 'Don't worry, Teresa, your food's already dead. You don't need to kill it all over again,' Mr Whattler said jokily. Mrs Whattler laughed softly.

No one had ever taught me how to use a knife and fork properly. I just used to hack my food to pieces, stab it and stuff it in my mouth. I didn't have the slightest idea about table etiquette or manners and so it didn't occur to me not to speak with my mouth full. No wonder they looked slightly alarmed during that first meal. I must have seemed completely primitive to them, especially as I was out of the habit of eating solids. But they were kind enough not to scold me. Instead they showed me how to eat properly and, conscious of my ignorance, I accepted the lesson gratefully.

Later on, when they began to show me how to do other basic things, I was eager to learn. I hadn't a clue about how to look after my appearance. My hair was in a terrible condition and it didn't help that I never brushed it. I didn't clean my teeth on a regular basis, so they were really yellow. When I did clean them, I gave them a five-second brush and that was it. 'You won't keep your teeth healthy if you do it that quickly,' Mrs Whattler told me, before showing me how to brush properly.

My nails were severely bitten, chewed down to the cuticles, and I chomped into the skin around them until it was ragged. Mrs Whattler put Stop 'n Grow on my nails to stop me biting them. I loved her for it but it didn't work. I just got used to the taste and went on chewing nervously.

After a few visits, I was allowed to spend the night at the Whattlers' house. Mrs Tarwin would drop me off there with an overnight bag and several envelopes of pills. Sometimes there were four or five tablets in each envelope, but other times there were as many as nine. Mrs Whattler used to pour them into my hand four times a day. She was shocked by how many there were.

'I don't want them. They make me feel weird. Can't we just throw them away?' I used to say.

'If we don't give them to you, they won't let us see you anymore,' she'd sigh.

So, of course, I took them because I loved Mr and Mrs Whattler and couldn't bear the thought of not seeing them. All I lived for were those visits.

Back at Kendall House, my days and nights continued to be disturbed by the tortured screams of the new girl Annie. Once when I was going to the bathroom, I caught a glimpse of her. She was a really pretty girl with glossy hair and a nice open face. I hated to think of what the staff were doing to her. Another time, I passed her in the corridor. She was being dragged along the landing by Harriet and Trinny. 'Don't let them break you,' I whispered, but I doubt she heard. Her eyes were half-closed and her body was limp.

I really began to worry about her after that, and with good reason, because it turned out that they were injecting her left, right and centre. A few weeks after I had first seen her, there was a huge kerfuffle just outside Sick Bay. I'd just come from the bathroom and Janice was about to lock me in when the sound of Annie's screams pierced the air. Janice rushed out of the room without locking the door, so I was able to take a peep at what was going on.

What I saw shocked me, even though I saw it through an anaesthetic film of drugs. While Annie struggled and yelled for help, Mrs Tarwin, Harriet, Janice and two other members of staff wrestled her to the ground with extreme force, grabbing, slapping and punching her. They pulled down her knickers and held her down while Mrs Tarwin injected her. Seconds later, she became motionless and utterly, eerily silent, as if dead. They dragged her into the room next to mine. I heard her body being dumped on the floor like a sack of garbage.

A few minutes later she woke up and began to vomit violently. I could hear her retching over and over again. Bleary as I was, I could tell that there was something seriously wrong with her.

The staff took her into the staffroom, which was almost opposite Sick Bay. She couldn't support herself or walk at all. There was vomit all over her and she continued to heave. She looked terrible, so bad that I really thought she might be dying. Judging by the expressions on some of the staff's faces, they were worried too. Someone rushed off for a bucket, someone else for a blanket. I heard Janice say that it was time to call a doctor. Meanwhile Annie just went on vomiting.

'What's going on? What's wrong with her?' I asked Janice.

'Get back to your room! She's got a tummy bug,' she replied.

'I don't think it's just a tummy bug,' I said. 'She's really ill. You'd better get an ambulance.'

'Who's got the Sick Bay key?' Janice shouted. Moments later, I was a prisoner again.

Was Annie lucky that she didn't die that night? I thought so at the time. I pleaded with the staff to let me spend some time with her and eventually we were allowed a few minutes together. She came into Sick Bay out of her head on drugs and sat on the bed, dribbling and jerking as she spoke. Her hair had lost its gloss. There seemed to be nothing shining within her, not even the tiniest flame of life.

'I want to die,' she said starkly.

'I know the feeling, but you must try not to give up,' I told her.

'I've already given up. I will kill myself. I promise I will. Even if I get out of here, I'll do it. I'm already dead anyway. My heart may be beating, but they've killed me. I hate them for it. I hate Mrs Tarwin. She has destroyed me. I'm a dead person in a living body.'

She slumped sideways on the bed and passed out. I sat beside her and gently stroked her hair, tears streaming down my face. I believed her when she said that she felt dead. She looked it.

I never found out why Annie was sent to Kendall House, or why she was being so heavily medicated. If her case bore any resemblance to mine, then there probably wasn't any logic behind the way she was being treated. Equally, was there any reason why I was being weaned off the heaviest drugs I had been taking while she was being knocked out? Who knows? Nothing made any sense at Kendall House. There were never any answers, only questions.

Around this time I was reintroduced to the group, which was a nightmare experience all of its own. The girls were like vultures and I was their prey. Bridget had brainwashed them into thinking I was bad, mad, odd, weird and dirty. No one apart from Jules had the least sympathy for what I had been through, and Bridget had become so powerful and intimidating that even Jules was reluctant to have anything to do with me now. When I was injected or sent to the detention room, Bridget would tell everyone that I deserved it. She said that I had been locked in Sick Bay all these months to protect the group from me, because I was wild and dangerous. I couldn't understand why she took so much pleasure in hurting me.

I was continually shunned. At mealtimes I'd sit on a table on my own while the girls made nasty remarks about me from across the room. The staff did nothing, not even when I had things thrown at me, and I was too scared to retaliate in case I was injected again. Whole days went past without one single girl saying a word to me. It was hell.

I was weak, a softie, a sucker for a kind word or gesture, and the girls took advantage of this, drawing me in by pretending to be nice only to reject me again and again. Ever hopeful and desperate to be liked, I fell for it every single time.

'I saved this sweet for you,' one of them would say and I would take it gratefully, only to find that it was a pebble wrapped in sweet paper.

'You look pretty,' someone else might say, before following up with, 'Pretty fucking ugly, I mean.'

When they suddenly said that they wanted me back in the dorms, I wanted to believe them so much that I went along with it. It was Nicole who went to see Miss Woods to ask if I could come out of Sick Bay. She told Miss Woods that the girls felt very sorry for being mean to me and wanted to make it up to me now. Miss Woods beamed as she related their conversation to me. 'Isn't it good news?' she said.

It was. I was thrilled, especially when the girls started to argue over whose dorm I would sleep in. By now I had been in Sick Bay so long that my old bed had been given to someone else, so I had the choice of sleeping in Bridget and Nicole's dorm with Sophie K, Zara and Tina, or in with Jules, Danielle, Estelle and a couple of others. To no one's surprise, I chose Jules's dorm. All the same, Nicole spat at me for turning down the bed next to hers.

My first night in the dorm felt really strange. I was so used to the isolation of Sick Bay that I couldn't get used to the sound of other people breathing in the same room as me. I lay there with my eyes closed, but sleep wouldn't come. I couldn't stop thinking about Annie. Images of her twitching, dribbling and telling me she wanted to die kept revisiting my mind.

The next thing I knew there was a pillow over my head and I was struggling to breathe. I kicked and thrashed, but the pillow stayed over my face. I could feel myself choking airlessly. Whoever was holding the pillow pressed it down. It felt like they were sitting on it. I began to panic. The fear of God ran through me. I was being asphyxiated. I am going to die, I thought.

A heavy weight fell onto my legs. Unable to kick out, I

lashed around with my arms and struck something or someone. I heard a yelp, and then the words, 'You bitch!' The pillow moved, the pressure momentarily lifted, and with one final effort, I pushed upwards and threw it off. I gasped, desperately gulping in air, then leapt from my bed and ran screaming out of the room – past Zara, Bridget and Tina. The pillow lay on the floor at Tina's feet.

I ran downstairs to the staffroom, where Ivy and Mrs Kale were nursing cups of tea. 'They've just tried to suffocate me!' I yelled.

Ivy sighed. She was very obviously unconcerned. 'Who has?' she said wearily.

Still finding it hard to breathe, I sobbed out a brief account of what had happened. But neither Ivy nor Mrs Kale wanted to know. 'I knew there would be trouble tonight,' Ivy said. 'Why they let you out of Sick Bay I just do not know.'

They sent me back to bed. I collapsed on the way upstairs, but neither of them came to help me. When I came to, I made my way back to the dorm on unsteady legs. Terrified that Zara, Bridget and Tina would come back for another go, I didn't sleep a wink that night. Too scared even to lie down, I spent the entire night sitting up.

CHAPTER SIXTEEN

'Teresa and that bloody cat!'

Everybody said it, from Mrs Tarwin to Bridget. I don't know why it annoyed people that I spent every spare moment in the laundry with Buttercup, but I ignored their comments and taunts just the same. Nothing would stop me visiting her. I loved her dearly and she was wonderful and loving back to me.

I felt that Buttercup was me in cat form. I identified with her because she was as lonely and scared as I was. It took months to win her over. I sat and talked to her endlessly until she got up the courage to poke her head through the hole in the wall. I was thrilled when eventually she ventured into the room. The biggest breakthrough came the first time I stroked her. She trembled with fear, but my patience had paid off. After a while she began to purr and rub her head against my face.

It meant a lot to me that she trusted me. She came when I called her, but no one else could tempt her out of hiding – apart from her owner Dot, of course. I'd make a really high-pitched squeal and she'd leap out of the hole in the wall and onto my lap. But if somebody else came into the laundry while I was stroking her gorgeous tabby and white fur, she'd run away and hide until the person had gone. She was extremely timid.

Buttercup was therapy and therapist to me. When I wanted to die I'd go to her and tell her all about it, safe in the knowledge that she wouldn't look down on me for crying or expressing how sad I was. No matter how drugged up I was, she didn't judge me. By loving me and making me feel wanted and needed, she was everything that the staff at Kendall House weren't. What's more, being with her and stroking her had a truly calming effect on me.

Once Bridget went into the laundry and mimicked my call. When Buttercup jumped through the hole in the wall, Bridget lobbed a heavy book at her. She boasted about it afterwards. I wanted to kill her so much that I cut my arms to shreds with a sliver of glass – turning my anger and frustration inwards, as usual.

Bridget was cruel and violent, but Tina was worse in many ways. She was a nutter. I was always having to defend myself against her. Although she was tiny and really quite pretty, she was scarily disturbed. After a petty argument over feeding the hamsters, she attacked me in the kitchen and stabbed me in the chest with a knife, causing a superficial but nasty wound. Another time she jumped on me in the upstairs schoolroom, because apparently I'd 'looked at her funny'. Ginger-haired Charlie managed to pull her off. He was constantly putting a stop to Tina's assaults.

I suppose that the difference between Bridget and Tina was that you just didn't have a chance with Bridget. If you punched Bridget, your fist made no impact. It would just disappear into her considerable muscle and fat. But I was able to defend myself against Tina, even though she was the dirtiest fighter you could come across. She was always attacking me from behind when I wasn't expecting it. Once I sat down to dinner and the next thing I knew she was hanging off my hair.

Tina was Mrs Tarwin's pet. She worshipped the ground Mrs Tarwin walked on, even though Mrs Tarwin used to inject her 'to calm her down'. If anyone said anything bad about Mrs Tarwin, or to her face, Tina would attack them. It was an odd kind of loyalty. I didn't understand it.

I resented Bridget, and to a lesser extent Tina, because life was already so awful at Kendall House that it was mean of them to make it even worse. How much better things could have been if the girls had stuck together. We could have supported each other through the hard times, instead of constantly being at each other's throats. Our stay in hell would have been so much more bearable if we had formed some kind of sisterhood. Perhaps it wasn't our fault. It was probably staff policy to divide and conquer, and it worked very well. But surely everyone – even the staff – would have been happier if there hadn't been so much squabbling.

As it was, practically every girl inside Kendall House was a miserable wreck. We bitched, scrapped, fought, self-harmed and regularly attempted suicide. Why the Council of Social Responsibility (who ran the place) or the local council (who helped fund it) didn't realise that there was something seriously wrong there during the early 1980s is anybody's guess.

Jules was having a very unhappy time. Her wrists were constantly bandaged. I tried my best to help her through, even though she wasn't supposed to have anything to do with me. When Bridget wasn't around we would exchange a few stolen words of mutual comfort, hoping that no one would grass us up later. And we still paired up for the ballroom dancing classes, taking care not to hurt each other's slashed wrists and arms as we bumped around the dance floor.

'Hey,' she said after class one day, 'let's try to get out again.'

We went to the toilets and sat in adjoining cubicles. Jules unscrewed a light bulb, smashed it on the floor and gathered up the glass pieces. After dividing the pieces in half, we set about eating a handful of glass each. I remember that it made a really weird crunching sound between my teeth. Strangely, it wasn't hard to swallow, and didn't hurt at all.

I hate to think what kind of damage it could have done to our insides, but we appeared none the worse for it afterwards. We were incredibly lucky; it could easily have ripped us to shreds internally. We told Harriet what we had done, but she didn't bother to call a doctor, as we'd hoped she would. Our plan had been to get to the local hospital – and run for it.

'Any more good ideas, Houdini?' I asked Jules.

'Give me time,' she said with a determined glint in her eyes. 'I'll come up with the perfect plan in the end.'

At least I had a form of escape in Mr and Mrs Whattler. I don't know what I would have done without them. By now I trusted them enough to know that they wouldn't peep as I changed into my swimming costume in the shed in the back garden, so I took up their offer of a swim in the pool. They understood my paranoia about my psoriasis scabs and swore that they wouldn't even come near the garden until I'd changed. Around this time they told me that I could call them Uncle Don and Aunt Betty.

They respected me every step of the way, which restored my confidence, and in the end it didn't matter to me if they saw my scars and scabs. While I swam and sunbathed, Uncle Don happily did his own thing, pottering around the garden.

Every now and then he'd call me over to look at a flower or an insect, never once remarking on my psoriasis. He taught me a lot about flowers and gardening, and as time went on, my skin began to clear up in the sun.

Occasionally I exposed it to the UV rays for too long. 'Oh my God, you're burnt!' Uncle Don said when I went to the kitchen for a glass of water one August evening.

Aunt Betty gasped. 'Go into the sitting room!'

They followed me into the sitting room with a great big bowl full of vinegar and water, which Aunt Betty gently dabbed all over my skin. It felt good to be tended to by someone who so obviously cared about me. Although my skin was on fire, I felt incredibly happy. What's more, the vinegar took away the stinging and I cooled down. It really did make a difference.

The Whattlers' kindness knew no bounds. To give me an incentive to keep my hair and nails nice, Aunt Betty took me to her local village beauty shop in Higham, Kent, where they permed my hair properly and gave my nails a manicure. She bought me my own nail file, clear nail varnish and two hairbrushes, and taught me to rinse my hair with cold water after washing it, to give it a shine. The perm was fine but it wasn't exactly modern in style. I was pleased with it, even though it made me look a bit old-fashioned.

I had my own box of muesli in the kitchen cupboard. Aunt Betty always made sure to buy the particular brand I liked at the Co-op. She showered me with little gifts that helped me to take pride in myself. I had my own personal products and sanitary towels, which meant that I didn't have to ask for them. My periods were often painful and she would rub my tummy and back. She constantly refilled my hot water bottle because the heat eased the pain.

She taught me a lot of basic things, like the value of money, how much a loaf of bread cost, how to shop sensibly, budget and work out the bill, how to make toffee and bake a cake. Uncle Don gave me lessons in wiring plugs and basic DIY. He even showed me how to gut a fish, which I didn't much like. All in all, they taught me how to look after myself.

Going back to Kendall House from the Whattlers' was always hard. I could never get to sleep the night before, whether I had been there for a week or just a night. A horrible fear would creep over me at the thought of what lay in store for me at the hands of people like Bridget, Harriet, Dr Peri and the men who hurt me while I was confined to Sick Bay. It wasn't like the fear of a spider or even of knowing a murderer was coming to get you. It was pure fear, fear in its largest form, sheer fear. I don't think anything could compare to that fear.

One night as I lay in bed contemplating my return to Kendall House, I became very distressed. I started panicking severely and it was a struggle to breathe. Aunt Betty came in with some kind of Vick's product, which she sprayed around the room. 'I don't very often use this,' she said. 'They don't sell it any more.' Somehow she calmed me down and talked me into breathing properly again, but I could tell that I'd really worried her.

Another night, Uncle Don came into my room while I was crying, concern written all over his face. 'Teresa, you've got to tell us what's going on at Kendall House,' he said. 'We know about the medication, but there's something else, isn't there?'

I couldn't bring myself to open up. I was scared that I'd be stopped from seeing them.

They hated having to administer my medication. On many

occasions they watched me vomit because of a bad reaction to the pills, and it worried them that I had such a small appetite as a result.

Since I never knew how many tablets I was supposed to be taking because the amounts varied so much, I unwittingly took a double dose one day. Someone back at Kendall House had made a big mistake, but we didn't realise it at first. It was lunchtime. I took my pills and went onto the back porch to lie in the swinging chair. All of a sudden I felt paralysed. I couldn't even move a finger. By the time Aunt Betty and Uncle Don called me for dinner, I was drifting in and out of consciousness and dribbling.

Uncle Don picked me up and carried me into the house. I heard Aunt Betty shouting into the phone. 'What the hell is it? What has happened?'

On the other end of the line, Mrs Tarwin told her to open up the other envelopes and tell her what was in them. She then phoned her son for advice. He was a doctor at one of the big London hospitals. When she rang back, she told Aunt Betty, 'She's been overdosed. We're going to come and pick her up.'

'We'll take her to hospital,' Uncle Don said, but Mrs Tarwin wouldn't hear of it. She insisted it wouldn't be necessary. She picked me up, took me back to Kendall House, injected me and stuck me in Sick Bay. Aunt Betty rang up to complain, but she was ignored.

The next time I went to visit, Aunt Betty told me that they had put in an application to adopt me. I was over the moon. The only time I felt anything close to happiness was when I was with them. 'But don't get your hopes up too high,' she said. 'We won't know for several months if we'll be allowed to.'

In early October, Dad came for a visit. It felt like I hadn't seen him for months and months, but because the drugs made it so hard for me to gauge time, it was impossible to know for sure. Unbeknown to me, the staff had been trying to keep him away with every excuse under the sun, no doubt because they were worried how he would react to my appearance. In the end, he turned up without an appointment and threatened to force his way in.

I met up with him in the dining room. He had a fit when he saw me. 'Oh my God! What have they done to you? You were in a bad way before but now you look forty years older, like an old woman,' he said.

I was shocked to see that he was crying. He took me in his arms and cuddled me, rocking and weeping and trying to comfort me while I sobbed out an account of what had been going on. He had never been emotional towards me in this way before. I felt so close to him.

Harriet came into the room. 'Mr Cooper, I'm afraid it's time to end the visit. Teresa has lessons to attend.' Her tone was brisk.

Dad gave her a withering look. 'You stop giving my daughter drugs *right now*, or I will take serious measures against you,' he said. 'What the hell do you think you are doing to her? I am going straight to the council, the Social Services and my MP to report you.'

Harriet bristled. 'I can assure you that Kendall House has Teresa's best interests at heart. Given her background and her mother's history of mental illness, you will understand that there are special concerns at play here. Of course, it's very difficult for a non-professional to understand . . .'

'Don't give me that!' Dad retorted, getting to his feet. His face was hot with anger. Harriet took a step backwards.

When Dad was in a rage, he could be pretty frightening.

'Teresa, leave us now,' she snapped. I had little choice but to obey if I didn't want an injection after Dad had left.

Poor old Dad didn't get anywhere with his complaints. Unbelievably, Wandsworth Social Services totally denied that I was being given drugs. He didn't get any further than their lies even when he and Nicole's dad got together to make their voices heard. Nicole's dad had already aired his grievances to the council and been ignored. He knew all about the drugs we were being given. He'd done a lot of research and was more than happy to share the information. Dad was outraged. He could see what they were doing to me was totally wrong, but he was helpless to do anything about it.

I dwelt a lot on Dad's comments about my looks. When I passed a window or a mirror and caught a flash of my reflection, I barely recognised myself. My self-image was poor anyway. I was constantly teased about being ugly. But things reached an all-time low when Shirley's daughter Mandy chose Nicole to be her bridesmaid at her upcoming wedding.

It was a massive humiliation for me, because Nicole rarely had anything to do with Shirley, whereas I was supposed to be close to her. Clearly she didn't love me as much as I had thought. I was gutted. I felt betrayed and angry. Nicole had only met Mandy once, whereas I had been to Shirley's house several times. OK, I didn't know Mandy at all well, but it was obvious that I had been passed over because I wouldn't look good in the photographs. I was the butt of everyone's jokes after that.

The taunting was constant: 'Your ugly mug would break the camera. You're too fucking hideous to put on a bridesmaid's dress. Mandy doesn't want her guests to run screaming out of the church!' On and on it went.

It was awful watching Nicole get all excited about her dress fittings. Shirley gave her a lot of attention in the run-up to the wedding, which made me feel that all the love and trust we had built up over my months in Sick Bay counted for nothing. At the actual wedding, I was shoved to the back while Nicole paraded around in her lovely dress. I felt so small and unloved that day.

Life dragged on. Christmas came and went. Easter came and went. I was devastated to hear that the Whattlers' application to adopt me had been turned down on the grounds of Aunt Betty's disability. Uncle Don and Aunt Betty seemed equally upset. We all felt that it was unfair. The staff went on injecting me. They'd jump on me, drag me onto the floor, grab my arms and legs and hair, hold me down on the floor – face down or on my back – kneel on me, with all their weight on me, hold my arms down, turn me on my side, pull my knickers down, exposing everything, and jab me with a huge needle.

When they put their knees into my back and neck, my jaw would click to the side, and I developed an unstable mandible, or loose, damaged jaw. I often vomited in reaction to the drugs. I was always covered in bruises. They went on locking me in the detention room and Sick Bay. I don't have any clear memories of further abuse while I was locked up, but I was treated for countless urine and genital infections.

Bridget and the others continued to scorn me. The torture just went on and on, and I wasn't the only one suffering. Jules attempted suicide again. Annie drank bleach and ate razor blades. A pretty, plump girl called Amanda arrived and screamed the house down for days. There was deep pain and sadness everywhere you turned.

One day it all kicked off when Mrs Tarwin and three other members of staff dragged a screaming Annie up the stairs after she refused to be quiet in assembly. It was a nasty scene and it upset us all. By now Amanda was very close to Annie and it hurt her to see her friend being treated so roughly. She complained loudly about the drugs we were being given. The remaining staff on duty started on her, telling her to shut up or she was next.

We could all hear Annie screaming, all the way from the ground floor. It was horrible to hear her in such distress. We didn't know what was going on upstairs but from my own experience I knew it wasn't good. The next thing I knew the staff were pulling Amanda up the stairs by her hair. She wasn't a small girl, either. At first Amanda laughed hysterically, like a mad woman, but the staff became more aggressive – yanking her hair, pulling her neck out of joint – and she began to shriek with pain.

Another girl called Shelley was so distraught at what was happening to Amanda that she started banging her head repeatedly against the wall. Her forehead split open and blood went everywhere. Now there were three girls shouting and screaming, one of them badly injured. The staff were obviously finding it hard to cope.

'Bridget!' Janice shouted as she struggled with Amanda. 'Come and help.' Bridget leapt to the aid of her pet member of staff. You could see that she relished dragging Amanda upstairs by her long black hair.

I don't know where they took Shelley, but Amanda was locked in the detention room and they stuck Annie in Sick Bay. A sudden hush descended over the house. It was almost scarier than the girls' screams of distress, because we all knew what had befallen them. That silence was deafening.

I hated Bridget for the way she treated me, but I hated her even more for helping the staff to control the girls. As time went on, I became so sick of being bullied that it became inevitable I would boil over with rage.

The moment finally came when Kate summoned me into the office for a phone call. I knew it had to be big news, because it wasn't a Friday, which was the only day we were allowed to take calls. I picked up the receiver. Bernadette was on the other end. She gently broke it to me that our nan had died. I was very upset, especially when Kate said that I wouldn't be allowed out to go to Nan's funeral. I left the office in tears.

At bath time, a girl called Ally came up to me in the bathroom with a big smile on her face. Ally was the tallest of all of us, even though she was only twelve. She was a very attractive girl who had been sent to Kendall House because she was highly sexually promiscuous, to the point that her mother couldn't control her.

'Your nana dead, is she? Is your nana dead?' she taunted.

I stared at her in shock. How did she know? I had asked Kate not to tell anyone, wanting time to grieve quietly on my own first.

'Ya boo diddums, your nana's dead as a doornail,' she went on.

A white hot rage shot through me. As she was running her bath, I flew at her furiously and ducked her head under the water. 'I'll give you bloody dead, you scumbag!' I howled, holding her head down. One of the staff had to pull me away before I drowned her. I broke free and lunged at her again.

Bridget came into the bathroom. Big mistake. I let go of Ally and went for Bridget instead.

Finally Bridget got a taste of her own medicine. All the rage that I'd built up towards her during my time in Sick Bay surged to the fore. It made me stronger than I had ever been in my life, giving me the power to beat her up.

'Stop!' she whimpered, finally. 'Please, you're hurting me.'

At last Bridget was scared of me, instead of the other way around! It was a sweet, sweet victory. Now it was me who was passing her in the corridor, saying, 'I'm going to get you later.' Not that I followed up on my threats – I was simply concerned with keeping her at bay. It worked too. She pretty much left me alone after that, which was a huge relief.

One day I woke up and Jules was gone. That was that – they hadn't even let her say goodbye. 'But where is she?' I kept asking.

'Forget about Jules. She's gone back to her family,' Mrs Tarwin told me.

Her absence created a huge hole in my life. I missed her terribly. But since I had no way of contacting her, there was nothing to do except continue with my miserable existence, without her. It seemed that there was nothing but loss in my life. One way or another I'd lost my mum, my dad, my brother and sister, my nan, my friend, my freedom, my peace of mind . . . the list was endless. So the last thing I expected was to find a long lost relative. It was one of the biggest surprises of my life.

It all began with an amazing coincidence. Nicole went home one weekend and while she was sitting on the toilet reading the newspaper, she noticed my mum and dad's names in a personal ad.

She brought the paper back to Kendall House and gave it

to the staff to follow up. I didn't actually see the ad, but it was a little notice that said something like, 'I'm looking for Georgina Cooper, married to Derek Cooper. If you have any information on their whereabouts, please call this number.'

My first thought was that they had been left some money in somebody's will. I wondered if I would get a reward for calling the number. My heart leapt. However, Kate wouldn't let me make the call. She made it for me instead.

She called me into the office. 'Good news,' she said, smiling. 'You've got a relative who wants to meet you.'

I didn't know what she was on about. 'What do you mean?'

She explained that a distant relation on my mum's side, Karen, had put the notice in the paper. Apparently Karen had played with us as kids and, even though she was a few years older, she still had fond memories of the family. An only child whose parents were now dead, she was looking to renew the connection.

I was thrilled. The idea of having a long lost relative definitely appealed. It was like something out of a fairytale and I couldn't help but fantasise about Karen in a fairy god-mother role. I was impatient to meet her, but it took weeks for Kendall House to arrange a meeting. She and her husband Trevor finally came to see me one Saturday. I was very nervous as I walked into the dining room, desperately hoping she would like me. Karen and her husband got up to greet me. She was around thirty and very pretty, with auburn hair in ringlets and large hazel eyes. I was disappointed that she wasn't very well spoken but she seemed nice and I decided I liked her. I was a little bit wary of Trevor though. He was tall and big set, with ice blue eyes and a skinhead haircut.

They didn't stay long, just long enough for Karen to

explain who she was and that she had been trying to find Mum for a couple of years. She asked me if I'd like to visit her at her house. 'Yes, I'd like that,' I said, but in my heart I wasn't so sure. Something in her attitude and way of speaking suggested to me that she wasn't the most desirable addition to the family. She did a lot of casual effing and blinding and came across as quite hard, as did Trevor.

Kendall House took girls up to the age of sixteen, so I was getting too old to stay there. Yes, I'd had another birthday, and no, I didn't get a cake or fifteen pounds that time either. My future seemed very uncertain. Wandsworth Social Services had care of me until I was eighteen, so I wouldn't be entirely free for another two years. In the meantime, I had to find somewhere to live, but there was nowhere for me to go. Dad couldn't have me, neither could Mum or Bernadette. My job prospects weren't exactly good either. I had no qualifications. I wasn't exactly unemployable, but the kind of work that would pay me enough to support myself was definitely out of reach for the time being.

Miss Woods called me into her office late in 1983. 'We've found you some foster parents to go to. They are wonderful people! You are going to be very happy with them.'

'What are they like?' I asked suspiciously. Obviously I didn't trust her. Not only was she in cahoots with Dr Peri, but as the head of Kendall House, I held her largely responsible for its cruel regime.

'Well, I haven't met them yet, but I've heard nothing but good reports of them.' She went on to tell me about the wonderful Novicks. The dad was called Doug. The mum was called Pam. There were three children, two girls and a boy. One was a baby. She blabbed on for a bit longer. She obviously knew very little about them apart from their names.

Typical, I thought. As usual there's a gloss on things, and it's bound to be a fake one.

I was desperate to leave Kendall House though. I was more than desperate. I was dying to leave, almost literally. So I agreed to have my photos taken for the forms, and I agreed to meet the Novicks. What choice did I have?

The first time we met, they came to Kendall House. They seemed OK. Pam was plump and a bit blousy. She wore bright flamboyant clothes and spoke in a low, husky voice with a slight lisp. Doug had a rugby player's build and was bald apart from a few brown tufty wisps. I noticed that he kept looking me up and down, as if I were an item in a shop. This made me feel slightly uncomfortable, but it was nothing serious. I hoped that I'd feel less nervous around him when I got to know him better.

The second time I met the Novicks I went to visit them at their house in Broadstairs. It was a big bungalow, big enough to accommodate two lodgers as well as the family. I liked it there. The children were really sweet and the appeal of having my own bedroom overcame any anxiety I had about living with strangers.

Doug Novick drove me back to Kendall House. In the car he told me that he was a keen golfer and he'd teach me how to play if I was interested. I said that I thought golf was a game for retired men, but he laughed and informed me that lots of young people were taking it up these days. I was aware of trying to like him, but not really managing to like him at all.

We stopped off at a McDonald's. I found that I couldn't eat in front of him. By now I knew that there was something about him I really didn't like. He kept looking me up and down and staring at me in the wrong places. But I continued making an effort to get on with him. I didn't want him and his wife to say no to having me. I was prepared to tolerate anything if it meant getting away from Kendall House. Or so I thought.

CHAPTER SEVENTEEN

Everything was arranged. After two overnight visits to the Novicks and a couple of sessions with my new social worker, Kerry Parker, and various members of Kendall House staff, it was agreed that I would move into the house in Broadstairs in early 1984.

I still had doubts about Doug Novick, even though I couldn't quite put my finger on what they were. I told Kerry that my biggest worry was that he looked at me in a sexual way. We jointly came to the conclusion that I was fearful of men in general.

I left Kendall House carrying a small bag of clothes and possessions and Patch my hamster in a cage. It was the greatest feeling on earth walking out of there for what I assumed to be the very last time. How often I had dreamed of this moment! On the other hand, there was something anticlimactic about the whole experience. As I looked back at its dismal exterior, I realised that the sad, lonely years I had spent inside that building were lost to me forever. I could never get them back. The pain would always be with me. One day the scars might heal, but there was no turning back the clock.

I stuck my head out of Doug Novick's car window as he

drove me away. 'Goodbye forever!' I screamed into the wind. Laughter bubbled up inside me. I was free! No more injections, no more Sick Bay, no more Harriet or Dr Peri – and no more Bridget. Yet the very thought of them all depressed me, despite the fact that I had finally escaped them. Images of what I'd suffered flashed through my mind. I hunkered down in my seat and spent the rest of the journey brooding.

I felt very shy when we arrived at the house. I just wanted to shut myself away. So after playing with the children a bit and cooing over the baby, I asked if I could go to my bedroom. Pam said that would be fine.

At first I spent most of my days in there. I needed my own space. It was so weird to be removed from the sights, sounds and smells of Kendall House that it was going to take a bit of time to adjust. With no routine to keep to, I played records and lay on the bed trying to blank out my most painful memories. And, like every teenage girl, I dreamed of falling in love, preferably with someone who looked like Christopher Reeve in *Superman*. I went downstairs for meals and to watch television in the evenings. Sometimes I'd play with the kids, chat to the lodgers or help Pam prepare food. But I kept my distance from Doug. There was just something about him that made my skin prickle.

His stepson Martin said that Doug had broken his arm in a rage once. He had then made him lie to his mother Pam about what had happened, so that he didn't get the blame. 'He told me to say it was an accident,' Martin told me. I didn't like the sound of that. I became even warier of Doug.

One night Doug, Pam and I sat down to watch a horror film. Halfway through, Pam yawned and announced she was going to bed. I stayed, caught up in the plot and desperate to see if the heroine would escape the forces of evil. There were lots of scary bits and I gasped out loud quite a few times.

'Don't be frightened,' Doug said. 'It's only a film.'

'I know, but look!' I pointed at the screen. The heroine was now being chased by something or somebody unknown, in the woods, in the dark, in the middle of the night. I was on the edge of my seat, nervously chewing my nails.

'Come and sit on my lap,' he said, patting his thigh.

I hesitated. Good memories of sitting on Dad's lap clashed with my natural aversion to Doug, but in the end I went for it, thinking that perhaps it would be a bonding experience. Plus, I was really scared. The film was reaching a terrifying climax and I imagined that it would be a comfort to sit with him, that he was offering a place of safety. How stupid and naïve I was.

I went over and sat on his knee. I felt uncomfortable immediately. I couldn't concentrate on the film. I just kept thinking, Why didn't I stay where I was? But I didn't move. I didn't want to seem rude or ungrateful.

I felt his hand slide down my back. A shiver of revulsion went through me. The woman in the film screamed. He started touching my legs. I tried to move away, but he held me firmly down. I could feel that he had an erection. He put his hands between my legs. I pulled away. I got off his lap and went straight up to bed without looking at him.

Disgusted by the memory of his touch, I wouldn't come out of my bedroom the next day. I wanted to run away while he was at work and Pam was out, but they locked the kitchen when they were out and my hamster and money were in there. The Novicks were keen on locking rooms. Their bedroom was always locked, as was the lodgers' room.

The first chance I had, I rang Kendall House. 'I don't like Doug. I think he's a pervert,' I told Harriet.

'I thought something like this would happen,' she replied. 'Now stop being silly. It's all in your head.'

I put the phone down and burst into tears. I had hoped so much that my nightmares were at an end.

One morning as I was taking a bath, I heard Pam call goodbye on her way out. 'I'll be back in a couple of hours. Don't forget to feed the dog,' she reminded Doug.

'Get going now, or you'll be late,' he replied.

I ducked my head under the bath water at the sound of his voice and held it under for as long as my lungs allowed. When I emerged into the steamy air, I heard a tap on the bathroom door. I ignored it and ducked back under the water.

There was another tap on the door, louder and more urgent than the previous one. 'Open the door. Your sister is on the phone,' he said.

I hadn't heard the phone ring. I didn't trust him. So I said nothing. But he started knocking harder on the door, insisting that Bernadette was waiting to speak to me. 'Don't keep her hanging on, she's in a phone box!' he said.

Perhaps it is true, I thought. Not wanting to miss the chance of speaking to Bernadette, I stood up, reached for a towel and wrapped it around me. I put my dressing gown over the top and fastened it at the waist.

I unlocked the bathroom door and stepped onto the landing. He was waiting for me. He grabbed me and pulled me across the landing. 'Don't!' I said. 'What about Bernadette?'

He dragged me towards the lodgers' room and unlocked the door with his key. He pushed me inside. I'd never been in the room before. There were two beds along the left side of the wall.

I was petrified. I froze with fear as he slammed the door.

He lunged at my dressing gown and tried to pull it off. I wrapped my arms around my body, trying to keep it in place, but he was so solid and strong that there was nothing I could do to stop him. Tears streamed down my face as he forced me onto the bed. He made me turn over so that he couldn't see my face. I cried out and begged him not to touch me. I tried to push him away and turn myself back over, but he forced me down flat.

He put an arm round my waist, pulled me up towards him and raped me. I screamed but no sound came out. He stroked my back as he repeatedly hurt me. Pain shot through me as he pushed and forced himself inside me. The more I struggled the more force he used. I begged him to get off. He kept telling me that he didn't want to hurt me, but he was hurting me terribly. I bit into the sheets as a way of coping with the pain.

He raped me several times. I don't know how long it went on for, but it was not a brief moment, it was ages. There was nothing I could do to stop him. He was too strong. Eventually it was over.

I pulled my towel over me, to cover myself up. Tears were still pouring down my face and I felt like my insides were going to drop out. I made a break for the door and got out of the room. As I ran to the bathroom, I saw blood running down my legs. I locked myself in the bathroom and sat on the toilet. I was bleeding really badly. I rocked in pain and cried so hard that I thought I'd never stop crying.

When at last I heard Pam come home, I left the bathroom and crept to my bedroom. He'd been there. My dressing gown was strewn on the bed.

I went on bleeding and had to use a pad to absorb the blood. All I could think about was taking Patch my hamster out of his cage and cuddling him. I barricaded my door with a chair and a chest of drawers. Pam called me down for tea but I ignored her. I felt that it was far better to starve than go downstairs and see his nasty face. I was in pain and I felt dirty. I knew hate, but I never knew hate like I felt it that day.

I played it as safe as I could from then on, making sure that I was never alone with him. I hated catching his eye, but I had to keep a look out for him at all times. I was obsessed by the thought that everything I owned was locked away in the kitchen. I knew that there was no way I could leave without my hamster. And if I did leave, where would I go? My family couldn't have me. The Whattlers loved having me to stay but it wasn't a permanent option. I had no other friends.

I tried calling Kendall House again, from a phone box down the road. Kate answered. 'Can you call me back?' I said, my voice cracking with emotion.

Harriet, rather than Kate, called back. 'What is it this time?' she said.

Sobbing, I told her that Doug Novick had done something very bad to me and I needed to go to the police.

'No, you do not need to go to the police,' she said crossly. 'You will go back to the house and stop being such a baby. When will you grow out of making up stories?'

So I went back. What choice was there?

Doug was always staring at me, smirking. I had nowhere to run and he knew it. He disgusted me. I felt like retching all the time he was around. One day, as he was cleaning the patio windows, he spat several times on the glass and delightedly watched his spittle dribble downwards, before wiping it off with some newspaper. 'Joanna' by Kool and the Gang was playing on the stereo. I wanted to puke.

Another time, Pam asked me to get some cheese from the larder. She was in the sitting room with the kids. Doug followed me in and pinned me against the larder wall. His rottweiler was lying on the floor. Doug started touching me. It was only when his wife called me that he took his fingers out of my knickers and let me go.

He raped me again in his bedroom while the baby lay in her cot sleeping. He put his hand over my mouth so that I didn't wake her. Out of the blue his stepson Martin walked into the bedroom.

Doug jumped off the bed and launched himself at the bedroom door. 'Get out!' he yelled. 'If you ever come in here again, if you ever say anything about what you saw in here, I will kill you!'

Martin never said a thing.

I rang Kendall House again from the phone box using coins I'd found down the side of the sofa. I cried my eyes out down the phone, but the response was always the same. 'Stop being stupid, go back to the house and behave.'

One of the lodgers found me in tears on a bench near the phone box. 'What is it, Teresa?' he said, his voice full of concern.

All I could say was, 'That man . . . he hurt me . . .'

'Do you mean Doug? Has he raped you?' he said.

Shocked that he had guessed the truth just like that, I managed to nod a yes.

'You must go to the police,' he said. 'There was a girl here before you. She ran away and was never traced again. I always wondered about her. I definitely thought something funny had been going on.'

He gave me some money to call the police, but my voice faltered when I came to speak to the duty sergeant. I just couldn't say it. I was too scared of the repercussions.

I stopped eating. I stopped sleeping. All I could think about was running away. I wondered whether my mum's relative Karen would take me in. I kept her phone number on me at all times, just in case.

Then my chance finally came. Doug, Pam and the kids left the house to go swimming, forgetting to lock the kitchen door. I rang Karen.

'I've got to get out of here. It's really bad. Can I come to you?'

To my relief she said yes. I almost fainted with gratitude. She asked if I had enough money to pay my bus fare. I admitted that I didn't. 'Get yourself down to the local bus station. Tell them I'll meet you at the other end and pay your fare,' she said.

I grabbed Patch's cage and a couple of other things and left the house without even shutting the front door. I walked as fast as I could in the direction of the bus station, racked with fear. What if they caught me? What would Doug do to me? I knew that he would be at swimming a while longer, but I had to hurry.

The wait for the coach to Watford was agonising. I kept scanning the bus station for Doug's thick-set figure, come to get me and take me back to hell. Finally the coach arrived. The driver let me on. We pulled out of the station. I burst into tears.

There was a nice young guy sitting next to me. I poured my heart out to him. He listened attentively, full of compassion. 'At least you're free now,' he said, patting me on the arm.

Karen met me at the bus depot at other end. She paid my fare and took me back to her house. I was in such a daze that

I barely noticed the peeling wallpaper or dirty, smelly carpets.

Karen was so nice to me that night. When we heard the ice cream van outside the house, she said, 'Would you like an ice cream?'

I didn't answer. My mind kept drifting to images of Doug raping me. I was still bleeding and in a lot of pain. My tummy was swollen. I started being sick.

Karen told her husband Trevor that instead she was going to take me to the petrol station to get an ice cream, so that we could have a private chat. On the way back I blurted out everything that had happened. She was aghast and full of sympathy.

The next day she took me to her GP for a pregnancy test. At the time we didn't know that Doug had had a vasectomy. She then informed Wandsworth Social Services and Kendall House of my whereabouts. They both insisted that I return to the house in Broadstairs.

'No way is she going back there to be raped again!' Karen said. She contacted her social worker Jo, who backed her up, although strangely she didn't report my rape claims to the police.

I was so grateful to Karen for taking the lead. I felt incapable of thought or action. It was as if I were in a trance. The shock of what Doug had done to me overruled everything. I could barely interact with Karen, Trevor or her kids. I left everything to her and blanked the world out.

But it gradually became clear that I had gone from the frying pan into the fire. Karen and Trevor were good about saving me from Doug Novick, but their charity went no further than that. I began to realise that it was in their interests to have me living with them because I provided free babysitting and cleaning services.

At first I was devoted to them, but in time the scales fell away from my eyes. The house was always cold. The heating was only ever on when Karen and Trevor were home. It didn't matter to them that I was freezing and could see my breath in the air.

The outhouse and back garden resembled a junkyard. They were full of car and bike parts and tyres. It was like a bikers' paradise. The house was dirty and there was rarely any food in the kitchen, although the makeshift bar in the dining room was always well stocked with booze.

Beer cans in hand, swearing and cursing and as loud as could be, they always managed to attract attention. I had to face the fact that I had moved in with what most people would consider to be neighbours from hell. They were the local problem family. Every neighbourhood has at least one – and, round here, they were it.

It was as unhappy a home for me as my dad's had been. Karen was not the nice person I had longed for her to be. She and Trevor made me go out to work and give them my wages in lieu of keep. I got a job in a leisure centre two miles from their house and they made me walk there and back in the dark, except on Fridays, when they'd be waiting outside in the car to collect my wages. I also sold Avon products door to door, and Karen got the commission.

One day I tried to run away. Trevor spotted me and dragged me back into the house by my hair. Once inside, Karen screamed at me that I was an ungrateful cow. 'I saved you from that foster father and this is how you repay me!'

I felt total and utter despair. Wherever I went, my life was hell. There was no stability, no love, no care and no freedom anywhere. There was no me. It was always about what everyone else wanted.

It got so bad that I approached Karen's social worker, Jo. She suggested that I return to Kendall House after she rang Kendall House and had a long chat with Mrs Tarwin, who had been promoted. Jo negotiated a temporary return for me, which stipulated that I wouldn't be drugged or locked up, and that I could go out by myself when I wanted to. I was ever so grateful to her. Anything was preferable to Karen and Trevor's house. It was a war zone. What's more, the rape allegations against Doug Novick had to be dealt with.

Mrs Tarwin picked me up. As we drove away, I didn't look back once. I never contacted them again. Mrs Tarwin took me to the Whattlers' house for the night. Aunt Betty and Uncle Don were terribly concerned about me. They believed everything I said about what Doug Novick had done to me. They offered every imaginable support. I loved them for it.

I was still bleeding and in pain. My condition seemed to be getting worse, rather than better. I didn't say anything to anyone at Kendall House, because I knew they wouldn't care. They'd just say that it was all in my head. Instead I took myself to the casualty department at the local hospital.

I cried miserably as I waited my turn, crippled with pain. Seeing how distressed I was, a nurse took me to a room on my own. She was so nice to me, I couldn't bring myself to tell her what was wrong. I was ashamed and embarrassed, and the pain was so debilitating that I could hardly speak anyway.

An Indian doctor came to examine me. He asked me my name and where I lived, but I was too scared to tell him. He tried to calm me down. 'I can't tell what's wrong if you don't let me have a look at you,' he said softly.

I flinched at the very thought of being touched down there, but I lay on the bed and let him prod my stomach.

When he felt my lower abdomen, I shrieked in agony. The nurse took my temperature. 'It's rather high, doctor,' she said.

Eventually I agreed to an internal examination. The nurse held my hand as he inserted a speculum. I wriggled in pain as he inspected me. 'Who has done this to you?' he asked in a firm but kind voice.

'I'll get in trouble if I tell you,' I replied.

'It won't be you who gets into trouble, it will be whoever has done this,' he assured me.

After I'd got dressed, he told me that my vagina and cervix were badly torn, as was the neck of my womb. I had an infection that had spread to my fallopian tubes, causing salpingitis, a serious inflammatory infection of the ovaries that can cause infertility. He recommended a short stay in hospital.

But I had to get back to Kendall House. If I stayed out any longer they would assume I had run away and I'd be in big trouble. 'At least let me report this to the police,' the doctor said. 'A crime has very obviously been committed here.'

'No, please!' I begged. Reluctantly he let me leave, taking copious antibiotics and painkillers with me.

Back at Kendall House, Nicole rushed up to me. 'Your foster parents are here!' she said.

I reeled in shock. The next thing I knew, Mrs Tarwin was calling me upstairs to the staffroom on the second floor. I walked in to find Doug and Pam Novick, Dr Harris, Miss Woods and Mrs Tarwin sitting in a circle. Dr Harris was a psychiatrist. He was standing in for Dr Peri.

All eyes fell on me as I entered the room. Without any preamble whatsoever, Miss Woods said, 'Sit down, Teresa. We need you to state your allegations against your foster father.'

I shuddered visibly. I was terrified out of my wits at the sight of Doug Novick. It was horrific being in the same room as him. 'Where's my social worker?' I asked.

'She is on holiday. Unfortunately, we are compelled to conduct this meeting in her absence.' I noticed that Miss Woods was speaking with unusual precision, and throwing her voice like an amateur actress. Little did I know that she was secretly taping the meeting.

'Sit down, Teresa,' Mrs Tarwin said. I looked wildly around the room. The only spare chair was the one next to Doug Novick.

'Not there,' I said.

'Sit down now!'

I did as I was told, my head spinning. Doug shifted uncomfortably in his seat and I cringed, expecting him to leap up and hit me. I could hardly believe what was happening. Here was the man who had raped me so badly that, earlier that very day, a doctor had wanted to report him to police.

'Now, clearly state your complaint against Mr Novick, please.'

I said nothing. I was too scared to move or speak.

'Let me just take Teresa outside for a five-minute break,' Mrs Tarwin said. She took hold of my hand and led me out of the room.

In order to involve the police, Teresa, you have got to say what your foster father did to you. If you don't tell us now, we won't be able to help you.'

I desperately wanted to see justice done. I couldn't bear the idea of Doug Novick getting away with it, especially when I was in so much pain. I asked to be excused to go to the toilet and promised to return.

In the toilet, I took out one of the bottles of painkillers that the doctor had given me. I pondered whether to take them. Once again, I didn't want to go on living. Suddenly I started knocking back pills, as many as I could cram into my mouth and swallow in one go. But then Mrs Tarwin came to find me. I hid the bottles behind the toilet and went back to the staffroom.

As I entered the room, I pointed at Doug Novick and screamed, 'You raped me and you hurt me!' What did it matter what I said now? By morning I would be dead. I ran out of the room in floods of tears.

Nicole came to find me. She cuddled me and asked me what was wrong, but I asked her to leave me on my own. Shortly after the tablets started to work I went into a daze. Mrs Tarwin asked me if I'd taken anything because I didn't look well.

'Yes, I hope it kills me so that none of you can hurt me anymore,' I yelled. I started running around in rage and fury, but then dropped to the floor in a dead faint.

When I came to, I was totally floppy, so Mrs Tarwin and a member of staff called Sally held me up and walked me to the local hospital in an attempt to keep me conscious. I heard Mrs Tarwin tell Sally that it was all an act, as usual. 'She loves attention. That's all she lives for,' she said, thinking I couldn't hear.

Not surprisingly, the pills soon wore off. After all, my body had been used to far worse in the past. The main side effect was that I couldn't stop crying. A psychiatrist evaluated me. He said I was a simple girl, but not mentally ill or disturbed.

It took Miss Woods two whole months to report my allegations to the police. Finally a policeman from Gravesend police station came to interview me at Kendall House. Not a policewoman, as was later logged at the station, but a policeman. *He* saw me in Miss Woods's office. After spending ages with Miss Woods, he gave me five minutes, barely listening to what I had to say. 'You don't have a leg to stand on,' he concluded. And that was that.

I will never forget those words. That's the story of my life, I thought. I ran out of Miss Woods's office so that he wouldn't see me cry.

CHAPTER EIGHTEEN

One good thing came out of my time at Karen and Trevor's – and that was their friend James. He was such a lovely guy and we built up a good friendship. There were no secrets between us. I told him everything that had happened to me. Eventually he became my boyfriend.

We didn't have sex. I was scared and he didn't want to rush me. Plus, I still had loads of problems down there as a consequence of the rape. Still, we kissed and cuddled a lot and he made me feel loved every time he held me.

His family didn't like me, but we didn't care. They were very well off and his parents were snobbish. His dad was always making snide comments about me when I went to their house in St Albans.

One evening, during a game of Trivial Pursuit, I answered a question correctly.

'JRR Tolkien!' I said.

'So you know something, then,' James's dad said, eyebrows raised.

James's mum told him off for that.

Finally I left Kendall House early in 1984. First I stayed at a place called Rivendale, and then I moved to Newhaven, where the staff were nice and I was treated like a human. At

Newhaven I was encouraged to write poetry and paint. The staff were hugely supportive of me in every way, especially Elaine and Sue.

I had written a poem at Kendall House, but my grammar and spelling were so appalling that it barely made any sense. A member of staff at Newhaven helped me to set it out properly, explaining the grammar as we went.

'This is very good,' she said, when we'd finished. 'You've definitely got a way with words.' I was so unused to receiving compliments that I walked around with a big grin on my face for days afterwards.

Newhaven was housed in one of the outbuildings of what had once been Friern Barnet Hospital in North London. I really liked it there. I was given my own little flat within the building. At last, freedom and my very own space! I grew up emotionally, and learned how to be independent. I learned a lot, in fact. My self-esteem soared.

The other girls were really naughty. I remember one of the staff went mad in a group meeting and said, 'Considering the kind of life Teresa's had, where she's come from and all those drugs she's been on, how is it that she behaves better than you lot, who didn't go through all of that?'

Although Kendall House had told Karen's social worker that they wouldn't drug me when I went back there after living at Karen's, in actual fact they had insisted that I continue with a certain level of medication, just as they had when I went to the foster home. So the staff at Newhaven had to see me through extreme withdrawals when I arrived there. It wasn't a pretty sight. I vomited everywhere, collapsed all the time and often couldn't get out of bed. It took weeks and weeks to get those drugs out of my system, or perhaps even longer – it's hard to remember. It got worse before it got better. After three years on heavy medication, it's not surprising that my body reacted so violently. I went through hell. But, my God, was it worth it.

I went back to being a normal girl again. It was amazing. I no longer had mood swings. I didn't once think about suicide during this time and I didn't self-harm again. The staff at Newhaven told me that these impulses had been a direct consequence of the drugs. Now I was off the drugs, I was myself again.

That's not to say that life was suddenly a bed of roses, of course. I was still very fragile and haunted by horrific memories of abuse. My struggle to come to terms with what had been done to me at Kendall House was only just beginning and I often found it hard even to contemplate what had gone on there. I tried to block it out of my mind, but it wasn't always possible. At least my mind wasn't fogged up though. At least I wasn't being injected or beaten up or raped anymore. Life was finally worth living.

James and I became ever closer. His kindness was wonderful. I was on my period a lot of the time as a result of the salpingitis, and my periods were incredibly painful, but he was very understanding and never tried to push me into having sex.

One night, during a rare break from bleeding, we got drunk together. The big day had come. Since I didn't want to go on being scared of men and sex, that night we took things further, and one thing led to another. Unfortunately no one had explained about contraception. Sex education had simply passed me by.

Inevitably I fell pregnant. I was over the moon – until a social worker told me that I had to have a termination.

'Why?' I asked.

'You are still only seventeen and still in the care of Wandsworth Social Services. When you are eighteen, you may do what you wish. Until that time, you must play by our rules. If you don't have a termination voluntarily, I'm afraid that Social Services will take steps to compel you to have one.'

I burst into tears. I was only a few weeks off my eighteenth birthday. 'The upside is that if you agree to it, we will be in a position to award you a holiday grant,' she continued. It was an extraordinary trade off. I wish I had contacted the local newspaper, or one of the tabloids. They would have had a field day, surely.

Reluctantly, I went to my GP and said I needed an abortion. 'Are you sure this is what you want?' she asked me.

Clearly I didn't want it. But what the doctor didn't realise was that I'd been through so much abuse at Kendall House that I was mortally scared of Wandsworth Social Services. I dreaded to think what they would do to me if I didn't comply. I had visions of being locked away in a mental hospital, for life. I had heard that poor Annie from Kendall House had been sent to an adult psychiatric institution. Poor old Georgie too. My freedom was too valuable to me to risk anything like that.

So I told the doctor, 'Yes, this is what I want.' And I had the abortion.

I went on holiday with Bernadette almost immediately afterwards. I hated myself. I hated Wandsworth. I couldn't bring myself to see James ever again.

I couldn't stop thinking about the baby I had lost. When I was given a one-bedroom flat in Tottenham, North London, only weeks afterwards, I felt utterly deceived. Surely I could have kept the baby?

Life got better though. I met a wonderful guy. I fell head over heels in love with him and experienced feelings I didn't even know existed. It was overwhelming. I couldn't get enough of him.

By now my dad had been diagnosed with cancer. I knew he was dying and threw myself into caring for him. We began to grow closer than we'd ever been, which made me very happy, despite my sadness at his illness. He often came to visit me and we spent hours chatting and laughing. We still had our moments, but most of the time things were good.

Christmas 1985 was fantastic. Bernadette, David, Dad and I went to Auntie Rachel's house. Rachel was Dad's sister. I enjoyed every minute of it, even though I'd been feeling sick for a couple of weeks and didn't much feel like eating a full turkey dinner.

'I bet a hundred to one that you're pregnant,' Auntie Rachel said in a quiet moment.

'Not a chance,' I laughed. 'With my periods?'

I did a test. It was positive. I was overjoyed. A whole new world opened up before my eyes. I was going to become a mother and I wanted this baby more than anything. My only worry was telling Dad, because he disapproved of children outside marriage.

Sure enough, when I told him he went ballistic. I hadn't intended to say anything, but it just slipped out one night while I was at his flat. 'You whore, you piece of trash, opening your legs without thinking!' he shouted. 'I bet that idiot you call a boyfriend won't help you now!'

It was the worst I'd ever heard him in terms of swearing. He hit me and told me to fuck off out of his house. 'You're no longer a child of mine!' he screamed.

I was very upset. I hadn't expected such a strong reaction, but I had no choice but to leave, even though it was late and I had a terrible feeling that the trains back to North London had stopped running.

I walked to the station and shivered as I waited in the freezing cold for the next train, which wasn't due for several hours. A drunk man nearby kept trying to talk to me. He scared the crap out of me. A tall black man with kind eyes walked up. He was wearing a British Rail uniform.

'What are you doing at an empty station in the middle of the night? There are no trains. You are putting yourself in great danger,' he said.

'My dad's thrown me out because I'm pregnant! I've got to get home to Tottenham but there aren't any trains until morning,' I blurted out.

'OK. Stay put,' he said and walked away.

I didn't feel scared. You could tell he was a good man. He came back with a big overcoat and wrapped it around me. When he was able to leave work, he drove me in his car to his parents' house. Taking my hand, he led me up to his bedroom. I got into his bed, still shivering with cold and feeling hungry yet sick – pregnancy sickness. He brought me some biscuits, which I ate greedily. He gave me a big cuddle and left me to sleep.

When I woke up this wonderful guy took me downstairs again. There were lots of people milling around. They turned out to be his family and church friends. They were so polite to me, even though I looked really rough. They gave me a cup of tea and biscuits before their son drove me back to the station so that I could get a train. I will never forget his or his family's kindness and concern.

Dad stopped talking to me after that, but my brother

David started coming to see me. He'd take me to Sainsbury's in Wood Green and help me back home with the shopping bags. By then I had huge cravings. I couldn't stop staring at the shelves of pickled onions. David bought me several jars, along with lots of other food. I was amazed; he actually paid for it! At the checkout he put his arm round me and said, 'You need to eat for two now, little sister. And proper food, eh? Not just biscuits and crisps.'

I felt a wave of tiredness overtake me, so David flagged down a cab. 'Ta da!' he sang, taking out a jar of pickled onions and opening it. We were about halfway home.

I grabbed the jar and ate one onion after another until there were none left. I was like a crazy animal.

Back at home, David emptied my bins and cleaned up the flat. 'Put your feet up,' he said. 'I'll make us a salad.' I scoffed it down so quickly, he couldn't stop laughing.

He left me curled up in a chair reading a Sheila Kitzinger book about pregnancy that I'd checked out of the library. I'd lost all my education at Kendall House, so it was hard to read it, but I painstakingly put the words together, and the pictures provided a lot of information. That night I had the most wonderful feeling of butterflies in my tummy. The next day the butterflies were stronger. I was thrilled when I realised that it was my baby moving around.

I didn't smoke or drink during my pregnancy. I was obsessed with this thing growing inside me. But one day I got very upset thinking about how I wouldn't be able to help my child with his or her homework. I wouldn't know where to begin. I was thick. So I started getting more books from the library and re-educating myself. I stopped swearing and took better care of myself. With this child inside me, I felt alive for the first time in my life.

My labour came and the father held my hand and saw me through every step of it. By now we both knew that the relationship wouldn't be continuing, but there were no hard feelings. I was happy to be a single mother.

With my last push, I gave birth not only to my first child but also to a new life for me.

By now I had a small circle of friends who lived nearby, so I knew I wouldn't be too lonely. Some of them came to visit me and my gorgeous new son Daniel in hospital. Much to my amusement, my friend Dave took him out of his crib and held him up to the window. The other guys gathered round. 'That's Tottenham football ground over there,' Dave said, nodding at the stadium. 'You'll be a football player because you've got such big feet.' Daniel promptly weed on him. He had already started making his mark.

It was time to go home with my new son. I was as happy as a person could be. My sister Bernadette and Auntie Rachel arrived, closely followed by – lo and behold! – my dad. Bernadette and Rachel were all oohs and aahs. Dad kept his distance. It broke my heart to see how thin and ill he looked.

All of a sudden, Bernadette took Daniel out of his crib, marched over to Dad and plonked him in his arms. Dad had no choice but to hold him, and he started crying. He cuddled Daniel like there was no tomorrow. He didn't want to hand him back. He had fallen in love with this new being, this new child, his own flesh and blood.

'What's his blood group?' he asked.

'It's funny you should ask because it's different to mine – it's A negative,' I said.

Then Dad really began to sob. It turned out that all these years he had suspected that I wasn't his child, because my blood group wasn't the same as his. Apparently Mum had started an affair with a man down the road around the time of my conception. (Or that's what Dad claimed. You could never tell with those two. They drove each other to distraction.) Since I resembled Mum so much more than I did him, he had become sure over time that I wasn't his. But Daniel's unusual blood group convinced him that I was his child because it was the same as Dad's.

His attitude to me changed completely. He became the proudest dad and granddad in the world. He immediately stopped drinking and smoking. He insisted on being a part of his grandson's life. I had waited all my life for him to be a proper dad to me – and this was it.

He regularly travelled all the way from south-west London – where he now lived – just to be with us for an afternoon, and I took Daniel to see him as often as I could. Dad often babysat for me. He bought Daniel toys and constantly played with him. He loved his grandson so much that when Daniel got his first tooth through, he came all the way to Tottenham and then took him all the way to the Fox and Hounds in Putney just to show his drinking friends his grandson's first tooth. Then, ill as he was, he travelled all the way back with him to me in Tottenham. That night he stayed the night and started bleeding really badly. I did my best to nurse him and make him comfortable.

Bernadette and I became a lot closer too and in the summer we took Dad and Daniel on holiday to Butlins. We had an absolute scream. I've got pictures of them riding on the choo choo train, of Daniel perched on Dad's knee and Dad pushing Daniel's pram. There was always a fight about who was going to push that pram and most of the time Dad won.

Back at home, Dad started to stay with me more as his

health deteriorated. We did the crossword together every day and always had a laugh over it. He would tease me about my crap ironing and insisted that he washed and ironed all of Daniel's clothes. I've got pictures of Dad and Daniel next to the cake I baked on Daniel's first birthday. It was an amazing time. I was finally getting to know my dad properly.

Sadly, he died shortly after that. Just before he passed away, he told Auntie Rachel, 'I hope Teresa forgives me for letting her down when she needed me.'

Of course I forgave him. He had made up for everything tenfold in those last couple of years. He had become my trusted friend, as well as a proper dad.

Losing him was the most painful experience I'd ever been through. It seemed so unfair that I'd got my dad back only to lose him again. At his funeral, I wept and wept.

On the way home, I stared into my sleeping son's face. It struck me that Daniel had given me back the father I'd lost for all those years. He'd given my dad the chance to make up for everything that had gone wrong. And he'd also given me my life back.

I had every reason to go on living. Sad as I was over my father's death, I had every reason to be happy.

Daniel was now my life.

EPILOGUE

I am now 40. I have three wonderful children, fifteen gorgeous cats, two naughty dogs and a budgerigar. I work as a volunteer with DEStiny (Disability Enterprise Support) CIC and I have set up and manage a website for survivors of abuse, www.no2abuse.com. The website provides survivors of abuse with an online community where they can share their experiences, learn from each other and help those who seek support. The site also welcomes those caring for vulnerable people and helping them to cope with their experiences. It is important that we unite in helping to bring about the changes needed to improve the lives of vulnerable people and children.

I have organised a petition to get the Statute of Limitations Act changed, at http://petitions.pm.gov.uk/statutebarred/

It has taken many years to come to terms with what happened to me while I was growing up. There are still so many unanswered questions.

For a long time I didn't talk about the terrible abuse I suffered at Kendall House because I was worried that no one would believe me. I also hoped that the pain and memories would fade in time, but they didn't. So in 1992, I decided to try to track down my files, or at least find out if they still existed.

Wandsworth Social Services refused to cooperate, so my social worker at the time suggested that I go to a solicitor, which I did. It was subsequently acknowledged that the first investigation into the rape allegation against Doug Novick, the foster father, had been inadequate. As a result, the police reopened their investigation into the rape, as well as Kendall House.

But Wandsworth Social Services still refused to make my files openly available to the police, to my solicitor or to me. The council initially said that it would make part of the files available to my social worker and me, but the Kendall House files were not included in this offer. When my solicitor requested full access, not only was it denied but the previous offer was also withdrawn. This hampered the police inquiry. One police officer wrote:

'I am troubled that a public service such as Wandsworth Social Services is not open to external scrutiny and the fact that they appear to be able to hinder and undermine a current criminal inquiry is most unsatisfactory.'

I went to see my local MP, Neil Gerrard, and he brought my case up in Parliament on 25 October 1994. He criticised Wandsworth Council on several counts, from their refusal to give me access to my files to their attitude to the rape allegations against Doug Novick. He was very concerned that Wandsworth did not treat my claims seriously. Here's an extract from his speech (he refers to me as 'my constituent'):

'In 1984, my constituent was placed with a foster parent and, shortly afterwards, she alleged that the man had raped her. The way in which that complaint was dealt with was dreadful and Wandsworth Council has more or less admitted that since. The rape allegation was not immediately reported to the police and, worse than that, a few days later my constituent was forced to confront the man who she alleged had raped her, and his wife, without the presence of a social worker. The files show that the social worker was away on holiday at the time. Shortly afterwards, the Social Services department agreed that, if she did not withdraw her allegation, it would write to the police and ask them to investigate. It is clear from the paper in which it agreed to do that that it had already made up its mind. The paper states:

"When we receive formal notification from them [the police] that the allegations will not be proceeded with because of lack of evidence, the Department's records will need to be amended so that it is absolutely clear that her allegations were totally unsubstantiated and merely a fantasy."

Clearly, the department had made up its mind. It did not believe her and it was not going to refer the matter in any serious way to the police.'

Neil Gerrard also seemed very worried by the way Wandsworth continued to withhold information from the police. He said:

'The problem all along has been the refusal of Wandsworth Social Services to make its files openly available . . . the continued refusal cannot but suggest that there is something to hide. Moreover, pressure has been put on my constituent to drop the case. In direct telephone conversations with senior Wandsworth Social Services officers, she has been told, "Forget all that stuff from years ago and just get on with your life", sometimes in a quite unprofessional manner.'

The law on access to files has since been changed, although it remains a sad fact that only a small percentage of children in care ever manage to get access to their full files when they leave.

It took me twelve years to get hold of my Wandsworth

files and when I finally got them, they were incomplete. (They also included a report on another Kendall House girl that should not have been in my files.) But there is enough evidence in the information that has been released to reveal the many mistakes the council made in the course of my childhood from the day my parents first contacted them.

They left me in the care of my violent father and kept sending me back to him between homes, even when they knew he had not paid the electricity bill, but they wouldn't let my mum have us because she'd had a breakdown. Mum wasn't violent to us. Many times she begged to see us and wasn't allowed to. So many times my dad asked for help and didn't get it. My parents had their problems and Social Services were supposed to help, but the council turned out to be the worst of the worst. It was not a system that cared. It was not a system that helped. It was a system that let children and families down.

Why was I sent to Kendall House? There was no valid reason. I wasn't naughty, I wasn't aggressive; I was liked and got on with most people. My schooling was average and the Social Services were trying to find excuses to put me where I didn't belong. Convenience? Who knows, but I do know that every evaluation I had prior to Kendall House made it clear there was nothing wrong with me mentally. In the end Wands-worth put me in Kendall House regardless. They took me out of a home I was happy in (Miss Foley's) and put me in the home from hell.

In my files there is a letter from Dr M A Sevitt, consultant psychiatrist at Long Grove Hospital, to Mrs White at the Inner London Education Authority, dated 19 June 1980, written during their discussions about where it would be best to send me to complete my education:

'I am writing following our Case Conference of Thursday last week to confirm that we are recommending a boarding school placement for Theresa [sic]. We feel that Theresa would be best placed at a small ordinary boarding school and will not require a maladjusted provision.'

The Inner London Education Authority agreed that a 'small ordinary boarding school' would be suitable for me. Social Services were copied in on the correspondence. Yet they insisted that Kendall House, with its drugs and punishments regime, its locked doors and its intake of violent and disturbed girls, was the right place for me. Why did they not tell me what it was like there? Did they have a vested interest in sending me there? In my files, five boarding schools are listed as placement possibilities for me, not including Kendall House. I was never supposed to be locked away.

There were newspaper reports even before 1980 slamming the drug regime at Kendall House. Complaints had been made by various individuals and establishments about Kendall House, but Wandsworth Social Services continued to put girls there. Why were none of my dad's complaints investigated, and why was he not told that I was being given drugs? The girls' complaints were also ignored. Miss Woods and Dr Perinpanayagam had free reign to do as they liked, and the devastating results included mental, physical and sexual abuse.

As soon as I learned that there were records of my time at Kendall House written by the staff, I rang all the archive centres in Kent and the surrounding areas to see if someone other than Wandsworth was holding a set. No joy. Then one day, out of the blue, I had a phone call from an archivist to say that she had found my Kendall House file.

I'm not sure what I was expecting, but I was astounded to

see that my file logged every single day I spent at Kendall House from June 1981 onwards. I couldn't believe what I was reading. There in black and white was an account of the drugs I was given and the abuse I suffered. It wasn't always reliable – the staff reported day-to-day incidents from their own warped perspective and there was quite a lot of covering up. What struck me above all were the lists of daily drugs and dosages I was forced to take.

As Neil Gerrard MP pointed out in his speech to parliament, the recommended Valium dose for children and teenagers, even in exceptional circumstances, is in the range of 5 to 10 mg, yet I was being given daily doses of up to 80 mg in tablet form – and 100 mg intravenously, which was combined with other serious drugs well over recommended adult doses. It is a wonder that my body was able to process these amounts. I could easily have died.

Other medicines I was forced to take included some extremely strong antipsychotic drugs, some of which were used to treat schizophrenia. Considering that I had not been diagnosed with any form of mental illness whatsoever, it seems extraordinary that I was being 'treated' with these powerful medicines. Or was I simply a guinea pig for drugs trials? Was it possible that Dr Perinpanayagam was attempting to induce symptoms of schizophrenia in me using psychotropic drugs like Valium, in order to then treat me in a series of tests using antipsychotic drugs? It sounds far-fetched, but I often ask myself, what other explanation could there be?

The drugs he used on us turned healthy girls into something they were not. Girls who arrived after me, like Danielle and Annie, came into Kendall House with clear eyes and complexions. Within days they looked ill and haunted. The drugs created a whole new me, a person who became almost unrecognisable to my family.

Why was I drugged less than twenty-four hours after I arrived at Kendall House? There was absolutely nothing in my past history or records to suggest that I required medication, and nothing in my Kendall House file to suggest that I was being disruptive. In fact that first night all I did was sleep. The psychiatrists who had assessed me prior to going to Kendall House found me to be mentally healthy, despite my unstable background. So why was I given Valium from the start? Surely it could not simply have been because I complained about being locked up.

Bridget and Tina were genuinely aggressive and disturbed, so why weren't they drugged?

My initial meeting with Dr Peri on my second day at Kendall House lasted five minutes, which obviously wasn't long enough for a psychiatric evaluation of any serious kind. Miss Woods had already made me take some medication, so the meeting with Dr Peri must have been just a formality.

Who was DR Perinpanayagam? This is his official title:

MBBS, FRC Psych, DPM, DCN, consultant psychiatrist and tutor, University of London, psychotherapist to the Home Office.

In other words, he was a highly qualified and highly respected psychiatrist and psychotherapist, a position he seriously abused.

Kendall House was not licensed to be a secure unit, nor were the staff authorised to administer the kind of drugs they were doling out. Why were untrained staff allowed to give out drugs without reference to a GP? Surely it was illegal?

An inspection visit in June 1984 by the Department of Health and Social Security (DHSS) found an alarming number of irregularities in the way Kendall House was run. The stocking and storage of medication was heavily criticised, as was the way the drugs were given. The Department report to Kendall House stated that:

'It must be absolutely clear that *no* drugs, except for simple, non-prescribable drugs, must be administered except with the direct involvement of either the general practitioner or Dr Harris [who replaced Dr Peri at the meeting to discuss the allegation against Doug Novick].'

According to the law, only a GP or doctor is permitted to administer prescription drugs like Valium. So the injections I was given at the hands of Harriet and Mrs Tarwin, aided by Shirley, Matthew, the bookkeeper and various teachers and members of staff were not legally given, setting aside the fact that undue force and cruelty were used when they pinned me down and injected me.

The drugs I was forced to take at Kendall House included: Sparine (sedative and antipsychotic), Kemadrin (used to treat symptoms of Parkinson's Disease), Droleptan (antipsychotic, discontinued), Haloperidol (used to treat schizophrenia and mania), Disipal (used to treat symptoms of Parkinson's Disease, not recommended for use in children), Depixol (used to treat schizophrenia and mania), Largactyl (used to treat mania), Phenergan (antihistamine), Sernace (used to treat schizophrenia and mania), Normison (sedative, similar to Valium). I presented many of the side effects of these drugs, from dizziness and trembling to nausea, loss of appetite and mood swings.

Samples of my blood and urine were taken – usually by Harriet – every two weeks, but the results of the tests were not logged with my GP or any of the local hospitals. Why not? Where were the samples sent and where were the results of the tests kept? Could it be possible that Dr Peri was using those results for his own, unauthorised, research?

Why were ninety-nine per cent of the drugs administered to me not registered with my GP? And why were untrained staff like Miss Woods and Mrs Tarwin allowed to request powerful prescription drugs from the local GP and get them without a consultation with the patient?

Why did the police never look into my complaints of drugging and abuse when they picked me up after I had run away?

What are the long-term effects of drugs like the ones I was given? A common birth defect in children born to mothers who use psychotropic drugs in or prior to pregnancy is a cleft palate, and my daughter was born with this and Pierre Robin syndrome. My second son was born blind, but fortunately recovered his sight after two years. Coincidence? It seems likely that there is a link. I have never used any drugs during, prior to or since my pregnancy. The only time I was on those drugs was at Kendall House.

The 1984 DHSS report also said: 'We still remain concerned about the amount of internal locking of doors . . . in particular the continued practice of locking the door between the ground floor and first and second bedroom floors at night is not warranted . . . this does constitute a 'restriction of liberty'.

Kendall House did not have permission from any governing body to lock up the girls in this way; in which case, surely, it was responsible for falsely imprisoning the girls there.

An earlier DHSS report in 1983 ordered Kendall House to open up the detention room and Sick Bay, stating that girls must not be locked within either room. Kendall House assured the DHSS by letter that the rooms had been turned into offices. Clearly this was not the case. My files show that I was still being restrained in the detention room and Sick Bay in 1983.

Other major DHSS concerns included 'the inadequate provision of qualified teaching staff'. The teaching curriculum was deemed to be 'too limited and traditional' and 'to have a number of serious deficiencies'.

In actual fact, the curriculum barely existed. Educational standards at Kendall House were farcically low.

The Department made a number of recommendations for change in Kendall House, including the removal from the premises of all non-prescription drugs. Perhaps if they had made their inspection a few years earlier, I would not have been subjected to daily overdoses.

Another huge question in my mind concerns my allegations of sexual abuse while I was in Sick Bay. In a letter dated 23 February 1983, Miss Woods wrote to the local GP saying:

'I enclose copy of report on anal swab taken from Teresa Cooper. It is likely that she has been sexually abused.'

It seems extraordinary that Miss Woods would make a written acknowledgement of this, when at no point did she acknowledge to me that she was taking my claims seriously. She accused me of making up stories and said that it was 'all in your head, Teresa', but this letter shows that she appeared to know a lot more than she was letting on.

It also seems incredible that not one member of staff reported my allegations of sexual abuse to the police, even after they had logged a wide range of physical problems I endured as a result of the abuse. Instead there almost seemed to be a conspiracy to keep my claims – and the evidence – contained within Kendall House. Otherwise, why did they do the swabs and examinations in house? Why all the secrecy?

Why was I given an anal stretch in hospital? I can only assume that it didn't occur to the medical staff that my injuries were sustained as a result of anal rape. They must have assumed that I had a medical problem that was causing rectal tears and fissures. Of course, I was too drugged up to have any say and the Kendall House staff spoke for me. I can only guess at the lies they told the doctors.

The foster father situation was terrible too; a serious failure by Wandsworth and Kendall House. Doug Novick was based in Kent, and he was prosecuted in later years for crimes against another person he was caring for. He is on the Social Services register and is not allowed to look after children or adults again. If Wandsworth had taken my rape allegations seriously, perhaps he wouldn't have had the chance to abuse again. As it was, they gave him free reign.

Despite numerous attempts to take legal action against Wandsworth, with full support from the legal aid board, I was unable to get around the fact that I was statute barred. The statute of limitations sets forth a maximum period of time, after certain events, that legal proceedings based on those events can be initiated. Because I had mentioned the abuse to my social worker many years before I started proceedings (and here 'abuse' refers to everything that happened at Kendall House and with the foster father) the maximum period of time had expired (six years) and I could not take civil action.

The Statute of Limitations Act crippled me, as it does many victims of abuse, by preventing me from taking civil action against my abusers and the local authorities. It blocks any redress for the abuse suffered and also prevents sufferers from getting recognition of what they went through. The care system failed many survivors of historic abuse and the Statute of Limitations Act puts survivors through further abuse by not allowing them the right to a fair hearing. The civil law as it stands contradicts fair law when it comes to survivors of child abuse. I feel strongly that the law must be changed so that it supports the abused and not the abusers and I am currently campaigning for that change.

The Criminal Injuries Compensation Authority refused me the right to seek compensation under the exceptional circumstances clause, despite all the evidence. No matter what route I took, they prevented any compensation claim.

Through the many years that I have been trying to seek some form of justice, not one of those involved in the abuse I suffered has shown remorse. I will not give up seeking an apology from those who had a duty of care for me and failed me.

The cruel regime at Kendall House is one that no child should endure and these regimes need to be highlighted in order to bring about much needed changes. The abuse I suffered violated every description of the word 'care' and it wasn't normal to be treated like that in the care system. Like many survivors we were put in care to protect us from abuse and bad family situations, but we were subjected to abuse in the care system that in many cases far outweighed any abuse we suffered at home.

My mum and dad are both dead, Mr and Mrs Whattler too. Bernadette now works abroad. I haven't had contact with my brother David for more than ten years. I don't see or speak to Karen, my mum's relative.

Last year I contacted Jules again and our friendship is stronger than ever.

Annie, the girl whose tortured screams I heard while I was

locked up in Sick Bay, committed suicide in 1987 by jumping in front of a train. I am in contact with Amanda, Annie's best friend and we have a good friendship.

I heard that Georgie was bundled off to a psychiatric hospital, but has since been released into the community.

I don't know where Bridget is, or what happened to Nicole. I haven't tried to find out.

The Council of Social Responsibility is now known as the Church of Social Responsibility. The church helped me to get hold of my Kendall House files and is currently aiding other Kendall House ex-residents in the search for their files.

I went to have a look at Kendall House recently. Back in the 1980s it closed down as a girls' home and was turned into rooms for the homeless, but it is now derelict. Standing on the pavement outside, I felt horrible. The windows were dirty. It looked dead. It was dead. There was no life in it. It's just a house now, just broken down bricks and mortar. The staff are no longer there; the girls aren't there. I didn't go inside. I felt relieved when I drove off. It was good to get home to my children and all my pets, where I am happy.

No Child of Yours

I saw a child hide in the corner
So I went and asked her name
She was so naive and so petite
With such a tiny frame.

'No one,' she replied, 'that's what I am called
I have no family, no one at all
I eat, I sleep, I get depressed
There is no life, I have nothing left.'

'Why hide in the corner?' I had to ask twice
Because I've been hurt, it's not very nice
I tried to stop it, it was out of my control
I feared for myself, I wanted to go.

I begged for my sorrow to disappear
I turned in my bed, oh God, I knew they were near
'So come on little girl, where do you go
A path ahead, or a path to unknown?'

With that she arose, her head hung low
She held herself, for only she knows
Her tears held back, her heart like ice
It looks as though she has paid the price.

The ice started melting, her tears to flow
The memories flood back, still so many years to go
The pain, the anger all built up inside
Nowhere to run, nowhere to hide.

It will get better, just wait and see
You'll get a life, though you'll never be free
Open your heart and love yourself
The abuse you suffered was NOT your fault.

Teresa Cooper